It was the ambition of Sammy Adams to make his fortune while he was still a young man. It was the opinion of Chinese Lady, his mother, that he thought too much about making money and not enough about finding himself a wife. But Sammy was quite definite about that – wives cost money and he had no intention of committing himself and his pocket, not even to blue-eyed Susie Brown. He put temptation out of his way by 'promoting' her to run his new ladies' wear shop in Brixton, far from his Camberwell office.

But he reckoned without Susie's ability to run rings round him, and it was she who had the final word concerning his future, showing him that a man who builds an empire is not necessarily king of all he surveys.

Also by Mary Jane Staples

DOWN LAMBETH WAY
OUR EMILY
RISING SUMMER
THE LODGER
TWO FOR THREE FARTHINGS

and published by Corgi Books

KING OF
CAMBERWELL

Mary Jane Staples

CORGI BOOKS

KING OF CAMBERWELL
A CORGI BOOK 0 552 13573 9

Originally published in Great Britain by
Bantam Press, a division of Transworld Publishers Ltd.

PRINTING HISTORY
Bantam Press edition published 1990
Corgi edition published 1990
Corgi edition reprinted 1990
Corgi edition reprinted 1991

This book is set in 10/11½pt California
by Colset Private Limited, Singapore.

Corgi Books are published by Transworld Publishers Ltd.,
61–63 Uxbridge Road, Ealing, London W5 5SA, in Australia
by Transworld Publishers (Australia) Pty. Ltd., 15–23 Helles
Avenue, Moorebank, NSW 2170, and in New Zealand by
Transworld Publishers (N.Z.) Ltd., Cnr. Moselle and
Waipareira Avenues, Henderson, Auckland.

Printed and bound in Great Britain by
Cox & Wyman Ltd., Reading, Berks.

CHAPTER ONE

'Mister Sammy?'

Sammy Adams, a young man of initiative and enterprise, looked up from his examination of a proposed lease on a Kennington shop. He met, as he feared he would, the deep blue eyes of Susie Brown, assistant in his shop below his office at Camberwell Green, South London. Invaluable, the girl was, but he wished her blue saucers would not always have the effect of making him feel he was going to say yes when his every instinct cautioned him to say no.

'What is it, may I ask?' he enquired.

'Boots said—' Susie hesitated. Boots was his eldest brother and the manager of the shop. 'Boots said you and Mister Tommy's goin' to move out of your house next month to live in the rooms here.'

'You have been informed correct, Miss Brown. Them selfsame rooms is presently being made ready for our desired occupation.'

Susie wrinkled her nose. She knew Mister Sammy was always on his guard when he called her Miss Brown and spoke to her in careful prose.

'Well, you see,' she said, 'Mum and Dad, well, what with Dad's bit of pension for his gammy leg, and what he earns doing odd jobs for you, and me earnin' my bit too, owing to your kind generosity, we'd like to move out of Peabody's and 'ave—' Susie stopped in recognition of her dropped aitch. Working in the shop with Boots, who spoke ever so educated, had brought about an instinctive improvement in her own speech. 'Well, we'd like to have a nice little house like the one your fam'ly's lived in so long. Mister Sammy, could you speak for us to your landlord, could you put in a word for us?'

'Eh?' Sammy sat back and rolled his fountain pen between his fingers. 'Are you makin' known a desire to take our old house over, Miss Brown?'

'We've got a likin' to, so could you speak for us?' Susie knew Caulfield Place in Walworth. It was off Browning Street, near Browning Hall and its clinic. At the clinic, kids could be treated for conjunctivitis, an eye condition not unknown among the poverty-stricken families of Walworth. Caulfield Place was one of the streets clustering around St John's Church and its school. The church was the centre and fount of social activities, and the little terraced houses in those streets, with their modest rents, were always well sought after, and none of them ever stood empty. Susie couldn't think of any house her family would rather have than the one that had known Mister Sammy's family. She was sure they had made a happy home of it. Her mum and dad said that when you moved into a new home you could always tell what sort of people the previous tenants had been. People always left something of themselves behind. 'Mum and Dad would be ever so grateful, Mister Sammy.'

Sammy, practical though he was, could not help being touched by the request. He said, 'In consideration of you being a credit to me business, Miss Brown, I am happy to inform you I'll use me highly regarded influence on your behalf.'

'Oh, I thank you considerable, Mister Sammy,' said Susie, who had learned how to respond in kind to Sammy's verbal indulgencies.

'Now, if you don't mind, I'll continue examining me business affairs,' said Sammy, his dark brown hair thick and well-brushed, his features pleasantly masculine, and his own blue eyes capable of wheedling glances.

'Yes, Mister Sammy,' said Susie. In her seventeenth year, she was fair-haired, slim and pretty, and acquiring an improving dress sense. She returned to the shop below in a state of high hope. Mister Sammy had given his word, and he never broke it once he gave it. He had funny ways, and was very droll sometimes, but he had good principles.

The following day, when Mr Eli Greenberg, a valuable business go-between, called to see Sammy, Sammy mentioned the house in Caulfield Place. It was occupied at the moment only by himself and his brother Tommy. Boots and his wife Emily had moved out two months ago, in January. And Sammy's mother was convalescing from TB in a Frimley sanatorium. She would live with Boots and Emily when she came out.

'In respect of same,' said Sammy, 'I am requestin' your kind co-operation, Eli old cock.'

Mr Greenberg, son of a Latvian father and a Russian mother who had escaped Tsarist pogroms when he was a child, put on a wise look. Wisdom was priceless, and added considerably to the value of co-operation.

'Vould you say it's goin' to be my pleasure, Sammy?'

'A trifling act of friendship is all I'm askin',' said Sammy. 'Kindly do the needful by seeing Susie Brown and her fam'ly get first option.'

'Ah,' said Mr Greenberg. He lifted his ancient black hat and resettled it until it roundly crowned his dark, majestic features.

'No ahs, Eli,' said Sammy. 'Kindly speak to the landlord, Mr Small, an old friend of yours.' There were few businessmen in South London who weren't old friends of Mr Greenberg.

7

'For you, my poy, I ain't averse, but there's a little matter of a vaiting list.'

'A waiting list? In this day and age?' Sammy looked disgusted. 'And in Walworth? It beats me, Eli, the way you can talk like that without hardly movin' yer lips.'

'Come, come, Sammy, such desirable residences,' said Mr Greenberg.

'Don't make me choke to death,' said Sammy. 'Kindly arrange for the Browns to go top of the list.'

'My life, should I do such a thing?' Mr Greenberg looked shocked. 'Could I do such a thing? The poor vaitin' families, Sammy, should they vait longer?'

'That's it, make me die laughin',' said Sammy. 'Listen, it's me that's kindly requestin', not some geezer you've only just met.'

'Sammy my dear, ain't I alvays treated you like my own son?' protested Mr Greenberg.

'It's been highly mutual and given me cause to love yer, Dad,' said Sammy, 'so you see Susie's fam'ly get the house.'

'Sammy, there is only vun Jesus, my poy. Should I be expected to valk on vater vhen I am only me? But I ain't saying a vhite vun von't help.'

'Hold on,' said Sammy, 'I don't think I'm hearing you right. You didn't mention a fiver in passin', did you?'

'It costs to climb a vaitin' list, Sammy, and love is vorth a little vhite vun, ain't it?'

'No such thing as a little white one,' said Sammy. 'They're all worth five nicker apiece. Wait a minute, what d'you mean, love?'

Mr Greenberg looked wisely knowing.

'Such a pretty smile, my poy, such sveet blue eyes. My vord, ain't such eyes the light of a young man's life? Vell, say four pounds, Sammy, and I'll see vhat I can do for her family.'

'Oblige me by leavin' off,' said Sammy. 'You're

hurtin' my ears and strainin' me pocket. Also, I ain't in love, I just happen to have a kind heart.'

'Vhy, Sammy, there ain't a kinder heart in the kingdom,' said Mr Greenberg generously, 'but—'

'All right, I'll slip yer five bob,' said Sammy.

'Sammy, Sammy.' Mr Greenberg showed pain. 'Say three pounds ten, my poy.'

'Thirty bob,' said Sammy, 'which offer means I'm off me chump.'

'Done at two pounds, my friend.'

'Some friend,' said Sammy, 'and I still got to get it back from Susie.'

'I should believe that?' said Mr Greenberg.

'I ain't a benefact'ry institution,' said Sammy. 'I'm kind, but I ain't daft. Also, this ain't the year of plenty, it's the year of the locusts.' It was 1921, and the Exchequer coffers were bare, according to the Chancellor.

'In such hard times, Sammy, friendship is dear to me. Ah, should I collect now?'

'Fair do's, if I can tell Susie it's on.'

'Vell, vhy not, Sammy, vhy not?' said Mr Greenberg, and Sammy handed over two pound notes.

'I'll tell her she can go round to the landlord at the end of the week, right?' said Sammy.

'Right it is, Sammy,' said Mr Greenberg. Going through the shop on his way out, he smiled at Susie.

'Good morning, Susie,' he said.

'Good morning, Mr Greenberg,' said Susie.

'Vould even the prettiest daughter of Abraham have such blue eyes?' said Mr Greenberg, and departed chuckling.

Susie was called up to Sammy's office later.

'Yes, what is it, Miss Brown?' he asked.

'Well, I like that,' said Susie protestingly. 'You called me.'

'Did I? Me mind's unconsciously occupied – oh, half

a mo', I remember now. The house, Miss Brown.'

'Yes, Mister Adams?'

'Tell your parents to go and fix things up with the landlord at the end of the week. I suppose they know the rent's fifteen bob?'

'Oh, Mister Sammy, ain't you a love?' said Susie rapturously.

'No, I ain't,' said Sammy, 'I'm yer employer.'

'But you did it, you spoke for us. Thank you, Mister Sammy, and we can afford the rent. I got to say it, you been a shinin' light to me fam'ly.'

'Shinin' lights come expensive,' said Sammy.

'Expensive?' said Susie. 'What d'you mean?'

'I mean—' Sammy saw her blue eyes flicker anxiously. He dropped his gaze and frowned at his blotter. 'I mean it's goin' to cost yer.'

'But if it's the rent, I just said we can afford that.'

'All the same.' Sammy cleared his throat. Miss Susie Brown, invaluable assistant, was getting worryingly pretty. 'You sure you can?'

'We got near to two pounds ten a week comin' in these days, Mister Sammy, really we have.'

Sammy said, 'Well, the donkey's been fed a carrot and you got to pay for it.'

'Oh, we don't have no donkey, Mister Sammy,' said Susie. 'What would we do with a donkey, and nowhere to put him, either? Mister Sammy, ain't you funny sometimes?'

Sammy sighed. It was no good. He couldn't do it.

'Well, all right,' he said, 'you can go back to your work, Miss Brown.'

'Yes, Mister Sammy.' Susie hesitated. 'Mister Sammy, you all right? Only you look a bit woebegone, like.'

'I'll get over it,' he said. Two quid, he thought, two quid, and I don't have the strength to even mention it, let alone ask for it. It's me who's the perishing donkey, and I've got a horrendous feeling it ain't going to get better. It had been like that for nearly a year, ever since he had taken her on. It was crucifying what she could do to his pocket, and at her age too. Those mince-pies of hers, supposing a feller had to live with them day and night, including week-ends? He'd walk about mesmerised, and his business would go to rack and ruin. He'd been in business on his own since he was seventeen, and he'd reckoned to be a self-made man by the time he was twenty-one. He'd miss it by years if he didn't cure his weaknesses. 'I am not proposing to fall ill, Miss Brown.'

'Oh, we'd all miss you dreadful if you was took queer, Mister Sammy,' said Susie, who often wondered why little intermissions with him always made her leave his office singing to herself.

'Should I pass away at me desk, Miss Brown, be so good as to inform Boots me eldest brother to let Mr Greenberg see to the funeral arrangements on account of Mr Greenberg knowing which undertakers will give the fam'ly the best discount.'

'Yes, Mister Sammy, I'll tell Boots that if it happens,' said Susie demurely, 'but I do hope it won't happen this week, like. We'd all be prostrated.'

'Hoppit, yer saucebox,' said Sammy.

'Yes, Mister Adams.' Susie went to the door, her neat blue frock a tribute to her improving taste. She turned and said, 'I just got to say it's heavenly thinkin' about leavin' Peabody's and movin' into your fam'ly's house.'

'I can't afford heavenly thoughts meself, not now I can't,' said Sammy. 'I just committed an act near to financial suicide.'

'Mister Sammy, don't you go jumpin' out of no high windows,' said Susie, and was singing to herself as she went down to the shop.

CHAPTER TWO

It was moving day for Sammy and Tommy Adams, a crisp cold March day. It was also early closing day for shops and the East Street market. Sammy arrived from his Camberwell Green shop at half-past one. Tommy, who looked after Sammy's china and glassware stall in the market, was already there. Sammy was not quite nineteen, but in his smart suit and his air of self-assurance, he looked a good twenty-one. Tommy, coming up to twenty-one, was the handsomest of the brothers, but was easy-going where Sammy was demanding and Boots cryptic. It was Sammy the youngest who was the family live wire, however, an engine of perpetual motion that constituted the driving force of Adams Enterprises, the family business.

Tommy quietly surveyed the kitchen, the place that had been the hub of family life. The glowing range had kept it warm in winter, its thick Victorian walls cool in summer. All the furniture was there, except for the old sewing-machine. That was the only thing Boots and Emily had taken from the kitchen when they moved to their new home near Denmark Hill. They had taken it because Boots's mother, Chinese Lady, was attached to it. Her family called her Chinese Lady because she had almond eyes and had once taken in washing to augment her meagre income.

'We only want some crockery, cutlery and a few odds

and ends out of here,' said Sammy.

'Let's take the dresser and coal scuttle,' said Tommy.
He looked on the ancient dresser and the wooden coal
scuttle as family heirlooms. The flat he and Sammy
were to live in above the shop at Camberwell Green
consisted of two bedrooms and a living-room with
kitchen facilities.

'The dresser's a bit big,' said Sammy.

'Not too big,' said Tommy, 'and we got to have somewhere to put things. Besides, it's an old fam'ly piece.'

'It's only a dresser,' said Sammy, regarding the move
in a more practical way than Tommy. 'Well, all right,
we'll take it.'

'Oi, oi, you there, Sammy my poy?' called a voice
from the open front door. Mr Greenberg had arrived.
The rag and bone man, known all over South London
and in some areas north of the river, had contracted to
do the removal job, as he had for Emily and Boots. He
was not only willing to cart what furniture Sammy and
Tommy wanted for their flat, but also to buy what they
didn't want. Two pounds was his price for the removal
job, which included five bob each for two sturdy Jewish
lads who were to do the humping.

Sammy and Tommy went outside. Mr Greenberg
had brought a horse and open cart. Sammy eyed the
ancient cart dubiously.

'You sure that unsalubr'ous vehicle ain't going to fall
to pieces under the weight?' he asked.

Mr Greenberg's pained look arrived.

'Now, Sammy, vould I hire a cart that vould deposit
your furniture in the Valvorth Road? Vhat good vould
that do to my business and your furniture? No, no, all
shall be delivered safe, ain't it? Of course. Ah, but it's a
sad day, Tommy, you and Sammy leaving your home as
the last of your kind family, and I veep tears over it. But
time is still money, so show me vhat you require to be

13

carted to your new home, and vhat you vould like me to take off your hands, for vhich service I von't charge you, no, not a penny.'

'Half a mo',' said Sammy. 'Eli, I'm frequent not hearing you too good these days. Just make a fair offer for what me and Tommy don't require, as was formally agreed, and then I won't have no further ear trouble.'

'Vell, you got a point, Sammy, and business between friends ain't like other business,' said Mr Greenberg, and began the task of discovering, in company with the brothers, what was to be loaded first, the unwanted stuff. Tommy was a little restrained, Sammy brisk and forthright. The sturdy Jewish lads, Russian Hebrew constantly alternating with South London cockney English, carried the relevant items of furniture out to the cart, Mr Greenberg making a pencilled note of each piece in his pocket book. When it came to moving the wanted items, Tommy began to wander about in the house. It seemed to him that his old home was being bruisingly dismantled. The kitchen, empty and bare eventually, was like a hollow ghost of its former self. And the parlour, once so alive on Sundays, seemed to become devoid of all life except for faint, lingering echoes. The smiling Jewish lads humped, hefted and carried, and the removal of each piece took a little more from the heart of the house.

'I don't know I've had a more depressin' time,' Tommy said to Sammy.

'Fair comment,' said Sammy, 'but when you got to go, you got to go.'

'Boots and Em'ly wouldn't like it like it is now,' said Tommy.

'Well, they're on their way to Frimley, to see Chinese Lady,' said Sammy. 'Cheer up, mate, it's not the end of the world. I'm pleased to remind yer that Chinese Lady her very own self said it was time we all moved.'

14

'I'm only trying to say it's been a good home to us,' said Tommy. 'I suppose you got some feelings outside of yer wallet, ain't you?'

'I got fam'ly feelings which I ain't ever goin' to let go of, and that's gospel,' said Sammy.

Booted feet clumped, and dismantled iron bedsteads were carried out. Finally, the house stood empty, although curtains still hung at windows. Tommy and Sammy were leaving them for Susie's family, as well as gas fittings and gas globes.

'Remember Sundays in the parlour?' said Tommy, he and Sammy now in the passage. His voice rang hollowly. 'And the Christmases?'

'Cost me money, Christmases did,' said Sammy. 'Still, they were good. So were Chinese Lady's Christmas puddings, all of us gettin' a stir for luck when she was mixin' them Christmas Eve. Look, we're movin' out, Tommy, but we got our memories to take. You can't leave memories behind. We've got 'em for life. And there's Susie and her fam'ly comin' in after us, they'll fill the place up again. They're a lively bunch and the old home'll take 'em happy to its bosom. Come on, we'll ride to Camberwell on the cart and save the tram fares.'

'You go,' said Tommy. 'I got Mr Greenberg to leave a broom and dustpan. I'll tidy the place up. Can't leave bits and pieces, or corner dust. Susie wouldn't think much of that, nor would Chinese Lady. I'll follow later.'

'Ah, my young friends.' Mr Greenberg entered the passage. 'All loaded up, all lashed. Now, for vhat you vish me to take off your hands, let me see.' He licked the end of his pencil and totted up figures in his notebook. 'Vell, you're my friends, and friends ain't the same as people. So I von't offer five bob, vhich I vould to people, it being a fair price, but ten bob, vhich is a friendly

15

price. Vill I lose on the deal? I vill, seeing most of it is only good for firevood, but vhat's a small loss vhen it's for the sake of friendship?'

'Don't make me fall over, I might never get up,' said Sammy. 'Heart failure can kill yer, Eli, don't yer know that? We'll talk about it on the way to Camberwell.'

'Vell, I don't mind being hurt a little, Sammy,' said Mr Greenberg, 'but at my age could I stand the pain of havin' you empty all my pockets before we reach Cambervell?'

'I'll just bargain with yer,' said Sammy, who was never going to be able to resist the challenge of fighting for an extra bob or two, however affluent he became. Mr Greenberg smiled in pleasure. To bargain with Sammy Adams was to make a day worthwhile for any man who appreciated the subtleties of wheedling financial dialogue. Sammy, giving Tommy a pat on the shoulder, walked out to the cart with Mr Greenberg. The humpers were already aboard, comfortably ensconced with the furniture. There were only little kids about, their elders all at school, but some women who had been watching from their front doors came over to the cart. There were old friends and neighbours among them, including Mrs Pullen, Mrs Blake and Mrs Higgins.

'Afternoon, Mr Greenberg,' said Mrs Blake, wife of a coalman, and Mr Greenberg lifted his black hat to her and smiled. 'Yer orf for good now, Sammy?'

'Not precisely for good if yer mean really for good,' said Sammy. 'As you know, my fam'ly and me has a high regard for all you ladies that's been our kind neighbours for years. Movin' elsewhere from here don't mean forgettin' you or yer fam'lies or yer kindnesses, which is what really for good would mean. We'll be with yer in spirit, don't you worry.' Sammy never minded making a speech. It didn't cost anything, except

16

a few minutes of his time, and people liked it. 'Me fam'ly wishes you to know it ain't goodbye, just so long, and any time I'm passin' I'll knock one of yer up for a cup of tea.'

'I'll be waitin' and willing, Sammy love,' said Mrs Higgins.

'You sure you said that right?' asked Mrs Pullen.

'I am referrin' to me kettle and teapot,' said Mrs Higgins.

'Appreciated,' said Sammy. 'On behalf of all me fam'ly, I want yer to know all good turns done by yer gen'rous selves during times hard and grievous is also appreciated. If me brother Boots was here he'd deliver educated talk about what yer neighbourliness has meant to us, but as he ain't, I hope yer'll accept my simple wordage in the spirit in which it's given.'

'Lor' love yer, Sammy, you got the gift yerself,' said Mrs Pullen, 'but I can't say I ever noticed you was simple; yer done me for more pennyworths of rotten apples turned good side up than I like to think about. Still, it ain't goin' to be the same round 'ere without you and yer mum and the rest of you. You make sure you give yer mum me best wishes for her consumption when you next see 'er.'

'Bless yer, Sammy,' said Mrs Blake, 'I ain't 'ad a dry eye since Boots and Em'ly moved in January, knowin' you and Tommy was goin' too, and yer mum. They don't make many like yer mum these days, nor like Boots.'

Sammy offered up a knowing smile. Boots was always bound to get a special mention from a female woman.

'Time we was off, Sammy,' said Mr Greenberg from the seat of the cart. 'Vould you kindly bring your fond farewells to a close?'

'Comin',' said Sammy. 'Now don't fret, ladies, you

got a nice fam'ly takin' our place next week. Being a thoughtful bloke concernin' old friends and neighbours, I took it upon meself to make sure our house, which is sacred to our much improved mum, wasn't taken over by some of them dubious geezers from the East End.'

'Well, God bless yer for that, Sammy,' said Mrs Higgins. 'We don't want none of them East End people in Caulfield Place, they don't have no manners nor any respectability, and their kids is all little tea leafs.'

'I give yer me word, yer goin' to have a real nice genuine Walworth fam'ly move in,' said Sammy. 'So long now, and may yer washing lines never collapse on a foggy Monday.'

'It's grievous to lose yer all, Sammy,' said Mrs Pullen, and wiped a tear from her eye with a corner of her apron.

Sammy climbed up beside Mr Greenberg, who lifted his hat again to the ladies and said, 'My dears, I concur vith my friend Sammy's vordage, who vouldn't?' He set the horse in motion and Tommy, from the door, watched the cart move off. Sammy turned his head, and Tommy thought that for a moment his younger brother showed human weakness by taking a last look at the house where they had all grown up together. There was even a little wave. Tommy acknowledged it, then went back into the house. He took up the broom and set about sweeping the floor of every room. He knew Chinese Lady would expect this to be done. He was quite willing. He felt the house deserved to be left clean and tidy. Boots had done a good job painting the doors and woodwork six months ago, as well as hanging new wallpaper. It was only right the floors should be cleaned up. He worked conscientiously. It did not surprise him, the amount of dirt and dust the broom found in some places, the places one could never normally get

18

at because of things like wardrobes and chests of drawers. Walworth grime was like that. It crept in invisibly and found places where it could stay invisible. He emptied panfuls of sweepings into the dustbin in the yard. When he had finished, he washed his hands under the sink tap in the scullery. It was time to go then. There was no more to be done. He thought of Chinese Lady. He spoke to her.

'Well, what d'you think, old girl, will it pass with a push?'

She would want to hold her head up about the state of the empty house. He thought she would be able to. The paintwork and wallpaper still looked new, the lino-covered floors looked clean. He began to say a silent goodbye to his old home, going back into every room to do so and to indulge a last, final look. He could not help himself. Tommy had a softer streak than anyone else in the family, even Lizzy.

This was where they had all grown up under the watchful eye and quick tongue of Chinese Lady, where in some miraculous way she had kept the worst effects of poverty at bay, and taught them that of all things in life family values were the most important.

In the bedroom he had shared with Sammy, Tommy looked out over the street. If the house was not the same in its emptiness, the street was as it always had been. Little kids not yet of school age were watching a man fitting a nosebag to the horse of a collecting van outside the printing works. There were always kids out there. The street was a place of homes, hard-working parents, and kids. In the summer it was a cul-de-sac playground.

Ghosts of the past intruded on his reflections. Chinese Lady coming down the street with her shopping bag and her upright walk. Chinese Lady at her sewing-machine, patching shorts or turning up the hem on a frock bought second-hand for Lizzy. Chinese Lady at the kitchen fireside, darning socks. She darned socks the moment they showed holes, and she tubbed her family every Friday night, making sure they scrubbed themselves free of Walworth grime. Sammy. Sammy with a gleam in his eye, counting his savings, his farthings, his ha'pennies and his pennies, earned by running errands or doing any kind of job. Sammy getting his ears boxed for careless language. Lizzy in the old pinafore dress she wore for school, playing forbidden street cricket with the boys and clouting the ball in reckless disregard of fragile window panes. Ernie Jones yelling in frustration because he couldn't bowl her out. Ernie Jones, killed in France at the age of nineteen during the victorious advance of the Allies in 1918.

Lizzy. Lizzy steel-combing her hair with the ferociousness of a girl determined not to suffer headlice. Lizzy beginning to sound her aitches at fifteen because she was in love and because she wanted to be a lady. Boots strolling home from his secondary school in his casual, lordly fashion, and consequently having the street kids call out, ' 'Ere comes Lord Muck,' and Boots not turning a hair. Boots the gent of the family, with Chinese Lady getting after him sometimes in case he got above himself. Chinese Lady again, going off to the pawnbroker, her shopping bag containing some article or other on which she hoped 'Uncle' would lend her a bob, but walking as if she was on her way to Buckingham Palace.

And Emily, Emily from next door, a living, breathing terror when she was a schoolkid. Skinny, scruffy and never standing still, coming into the house with a rush, her eyes darting quick, flickering glances, and mostly at Boots. No one realised she was more of a terror to Boots than anyone else simply because she craved his attention. Emily at thirteen, stringy as a bean, pointed of nose, auburn hair tangled and unwashed, who would have thought she could have turned herself into a well-dressed young lady and become a godsend to the family?

Tommy wondered where all the years had gone. The family had been poor, yes, bleeding poor, but they'd still been good years, the house warm to come home to in winter, the kitchen range welcoming and the spicy aroma of a hot, fruity bread pudding mouth-watering. They'd gone, all those years, and not one single day could be pulled out of all of them to be lived again.

In the parlour, there were marks on the lino where the old upright piano had stood. It was now standing in the new home of Emily and Boots, because Emily had begged to have it, as well as the round mahogany table. The piano and table represented to her all that she had enjoyed most about Sundays, tea in the parlour and music after tea.

Tommy thought of cousin Vi then. Vi had enjoyed coming to Sunday tea as much as Chinese Lady had enjoyed always having a guest or two at the table. Vi was just about the nicest girl he knew, but he hadn't seen much of her since Christmas. The fact was that in running the market stall for Sammy, he didn't have much to offer a girl like Vi. Her mother, Aunt Victoria, was quite certain about that. She also thought stall-holders were common. For his part, he was glad to have the job, even if he did feel it was going to pull him into a rut. Still, it would be nice to see Vi again, just as a friend. Vi had no side herself. He ought to look her up, she was a pleasure to be with.

He took a last look at the kitchen. Endless chatter, that was what the kitchen had known. Perhaps it was glad to enjoy some silence. Sammy had pulled his weight last night by cleaning the range and emptying the ashcan. The grate, the hearth and the range itself couldn't be faulted.

The chimney sighed to a sudden draught of wind, and a little soot fell. Tommy cleaned it up and used the dustbin for the last time. In the yard the clothes line drooped in a neglected way. He was lingering uselessly, reluctant to make the final break. He walked through to the passage. He thought the house itself was sighing, as if it did not like being empty. Did bricks and mortar have feelings? He grimaced at his imaginings. Still, Susie and her family would soon be moving in, and he thought Chinese Lady wouldn't mind handing the old place over to them.

He opened the front door. He turned, looking back through the passage that had known endless comings and goings. He closed the door quietly as he left. The latchcord was still hanging from the letter-box. Well, the dustmen would want to get in tomorrow, to get to the dustbin. He went on his way, up towards Browning Street. At the corner he stopped to take a last look back, as Sammy had done. He knew he was in a right old state then, because as he looked back he thought he heard laughter, just like the clear bright laughter of his sister Lizzy as a young girl.

CHAPTER THREE

That evening, Aunt Victoria answered a knock on the door of her house in Foreign Street, near Coldharbour Lane, Camberwell. Tommy was on her doorstep, the collar of his overcoat turned up against the chill of March. He lifted his hat. Well, I'll say this much, thought Aunt Victoria, he's got polite ways. But he ought to be doing something better than running a stall.

'Evening, Aunt Victoria,' said Tommy, and smiled at her.

Aunt Victoria, a handsome woman in her early forties, said, 'Why, it's you, Tommy.'

'Right first time,' said Tommy. 'Is Vi in?'

'Vi?'

'Your daughter,' said Tommy amiably. 'You must remember her. She's this high, with two feet and all her teeth.'

'Oh, you and your jokes,' said Aunt Victoria. 'No, she's not in. Did you want her for something special?' The question was asked a little discouragingly.

'Just to know if she'd like to come to the pictures on a convenient evening,' said Tommy.

'I don't know about that,' said Aunt Victoria. 'She's out with her young man just now.'

'Is that a fact?' asked Tommy, and looked rueful. Something like that was bound to happen. Vi was getting very attractive.

Uncle Tom appeared in the gaslit passage. He was a kind man and mild of nature, electing mostly for peace and quiet instead of argument. ' 'Ello, Tommy,' he said. He liked Tommy. 'Glad to see yer, but don't stand on the doorstep, come in.' He glanced at Aunt Victoria. He knew Tommy's mother wouldn't keep a relative standing on the doorstep, especially on a cold evening. 'Come on, Tommy, yer can probably do with a hot cup of tea.'

'He hasn't come for a cup of tea, he's come to ask after Vi,' said Aunt Victoria. 'Still, if he feels like one —?'

'It's all right, I've got things to do,' said Tommy. 'Sammy and me moved into the flat above the shop this afternoon. I thought I'd take a rest from me labours of gettin' straight, and walk round and see Vi. Thanks all the same for yer offer, Uncle Tom. Well, give Vi my regards.' He walked to the gate. Uncle Tom called to him.

'How's yer mother, Tommy, when's she comin' 'ome?'

'Some time in May,' said Tommy, 'and she's doing fine. So long.'

'Vi'll be sorry she missed yer,' said Uncle Tom. 'Drop in any time yer like, Tommy, now that you're livin' much nearer, you're very welcome.'

'Thanks,' said Tommy, and went on his way.

Uncle Tom closed the door. Aunt Victoria attacked.

'I wish you wouldn't go against me,' she said. 'You know I don't want anyone encouraging him to come after our Vi.'

Uncle Tom decided to stand up to her.

'That's up to Vi,' he said, 'it's not up to you, it's not up to neither of us. It's Vi's business who she wants to go out with. And why not Tommy? I don't know a nicer young bloke meself.'

'He's common,' said Aunt Victoria. 'Vi don't have to

24

go out with anyone common, she's good enough to take her pick of respectable young men, she is.'

'Tommy ain't any more common than I am, or you are,' said Uncle Tom.

'You mind your tongue!' snapped Aunt Victoria furiously.

'All right, I'll mind me tongue, and I recommend you mind yer business,' said Uncle Tom, at which Aunt Victoria launched herself into a new offensive. 'I'm not listenin',' he said, and went and shut himself up in the parlour.

'That's it, have a sulk!' she shouted at the door. 'Go on, sit in there and freeze yourself to death!'

He was still there an hour later. Biting her lip, she went and rattled the door handle. He had locked himself in. At which point a key slipped into the front door lock. The door opened and Vi came in, warmly wrapped in a winter coat, with a close-fitting hat snug on her head. Her brisk walk from the tram stop had put a glow on her face.

'Mum?' she said.

'It's your silly father,' said Aunt Victoria, 'he's sittin' and sulkin' in the parlour, and gettin' 'imself—' She stopped, biting her lip angrily at dropping an aitch. She had long since taught herself to speak in what she called a respectable way. 'Yes, getting himself frozen stiff, I shouldn't wonder.'

'Course he isn't, Dad's not as silly as that.' Vi knocked on the locked door. 'Dad? It's me, Vi.'

Uncle Tom called, 'Comin', Vi.' He unlocked and opened the door. The room was warm. He had the fire going, something Aunt Victoria never allowed except on a Sunday. He had his *Evening News* in his left hand, his pipe in his right. He had even been smoking in there.

'Dad, what you up to?' asked Vi. She caught a wink from him. She smiled. 'You cheeky thing, you've lit the fire.'

'What d'you think you're doing, playing me up like this?' stormed Aunt Victoria.

'Just gettin' a bit of peace and quiet,' said Uncle Tom.

Vi smiled again. She took her hat off and pushed at her compressed hair. It fluffed into wavy softness. Uncle Tom felt a pride in her looks and her niceness. No one could say his warm-natured daughter hadn't grown up attractive, and it was good that she'd stopped hiding her light under a bushel.

'Mum,' she said, 'you two have got to stop gettin' at each other.'

'Oh, yer mum's all right, love,' said Uncle Tom, 'it's just that we don't always agree. By the way, Tommy called to see yer about an hour ago.'

'Tommy?' Vi quickened, then said casually, 'Well, it's nice to know he remembered where we live.' She unbuttoned her coat. 'What did he want?'

'Nothing special,' said Aunt Victoria, fiddling with her brooch.

'What's nothing special?' asked Vi.

'Well, he wanted to know if you'd like to go to the pictures with him some time,' said Aunt Victoria, sounding a bit ratty. 'I told him you were out with your young man.'

'Mum, you didn't have no right to say that,' said Vi quietly. 'He's not my young man, just a friend from the offices, and we only spent a bit of time at Lyons Corner House together.'

'Still, being in insurance makes him a nice, respectable young man with a safe job.'

'That still doesn't make him my young man,' said Vi.

'I'm sure he'd like to be,' said Aunt Victoria. 'Next time you go out with him, bring him home after, so I can meet him.'

'Just you?' said Vi. 'Not Dad as well?'

'Your father don't understand these things like I do.'

26

Vi looked at her dad. He gave her another wink.

'I don't know about bringing him home, Mum,' she said, 'he don't have very much conversation. Not like Boots and Sammy and Tommy. Dad, would you like a cup of tea if I put the kettle on?'

'You needn't ask me twice, Vi,' said Uncle Tom, and smiled because Vi, once so much under her mother's thumb, had found her feet.

Tommy received a brief letter from Vi on Friday.

'*Dear Tommy, Dad said you called last night while I was out. We were all relieved to know you were still alive, not having seen anything of you lately. Mum said you asked about taking me to the pictures, which was very gracious of you. I'm giving it consideration. Yours truly, Vi.*'

Jesus, thought Tommy, that's the kind of letter that's a bit hard to take.

Vi, on her way home from her Saturday morning's work in Holborn, got off the tram at East Street, off the Walworth Road. She entered the crowded market. The day was fiercely frosty but brilliantly white, and even the drabbest roofs of Walworth were sparkling and glittering, except around the smoking chimney pots. The smoke smudged the sky, but did not reduce the clarity of the light, which, combined with the cold crispness, had an exhilarating effect. The light and the cold touched the faces of people, and faces tingled, and the light sharpened the faded colours of women's shabby coats. The voices of stallholders declaiming their Saturday bargains cut briskly into the market hubbub.

Vi made her way along the pavement behind stalls until she reached the one run by Tommy. His display of china and glassware was mountainous. He was there. He was always there on Saturdays, from nine in the morning until seven or eight in the evening. He had a mug of hot Bovril on the back of the stall, together with a half-eaten sandwich. His assistant, Mrs Walker, was serving customers at the front of the stall. Tommy was saying cheerio to one he had just served himself. Vi, sneaking up behind him, said, 'Got any cracked cups, mister? If yer have, why don't yer mend 'em?'

Tommy turned. Vi's smile changed into a challenging look. Her red winter coat and her black astrakhan hat, picked up cheap in a Soho market one lunchtime, gave her a picture postcard look. Help, thought Tommy, she knows how to make herself look good.

'Is that you, Vi?' he asked.

'Yes, you may well ask,' said Vi, courage fortifying her.

'Ask what?'

'Is it me. I mean, I don't suppose I'm hardly recognisable to you these days.'

'Good to see you, Vi, and I'd know you anywhere.'

'I bet,' said Vi.

A woman, brushing Vi's elbow, leaned over the stall and searched the display.

'Got any brown china teapots?' she asked. 'Ours got broke. Me old man, as usual. Got 'ands like two left feet. Still, you can't say nothink. Navvying with a pick and shovel all day don't make a man dainty. Well, come on, where's a brown teapot?'

'You're lookin' at one,' said Tommy.

'Call that brown? I call it anaemic. Me sister's anaemic, 'ardly got no colour at all, and she eats her fried liver nearly raw, would yer believe. Don't you have brown?'

'That's brown, lady,' said Tommy, 'light brown.'

'Oyster, that's what that is. Oyster won't go with me brown milk jug, me brown slop basin, and me brown

28

sugar bowl. Come on, you surely got a brown teapot in all this lot. You look as if you know what brown is, you don't look as if yer mum dropped you on yer 'ead when you was little.'

'Oyster brown's very fashionable,' said Tommy, with Vi looking quite fascinated.

'Listen to that,' said the woman to Vi. 'I don't know you can even get sense out of grown-up men these days. It must of been the war. I mean, did I say I wanted a fashionable teapot? We don't get any visits from the Duke of Connaught, yer know.'

'Tell you what you can get out of me,' said Tommy in his amiable way, 'and that's an oyster brown teapot, milk jug, slop basin and sugar bowl. All genuine imitation Stoke pottery.' That little touch he had got from Sammy. It made a silent laugh spring to Vi's hazel eyes. 'I can't make more sense than that, even in front of me female cousin, Lady Vi.'

The woman, casting a glance at Vi, said, 'Well, you're a nice improvement on 'is teapots, I must say. Can yer credit it, not a brown one in sight? There's nothink looks nicer on a table than a good, old-fashioned brown teapot.'

'I like that oyster colour myself,' said Vi, 'it's sort of delicate.'

Mrs Walker, attending to customers on the other side of the stall, looked up, a slightly anxious expression on her face. A homely widow in her early thirties, she needed her job with Tommy. She hoped he wasn't thinking of replacing her with that attractive young lady. Tommy, catching her anxiety, gave her a reassuring smile. The woman in search of a brown teapot was taking a new look at the light brown one.

'Well, I suppose you could say it's more delicate, like,' she said. 'Except I'd 'ave to keep me old man out of its way, and I'd 'ave to 'ave the jug, basin and bowl as well. 'Ow much, then?'

'Ninepence the teapot, sixpence the jug, fivepence the bowl and fourpence the basin,' said Tommy cheerfully. 'And I'll do yer a favour, let you have the four pieces for two bob. Me lady cousin's me witness.'

'All right,' said the woman, 'seeing you're doing me a deal, I'll 'ave 'em.'

When she had gone, Vi said, 'Tommy, you crook, two bob wasn't a favour.'

'Never mind, she's gone off happy,' said Tommy, 'and I did put the stuff in a dec'rative box for her. And she's still got a bargain. Nice you were a help, Vi. Anyway, what're you doing down this way? Meetin' your young man?'

'Don't you start, I've had all that from Mum,' said Vi. 'I don't know why people want to push me where I don't want to go. And didn't you ask if I'd like to go to the pictures with you?'

'I got your letter about considering it,' said Tommy, leaving things to Mrs Walker for the moment.

'Yes, well, I was considering if you wanted me to fill in for someone else,' said Vi, an unusually crisp bite to her voice. 'Seeing you've been socialising with other girls, I suppose I'm being graciously required as first reserve, or second, perhaps.'

'Eh?' said Tommy, flabbergasted.

'I mean, have all your other girls got flu?'

'Hold on,' said Tommy, 'that's not you talkin', is it, Vi?'

'Oh, I do talk sometimes,' said Vi. 'Well, I've got to get home now, I really only came to make sure you hadn't fallen down dead.'

'Ouch,' said Tommy.

'See you at Christmas, perhaps,' said Vi.

'Hold on,' said Tommy. He spoke across the stall to

Mrs Walker. 'Daisy, can you manage by yourself for ten minutes while I see me lady cousin to the tram stop?'

'Be pleased to,' said Mrs Walker, and Tommy began to walk with Vi through the market.

'You don't have to,' said Vi. 'I can see myself to the tram stop.'

'I don't know you can,' said Tommy. 'The way you've been goin' on at a certain innocent party you're more likely to go up in fire and smoke before you reach Walworth Road. Your mum and dad wouldn't like that, and nor would I.'

'You probably wouldn't even notice,' said Vi.

'My eye,' said Tommy, 'I didn't know you could get ratty.'

'Well, I didn't know you were goin' to act as if you'd passed away,' said Vi. 'I thought we were gettin' to be really nice friends together, I didn't know I was only goin' to be asked out when it suited you.'

'Look, I know I haven't seen much of you since Christmas, but what with Em'ly and Boots movin', then Sammy and me, and our mum away convalescing, things ain't been exactly like I'd like, and you get a bit low just running a stall.'

'Oh, that's silly,' said Vi. 'I mean, all the people you must meet, specially people like that woman who wanted a brown teapot.'

'Well, yes, you get characters,' said Tommy, 'but a feller's got to think about lookin' ahead.'

'He don't have to think silly,' said Vi, who thought the atmosphere of the market stimulating.

Tommy smiled. Vi was turning into a character herself.

'Anyway, have you been goin' out with someone else?' he asked, as they manoeuvred a way through shoppers.

Vi said, 'Well, I do happen to be acquainted with insurance men.'

'That's fair, I suppose,' said Tommy, 'seeing your office building must be full of them. Can't say I like the sound of them, though.' He stopped as they emerged from the market. 'You're me favourite cousin, Vi, and that's a fact.'

Vi made a little face.

'That's an old record,' she said. 'Are you goin' to take me to the pictures or not?'

'Tonight?' suggested Tommy.

'Golden Domes cinema, eight o'clock?' offered Vi.

'I'll be there, I'll leave the stall early,' said Tommy.

'Well, I'll be there too,' said Vi, and went home feeling she'd won a little battle.

Aunt Victoria expressed displeasure.

'Well, I don't know, I should've thought you could have found someone better than Tommy,' she said. 'I'm not saying anything against him—'

'Yes, you are,' said Vi.

'Well, workin' in a market won't do much for him, Vi.'

'What you work at don't mean as much as what you are,' said Uncle Tom.

'I wish you'd keep out of it,' said Aunt Victoria.

'Wish away,' said Uncle Tom.

'Dad's got rights too, you know,' said Vi.

'I don't like him speaking out of turn,' said Aunt Victoria.

'He don't speak out of turn,' said Vi, 'he works hard and he likes a bit of peace and quiet when he comes 'ome.' She dropped the aitch deliberately. She was like her cousins. They could all sound their aitches and moderate their cockney when they chose to. They had come to speak 'more proper' because of Aunt Maisie sternly persisting with them.

Chinese Lady, although a Kennington cockney herself, had always tried not to murder the English language, which was what she thought the broadest cockney did to it. She was proud of her country and its language, and she was proud too of the way her late husband had risen above his Old Kent Road beginnings to self-educate himself by comprehensive reading. He had always carried books in his kitbag, and during the Boer War had read any amount of Dickens.

Aunt Victoria, shocked by her daughter's attitude, said, 'And what d'you think I do all week? Not sitting around, I can tell you. Making beds, doing the washing and ironing, cleaning up, suffering headaches and goodness knows what else. It's all right for him—'

'Who's him?' asked Vi.

'Your father, of course.'

'Well, you ought to say that, not just "him",' said Vi. 'Saying "him" like that's demeanin'.'

'Now, Vi,' said Uncle Tom placatingly.

'Well, it is,' said Vi.

'What's come over her?' Aunt Victoria put the question accusingly to her husband.

'She's all right,' said Uncle Tom.

'No, she's not, you heard how she spoke to me. What's come over you, Vi?'

'Mum, do leave off,' said Vi.

'Well!' Aunt Victoria fumed. It was true she thought the world of her daughter, but only as long as Vi was placidly obedient. 'I'm not havin' that. Go to your room.'

'Mum, don't be silly,' said Vi, 'I'm twenty years old.'

'Well, you're not actin' like it,' said Aunt Victoria, 'you're actin' like you've spent too much time in Walworth with your Aunt Maisie's family. Going there all those Sundays last year hasn't done you any good, I can see that, it's made you pick up too many of their common ways.'

33

'That's talkin' daft,' said Uncle Tom, 'so stop it. I never heard such a carry-on just because Vi's goin' to the pictures with Tommy.'

'I don't want any lip from you,' said Aunt Victoria.

'Mum, I don't like you calling Aunt Maisie's family common,' said Vi. 'All the boys are lovely, and so's Emily, and so's Lizzy and Ned, and so's Aunt Maisie. And nor do they have carry-ons like we do in this house.'

'Well, I don't know, I just don't,' said Aunt Victoria, 'speakin' to your own mother like that. I won't stand for it, nor any of them ideas you've got in your silly head.'

'Vi, don't have a silly head,' said Uncle Tom. 'Vi, go and put your 'at and coat away.'

'Yes, all right,' said Vi, and gave him an encouraging look as she left the kitchen.

'Now,' said Uncle Tom, and thereupon got his face smacked by his angry wife. 'That's done it,' he said, and took hold of her. Only then did she realise just how strong her husband was. Uncle Tom was a man who dug up roads and pavements, and laid gas conduits. He had whipcord muscles. He made a puny thing of his furious, struggling wife. Aunt Victoria choked back every outraged yell as she found herself face down over his knees. She refused to shriek, she refused to let Vi hear a single sound from her as Uncle Tom delivered a single hard smack on her bottom. Then he let her go and she fell from his knees in a collapsing heap. 'Victoria, that was to show yer what I could've give yer, but what I can't give yer, because I don't 'old with bruisin' a woman, and if I can't bruise a woman, even more I can't bruise me wife. But just don't go on at Vi any more. You got a good daughter, a sweet girl who's never give either of us no trouble, and it's time you let 'er live 'er own life, it's time you stopped livin' it for 'er.'

Aunt Victoria sat up, face flushed with fury, eyes glittering.

'You disgustin' brute!' she cried.

Uncle Tom slipped from the chair and sat on the floor beside her.

'Come on, old girl,' he said, putting an arm around her, 'we've lasted twenty years and more, we can last another twenty without makin' a misery of ourselves, can't we? You've got yer funny ways, but I'm still fond of yer or I'd 'ave walked out long ago. When you're in yer 'andsome moods, there's nothing Vi and me wouldn't do for yer. If Vi's sweet on Tommy, which I reckon she is, that ain't so bad, yer know. Yer won't find too many as nice as he is, and they're not close blood relations. Yer know he's nice really, don't yer, love?'

Aunt Victoria put her face in his shoulder and cried.

When Tommy brought Vi home from the pictures that night, Aunt Victoria said, 'Stay for a cup of tea, Tommy, and I've made some nice sandwiches too.'

At which, Vi gave her mum a kiss.

Mr and Mrs Brown and their family moved into the house in Caulfield Place the following Monday. Mr Greenberg did the removal job for them, quoting a highly favourable all-in price of thirty bob on account of Susie being dear to Sammy's heart. So he said to Sammy. Sammy, alarmed, repudiated what he termed a slanderous accusation, and did so with some choice verbiage. It put a twinkle into Mr Greenberg's knowing eyes.

Susie asked if she could have Monday afternoon off. Boots said of course. Sammy said she wouldn't get paid. Susie said she didn't expect to be, not for time off. All right, then, said Sammy.

At the end of the afternoon, with the job finished and the gas lamp alight in the passage, Susie sat on the top of the stairs in the family's new home. Her mum and dad were in the kitchen, her mum preparing a large pot of tea. With them were William, Sally and Freddy. William was fourteen, Sally nine, and Freddy seven.

Susie sat dreaming. She'd been right. You could tell the Adams family had made this a happy house, a warm house. They'd left something of themselves behind. It was so easy to imagine Boots and Sammy and Tommy and Lizzy all growing up here, and growing up in a lovely boisterous family fashion. If you closed your eyes and really listened, you'd be able to hear the echoes of their voices. If you wanted to. Those kind of echoes were always left behind in a house that had been a warm and happy home to a family. It was nice knowing that family so well, and knowing too that the mother, Mrs Adams, was recovering from her illness in a convalescent home. She'd brought them up all by herself most of their lives, and could be proud of what she'd made of them.

They'd left the house looking ever so clean, and all the paintwork and wallpaper was just like new. Mum had said you could have eaten a meal off the kitchen floor. Imagine that in Walworth.

The echoes were there, floating up from the passage like faint whispers of laughter, she was sure. They made her feel dreamily happy.

'Susie?' Mrs Brown, plump and equable, came out of the kitchen and called. 'Susie?'

'I'm up here, Mum.'

Mrs Brown appeared at the foot of the stairs and looked up at her eldest child, the apple of her dad's eye.

'What you doing, Susie, sittin' up there on the stairs?'

'Oh, just thinking. Ain't it grand, Mum, movin' out of Peabody's into a house all to ourselves?'

'Your dad's that pleased with himself he's said I can have a new hat an' coat. But the tea's ready, love, and you don't want to stay sittin' up there. You'll get cold.'

'No, it's not cold here, Mum, nor anywhere. It's a warm house, don't yer think so? It's the way Mister Sammy and his fam'ly made it and left it. We're goin' to be ever so happy here, and it's goin' to be so nice for you and Dad, havin' lots more room and everything.'

'Well, the kitchen's really nice just now, Susie, your dad's lit the stove fire, so come on down and have your tea.'

'Yes, Mum.'

CHAPTER FOUR

Rosie, the foster-daughter of Boots and Emily, was six. For her birthday party, they had bought her a new frock. Boots and Emily were the sunshine of her life. Her natural mother, having conceived her out of wedlock, resented her, disliked her, and had done her best to reduce the child to a negative being before finally deserting her. With the approval of Rosie's grandparents, Boots and Emily had agreed to foster her.

She had a rapturous birthday party on 5 May 1921. All the family were there, except Chinese Lady, whom she called Nana and who did not forget to send her a birthday card and a postal order from the Frimley sanatorium. Rosie had been to see her lots of times, in company with Boots and Emily, and the awe in which she held Chinese Lady was turning to shy affection. She adored all the family, Uncle Sammy, Uncle Tommy, Uncle Ned and Aunt Lizzy included. And she was also very attached to Annabelle, the bonny-looking daughter of Lizzy and Ned.

Boots thought Rosie the sweetest and most affectionate child ever. Lizzy told him he was soppy about her.

'Is that good or bad?' he asked.

'What a question,' said Lizzy, a vital and colourful mother of two.

'I only asked because Ned's soppy about you,' said Boots.

'Well, I'm special,' said Lizzy.

'So's Rosie,' said Boots.

'And Em'ly?' said Lizzy.

'And Emily,' said Boots. Emily was expecting their first child.

'Pleased with yourself, are you?' said Lizzy.

'So-so,' said Boots.

'Mum'll be home soon,' said Lizzy.

'I'll buy a red carpet,' said Boots.

'You do that and she'll box your ears,' said Lizzy.

Mrs Maisie Adams, otherwise known as Chinese Lady to her family, left the sanatorium during the third week in May. In her forty-fifth year, she was a pleasant-looking woman who still owned a firm bosom and straight legs, and who carried herself in proud upright fashion. Illness had taken its toll during her time in hospital, but she had fought the weakness of a badly infected lung with the resolution of a woman who had always been enduring. She emerged from four months' convalescence entirely to the satisfaction of her physician, and to not a little satisfaction of her own. Emily and Boots, arriving at the sanatorium to take her home, saw that the shadows of illness were gone, and that her colour was healthy. She had spent as much time as possible out of doors.

When she reached Emily and Boots's new home in an avenue off Red Post Hill, near Denmark Hill, she expressed pleasure on discovering how bright and airy the house was, and how nice the garden looked. There were four bedrooms, and the one Boots and Emily had chosen for her overlooked the garden. And in addition to a large front room and adequate kitchen, there was actually a room specially for eating meals. It was a dining-room. Imagine that. With Lizzy and Ned having one too, the family was coming up in the world.

Still, she would never mind eating in the kitchen herself. Kitchens were cosier.

'Well, we always do eat in the kitchen, Mum,' said Emily, 'unless we got company for dinner.'

'My goodness, Em'ly Adams,' said Chinese Lady, 'you invite company in for midday dinner?'

'It's called lunch south of Camberwell Green,' said Boots, 'and the evening meal's called dinner.'

'Well, I never thought I'd hear you and Em'ly had taken to livin' upside-down,' said Chinese Lady. 'Still, everything's getting new-fangled since the war. I don't hardly know what's round the next corner these days. Still, you got a nice bright kitchen.'

The kitchen faced the garden, and was very airy, but Chinese Lady couldn't think how Emily managed without a scullery. Fancy having the mangle in the garden shed. But it wasn't for Chinese Lady to say so, specially as she'd wanted them to have the house. Boots said he'd been putting in some work on the lawn and flower beds. Chinese Lady asked if there were any roses. Everyone with a garden ought to have roses, she said. Boots said there were rose bushes and took her out through the back door to look at them. He'd pruned them in March, and he showed her the new shoots. He had acquired a gardening book, and also a second-hand mower, the latter having been sold to him by Mr Greenberg for seven and six. He had cut the lawn for the first time in April.

'Well, it's made the grass look nice,' said Chinese Lady, breathing the fresh air. 'I always hoped you'd come to be a proper grown man one day, with a proper consideration of your responsibilities.'

'I expect one day might arrive eventually,' said Boots.

'Is that one of your comic remarks?' asked Chinese Lady.

'Oh, he don't change his spots very often,' said Emily,

arriving in the garden with Rosie. 'He still makes porridge sound like mashed potatoes, if you know what I mean, Mum.'

'But he's not naughty, Nana,' said Rosie, 'we don't have to be too cross with him.'

'Well, it never did him much good, lovey,' said Chinese Lady, putting a light hand on the child's shoulder.

'I'll make a pot of tea,' said Emily, 'and you can come in and sit down as soon as it's ready to pour.'

'Em'ly, all that sittin' down I've done on the train home,' said Chinese Lady, 'I don't need more sittin' down now. Still, I must say you've got nice kitchen furniture.'

'Well, except for what we brought with us, like your pianner, parlour table and sewing-machine, we got everything else from Mr Greenberg,' said Emily.

'At knockdown prices,' said Boots, 'and probably allowing ten per cent for Sammy, who was in on the deal.'

'That boy, makin' money at the expense of his own fam'ly,' said Chinese Lady, 'he'll aggravate me into an early grave, I shouldn't wonder.' They all returned to the kitchen, where she sat down, her hat still on. 'Still, now Boots has shown he's got good points, I dare say Sammy will show he's got some too. Em'ly, you comin' along all right?' That was a reference to Emily's expectant condition.

'I'm fine, Mum,' said Emily, warming the teapot, 'and the doctor says so as well.'

'Nana,' said Rosie in sudden excitement, 'did you know the doctor's going to bring us a baby?'

'Yes, I know, lovey,' said Chinese Lady.

'A real one, Nana, a real one,' said Rosie.

'It had better be,' said Boots. 'If it's not, we'll send it back.'

'Yes, we don't want one that doesn't work, do we,

Daddy?' said Rosie. 'Will the doctor bring it himself?'

'You bet,' said Boots, 'he's responsible for delivery. I'll remind him we want a real one.'

'Mummy, when's the doctor bringing it?' asked Rosie.

'In a few months,' said Emily, milking cups.

'Can't we have it tomorrow?' asked Rosie, blue eyes earnest. 'Daddy, can't we?'

'That's a question only mummies can answer,' said Boots. 'Daddies can't do much about it, except walk about, bite their nails and fall ill.'

'Oh, crikey,' breathed Rosie in alarm, 'isn't that awful, Mummy?'

'It would be,' said Emily, pouring tea, 'if it wasn't a big laugh.'

In the evening, Sammy, Tommy, Lizzy and Ned arrived to pay their respects to Chinese Lady and to welcome her home. Lizzy sat with her eight-month-old son Bobby on her lap, while her daughter Annabelle played with Rosie up in Rosie's bedroom. The two little girls were already forging a faithful friendship.

Chinese Lady regarded her family with the satisfaction of a woman who knew herself home again, even if the home was a different one. Her affection for Ned, her son-in-law, stemmed from her pleasure in his qualities as a good husband and provider. Her fondness for Emily, her daughter-in-law, was constant. Emily had been a godsend to Boots, especially during the four years he had been a blinded war casualty. He still couldn't see properly out of his left eye, and it looked lazy sometimes.

They all seemed to be talking at once. Except Boots, of course. He sat with that sly smile of his showing from time to time, and making only occasional remarks.

'Yes, well,' she said, 'it's nice you're all here on my

first day back and my first day living with Em'ly and
Boots. I kept thinking in the sanitorum about how you
were all gettin' on, and what Sammy was up to, and if
Ned was takin' proper care of hisself. I didn't like what
you said in your last letter, Lizzy, that he'd been climbing ladders with that wooden leg of his.'

'It's not wooden, Mum, it's artificial metal,' said
Lizzy. Sammy grinned, Ned smiled, Tommy coughed
and Boots looked at the ceiling. 'Have I said something?' asked Lizzy haughtily. 'Pardon me, I'm sure.'

'Climbing ladders with a leg like that,' went on Chinese Lady, 'I thought the next thing I'd hear was that
he'd fell off. I don't know it would do any husband any
good to fall off a ladder, nor his wife, either. Still, I
won't say a husband shouldn't do decoratin'. Boots did
our Walworth house up very fetching, which was a nice
surprise to me, seeing how airy-fairy he's always been.
Who'd of thought it, I asked myself, my only oldest son
pastin' up new wallpaper and paintin' all the doors like
he'd suddenly turned serious-minded. Is that one of
them smiles of yours on your face, Boots?'

'Just a passing one,' said Boots.

'I'm only saying you get to thinking of worrying
things when you're in hospital,' said Chinese Lady. 'I
feel better now I'm out and can keep more of an eye on
all of you. You're all still young yet.' Ned coughed.
Chinese Lady gave him a look. 'First Tommy coughing,
now you, Ned. Have you got a cold?'

'Just a tickle in my throat,' said Ned, a good-
humoured man of twenty-six, who made light of his
artificial leg, but was presently having a job to keep his
face straight.

'Where was I?' asked Chinese Lady.

'Keepin' an eye on all of us,' said Sammy, who thought
she was already in fine form.

'It'll be my death the day I don't keep a special eye on

you, my lad. I been hearing you're up to all kinds of tricks, includin' consorting with people in Shoreditch, which is full of foreigners and suchlike.'

'Well, Ma, if you must know—'

'There you go, calling me Ma as if I'd brought you up common,' said Chinese Lady. 'And you're fidgetin'. I noticed you'd picked up fidgetin' habits when you visited me at Christmas. That's what comes of spendin' all your time at business and going to foreign places like Shoreditch instead of takin' up with a nice ladylike girl who'd make you a good wife later on, when you're old enough.'

'Here, watch it, old lady,' said Sammy, 'I'm not goin' to be old enough for that kind of caper till I've made me fortune and can settle down to take care of it.'

'Count it, you mean,' said Tommy.

'Sammy Adams, don't you call marriage a kind of caper,' said Chinese Lady. 'Marriage is holy wedlock, as ordered by God, not a dance round a Maypole. And while you're makin' your fortune, just remember a good wife's worth a lot more than money.'

'Well, I won't mind a good wife as long as she spends her own money and not mine,' said Sammy. 'Not now, of course, Ma. Later on.'

Lizzy rolled her brown eyes. In her twenty-third year, she was a vivid brunette of picturesque looks who always seemed richly fulfilled.

'Em'ly, that Sammy,' she said, 'can you hardly believe he's real? I mean, when you're listening to him, don't it make you feel he's come from somewhere dubious?'

'Madame Twoswords?' suggested Emily.

'Chamber of Horrors?' said Lizzy.

'That's dubious,' said Ned.

'I tell most people I don't know him,' said Emily, 'then I don't get funny looks.'

'Don't mind me,' said Sammy, who didn't mind himself. He was immune to this kind of repartee, which had followed him about since the days when he had lent Chinese Lady money out of his savings at exorbitant interest rates.

'Tommy,' said Chinese Lady, 'are you and Sammy set up proper in that flat over the shop?'

'Fairly proper,' said Tommy, liking the way she was going on in her old style. He knew she wasn't going to say a word about her illness, nor allow anyone to suggest she wasn't as able as she'd always been.

'I think I'd best come round and have a look at the place,' she said. 'I hope I don't find the two of you livin' in a mess. I didn't bring none of you up to live in a mess.'

'It's no mess, Mum,' said Sammy, 'except Tommy could improve his cookin'.'

'I heard that,' said Tommy, who had been missing his mother's spotted dog and all other forms of roly-poly puddings. 'D'you mind me pointin' out you can't cook at all?'

'I got other talents,' said Sammy, 'which Ned has complimented me on, I'm honoured to say. Ned don't have aggravatin' turns of speech like me sister Lizzy.'

'Well,' said Ned, 'I did once say that if Sammy got marooned on a Pacific island, he'd be selling the natives their own coconuts by the end of his first week.'

'Can't no one do anything about Sammy?' asked Lizzy. 'Can't you, Boots? You're our oldest brother.'

'There's room for him in our garden shed,' said Boots. 'If we took the mangle out.'

'What's wrong with putting him through it?' asked Tommy.

'Oh, I like that, Tommy,' said Emily, green eyes joyful, 'he'd come out flat and we could hang him on the line.'

'Very comical,' said Sammy.

'Could we have some sensible talk?' asked Chinese Lady.

'Speak your piece, old girl,' said Boots, who thought there was something more on her mind than a need to deliver typical little homilies. She gave him one of her suspicious looks. He gave her one of his disarming smiles.

'Tommy,' she said, 'where's Vi?'

'She'll be here any moment,' said Tommy. 'She said she'd pop in to see you.'

'That girl's so thoughtful,' said Chinese Lady, 'and she's grown up as nice as Lizzy and Em'ly.'

At which point Vi arrived on cue. Boots let her in, helped her off with her raincoat, and brought her into the front room. The family greeted her exuberantly, and she traded kisses all round before swooping on Chinese Lady, seated in a fireside chair.

'Aunt Maisie, oh, it's really lovely to see you,' she said, and kissed her. 'Don't you look wonderful? Almost like you've been on holiday, you've got such a good colour. Mum's goin' to pop in tomorrow afternoon to have a nice chat with you, and Dad's goin' to call in on his way home from work. They won't hardly believe how well you look. Don't she look well, everyone?'

'Is that our Vi?' murmured Sammy. 'Our Vi on stage?'

'I've had a few surprises meself lately,' said Tommy.

'Nice you've come, Vi,' said Chinese Lady, 'let's look at you. Well, I never seen you more ladylike, I couldn't be more proud of you.' If Vi wasn't quite the beauty Lizzy was, she had a soft, fair attractiveness that Tommy found very appealing. 'Sit down, Vi.'

'Love to,' said Vi, who always enjoyed being among the family. Tommy made room for her on the sofa.

'I been havin' a talk with everyone,' said Chinese Lady, 'just to make sure the ones in trousers haven't been actin' up while I've been away.'

'Oh, I think they've all been good boys, Aunt Maisie,' said Vi.

'Did Vi say that?' asked Sammy. 'Was it her again?'

'Was it?' asked Ned.

'Her lips moved,' said Boots.

'Was it something funny that came out?' asked Tommy.

'I don't understand women,' said Sammy, 'they don't make sense to me. That's excludin' you, Ma. And Rosie and Annabelle. Those two angels ain't women yet, for which I'm gladly thankful. And gratified as well.'

Little Bobby woke up, yawned, gazed up at Lizzy, yawned again and fell asleep again.

'Little pet,' said Chinese Lady. 'Well, with the summer comin' on, I don't want anyone to think I won't be gettin' out and about, which I will be regular.' Boots looked at the ceiling. 'I happen to have a gentleman friend.'

'A whatter?' asked Tommy, sitting up.

Lizzy, delight in her eyes, said, 'I bet I know who.'

'I don't,' said Sammy, whose mind was nearly always on business. 'Who is the geezer, Ma?'

'Sammy Adams, kindly don't give me no costermonger talk,' said Chinese Lady, and went on to inform her family that Mr Finch, once her lodger, had been taking a kind interest in her well-being, and now she was home he felt she should enjoy regular country air. Accordingly, he was arranging to take her out in a hired motorcar once a week to the Surrey Hills, and would provide a picnic hamper.

'I don't know what's happening to me facilities,' said Sammy, 'but just recent I keep havin' days when I don't hear so good.'

'Faculties,' said Boots, a smile surfacing.

'No difference,' said Sammy. 'I mean, I didn't hear

47

casual talk about motorcars and picnics and Mr Finch, did I?'

'Mum, you talkin' about wedding bells?' asked Lizzy.

'Yes, are you, Mum?' asked Emily.

'I don't recall mentioning wedding bells,' said Chinese Lady, who had no intention at this point of telling her family that Mr Finch had proposed to her at Christmas. They would make the kind of comments she didn't want to hear, particularly as she hadn't yet made up her mind whether to say yes or no. 'Mr Finch has done me the compliment of being a gracious friend, and I thought I'd best let you all know. I don't want Boots comin' out with clever remarks no one understands except hisself.'

'Box Hill, that's the place,' said Boots.

'Box Hill?' said Emily. 'What d'you mean, Box Hill?'

'It's near Dorking,' said Boots. 'Beauty spot. Lovely views. Highly romantic. You go up single. You come down nearly married.'

Emily smothered a giggle. Ned coughed.

'I knew it,' said Chinese Lady. 'Ever since that oldest son of mine learned to talk he's been makin' clever remarks. I wouldn't know where this Box Hill was myself, so can anyone tell me what he means when he says you go up single and come down nearly married?'

'He means something it's best not to listen to,' said Emily.

'I've heard of Box Hill,' said Tommy, 'I don't know what happens when you get to the top of it.'

'It's high up,' said Ned.

'Is that why Boots said it was highly romantic?' asked Vi.

'Intoxicating,' said Ned. 'Rarefied oxygen.'

'What's rarefied oxygen?' asked Lizzy.

'Heady,' said Ned, and Emily smothered another giggle.

'Now I know,' said Lizzy. 'That Uncle Boots of yours,' she said to her sleepy, dribbling infant, 'he'll finish up in purgat'ry, he will.'

'Go up single, come down nearly married?' said Sammy. 'Well, good luck to you, Ma old sport, but I beg to inform everyone I'm seriously uninclined to go up singular with any female woman meself. I can't afford to get intoxicated, not yet I can't.'

Chinese Lady regarded her family aloofly.

'If I'd known I was comin' home to a circus,' she said, 'I'd of stayed where I was. It makes me wonder if you've all been goin' regular to church. I don't want any of my fam'ly gettin' clever and disreligious by not goin' to church. You all need some religion. It learns humility, and Sammy and Boots specially could do with a lot more humility than they've got at present. Well, I think that's all. I just want everyone to know Mr Finch is goin' to keep me company at times. Perhaps we could have a pot of tea now, which I'll be pleasured to make.'

'I'll do it,' said Emily, always alive with nervous energy. 'You sit there, Mum, you don't need to—' She halted, then gave Chinese Lady an understanding smile. 'All right, you make it, Mum. By the way, Mr Finch has been here a few times. Boots and me have been invitin' him.'

'Just to help the cause along,' said Boots.

'What cause?' asked Chinese Lady.

'The cause of kind and gracious friendship,' said Boots.

'Anything else to say, my lad?' she asked.

'Not at the moment,' said Boots.

'I'm sure we're all grateful for that,' she said.

Lizzy laughed.

'Mum, it's lovely having you home again,' she said.

CHAPTER FIVE

Mr Edwin Finch, a man of vigorous, worldly maturity, whose affection for Chinese Lady was born of his admiration for the way she had brought her family up in the face of grinding poverty, called for her at ten on Sunday morning. He arrived in a hired motorcar, which Rosie thought awesome. The day being fine, Chinese Lady had elected to wear a brown costume and a brown hat. Boots suggested she took a coat with her, just in case.

'Just in case of what?' she asked.

'Well, a snowstorm, perhaps?'

'A snowstorm in May?' she said.

'Just in case,' said Boots, and she gave him a faint smile. She knew he and Emily were going to regard her as something of an invalid for the time being.

'You're fussin',' she said.

'I think I agree with Boots,' said Mr Finch. He and Boots had a rapport. 'A coat just in case.'

'Well, if you think so,' said Chinese Lady, and fetched a coat. 'By the way,' she said with a forthrightness that was for the benefit of her eldest son, 'I don't want to go up Box Hill.'

'Box Hill?' said Mr Finch. Emily hid a smile.

'It's too rarefied.'

'I wasn't thinking of Box Hill,' said Mr Finch, 'but a place that would offer us a pleasant walk and a pleasant picnic spot.'

'Sounds very attractive,' said Boots. 'Enjoy your-selves.'

When they had gone, Emily said, 'Did you notice how she fell in with his advice about takin' a coat? I wonder, d'you think it could lead to weddin' bells? D'you think they'd suit each other, seeing there's differences?'

'Different worlds, you mean?' asked Boots.

'Well, different class, really,' said Emily. 'We're all working class, and Mr Finch is 'ardly that, is he?'

'I don't believe in these labels, Em, and I don't think Mr Finch does, either,' said Boots. 'I'm against any labels being stuck on us because of what we work at, or what our fathers worked at, or where we live. It's behaviour that casts you as to what kind of a person you are, and I couldn't fault Chinese Lady's behaviour, could you? Further, not many of us stick labels on our-selves, they're stuck on for us, mostly by people with axes to grind, political axes usually, by fatheaded Conservatives, granny-minded Liberals, and class-conscious Socialists. Have nothing to do with it, lovey, it's something they use for their own purposes. Don't go around saying you're working class and proud of it, when we all know we'd rather be filthy rich. I know we've been poor, perishing poor, but it was never a virtue, it was a condition. Sammy saw that before he was ten, when he began to fight his way out of it. He knew that to improve things for yourself, you don't rely on a political party, you roll up your own sleeves. Wit-ness his advancement. All his own work, Em. And it wasn't any political party that took us out of Walworth and put us into a house with a garden and a bathroom. It was you and me.'

'Help,' said Emily in astonishment, 'you just made a serious speech, you just give me a serious talk for the first time ever.'

51

'As a married woman, you've got a vote,' said Boots. 'Who did you give it to at the last election?'

'Not telling you. I didn't tell you then, I'm not telling you now. It's not your business. But you didn't vote at all. That's criminal backslidin'. Still, it's a change to hear you talk like this, all serious for once.'

'Don't you like me being serious?'

'Well, yes, in a way,' said Emily. 'But don't be like it all the time, will yer, because—' She stopped, and smiled.

'Because?' enquired Boots.

'It sounds as if it could be a bit boring,' said Emily. 'Me Dad always said keep politics in the back of your head and don't let 'em get out. He said people liked talkin' about other people best.'

'You had a good old dad,' said Boots.

'Liked his beer, he did,' said Emily, 'and he liked you. Ain't it a rotten shame he's not around to see we've got a house and garden and each other? And wouldn't he have been glad about Rosie, and me havin' our own baby?'

'Oh, I expect the angels are keeping him informed.'

'You get to sound more like Lord Muck all the time, d'you know that?' Emily gave him a little dig with her rolling-pin. 'Love me, do yer?'

'Love yer, Em. What's for Sunday dinner?'

'Men,' said Emily in disgust.

'I don't know I fancy a joint of roast men,' said Boots.

'Oh, very funny. Peel the potatoes for me.'

Rosie danced into the kitchen.

'Daddy, can you come and play in the garden?' she asked.

'Not yet, kitten. I'm on cookhouse fatigues. How about giving me a hand and helping me peel potatoes?'

'Oh, could we have lots of water for splashing?' asked Rosie.

'A bucketful,' said Boots.

'That's it, flood me kitchen,' said Emily. 'I don't know

what I'm goin' to do with you two sometimes, you're a daft pair together, both of you.'

'Oh, crikey,' whispered Rosie, one of the family, 'does Mummy mean you and me's potty, Daddy?' Boots said yes, and Rosie looked quite proud. 'I don't suppose everyone's potty,' she said.

'No, just you two in this fam'ly,' said Emily.

Chinese Lady went on her Sunday outings with Mr Finch, without saying much more about them than that she'd had a very nice time. On other days she went shopping with Emily or out by herself. She called frequently on Lizzy, who was close by. She took bus rides down to Camberwell Green to visit the family shop, now called the Bargain Bazaar, where she spoke her mind to Sammy about his improper practice of stocking ladies' female garments along with men's garments. She was quite sure, she said, that it was unlegal, and that he'd have a policeman come in one day and ask him uncomfortable questions. Didn't lady customers get embarrassed? Sammy said not to his knowledge, not as long as they could get Boots to serve them. Further, he said, it was a good way of doing business, because some ladies buying things for themselves alighted on unresistible bargains for their husbands.

She inspected the flat above the shop more than once, drawn compulsively to the habitation of her younger sons. It was adequate, she thought, but not her idea of a home. It had hardly any atmosphere. She did not, in any case, like this new-fangled notion of men having what were called bachelor flats. Men had no right to live shut off like that. It was against God's human designs. It was unnatural and selfish. There were hundreds of thousands of women robbed of marriage by the war. Men shouldn't set up as bachelors, specially not when so many of these women wanted affection, marriage and a family. God hadn't put men on earth to live like hermits, but to be responsible husbands and fathers. Not on any account was she going to let Tommy and Sammy live in that flat for longer than was decent and right. She'd set it on fire first.

Still, she did cook them suppers on a few occasions. She also visited her old hunting ground, the East Street market, to see Tommy while he was working at the stall. Among other questions, she asked him one day if he was walking out formal with Vi.

'I can't talk to you personal here, Mum,' he said, 'not with Mrs Walker around.'

'She's not listening, she's servin' a customer. Not that I know why you get the customers you do, it's all Birmingham stuff, I'll be bound. And what's that mean, "Genuine Imitation Worcester China"? I never saw such a silly thing as genuine imitation.'

'It's a bright idea of Sammy's,' confided Tommy. 'It tells the truth, but makes people feel it's superior to ordinary imitation.'

'They want their brains testin', then,' said Chinese Lady. 'That Sammy, he's got more hoodwinkin' ideas than that man the police took to court for selling the Houses of Parliament to a Persian gentleman. I wouldn't put it past Sammy to try that sort of thing hisself, and next thing we'd hear would be he'd sold Tower Bridge to Lord Rockinfeller.'

'He's an American, Mum, not a lord.'

'Makes no difference, you know how smart Sammy is.' Chinese Lady let a flicker of pride show. 'Anyway, I asked you about Vi.'

'Vi's fine.'

'It's not my business, of course, but I shouldn't wonder if a nice girl like Vi don't get attention from young men she meets at her work.'

'I shouldn't wonder, either,' said Tommy.

'Well, you've got to think about your future.'

'I just run a stall,' said Tommy. 'That's my future.'

'What's that mean?'

'It means you got to offer a superior girl like Vi a bit more than I can.'

In high dudgeon, Chinese Lady said, 'I'll box your ears if you talk like that. I don't want to hear any of my fam'ly puttin' theirselves down. You're makin' an honest and steady livin', which is more than some men are. All this unemployment still about. Criminal, I call it. All them men who fought in the trenches should have jobs. Now, that flat you and Sammy's livin' in. It's all right, but it's not a proper home, it don't have a woman's touch, and I don't want you and Sammy thinking it's more than temp'ry. Well, you've got some customers lookin' things over now, so I won't stay longer. Just remember what I've said.'

'I'm not sure what you want me to remember,' said Tommy.

'I don't know why I've got three sons all more argufying than your Aunt Victoria,' said Chinese Lady, and went briskly on her way.

'Sammy, it won't be long before you're twenty.'

'Quite correct, Ma,' said Sammy. Chinese Lady had him cornered in his office.

'Time you found a nice girl to walk out with.'

'Not at my age,' said Sammy. 'It ain't decent, not at my age. I'm not matured. If I was I wouldn't keep saying yes when I ought to say no.'

'Yes what? And who to?'

Sammy decided to ignore that. 'I got business brains, I grant yer, Ma, and they're currently pointing me to a new shop in Kennington, not at any young female woman. I ain't ready for that yet.'

'I'm not askin' you to get married.' Chinese Lady,

sitting opposite her youngest son, gave him a firm look across his desk. 'I'm just saying it's time you thought about how to get on with girls. I shouldn't like to think you was afraid of them.'

'Well, I am,' said Sammy, 'they've got horrendous ways of weakening a bloke and turnin' him upside-down in a manner of speakin'. I ain't partial to ending up lookin' as if I don't know which way up I am, it's bad for me business reputation. I know yer got romantic ideas for all yer fam'ly, which is natural and also kindly thoughtful, but like I've said before, Ma, I think I'll wait till I'm forty and matured before I start takin' up with skirts.'

'What your dad would of thought of a son of his makin' remarks like that, I can't hardly think,' said Chinese Lady. 'He wasn't afraid of girls, he was very sociable when he wasn't soldiering, though I had to put a stop to that, of course, when we began walkin' out formal. I'm not havin' you shut yourself up in that flat doing your business books and gettin' seclusive. I didn't bring you up to be a hermit. You've got to learn to be sociable, otherwise you'll never know how to treat girls.'

'I ain't desperate to treat any of them,' said Sammy. 'I need all the money I've got to capitalise me ventures.'

'I don't mean that kind of treatin',' said Chinese Lady patiently, 'I mean how to treat them kind and gracious. Girls like young men to be kind and gracious. I was thinking, that's a very nice girl who's assistant to Boots in the shop.'

'Oh, gawd,' breathed Sammy.

'Pardon?' said Chinese Lady.

'I got some telephone calls to make.'

'Never mind them. That nice girl, her name's Susie Brown, isn't it?'

'Something like that,' said Sammy.

'Well, she's very cordial and pleasing, except she could learn to speak a bit more proper. I noticed her when I first saw her last year, workin' on the stall for you, and I thought then, now there's a nice-lookin' girl with nice mannerly ways. Sammy, is something hurtin' you?'

'Just me ears,' said Sammy. 'I been gettin' every kind of ear complaint for a year now.' Susie had been working a year for him.

'You better see the doctor,' said Chinese Lady, 'you don't want to go deaf at your age. Now I don't want to interfere in your life, I just want to see you and Tommy set up like Lizzy and Boots, with nice homes and fam'lies. You've got your good points, Sammy, you only need to remember what God give you life for.'

'Yes, to make me fortune and not to get married till I know how to take care of me fatal weaknesses,' said Sammy.

'Say in a few years,' said Chinese Lady, and gave him a pat as she left.

She spent a fair amount of time thinking about things, and eventually decided all her sons had grown up and become independent of her. They were all living their own lives and developing their own ideas. Tommy had certain ideas about Vi, and Chinese Lady could only hope he wouldn't be silly about his own self. Sammy had his business, and she didn't think he was going to be distracted from it, not until he realised it wasn't natural for a man not to have a wife. And Boots was absorbed in his life with Emily and Rosie, with a baby to look forward to.

As for Lizzy, her only daughter, well, her life was just what she'd always wanted it to be. She and Ned were always going to be right for each other, specially now they had two children, and specially now Lizzy knew how to manage Ned, just as Emily knew how to manage

Boots. That was always the best way in a marriage. Women being more sensible than men, they were the ones who knew how to hold a marriage together. All they needed first of all was to learn how to manage their husbands. Sometimes it depended on who had the stronger will, of course. Lizzy had a very strong will. Emily had a very sharp mind, which was as good as a strong will, and she didn't let Boots give her any trouble. Those two marriages would be all right.

Well, she thought, seeing my family don't really have too much need of me these days, which is a bit sad but can't be helped, and seeing I feel fine, I don't think I need to wait any longer to give Edwin an answer.

CHAPTER SIX

It was no real surprise to the family when Chinese Lady announced she was going to marry Mr Finch. They happily accepted the expected, although Emily was a little regretful that she was no longer going to have her supportive mother-in-law living with her and Boots. Lizzy, however, made no bones about the fact that she was delighted for her mum. She had felt years ago that she would like Mr Finch as a father.

The wedding took place in the church on Denmark Hill, on a Wednesday afternoon in July, when the shops and market were shut, and Boots, Tommy and Sammy were free. Ned took the day off, and Vi was allowed to leave her work at noon. Many of Chinese Lady's old friends and neighbours from Walworth attended. So did Emily's large, hearty and florid mother, who managed to fortify herself with a glass of rich, nourishing stout on her way to the church.

Also present were Susie Brown and Mrs Rachel Goodman. Susie, hearing about the wedding, asked Sammy if she could come to the church. Sammy said as she knew all the family, she could come to the house as well, Boots's house.

'Mister Sammy, oh, I didn't mean—'

'You're invited, Susie, and you can help hand round the sandwiches and suchlike.'

'Oh, if I can be a help, I'll be overwhelmed with pleasure,' said Susie.

'Very good, Miss Brown, consider yourself over-whelmed, and me family'll be pleasured themselves to have you.'

That same day, Mrs Rachel Goodman telephoned Sammy. She was a young woman of the Jewish faith, married to Benjamin Goodman, a rising course bookie. She knew all of Sammy's family extremely well, having enjoyed Sunday teas with them during the time when she had been Sammy's only girl friend. As a schoolgirl, she had given her heart to him, and he still had a large part of it.

'Sammy, I should believe your darling mother is to be married? Is this what I hear?'

'You've heard correct, Rachel.'

'Sammy love, how delicious. Ah, such a good mother to all of you. So?'

'So what?' asked Sammy.

'I have not had my invitation.'

'Well, it don't happen to be my weddin'.'

'My life, I should want to come to your wedding? Have a heart. But to see your mother married, that I could enjoy when she was so good to me, a shy little Jewish girl.'

'Shy?'

'Is it right, Sammy, that you should keep your only sweetheart from your mother's wedding?'

'There's something wrong with this line,' said Sammy, 'it's handin' me peculiar wordage.'

A little laugh escaped Rachel and travelled vibrantly to Sammy's ears.

'Sammy, you're so funny, and I'm only pulling your leg, I'm only phoning to ask you to give your mother my loving regards and my very best wishes.'

'Come and give 'em to her personally. Come and join

the fam'ly. Boots'll be pleased to give yer a grateful smacker for the loan yer made him on his house.'

'A smacker from Boots? Yer temptin' a girl, Sammy.' The cockney in Rachel surfaced. 'Yer invitin' me official?'

'Official nothing. You're a fam'ly friend and welcome.'

'I should be proud?' said Rachel. 'Well, I am. Shall you take me to lunch this week?'

'I'm a bit short of lunch dibs,' said Sammy. 'Besides which, I ain't disposed to make a habit of lunching with married wives, as yer well know.'

'A habit? Last time was February, five months ago.'

'That's it, like I've just said. It's gettin' a habit. People'll start talkin', and Benjamin'll send his runners round to smash me shop window.'

'Say Thursday, lovey. I'll be at your office at noon.'

'At noon on Thursday I'll be ill in bed,' said Sammy.

'No, you won't. Sammy, it's only for company and a talk. My life, don't be such a skinflint with your affections.'

'My affections for you, Rachel, are considerable. Ain't they always been?'

'I like to think so, lovey,' said Rachel.

Emily had asked Chinese Lady what she was going to wear. Not white, said Chinese Lady, a woman should only go once to the altar in white. Sammy spoke to Mr Greenberg about a new costume, and Mr Greenberg turned up with a swatch of sample materials. Lizzy and Emily helped Chinese Lady to select a dove grey. Mr Greenberg, delighted about the wedding, returned a few days later with the made-up costume at a fitting stage. Only one alteration was required, to the sleeves. When the versatile rag and bone man brought it back two days later, it fitted perfectly. It gave Chinese Lady elegance.

'Lord,' she said a little breathlessly, 'I daren't hardly ask how expensive it is, but you'd best speak up, Mr Greenberg.'

'Vell, Mrs Adams, I ain't saying fetching and carrying don't come a bit costly,' said Mr Greenberg, black hat held to his chest, 'there being vear and tear on my horse and cart. Vill a bob be acceptable?'

'A bob?' said Emily.

'I can't make sense of that,' said Chinese Lady.

'Speak up, Eli,' said Boots with a smile.

'Vell, seeing times is still hard, I'll take ninepence,' said Mr Greenberg.

'Mr Greenberg, ninepence for what?' asked Emily, seven months gone.

'For fetching and carrying,' said Mr Greenberg, 'all else being friendship, vhich is a precious thing to my people and ain't to be found in every country. From Russia my father and mother came, and vith nothing except a hope and a vish to live in peace. Vhy, I have seen my old mother in tears because here the police protect us, vhich vas an astonishing thing to her. Don't I have more gentile friends than Jewish? I vish to charge only for the fetching and carrying. All else is a privilege of friendship. Vhat more can I say?'

'Have a whisky,' said Boots.

'If you vill join me, my poy, that vill be a pleasure.'

'You must come to the wedding,' said Chinese Lady.

'Vhy, Mrs Adams—'

'Of course you must,' said Emily, 'and to the house afterwards.'

'An honour,' said Mr Greenberg, and blew his nose.

Uncle Tom gave the bride away. Aunt Victoria seemed genuinely pleased about that. She looked mellowly handsome on the day. Uncle Tom looked rugged and homely. He was losing half a day's pay, but it was worth that and a bit more to officiate, for he was

62

very fond of his cousin Maisie.

In the church, Mr Greenberg followed the ceremony solemnly. Susie was entranced. Emily and Lizzy were moist-eyed because Chinese Lady not only looked lady-like in her new costume and matching hat, she also looked visibly pleased with herself. Mr Finch in dark grey stood square-shouldered beside her, with Boots as his best man. Chinese Lady made her responses quietly but firmly, believing in what they meant. Mr Finch's responses were just as firm. Rosie and Annabelle were in wide-eyed wonder as Uncle Tom gave the bride away, Rosie's hand clinging tightly to Emily's. Vi sat between Tommy and Sammy, thinking how moving all the family weddings had been.

Mr Finch gave Chinese Lady a gentle kiss at the end. It signified his understanding of their new relationship. Their marriage was to be one of companionship, which Chinese Lady considered entirely suitable for people their age. He was forty-seven, she nearly forty-five. She saw companionship as mutually satisfying, and liked the thought of it when they were both old. It was best for a woman to grow old with a man and not to be a burden on her children. She was not a woman who could live alone, with no one to talk to, and to have a husband again was something she reflected on with pleasure, particularly as she knew she and Mr Finch had affection for each other. Her late husband Daniel, a soldier, she had loved. She still had love and respect for his memory. He had been killed on the Northwest Frontier years before the Great War. She always said it had been very careless of him to get himself blown up like that.

The reception at the house of Emily and Boots was a crowded crush. So many people swarmed in, all jostling to pay their respects to the bride and groom. Old friends and neighbours were amazed at how posh everything looked compared with Walworth homes, and at there actually being a bathroom as well as a garden. And electric lights. My, that Boots and Emily, hadn't they come up in the world? Mrs Pullen asked Lizzy if electric lights were dangerous, and Lizzy said well, Emily and Boots hadn't been electrocuted yet.

Aunt Victoria paid handsome respects to the newly-weds. Vi paid affectionate respects. Susie paid shy respects. Rachel's tribute was warm and sincere, and it delighted her that Chinese Lady remembered her so well.

'Nice you've come to my weddin', Rachel. My, you've grown up lovely, but then you always was a lovely girl. That Sammy of mine, a pity he gave you up on account of always wantin' to make his fortune. Still, I suppose – well, you know, I'm sure.'

'Yes, I know,' smiled Rachel, well aware she could never have married outside her faith. She could not resist adding, 'And I suppose you know you've brought up the three loveliest young men south of the Thames?'

'Rachel,' said Mr Finch, who had known her before he left Walworth, 'I couldn't agree more.'

Chinese Lady allowed herself a faint smile of pride.

Susie and Vi helped Emily and Lizzy distribute food to guests in the house and garden, the afternoon being warm and sunny. Boots, Ned, Tommy and Sammy saw to the supplying of drinks. There was some first-class Spanish sherry contributed by Ned. Sammy carried a gramophone into the garden and put on a record, 'If You Were the Only Girl in the World'. The Walworth guests began to dance and sing. A loud voice sounded from the garden next door.

'Here, what's goin' on? Hampstead Heath on a Bank Holiday?'

'Come and join us, Mr Mitchell,' called Boots.

'Eh? Well, don't mind if I do.'

'Bring the missus,' called Boots.

Chinese Lady and Mr Finch, snatching a few moments to themselves at last, turned to each other.

'You're not tired, Maisie?' he said.

'My fam'ly fuss,' she said. 'I hope you're not goin' to.'

'Oh, I'll fuss,' he said, 'I'm looking forward to that. Do you know, by the way, how well you look, what a nice-looking woman you are?'

'You already want to borrow something when we've only been married five minutes?' she said.

He laughed.

They left shortly afterwards, to drive to Cromer in a hired motorcar, where Chinese Lady could expect to enjoy the ozone of the East Coast for a fortnight. The farewells were many and prolonged. Chinese Lady had a last word for Boots just before she entered the car.

'Boots, you mustn't think your dad would of minded.'

'I don't think that,' said Boots, 'I think our dad loved you. We all love you. Good on yer, young lady, enjoy yourself.'

'You've not grown up a bad boy,' said Chinese Lady.

Mr Greenberg lifted his hat to the departing motorcar and its trailing old boot.

'A fine lady, my poy,' he said warmly, 'and a fine gentleman, ain't it? Vhich reminds me of your own fine lady vife Em'ly. Such a mangle she has.'

'Inherited from the previous owners,' said Boots, watching the car disappear.

'Should any vife in her happy condition have such a big mangle in such a little shed? I vill bring a smaller vun, as good as new, vith rollers to squeeze tears from the finest silk sheets. Vould you say five bob for such a mangle and to take the other off your hands, Poots?'

'Done,' said Boots.

'Such a beautiful day, my young friend, ain't it?'

*　　*　　*

The hotel at Cromer was grandly Victorian, and accordingly spacious. The journey there had given Chinese Lady time to reflect on her wedding vows, and on a marriage of companionship. In her old-fashioned way she had felt that at their respective ages, passion would be undignified and also make her unfaithful to her long-dead Daniel. There were separate rooms for them at the hotel. Adjoining, but still separate. They would have separate rooms in their house on the outskirts of Dulwich. That was not being married, that was not being man and wife. What would people say if they knew? She and Edwin had taken vows as man and wife. To have separate rooms, not to be properly man and wife, couldn't be right in the eyes of God.

She braced herself and spoke to her husband after they had finished dinner in the grandest dining-room she had ever seen. She had drunk wine for the first time. It gave her a heady courage. So she spoke to Edwin.

She woke up early the next morning, and actually blushed at what had happened. Edwin was beside her, still sleeping. She did not disturb him. She lay in quiet thought. It all came down to one thing, really.

She and Edwin were man and wife, as ordered by God.

After Cromer, they set up home together, their surroundings a great improvement on the crowded and sooty neighbourhood of Walworth. Mr Finch kept a watchful eye on her, accompanying her once a month to Brompton Hospital for a check-up. His work with a Government department allowed him generous flexibility, and it was a pleasure to Chinese Lady to realise she was now more important to him than the department. She did the cooking, the housework and the Monday washing, all with the pleasure of a woman who prided herself on knowing what was the role of a wife and what was the role of a husband. There was also the pleasure of finding herself perfectly able.

If she missed close contact with her family, she did not say so. She knew where they all were and visited them regularly. And they all came to see her from time to time. That Sammy, though, he was no sooner in the house than saying he had pressing business to see to.

It was a little after half-past three on a September afternoon that Emily gave birth to a son in King's College Hospital. A nurse took the waiting father to see the baby at a few minutes after four. The mother was being given time to relax, to have her perspiring face and neck washed, to have her hair tidied and to be lightly made up. Emily insisted. She felt wonderful at being relieved of a dragging, painful and obstinate weight, and was dying to see Boots, but not before another nurse had helped her to look presentable. She knew she always had to make the most of her good features, her hair, eyes and mouth. It was her peaky nose, her thin cheeks and her pointed chin that were unkind to her.

The first nurse regarded Boots with a smile.

'Well, say something,' she said.

Boots, not an unsophisticated man, gazed in curiosity at the crinkly face and screwed-up eyes of the infant child.

'That's a baby?' he said.

'It's not a turnip,' said the nurse.

The baby's mouth wriggled and bubbled.

'It's talking,' said Boots, 'it's a miracle.'

'A seven-and-a-half-pound one, Mr Adams.'

'Bless you, Nurse Nightingale.'

'I'm Nurse Caldwell.'

'You'll always be Florence Nightingale to me. Where's my wife, the miracle performer?'

'Just a moment, I'll get my lamp and see if she's ready to receive you.'

Emily was quite ready. Boots came in. She had pillows piled under her head. Her face was a little pale under her light make-up, the shadows of strain beneath her eyes faintly visible, her auburn hair brushed and her nose powdered. He leaned and kissed her. She smelt of face powder and disinfectant. She put her arms around his neck. It was a moment of wonder for the two of them, the wonder of two having become three. Boots reflected on precisely what a woman experienced in conceiving, carrying and giving birth. Apart from the moment of conception, which she would not even be aware of, he could only associate the life-forming process with a long period of discomfort, and the birth itself with inescapable pain. And in giving birth, a woman divided herself to become two separate living bodies. It had to be considered some kind of a miracle. No man could ever know precisely what it all meant, what it entailed, and what it all did to a woman.

'Pleased with me?' murmured Emily.

'You're a living wonder, Em. And I've just seen the other one.'

'It's a boy, would you believe.' Emily relaxed on the heaped pillows, her eyes looking large and dewy. She felt dreamily loving towards him. If there had been moments, a few moments, when she had wished him to be as vigorously active as Sammy and not so airy-fairy, such moments had not lingered. It was his airy-fairy nature that made him so likeable. Strangely, although she was closest to him as his wife, Emily had never noticed the little gleam of steel in her husband. Mr Finch was aware of it, so was Sammy, and so was a certain Mr Ben Ford, who had once clashed with Boots to his cost. 'It was no trouble, Boots, not really. It tried to play up, but I wasn't havin' that. We've got a son, darling. You and me.'

'All your own work, lovey, and I mean the work.'

'And you're really pleased with me?'

'You're my one and only,' said Boots.

Nurse Caldwell brought the infant in and placed it in Emily's arms. Emily held it with all the sensitive tenderness of a mother in wonder at her first-born. It opened its eyes. It opened its mouth.

It yelled.

'There, it knows us already,' said Emily.

'Does it?' said Boots. 'What's all the noise about, then? Has it decided it doesn't like us?'

'That's not noise,' said Emily, softly cuddling the bawling mite, 'that's it talking to us.'

'That's not the kind of talking I heard when I first saw it,' said Boots. 'What's your opinion, Nurse Nightingale?'

'New babies are loudly talkative,' said Nurse Caldwell.

'Well, my wife and I wouldn't want an old one, of course, but I hope our new one won't be as loud as this when he arrives home.'

Nurse Caldwell laughed. Emily smiled. Infant babies always yelled when they found their world was no longer dark, warm and cosy, she knew that.

The baby stopped yelling. It nuzzled.

'Oh, lor',' said Emily with a distinct blush, 'it can't, not already.'

'I'll go and look for Rosie,' said Boots tactfully. 'Lizzy said she'd bring her here from school.'

Rosie, after her first look at it, thought the baby wonderful, although not quite the colour she had imagined.

'Mummy, fancy the doctor bringing us a red one,' she said.

'Better than a striped one,' said Boots.

'Oh, yes,' said Rosie, 'and it is real, isn't it?'

Emily asked for her son to be called Timothy, her father's second name.

CHAPTER SEVEN

Vi put the cover on her typewriter at the end of her day's work. Miss Anderson, in charge of the typists, liked every girl to leave her machine neatly covered and her desk clear. She also liked the girls themselves to look tidy and fully covered, preferably in dark grey dresses with white cuffs and collars, a distinctly pre-war office fashion that did not find much favour with the post-war girls, especially as their supervisor expected such attire to be ankle-length. Miss Anderson looked askance at typists who arrived for work showing their calves.

Vi had defied conventions today by wearing a light summer dress of azure blue. Miss Anderson, quivering with shock, suggested its look and its length were not at all appropriate. Vi respectfully suggested it was the only thing she could think of for a hot tenth of September. At which point a departmental manager came in to speak to Miss Anderson. Noticing Vi, he said, 'Charming.' Miss Anderson was defeated.

Ready now to go home, Vi was not in her brightest mood. She could think of nothing more dull and boring than to be a typist all her life. Emily had been a typist. She wasn't now. She had her own home, she had Boots and Rosie, and now a baby boy. And Lizzy was just as well off. Typing, ugh.

She could hardly believe her eyes when, emerging from the building with other girls, the first person she

saw was Tommy. She didn't know anyone she liked
being with more than Tommy. She had been out with
three other young men who had shown interest in her,
all of them in the insurance company. One had been
impossible, gawky, inarticulate, and no fun at all. As
for the other two, one had actually been disgusting
enough to put his hand up her clothes in the cinema, he
had actually tried to push it between her legs. The
other had been quite nice, quite good-looking, but was
so serious it was painful. Vi could not help always
comparing young men with Aunt Maisie's sons. Boots
and Tommy and Sammy, oh, they were such fun, and
Vi had an instinctive feeling that one couldn't make a
go of marriage unless a sense of humour was always
lurking about. She did go out fairly regularly with
Tommy, but he was really never definite in his attitude, and he had no idea how much she wanted him to
be. Tommy was not only fun, he didn't grope and he
didn't have hot hands. Aunt Maisie hadn't brought any
of her boys up to have hot hands, she was sure.

Her eyes brightened. Tommy was just the tonic she
needed, never mind why he happened to be here. He
didn't half look handsome. She detached herself
quickly from the other girls in case any of them got
competitive ideas. Prospects for any girls of twenty-one
and over were hardly wonderful. A million men whose
average age would have been about twenty-eight now
had gone. In a park on a Sunday, in the streets of the
West End any evening, or at Hampstead Heath on a
Bank Holiday, one saw young women by the dozens
and so few men of the right age. Boys, yes, but not men.
And the young women were lonely. Vi, who had found
her feet, but still did not have too much self-
confidence, prayed that she would not be lonely when
she was twenty-four or twenty-five.

Tommy came towards her. It was Wednesday, the

71

East Street market closed for the afternoon, and he had had plenty of time to call on Aunt Victoria and get to Holborn by five o'clock. He picked Vi out very easily. She looked so colourful in her light blue dress and little dark blue hat. And Chinese Lady would have approved her very ladylike white gloves. Just as well he'd put his best suit on. Just as well he had a best suit. Not every feller did.

'I think you're my cousin Vi,' he said, and Vi liked it that he could greet a girl without being loud and brash. Boots had always been like that, and Tommy and Sammy both knew how to take him off. 'I don't mind a bit that you've kept me waitin'.'

'Well, I like that,' protested Vi, 'I didn't know you'd be here, and, anyway, I've come out at my usual time. Tommy, what're you doing here?'

'Lookin' at you,' said Tommy, 'and you look like Sunday on Wednesday. I'll tell you something, but keep it under your pretty titfer.' They stood on the edge of the pavement, away from the swirling rush of office workers hurrying for tube stations or railway stations or trams, or for the growing option of open-top omnibuses run by the London General Omnibus Company, now making a name for itself. Most workers always hurried in an attempt to avoid what usually proved unavoidable, scrambles and crushes at pick-up points.

'Nice you think my hat's pretty,' said Vi, 'and all right, tell me something that you want me to keep under it.'

'I've formed a guard unit,' said Tommy solemnly.

'A whatter?' asked Vi. 'A guards' unit?'

'Guard,' said Tommy. 'Guard singular.'

'Guard singular?' Vi laughed. 'Yer showing off.'

'I get it from Boots, he's been showing off his vernacular since he first opened his mouth. Well, I'm the unit, just me. For special duties. Like the constabulary specials.'

'I didn't know you could say that,' said Vi. 'I couldn't. What duties you talkin' about?'

'Protective.'

'Protectin' what?' asked Vi, happy to linger and talk.

'You,' said Tommy.

'Me? Me?' Vi looked as if the boredom of her day had come to a sudden end. 'What from?'

'Insurance men,' said Tommy.

'You said that before, that day I came to your stall.'

'It's serious now,' said Tommy. 'I said to your mum this afternoon, I said Vi's gettin' too pretty for her own good. I'll go and protect her from all those insurance men she works with, I said, or one of them might sell her a policy that'll bind her hand and foot. I don't want her gettin' tied up like that, I said.'

'Yes, I can hear you talkin' to my mum like that, I don't think,' said Vi.

'I said to her, I'll go and carry her off.'

'I don't know I can hardly wait,' said Vi. 'Where to?'

'Well,' said Tommy, 'I thought a Lyons teashop first, for tea and toasted tea-cakes or suchlike, and then two-bob seats at a theatre, or a ride to Hyde Park, where there's a band playing this evening.'

'What?' said Vi in delight.

'Your lovin' mum said it was all right, she said she was near worn out takin' care of you all yer life up till now, and wasn't goin' to mind a bit if I took up a share of the burden.'

'She didn't say that, I bet she didn't,' declared Vi.

'Well, something like it,' said Tommy, 'so here I am, your protective guard unit.'

'Oh, you idiot.' Vi laughed. 'But go on, then, carry me off to a Lyons and then to Hyde Park. A band concert'll be lovely on an evening like this. Better than a hot theatre. Did you really come all this way to treat me to a nice evening?'

'I like treatin' my favourite cousin.'

'There, I was just thinking you were fun, and then you come out with that boring old bit about me being your favourite cousin.'

'I meant favourite girl. Come on, let's walk to Lyons.' They began to walk, Vi's light dress fluttering a little. Holborn and High Holborn never seemed to be affected by the depression, its shops and offices always appeared to reflect prosperity. 'I've been thinking, Vi.'

'What about?' asked Vi. Tommy took her gloved hand. She gave it to him willingly. His clasp wasn't hot and sticky, it was cool and firm.

'About you,' said Tommy.

'Me?' A little nervous beat momentarily disturbed Vi's pulse rate. 'Tommy, did you really go and see Mum this afternoon?'

'I thought I'd better let her know I was comin' to meet you out of work, so she wouldn't worry if you didn't get home at your usual time. Highly charitable, she was, as Sammy would say. Gave me a cup of tea and a slice of cake.'

'Oh, I'm so glad,' said Vi in a soft little rush.

'Here we are,' said Tommy, and took her into Lyons. There were a number of young people at tables. Girls met their boy friends here after work. Tommy and Vi sat down. A plump waitress appeared. Tommy said hello. She gave him a tired smile.

'Wish I was you,' she said to Vi.

'Why?' asked Vi guardedly.

'I could be where you are, sittin' down. Me feet's killing me. Never believe it, you wouldn't, but I took this job to get me weight down, and all it's doing is wearing me legs out. What can I get you?'

'Toast and toasted tea-cakes, Vi?' suggested Tommy.

'Lovely,' said Vi.

'Don't want to wear you down to your knees,' said Tommy to the waitress, 'but could you make that for two, and a pot of tea for two?'

'Be glad to,' said the waitress, 'if you could lend me your feet when I finish at six.'

'Be a pleasure,' said Tommy, 'only I'm using them meself this evening.'

'It's not my lucky day,' said the waitress, and limped away.

'I was saying,' said Tommy.

'That you'd been thinking,' said Vi.

'You're a lovely girl, y'know.'

'How much d'you want to borrow?' asked Vi.

'It's not much of a job I've got, runnin' the stall.'

'Why'd you say that?'

'Well,' said Tommy.

'Yes?' said Vi, on edge now.

'I've been thinking,' said Tommy.

'I'll hit you,' said Vi.

'No, it's a fact, Vi, runnin' a stall's not much to offer.'

'Tommy Adams, why're you goin' round in daft circles?' asked Vi.

'Dunno,' said Tommy with a wry grin, 'I don't usually come all over serious nerves. It's being in love, I suppose. Gives me a headache as well.'

Vi took a deep breath.

'Who you in love with?' she asked.

'That ain't a serious enquiry, is it?' asked Tommy.

'Tommy?' Vi was suddenly misty-eyed.

'Best girl I know, you are,' said Tommy. 'I've been thinking that if you happen to have fairly affectionate feelings for me, and it don't worry you too much that I'm only runnin' a stall—'

The pot of tea and the rounds of toast arrived, and the waitress said, 'Bring you the tea-cakes in a minute,

75

if I can last out. Or was you thinking of eating them first and the toast second?'

'You got it the right way round, love,' said Tommy.

'Makes a change,' said the waitress, and left them alone again. Vi, a little flushed, jerkily tugged her gloves off.

'I was saying something,' said Tommy.

'Tea?' said Vi.

'No, not about tea.'

'I mean, shall I pour?' asked Vi, hiding her flutters.

'Yes, you pour, Vi. You all right? I mean, have you been following me?'

'Yes, and I'm very happy, thank you.'

'That's encouragin'. Well, then—'

'Could you wait till we get to Hyde Park and the band's playing?'

'Come again?' said Tommy.

'I'll like it better in the park, with music and everything.'

'It?'

'It won't sound right while you're eatin' toast,' said Vi.

Tommy laughed. People looked.

'You'd like music with it?' he asked.

'Yes, if it means you're goin' to propose to me.'

'Well, I'd like to,' said Tommy.

'In the park,' said Vi, and Tommy enjoyed his toast hugely then, and the tea-cake that followed. Vi, trying to cope with emotion, wasn't sure what she was eating.

The evening air in Hyde Park was balmy, and any amount of people had come to listen to the military band. The outward signs of the economic depression never seemed to touch Hyde Park, any more than it did parts of the City and West End. Seated in deckchairs at threepence a time, Vi and Tommy listened to 'Soldiers

76

of the Queen', a great favourite with Chinese Lady. The music was stirring to Tommy, romantic to Vi. He proposed midway through a Sousa march. Vi heard it. No one else did. She squeezed his hand tightly.

'Does that mean yes?' he asked.

'It's been yes for a whole year,' said Vi, and thought the rest of the programme was made up of the most exhilarating music she had ever heard. Tommy thought that if he'd been unemployed, it would have made him join the Army.

They had the top deck of a tram to themselves on the way home. Tommy said he thought two years would be about right.

'Two years?' said Vi. 'Two years engaged? Tommy Adams, I'm twenty-one, as you well know, and I'm not waitin' two years.'

'I was thinking I need time to give me a chance to add to me savings, so we could furnish a rented house. And me prospects might be better by then.'

'I'm not waitin' two years.' Vi was surprisingly firm in defence of her rights and her expectations. 'I've got a job, you know. We could get rooms to start with, and save together.'

'I don't fancy goin' into lodgings, not with you, Vi. Nor would my mother like it. She'd read me the riot act. It's got to be something better than lodgings. I'll get to work on it.'

'You'd better,' said Vi, sounding even firmer. She felt so heady she could have taken on the Prime Minister. 'You'd better, because I'm goin' to ask my vicar to read the banns.'

'When for?'

'Six weeks,' said Vi.

'A weddin' in six weeks?' said Tommy.

'There, you said that quite nice,' smiled Vi, the tram gliding smoothly over the lines on the straight run of

Walworth Road. 'I never heard anything more silly than two years.'

'I wasn't saying that six weeks—'

'The last Saturday in October would be just right,' said Vi. 'It might turn out one of them really nice autumn days. I think you're awf'lly sweet, not arguing about it.'

'I could argue, I could say where're we goin' to live, then?'

'We'll find somewhere. A nice little flat, not too expensive, say between Camberwell Green and Brockwell Park, so that we'd be able to save for something better.'

'I think I'll ask Sammy to mention it to Mr Greenberg. If anybody ever wants anything special, Eli's the feller. He's a walkin' notebook.'

But it was Aunt Victoria who came up with the answer. Not only did she accept the news of the engagement with handsome good grace, she also gave practical thought to the problem of suitable accommodation. She spoke to Uncle Tom about it. In times past she would not have bothered to consult him. Uncle Tom agreed with her suggestion, he being delighted about the engagement and very willing to help them all he could. When Tommy came round the following evening, Aunt Victoria talked to him and Vi. She agreed with Tommy, she said, that they mustn't start their married lives in common lodgings, that sort of thing soon turned dispiriting for young married couples. So she and Uncle Tom were willing to make a flat for them of their upstairs rooms. She and Uncle Tom would live downstairs, turning the back room into a bedroom. The three rooms upstairs would provide a bedroom and a little living-room, and the third could be turned into a kitchen. Vi and Tommy could live separate from her and Uncle Tom, and not be interfered with, but perhaps they could all have family dinner together on Sundays. Now, what did they think about it?

Vi looked at her father. Uncle Tom smiled and nodded.

'But it's up to the two of you,' he said. 'Mother and me ain't goin' to force yer.'

'Oh, it's so good of you and Mum,' said Vi, and looked at Tommy. Tommy was giving it thought. 'Tommy, what d'you think?'

'It's gen'rous of your mum and dad, and that's a fact,' said Tommy soberly, and Aunt Victoria thought then that he was going to turn the suggestion down, that she wasn't going to enjoy the pleasure of still having Vi under her roof.

'Emily and Boots lived with your mother, Tommy,' she said, 'and it seemed to work fine.'

'Well, Em'ly and Boots like a good old fam'ly atmosphere,' said Tommy, and smiled. 'So do I, and at Sunday dinner especially. You sure you don't mind splittin' your house in half?'

'We don't mind a bit, partic'larly for you and Vi,' said Uncle Tom.

'And you needn't pay any rent,' said Aunt Victoria, 'and that'll help you save more for your own proper place later on.'

'I think we should pay rent,' said Tommy.

'Yes, Mum, we ought to pay something,' said Vi. 'Oh, it really is good of you and Dad.'

'I see yer point about rent,' said Uncle Tom. 'Five bob a week suit yer, Tommy?'

'That's not very much for the whole of the upstairs,' said Tommy.

'Well, what d'you think, then?' asked Uncle Tom.

'Seven and six would be fairer,' said Tommy, wisely not wanting to be too beholden.

'All right,' said Uncle Tom, 'but we won't mind

knockin' it down to six bob if Vi stops workin'.'

Which meant if a baby came along, of course. Vi, not worldly, coloured a little as she drew the inference, then she laughed and hugged her father, and then her mother.

Aunt Victoria let the young couple have the parlour to themselves afterwards, where they talked and made plans, Vi in excited fits and starts, Tommy in his thoughtful and agreeable way. And for the first time they cuddled, kissed and caressed like lovers. Tommy discovered Vi had exciting legs and a warm, loving mouth, and Vi discovered Tommy was a healthy pleasure to her. All the same, she had to make some protest. It was only proper to.

'Tommy, you cheeky devil – well, I don't know!'

'What's up?' murmured Tommy.

'My dress.'

'Can't think how that happened,' said Tommy. 'Still, can't be helped, and it's all in a good cause.'

'What good cause?'

'Mine,' said Tommy.

Chinese Lady could hardly disguise her pleasure when Tommy called on a Wednesday afternoon to have a cup of tea with her and give her the news that he and Vi were going to be married.

'Well, I never, imagine that,' she said. 'You and our Vi, who'd of thought it?'

'You would,' said Tommy, 'you thought of it when I was one year old and Vi was still in nappies.'

'Don't you start soundin' like Boots,' said Chinese Lady, 'I get enough clever remarks from him. Still, you got sense, Tommy. Best for young men to marry lady-like girls with all them flighty ones about since the war. Our Vi'll be a nice wife. Always been a sweet girl, she has.'

'Tell you what,' said Tommy, letting his mother refill his cup, 'this fam'ly's gettin' the best collection of legs that ever knocked 'em in the Old Kent Road. Lizzy's always had corkers, Em'ly's grown two unbeatable ones, Vi's got sparklers, and I 'ad it on good authority from Sammy once that you got—'

'I'll box your ears!' said Chinese Lady.

'Help yerself, Mum. Still, you can't argue with what's fact. Makes you feel proud what this fam'ly could show the world when Vi joins up.'

'If I thought you was goin' to turn vulgar, Tommy Adams—' Chinese Lady stopped. Her mouth twitched. 'You better finish up that cake and tell me about the wedding and everything.'

She had her own news to impart, but kept it to herself for the time being. Edwin had been very thoughtful, very observant, and had come to know how much she missed being near her family. She had been fretting lately about how Emily was coping with her first baby. She'd have liked to keep a daily watch on the infant.

Mr Finch knew this. He suspected it was because it was Boots's first child. She had never shown favouritism, but he knew, as Lizzy knew, that she had special feelings for Boots, her own first child. He also knew that her sons and her daughter were an indivisible part of her life. So he had recently had a long conversation with Boots and Emily, both of whom had been entirely responsive. Accordingly, they were now looking for a large house, one that could accommodate all of them, but without getting in each other's way. Boots knew his mother would protest at the arrangement, but welcome it, and Emily could hardly wait. An only child, Emily craved a home full of family sounds.

A month after Vi and Tommy were married, the move

took place, to a very commodious house near North Dulwich railway station. Chinese Lady could not have been more contented. She had a husband, a son, a daughter-in-law and a grandson to keep an eye on. And she also had Rosie, for whom she had a special affection.

CHAPTER EIGHT

In 1923, when Susie was nineteen, Sammy opened a
ladies' wear shop in Brixton and put her in charge as
manageress, thus keeping a promise he had made to
her. He was fully acquainted with her talents and her
acquired self-confidence. He was sure she could do the
job, with the help of an assistant. Susie quickly proved
herself. Sammy kept the shop stocked with every kind of
ladies' wear, including coats. Most items emanated
from a Shoreditch sweatshop at prices the owner, Mr
Reuben Morris, swore would bankrupt him. Talk like
that bounced airily off Sammy, who didn't believe it,
anyway.

After a successful first year, he added a lingerie
department and engaged a second assistant for Susie.
He called in once a week to see how things were going,
to check takings and stock, and to pay the wages. He
never failed to compliment Susie, conducting his dia-
logues with her with the ease of a man who had freed
himself of distractions. Apart from his weekly visits,
Susie and her mesmerising blue eyes were out of the
way in Brixton, and he carried on unhindered in
Camberwell.

He was making money. His three shops – he had a
third in Kennington – were renowned for offering bargains. The Kennington and Camberwell shops dealt in
clothing, household linen and household goods, mostly

WD surplus. The ladies' wear shop at Brixton offered up-to-date styles of very passable quality and excellent stitching at prices that were irresistible. His mark-up was low, but it ensured an increasing turnover and a reasonable profit. He was building steadily on that.

However, during the second year as manageress at Brixton, Susie began to feel the challenge was losing its flavour. She felt she was actually out of things, that everything exciting about the progress of Adams Enterprises was happening in Camberwell, not Brixton. She felt something was missing from her life.

There was another young girl in the house in Caulfield Place where Rosie had once lived. Nine-year-old Daisy was the daughter of Mr and Mrs Cook. She had black hair and eyes as bright as polished brown buttons. She was a little plump and the street kids called her Pudden.

On his way home from school one day, ten-year-old Freddy Brown, Susie's younger brother, saw Daisy in the middle of a group of street kids. Charlie Higgins, eleven, and the leader of the kids, had Daisy's woollen hat on. It had two pom-poms. He was holding Daisy off as she tried to snatch her hat back. The other kids were laughing. Freddy liked Daisy. She was a newcomer but a sport. She had spirit too, and was showing it now in her attempts to kick Charlie. Her teeth were gritted in determination.

There was no great harm in the general antics of street kids. Dads walloped erring offspring who went too far, or the local bobbies tweaked their ears and spoke magisterially to them about the terrors of Dartmoor. It was a fact that boys sometimes picked on easy targets, and they all liked to tease girls.

Freddy stepped off the pavement, pushed inside the group and whipped Daisy's hat off Charlie's head.

' 'Ere, whadyerdo that for?' asked Charlie, peeved.

'It don't suit yer, Charlie,' said Freddy, 'not unless yer wear a frock with it.'

'I'll bleedin' spiflicate yer,' said Charlie.

'What for? Was yer actually thinkin' of buyin' a frock, then?' asked Freddy, who was as tall as Charlie and a lot more cheerful.

'That's done it,' said Charlie amid the guffaws of other kids. He spat on his hands. 'I'm goin' to bash both yer mince pies to the back of yer bonce so's yer won't know if yer comin' or goin'.'

'Nasty, that sounds,' said Freddy. Charlie balled his right fist and began to wind his arm up. 'Charlie, yer showing off.'

'Watch yer conk,' said Charlie, 'it's in me way.'

'You Charlie!' Mrs Higgins called from an upper window. Her head was out of it. 'What you doing?'

'Nuffink, Ma,' said Charlie. 'Yet,' he muttered.

'What's that?'

'He's talkin' about buying a frock, Mrs Higgins,' called Freddy, and Daisy, standing beside him, hat back on her head, giggled.

' 'E's talkin' about what?' yelled Mrs Higgins.

'It's to go with a pom-pom hat,' called Freddy.

'Oh, yer bleedin' monkey,' hissed Charlie. The other kids were all huge grins.

'What's that?' shouted Mrs Higgins. 'I'll give 'im pom-pom 'ats. Charlie, you come indoors so I can find out what you're up to out there.'

'Me?' said Charlie. 'Me? I'm just standin' 'ere, Ma, that's all I'm doing, just standin' 'ere.'

'Well, all right. But don't let me see yer 'elping yerself to young Daisy's 'at, if that's what it's all about. You treat girls nice, you 'ear?'

'Yus, Ma,' growled Charlie.

'Just jokin', he was, Mrs Higgins,' said Freddy. 'Come on, Daisy, I'll treat yer to one of me mum's jam tarts.'

'Oh, ta and fanks,' said Daisy, and went with her champion.

'Then yer can 'elp me with me Meccano,' said Freddy generously.

'I'm good at Meccano,' said Daisy. She thought. 'I fink.'

She enjoyed two jam tarts under the motherly eye of Mrs Brown, then helped Freddy finish the building of a Meccano crane.

In January 1924, the poor people of London danced in the streets. So did some Russian exiles, to celebrate the death of Lenin, and in ignorance of the fact that the cold mercilessness of Lenin was to be replaced by the savage butchery practised by Stalin.

The poor people danced because a Labour Government, under the Premiership of Mr Ramsay MacDonald, had been elected for the very first time. There was great hope at last of a better deal for the poor. The Labour Party had made firm promises. Ex-suffragettes also celebrated, for among the promises was a better deal for women. Ellen Wilkinson, a member of Mr MacDonald's cabinet, was a fiery redhead and a champion of women's rights.

Everything pointed to an improvement in the lives of the oppressed. Emily said a Labour Government certainly couldn't be worse than a Liberal or Conservative one. Chinese Lady said she'd wait and see what Labour did for the war widows, the war disabled and the unemployed ex-servicemen before giving any opinions. She didn't trust any politicians, she said. If she favoured any of them at all, it was the Conservatives, simply because she secretly felt they were the most respectable. She did say she didn't think there were any good Parliaments anywhere. Mr Finch said he thought the British Parliament was an improvement on most others. Boots said Sammy had bought a new overcoat of herring-bone grey. Chinese Lady said she'd given up hoping the day would come when her only oldest son might start talking sense. What, she asked, was Sammy's new overcoat to do with a new Labour Government? Boots said not very much, but he just thought she'd like to know Sammy looked a prosperous businessman in it. Chinese Lady said she was gratified to hear it, but it still didn't make sense to her. Emily said Boots never took much interest in politics, and hadn't bothered to go and vote again, which was a backsliding act. Mr Finch said it was a privilege to have a vote, and that not to exercise it was an expression of democratic freedom. Emily insisted it was backsliding, and that if too many people backslided you could lose that freedom. Boots said he hadn't come across the word backslided before. Chinese Lady said nor had she, but it sounded all right to her and made sense, which was more than he did. Mr Finch said that not making sense could be very entertaining. Chinese Lady at once said she hoped he wasn't going to go the same way as her comedian son.

The Labour Party, the voice of the people, probably had the shrewdness to realise that conversations expressing both hope and doubt were going on all over the country, for they committed themselves enthusiastically to their manifold tasks. They had an excellent Chancellor of the Exchequer in Philip Snowden, but almost at once he came up against the same economic problems that had bedevilled previous Governments. But he persisted, and so did his Party.

Alas, the first Labour Government did not last long. It fell in November. The Conservatives returned to power, with Mr Stanley Baldwin as Prime Minister. Emily said it was a crying shame. Chinese Lady said it was more trying than crying, that people ought to know by now politicians all made promises they knew they couldn't keep or weren't going to keep. Rosie, now nine, said everything was awful confusing to girls her age. Mr Finch said it was just as confusing to men his age. Emily said she hoped the Labour Party would get another chance, she thought they were at least more honest than the Conservatives or Liberals. Chinese Lady said honesty was all right, but not much good if they were mental deficient. Emily said, oh Mum you can't really say that about the Labour people. Chinese Lady said she was saying it. Mr Finch said he thought it was ministerial inexperience due to the fact that the Labour Party had never governed the country before. Same thing, said Chinese Lady. Boots said Vi was giving up her job. What, asked Chinese Lady, was that to do with Labour's minist'ral inexperience? Wait a moment, she said, giving up her job? Our Vi? Boots said Tommy had called at the shop to give him the news. Mr Finch asked if that meant a happy event was expected. Boots said Tommy hadn't mentioned happy event, only that Vi was nicely in the family way. Chinese Lady, delighted, nevertheless said don't be common. Rosie asked what the family way was. Emily said the doctor was going to bring Uncle Tommy and Auntie Vi a baby later on.

Emily had a part-time job herself, with the Camberwell Green estate agents, from nine until one o'clock. Chinese Lady was not too sure she approved, but all the same she happily looked after three-year-old Timothy while Emily was at work. Emily said she had prospects with the firm. Chinese Lady spoke to Boots. She said she was afraid Emily was forgetting she was a wife and mother, and the time might have to come when he'd have to put his foot down, which was what a husband should do when his wife talked about prospects outside her home and family. Weren't they going to have any more children? Two wasn't much, especially as only Timmy was their own. Boots said he was hoping for others, and had been during the last year or so. Look at Lizzy and Ned, said Chinese Lady, they've got four now, Annabelle, Bobby, Emma and Edward. Yes, lovely, said Boots. I don't know what's coming over our Em'ly, said Chinese Lady. She likes having a job, said Boots. That's all very well, said Chinese Lady, but there's wives whose husbands don't have any job at all, and half the time she's not here being a mother to little Tim.

Boots thought about it and spoke to Emily, without mentioning his mother's opinions. Emily sprang to her own defence and would have quarrelled with him, except that Boots wouldn't let her. He simply told her to take it easy, and that if what she was doing was what she really wanted to do, to carry on doing it. Did she want to work for the firm some time, by the way? Emily said she thought she liked it better being on her own, like, it was more of a challenge.

Boots said it was a pity there had been no more children. Emily said well, they had Rosie and Tim, they couldn't grumble.

Vi gave birth to a baby girl in May 1925. She and Tommy called her Alice. Aunt Victoria lost her head and acted as if she was the only woman who had ever been a grandmother. She frequently called on Chinese Lady and regaled her with minute accounts of the baby's amazing activities. Chinese Lady did what she could to fill Aunt Victoria's mouth with home-made cake and to get in a few words of her own, every one of which sailed over the top of Aunt Victoria's head. Uncle Tom's feelings were expressed less verbally. His beaming smile told all.

Vi was entirely happy with Tommy and her infant daughter in the flat she and her husband had fashioned for themselves in her parents' house. Tommy, however, had his mind on a house of their own. Things, perhaps, were a little better than they'd been in 1921, unemployment a little less acute, and business in the market quite brisk. All markets did consistent business, for every market offered people the lowest prices they could get. Tommy thought a great deal of Vi. She had a very warm and affectionate nature, and if she had learned to stand up for herself, she did so with him in an unquarrelsome way. Tommy, who was like Boots in that he did not ask for the moon, nevertheless wanted something better for Vi than a flat in her parents' house. Lizzy and Ned had a house with a garden. Boots and Emily lived with Mr Finch and Chinese Lady in a house with a garden. Tommy thought he ought to work to provide Vi with no less. He told Sammy he was keeping his eye open for an engineering job with prospects. Sammy almost fell down.

'Not on your Nelly,' he said, recovering.

'Did you say that for a laugh?' asked Tommy.

'Did I hell,' said Sammy. 'Let me inform you, mate, I owe me advance to a limited company to me rigid inclination never to say anything for laughs.' Adams Enterprises had become a limited company late in 1924, Sammy the managing director and major shareholder, Boots the chairman. 'Kindly let it be known my reliance on you as manager of the market stall is one of fam'ly faith. All right, I'll give yer a rise. Five bob. From this week. How's that?'

'Bloody enormous,' said Tommy, 'and I'll still be keepin' my eyes open.'

'You'll upset me considerable with that kind of language and that kind of ingratitude,' said Sammy, 'and you a husband and father too. Yer know I was brought up respecting these things. I might be a husband and father meself one day. If I can find the time.'

'It'll cost yer,' said Tommy.

'Jesus,' said Sammy, 'you've already given me a nasty turn, don't give me a gorblimey headache as well.'

' 'Strewth,' said Tommy, 'I never heard anyone carry on like you do about the 'orrors of affordin' a wife. Yer missin' out, cock, and yer don't know it. It's me honest opinion you're running scared. You got Susie out of yer way by sendin' her to Brixton, didn't you?'

'Susie?' said Sammy. 'What Susie? Oh, Susie Brown. Good business move that was, Tommy, makin' her the manageress. She's a natural. I ain't askin' to be complimented on me business savvy, but I'd be obliged if you'd make yer conversation more cultural.'

'You're killing me,' said Tommy.

'It's a furnished room,' said Mrs Stubbs of Westmoreland Road. Her caller was obviously a widow, for she wore a black coat, a black hat and a black veil.

'Furnished?' It was a soft-spoken enquiry.

'I only let furnished. It's five shillings a week.'

'How kind. Thank you.'

'I don't know about kind,' said Mrs Stubbs. 'I couldn't ask less, and I'm not askin' more. D'you want to see it?'

'Thank you.' The veiled woman murmured to herself. 'Yes, may I see it?'

She speaks very nice, thought Mrs Stubbs, she must have come down in the world to be looking for lodgings.

'Come in. I'll show you the way.' Mrs Stubbs led the woman up the stairs to the back room. It was adequately furnished and looked clean and tidy. A companion set stood in the hearth, but there was no fire laid. The room was cold on this late autumnal day. 'I can order some coal for you, it's a nice cosy room when the fire's goin', and there's a gas ring in the corner.'

'How kind.' The woman's soft voice was not much more than a murmur. 'Yes, thank you, I'll take it.' She looked down at the suitcase she was carrying. She placed it on the floor with a sigh of relief.

'All right,' said Mrs Stubbs, who preferred gentleman lodgers on the whole. But she felt sympathetically disposed to a woman obviously recently widowed. 'Come down and I'll make a pot of tea. I expect you'd like a cup of tea, carrying that heavy suitcase and all. Then I'll make out a rent book. The rent's in advance, of course, y'know. Could I 'ave the pleasure of knowing your name?'

'Yes. Thank you.'

'Mrs—?'

'Pardon?'

'You're Mrs—?'

'Oh, yes, my name.' The woman smiled beneath her veil. 'Mrs Smith.'

'I'm Mrs Stubbs, and pleased to know you, Mrs Smith.'

'Such a problem, you know.'

'What?' asked Mrs Stubbs.

'A cup of tea will be so nice. Thank you.'

There was hardly anything to be got out of the woman over the tea. She offered no information about herself, and answered questions only in a vague way, but Mrs Stubbs thought her a nice, gentle person.

The woman went out the following day. She was dressed in a dark blue coat, a matching hat and a blue veil. She descended from the tram at Manor Place and stood in the road, looking about her. The tram went off, and the driver of a corporation water cart brought his pair of horses to a sudden stop. The pair reared and plunged. He bawled at the woman.

'Don't stand there waitin'. for Christmas, missus! Gedoudavit!'

The woman neither answered nor looked at him. She crossed the tramlines heedless of the traffic and was bawled at again, by the driver of a fruit wholesaler's van. She took no notice. She reached the pavement and proceeded down Browning Street in a leisurely and almost dreamy way. She passed Caulfield Place. She stopped, seeming unsure of where she was. She retraced her steps and entered Caulfield Place. She halted midway, her heavy veil masking her face and her expression of uncertainty. Mrs Higgins, cleaning her front bedroom, raised the window and put her head out.

'Who yer lookin' for, love?'

The woman, startled, turned about and walked back to Browning Street. She turned left. She walked to St John's Church. She went in. It was empty. She sat down in a pew.

Her lips moved, as if she was praying.

CHAPTER NINE

On a morning in November 1925, Miss Polly Simms, teacher at St Luke's Church School, which lay to the west of Ruskin Park in South-East London, stood at the entrance and peered through the fog. She picked out the vague shapes of children coming in through the gates. They could be better heard than seen, but even the clarity of their young voices was muted by the blanket of yellow.

' 'Ere comes old Beaver,' said the voice of a boy invisible.

Poor Mr Stokes. Due to retire soon, his beard had always provoked sly cheekiness behind his back. This time, however, the miscreant had been heard.

'Stay in after school, Potts,' said Mr Stokes, headmaster.

Polly heard Potts say in shocked innocence, 'What, me, sir?'

'Stay in after school. Report to me.'

'Me, sir?'

'Yes, you, sir.'

'Whaffor, sir?'

'Impertinence.'

'Crikey, I ain't done nothink.'

'Impertinence is not nothing, Potts. Impertinence is punishable by death.'

The dialogue sounded hollow in the fog hanging

thickly over the school playground. Mr Stokes emerged from the yellowness. He was coated and hatted, and wore a woollen muffler around his neck. He gave Polly a nod and a smile.

'Good morning, Miss Simms. This is going to last all day.'

'I hope not,' said Polly, twenty-nine and quite the most attractive teacher growing boys could ever get a crush on. The frontal points of her bobbed dark hair curved in the fashion of film star Colleen Moore. Mr Stokes entered the school. Polly looked at her watch. Seven minutes to nine. She heard other voices, girls' voices, then Potts again.

'Lummy, 'ere's our Lady Mucks. Didn't yer get lorst, then?'

'Ugh, it's spotty Potty,' said ten-year-old Rosie Adams.

'Blessed urchin,' said Annabelle Somers, almost nine.

'Gertcher,' said Potts, a shifting figure in the fog.

'Rosie? Rosie Adams?' called Polly, who had taken up teaching in a spirit of defiant challenge. Her father, a general, had helped her secure a position at St Luke's two years ago. St Luke's, because it taught children of working-class and lower middle-class parents, was another challenge, and it was also in the right spot. It kept her in touch with the father of one of the pupils. She was a first-class teacher and it exhilarated her to know it.

Rosie appeared, Annabelle beside her. Both girls were in warm winter coats. Rosie's honey-coloured hair, showing two pigtails tied with dark blue ribbons, was crowned with a straw boater. Annabelle wore a beige tam-o'-shanter over her chestnut hair. Rosie was extraordinarily pretty, her blue eyes already long-lashed. Annabelle was round of face, brown-eyed and bubbly. She and Rosie were fast friends and destined to be so all their lives.

'Good morning, Miss Simms,' said Rosie in her precise little way. 'Isn't the fog just awful? Annabelle and me – oh, lor', Annabelle, where's Bobby?'

Bobby was Annabelle's five-year-old brother, and this was his first term at St Luke's.

'You Bobby!' called Annabelle. 'Where are you?'

'Here,' called a young boy's voice. Then, 'Girls, don't they fuss, Olly?'

'That boy,' said Annabelle, 'I don't know what we're going to do with him sometimes.'

'Yes, we both had to hold his hands when we left the bus, Miss Simms,' said Rosie, earnestly informative. 'It simply crawled, the bus. Daddy came to the school gates with us—'

'Is he there?' asked Polly.

'Oh, no, he's gone on to his work, Miss Simms, and Mummy left earlier. I hope he doesn't get lost, he can only see out of one eye, you know. He said the pea soup was so thick you could eat it, if you had a knife and fork, and I said you need a spoon for soup. Daddy said no, you can slice it into chunks when it's as thick as this, and Annabelle said ugh. It's not quite as bad as this at home, thank goodness for our grandmother, who used to be consumptive, you know, but is much better now. Did you want specially to see me, Miss Simms?'

Polly smiled. Words always poured from Rosie.

'Only to ask if your father is coming to see me this afternoon, Rosie.'

'Oh, yes, Miss Simms, I asked him last night and he said he would, he said how could he refuse? He said he'd take time off from his work, and was there going to be a cup of tea for him in the teachers' room which wasn't stewed like one you gave him before. I told him it wasn't very nice to say something like that, and he said fathers had to face facts in the teachers' room. Nana – my grandmother – said to tell you to try and excuse him, that he'd been a comedian all his life, and she'd never been able to do anything with him.'

'Nor have I,' said Polly.

'Not with my Uncle Boots?' asked Annabelle in innocence.

Polly wrinkled her nose. She thought a nickname like Boots for a man like Robert Adams a disastrous family accident.

'Oh, some fathers are more comical than others, Annabelle,' she said. 'So are some uncles, of course.' She laughed to cover emotions she showed to no one. She had an effervescent personality that struck a responsive chord in her pupils. She shed her vocationary role at week-ends, when she participated with the Bright Young Things in extrovert activities. There was still something of the madcap in Polly Simms, an ambulance driver during four years of war. But she had a warm, enduring affection for the men who had fought in the trenches, and she regarded Boots as very special.

'Daddy's really quite nice,' said Rosie, which was an understatement of her true feelings for her foster-father.

'Why, of course, Rosie,' said Polly. She checked the time again, and began to ring the bell. The girls and boys still in the foggy playground started to troop in. St Luke's was a good school, offering a sound primary education, including reading out loud in class in an attempt to make the young cockney pupils cure themselves of gabbling. The brightest pupil by far in Polly's estimation was Rosie Adams, and Mr Stokes considered her a natural scholar. Since the beginning of 1925, Rosie had achieved top marks in every end-of-term exam.

Other things had happened in 1925. Oxford sank in the Boat Race. Mr Winston Churchill, Chancellor of the Exchequer, took sixpence off income tax, much to the disgust of the Labour Party. But Mr Churchill said it would provide more spending money and stimulate the economy. Old-age pensions at sixty-five and widows' pensions were introduced. Madame Tussaud's waxworks exhibition took fire and burned down. Legislation to increase summertime was passed. It entailed putting clocks forward an hour in April, and putting them back in October. People who thought God had invented clocks said the Bill was sacrilegious. Hindenberg was elected President of Germany. That did not stop a political firebrand called Adolf Hitler being an irritation to him. Amundsen of Norway flew over the North Pole. Charlie Chaplin and Pearl White established a new ascendancy in the cinema. A peculiar type of aeroplane made a vertical take-off at Farnborough, Hampshire. This eccentric flying machine impressed nobody of importance. By way of a minor happening, Adams Enterprises Ltd acquired the scrap metal business of a certain Mr Ben Ford, and an East End sweatshop at the beginning of November.

In the kitchen of the Browns' house in Caulfield Place, Walworth, Susie Brown buttoned her dark red winter coat. A navy blue cloche hat hugged her shingled hair.

'I'm off now, Mum,' she said. 'I've got to meet Mister Sammy at his new fact'ry in Shoreditch, the one he's just bought.'

'What's he want you to go there for?' asked Mrs Brown, a plump and jolly woman. 'And who's managin' your Brixton shop?'

'I shan't know what he wants till I get there,' said Susie. 'I don't see him often enough or long enough to be told anything much. The assistants are lookin' after the shop.'

'Well, he must have your good at heart, love, seeing you're still manageress at Brixton and bringing home two pound a week. I hope the fog don't hold you up. Oh, and when you see Mister Sammy, tell him we're still very 'appy in his fam'ly's old house.'

'Yes, Mum,' said Susie, pulling on fine kid gloves. She was able to buy all her clothes and accessories at trade price.

'You look ever so chick, love,' said Mrs Brown. She meant chic.

'Yer mean posh,' said thirteen-year-old Sally, still eating her breakfast porridge. Her brother Freddy, eleven, had just departed for school, and her elder brother, eighteen-year-old William, was in the Army, having been accepted as a drummer boy when he was fifteen.

Susie had a well-dressed look. Mrs Brown thought her a picture. Her prettiness as a girl was now the loveliness of a young woman. Why at twenty-one she wasn't married, Mrs Brown couldn't think. She had had any amount of boy friends, all ever so keen on her. And last year a nice young man she had met in Brixton had started to call on her. Susie lost interest after only a few months.

'So long, then,' she said, and Sally took a peek at her sister's legs as she walked to the door. Susie's coat, an inch longer than her skirt, was no more than three inches below her knees. Hemlines had become progressively higher, and some people said the limit had been reached.

'Crikey, Mum,' said Sally, 'Mister Adams'll lose 'is eyesight when Susie gets close. Can't I wear silk stockings?'

'No, you can't,' said Mrs Brown, 'and they're imitation silk, anyway.'

'Ta-ta, Mum,' said Susie. 'Toodle-ooh, pudding-face,' she said to her sister, and left.

'She's gettin' posh,' said Sally.

'Course she's not,' said Mrs Brown, 'she just looks nice, like you will when you're twenty-one.'

'It ain't fair,' said Sally, as if her sister had no right to be grown up when she herself was only thirteen and boys called her Shorty.

'Finish your porridge, lovey, and get off to school,' said Mrs Brown. 'Freddy's already gone.'

'Gone off, that's what 'e's gone,' said Sally.

'You pickle,' said Mrs Brown, and smiled her jolly smile.

The fog crept into the house.

Sammy looked pointedly at his pocket watch when Susie arrived in the office of the garment factory in Shoreditch. Susie did not miss the look. It was a quarter to ten, and he had asked her to be there at half-past nine.

'I'm sorry,' she said, 'but the fog was terrible. The buses stopped running, and I had to come on the Underground from Kennington Oval.'

'Have I said anything?' asked Sammy.

'You looked at your watch,' said Susie.

'I happen,' said Sammy, 'to own a real rolled gold watch to which I refer constant and out of habitual habit, it being my firm belief that time costs money, which is hard to come by.'

'Yes, it is, for most of us,' said Susie. Sammy glanced at her. Whatever the cold foggy weather was doing to other people, it had given Susie a glow and made her look a young lady tingling and alive. What a problem she was to him, even out of the way at Brixton. He doubted if he would have the strength to endure one more year without something drastic happening. There had been a change in her during these last few months. Very cool and quiet, she was. Not that it didn't suit her. It gave her the kind of ladylike air his mother liked best in a girl. All the same, he thought he preferred the old Susie, hiding nothing of her feelings and declaiming her faith in the goodness of God and His wondrous works. She had turned the Brixton shop into a small gold mine, and he had asked her two months ago to spend a few days at his new shop in Peckham Rye, to find out why it was more like a lead mine. Susie consented, but in very straight-faced fashion, and took only a short time to make the shop a going concern, simply by rearranging the displays and teaching the manageress and assistant how not to make customers feel inferior to them. Sammy thought about sacking the manageress. Susie reacted quite coldly to that, telling him if he did sack the woman then he ought to sack himself too, because he was responsible for giving her the job in the first place. Sammy, shocked, said he'd be obliged if she'd kindly remember not to give him that sort of advice. But he kept the woman on, and she was doing a much better job in the Peckham Rye shop now.

He interrupted his reflections to ask, 'Is something wrong?'

'I don't know, is there?' said Susie.

'I'm suffering a discomfortable feeling you've got problems.'

'Really?' Susie's speech had improved considerably during her time at Brixton. She could put a very lady-like inflexion into the word really. Of course she had problems, and if he of all men didn't know what they were, she was always going to be stuck out there in the wilderness of Brixton. 'Please don't concern yourself, Mister Adams. Kindly have the goodness to explain what you require of me now I'm here.'

Sammy, not for the first time lately, could hardly believe what came out of her mouth sometimes, nor the way it was said.

'I'll excuse that piece of peculiar wordage, Miss

Brown. It's my pleasure to explain this fact'ry represents the advantage of manufacturing for ourselves.
Profit not being come by easy, we're eliminatin' paying
someone else for makin' our garments, so we've got rid
of his hurtful profit by buying him up.'

'We?' enquired Susie.

'It's my pleasure to consider you inclusive.'

'Inclusive of extra profit?'

'Eh?' said Sammy.

'Or did me last Christmas bonus of three pounds
make me inclusive, Mister Adams?'

Astonished, Sammy said, 'Is my ears deceivin' me?
You sounded like a disbelievable little ingrate.'

'I'm not little, Mister Adams, and you got no right to
call me an ingrate.'

Sammy shifted his feet and muttered. She'd got him
off balance, like she had umpteen times before. All
right, so she wasn't little, not at five feet seven, but it
was still painful to hear her talking like this.

'Well, maybe I spoke a bit hasty,' he said.

'You spoke very hurtful,' said Susie, her heart a sensitive ache. For nearly a year now she had felt detached
from the firm. She felt detached from him, and from
Boots and Tommy, both of whom she had worked for in
the past. For all the challenge of her job in the Brixton
shop, she felt out of things. She hankered after
Camberwell and Walworth, Walworth being where the
market stall and the scrap metal business were. She
eyed Sammy in her direct way, thinking how tall and
manly he was at twenty-three. He wasn't burly or
thickset, his activity and energy kept him lean. He
dressed distinguished too, nearly always in light grey in
summer, and charcoal grey in winter, with plain ties
instead of the natty ones he had favoured when running
the stall in East Street market. Oh, happy days, she
thought. He used to smile a lot then, in between his

funny muttering moments. He was too busy to smile these days, and was always rottenly businesslike with her each time he visited the Brixton shop. But she could not forget how he had virtually picked her out of the gutter, employed her, forgiven her her mistakes, and kept his promise to make her a manageress. It had induced in her a loyalty she thought would never change. A hugely round man called Ben Ford, known as Fatty or Fat Man, with business interests all over South London, had several times offered her a job at a better wage than Sammy paid her. She had always refused, but it made her wonder what her actual worth was.

'If we could refer to business,' said Sammy, 'I'd like to begin by saying this place wants puttin' in order.'

'Yes,' she said.

'I can't stand this,' he muttered, 'it's like talkin' to nobody. It's upsettin' me, Susie. I've done something I shouldn't. All right, what is it?'

Susie could have said it was simply that he made her feel she was only another cog in the wheel of his business, that he took her for granted and never held a sociable conversation with her.

'You haven't done nothing, Mister Adams,' she said, and there was a world of meaning in that. It passed right over his head, of course.

'Well, all right,' he said, but uncertainly, and he hated to feel uncertain about anything. 'Anyway, what d'you think about this place?'

Susie looked around the office, such as it was. It was indescribably mucky, it looked as if it had never known a broom or a duster. The plain, distempered walls were a dirty brown. There were files, papers, garment oddments, discarded samples, overflowing cardboard boxes and other things everywhere. On top of a filing cabinet was a jumbled mess of stuff, and the desk was crowded with yellowing papers stuck on spikes with cork bases.

'It's disgustin',' she said.

'It don't look too promising, I grant you,' said Sammy, 'and when you see the workshop itself you'll find there's room for improvement there too. Anyway, to start with, I'd be much obliged if you'd knock this office into shape. Mr Morris said he'd lend a hand.' Mr Morris was the previous owner.

'If Mr Morris is responsible for this disgustin' mess,' said Susie fiercely, 'I don't want his help, thank you.'

'Now calm down,' said Sammy. 'Just say if you can put this office to rights, and then we'll talk about—'

'I will say! I'll say no, I won't!' It all came to a head then, everything, including the heartache. The words burst from her. 'It's a job for a navvy, and I'm a young lady, I am, come of age, which I don't suppose means anything to you, oh, no. I've give you the best years of me life, I have, and what's it done except make you think all I'm good for is clearing up someone else's filthy mess? A bloody cheek you've got! You find someone else to do it, and you find someone else to run the Brixton shop and put other shops right. Keep all your rotten jobs, I don't want any of them no more, and may God forgive you for what you've done to me!'

Sammy could not believe it. Nor could he believe her rushing act of disappearance. By the time he had come to she was well on her way, but his ears were still ringing.

'Susie?' said Mrs Brown, as her daughter came into the kitchen. 'What you come back home for?'

'Nothing,' said Susie.

Mrs Brown gave her a long look, noting the flush on her face, the fierce set of her mouth, and the glitter in her eyes.

'There's something wrong, Susie. You'd better sit down.'

Susie sat down at the table, the yellow fog hanging against the bay window and blotting out the yard. The range fire was glowing. She stared into the hot coals.

'It's nothing,' she said.

'Now, Susie, don't tell me no fairy stories,' said Mrs Brown.

'Oh, if you must know, I fell out with Mister Sammy.' The words were wrenched from Susie. 'I've given up my job. I'm not goin' to be walked on nor treated as if I was just a bit useful now and again.'

'Susie, oh, lawks.' Mrs Brown was aghast. 'Susie, you can't give up your job, think of all the people who don't have one. You can't bring no wages home. And Mister Sammy's been good to you—'

'He hasn't.' Susie was bitter. 'He's been rotten to me, he hasn't got a ha'porth of ordinary human affection for anyone or anything except his business.'

'Now, Susie,' said Mrs Brown gently, 'you know that's not true. You shouldn't say unforgivin' things like that. Why, I remember the time you had mumps cruelly bad and he come round right away to see you.'

'Yes, to see what a sight I was, he did that all right. Well, if he comes round again and goes down on his bended knees beggin' me to go back, I won't. I can get another job easy, with a man called Ben Ford. He's offered more than once. I'll go and work for him, I will.'

'Susie love, don't talk like that,' said Mrs Brown in concern. 'Mister Sammy can't have been roaring and bellowing at you, can 'e? He wouldn't, not Mister Sammy. He treats your dad very good down at the scrap metal yard.' Mr Brown had full-time work at the yard now. 'Susie, Mister Sammy hasn't got cross, he hasn't shouted at you, has 'e?'

105

'I wish he had, it might have meant he cared a bit, then, it might—' Susie stopped and turned her eyes on the fire again.

'Susie?' Mrs Brown was maternally enquiring. 'Susie?'

Susie got up.

'I'm goin' out again,' she said. 'I'm goin' to walk to Kennington and see Mr Ford. He'll give me a job on the spot, I know he will, and at more than that Sammy Adams pays me.'

'No, don't do that—'

'I'm goin' to,' said Susie, and left the house with her bitterness still fierce. She walked through the fog, the fog that was choking Walworth and muffling every familiar sound.

Four minutes later, the worried Mrs Brown answered a knock on her front door. Sammy stood there, in a trilby hat and a grey herring-bone overcoat. He had left the factory as soon as he had recovered his wits. His first clear thought had appalled him. It told him he couldn't do without Susie.

'Morning, Mrs Brown, is Susie home?' he asked, and Mrs Brown thought he looked as worried as she felt.

'Mister Adams, go an' catch her before she does what she shouldn't. She's walkin' to Kennington to get a job with a man called Ford. She'll go up through Manor Place, she's awful upset about things – Mr Adams?'

Sammy was gone, striding recklessly fast through the fog.

He caught her up just as she turned the corner of Penton Place into Kennington Park Road. He considered himself lucky. Visibility was chronic, and he heard her before he saw her. He heard the click of her patent leather shoes on the pavement. He came up beside her. She gave a startled little gasp, but continued walking, mouth shut tight, chin up and nose high in the fog.

106

Sammy spoke penitently. 'Susie, I upset you. I'm sorry. I'd be grateful if you'd let me take you back home and talk to you.'

'Go away,' said Susie.

'I can't do that, Susie, I've got to talk to you.'

'Then I'll call a policeman, the first one I see, and complain you're molestin' me.'

'Look, if I did yer wrong, I'm in Christian repentance, on the Bible I am.'

'Kindly don't make me laugh, I'm not in the mood,' said Susie. 'I decline to speak to you, Mister Adams, I am declining to speak to you ever again. That kind gentleman Mr Ford has offered me a job more than once, and I'm goin' to take it.'

'The Fat Man ain't kind, nor a gentleman,' said Sammy, 'and you're not takin' any job he offers.'

'Who's goin' to stop me, may I ask?'

'I am,' said Sammy.

'Is that another joke?' asked Susie.

'It's no joke,' said Sammy. 'I mean it, even if it costs me two broken legs and a hole in me head.'

'Have a nice time in hospital.'

'Susie, is that a nice thing to say? I never thought I'd hear you talk so uncaring.'

Susie, walking stiffly through the fog, said, 'Yes, you still think I'm a Sunday School kid that wouldn't speak ill of anyone. Well, I'm pleased to inform you, Mister Adams, that I'm considerably grown up.' While growing up, Susie had learned to confound Sammy with his own kind of vernacular. 'I am now a grown woman and don't wear rose-tinted spectacles any more, but that don't mean I've given up believing in the Christian faith, only that I can see certain people for what they are.'

'Oh, my suffering head,' said Sammy, 'I never heard such obstreperous wordage. Look, Susie love—'

107

'Susie what?' She stopped then, much to his relief. Trying to talk to her while blundering through the fog, with other pedestrians a menace, was hardly promising. He faced her. They became two static figures shrouded in yellow. 'I hope you ain't – I hope you're not being familiar, Mister Adams.'

'Now what've I said?' Sammy cleared his throat. Susie's eyes searched him. He cleared his throat again. 'All right, I've got to say it, you've grown up very creditable, you look as good as Pearl White, and I'm proud of you.'

'I've heard all that before, thank you,' she said, but she was thinking he must care a bit, he must, or he would never have come after her like this.

'Now, Susie—'

'Oh! Don't say that! I won't be condescended to!' Susie actually stamped a foot.

'Now, Susie—'

'Oh, you done it again, I'll hit you!' cried Susie, and was mortified then as a figure came out of the fog, bumped into them and made known it had heard what she said.

' 'Ere, yer'd better cart yerselves orf 'ome an' do yer wallopin' there, 'cos I'm tellin' yer, yer dangerous hobstructions to innocent walkers while yer standin' there an' not showin' no fog lamps.' And it went grumbling on its way.

'Never mind that prime specimen of how not to make friends in the dark,' said Sammy. 'Here, Susie, where you goin'? Oh, me gawd.'

Susie, still too proud to encourage reconciliation, had stepped off the kerb into the fog that blanketed the road. He heard the heavy sound of a slow-moving vehicle. He rushed, flung both arms around her from behind, lifted her and plunged back on to the pavement as pale fog lamps loomed up. A corporation watercart

108

passed by. Susie turned in his arms and for a moment he felt her warm body alarmingly close to his. There was even a calamitous urge to pull her closer. Susie broke free, her breathing a little quick and noisy.

'If you don't mind,' she said, but there was a catch in her voice.

'Susie, don't you ever do that again, don't you ever step off a kerb like that in fog like this.'

'Can I help it I'm upset?'

'You're not the only one,' said Sammy. 'How d'you think I feel about all this carry-on?'

'It's nice to know you've got feelings,' said Susie. 'I didn't think you had, seeing you've kept me locked away in Brixton all these years.'

'Locked away?' Sammy's astonished breath escaped. It steamed into the fog.

'That's what it felt like,' said Susie.

'Well,' said Sammy helplessly, 'I just don't know what I'm goin' to do with you, Susie Brown. Didn't I keep my promise to make you manageress of my first ladies' wear shop?'

'I didn't know I was goin' to be eternally banished.'

'Eternally banished? I'm goin' to fall unconscious in a minute from all this ringing in me ears.'

'Someone will pick you up, I'm sure,' said Susie, experiencing little leaps of exhilaration because he was so obviously on the rack. 'I can't stop here talkin', Mister Adams, I have to proceed on my way to the offices of Mr Ford, the gentleman mentioned previous.'

'Nothing doing,' said Sammy, 'you'll get run over for sure next time. Besides which, the mentioned gentleman is a dubious geezer who's not goin' to be your employer except over my dead body. And would you do me the favour of not talkin' about being banished?' Sammy was having a terrible time fighting the ruinous urge to give in. And Susie was watching him, watching

109

his eyes trying to avoid hers. 'Look, if I was displeasing to you this morning, I'm sorry, specially as I had a proposition to put to you after we'd worked things out at the fact'ry. It so happens I'm up to my eyeballs in work at the office, and I need a personal assistant, someone who looks highly creditable and has got considerable mental engineering works. Which is you, Susie. I'd be more than gratified if you'd come back to Camberwell as me private secretary and personal assistant, which is a necessary appendix to any businessman of reputable standing. I can get another manageress for the Brixton shop. There's smart women lining up for that kind of job. Well, what d'you say, Susie?' Sammy had given in. He knew what it would do to him, bringing her back into his daily business life.

Susie's blue eyes turned misty. Sammy sighed. Calamity was in the offing, he could feel it. Sooner or later he was going to chuck away all the benefits of remaining a bachelor businessman.

'Mister Sammy?' she said, a little husky. 'Do you mean that?'

'I never make unmeaningful business propositions,' said Sammy. 'Would twelve pounds a month suit you?'

'Twelve pounds? Three pounds a week?' Susie knew few young ladies of twenty-one earned that amount. But it was not the money alone that mattered, it was something else, something far more necessary to her.

'I'd like you to go to evening classes and learn typing, of course,' remarked Sammy.

'Yes,' said Susie and drew a breath. 'Mister Sammy, I'm sorry I said all those awful things about you, and you mustn't ever think I didn't know how good you were givin' me the job as manageress. Only – only I don't want Brixton for always, I'd love to come back to Camberwell. I did get upset at the fact'ry, thinking you didn't have any regard for me—'

110

'Susie, my regard for you is highly affectionate,' said Sammy.

'Oh,' said Susie, eyes mistier.

'Which, of course, don't mean I'll make improper advances,' said Sammy, stepping hastily back from the brink.

'Why, Mister Sammy, as if you would,' said Susie, wondering what he thought an improper advance was, and wondering too what it would do to her. 'I'm sure any girl could trust you to advance very proper on her.'

'Well,' said Sammy vaguely and helplessly, 'well, yes, I hope so, Miss Brown.'

Silent laughter welled up inside Susie then. He was so funny, just like he had always been. He looked mature, he really did, but he didn't know a thing about girls. He had no idea that during the last year she had been longing to get back to Camberwell. His regard for her was highly affectionate? He was still so droll.

With her tongue in her cheek, she said, 'Twelve pounds a month is wondrous gratifying, Mister Sammy, specially as it won't come with improper advances.'

Sammy coughed.

'Fog in me throat,' he said. 'Well, I'm glad you've accepted.'

'When do I start?'

'Tomorrow.'

'Utter bliss,' said Susie. 'I'll come back to Shoreditch with you now, if you like, on the Tube. We can talk about the office and fact'ry when we get there.'

'We'll do that tomorrow, I've got other calls to make now, includin' one on an unemployed female manageress I happen to know, concerning takin' over the Brixton shop. You meet me at the fact'ry same time tomorrow and we'll sort things out. I'd like the fact'ry to look a bit better than a sweatshop, it's a principle of

111

mine not to have any part of Adams Enterprises lookin'
discreditable. All right, Susie, you've had an upset
morning, so take the rest of the day off. I won't dock yer
wages. You go home and enjoy a mug of hot revivin'
Bovril.'

'Yes, Mister Sammy, thank you.'

'My pleasure,' said Sammy, and they parted, he conscious his future was doomladen and Susie utterly and
blissfully sure he cared for her.

The woman wore a black coat and hat on this day, with
a heavy black veil. She wandered along Walworth
Road, murmuring to herself. She went into Maypole's,
the grocers. A counter assistant, sympathetic about her
widow's weeds, asked her in kindness if he could serve
her. She shook her head in a startled negative and left
the shop. Reaching Browning Street, she turned into it,
hurrying her step. At Caulfield Place she stopped. Her
veil moved to her murmuring voice. A passer-by looked
at her. She went quickly on, to Walcorde Avenue, and
from there to the church.

The vicar found her there twenty minutes later,
seated in a pew, her veiled face bent. He did not
interrupt her. She left when she became aware of his
presence.

She wandered murmuring through the fog.

CHAPTER TEN

At three o'clock that afternoon, Boots entered Sammy's office. Sammy had just returned from making a number of business calls. He had always believed in the benefits of personal contacts. The telephone on his desk was a useful piece of equipment. Once installed, it could not be done without. But it was not the same as being face to face with people, shaking hands with them and showing them an honest countenance.

Boots placed a slip of paper on the desk.

'Plonk your peepers on that, Sammy.'

'I'm plonking,' said Sammy, 'but why do I have to?'

'We're spending a small fortune on collection and delivery charges. Look at the amount we've paid Carter Paterson for the first six months of the current financial year.'

'What?' Sammy studied pencilled figures.

'Wake up, Kruger.'

'I ain't aware I'm asleep.'

'We need a van.'

'Pardon?'

'A van. For collecting and delivering, and serving all our shops. A motor van, not a horse and cart.'

'Cost a fortune,' said Sammy.

'That's a fortune in those figures,' said Boots, 'and it's increasing every year. Don't muck about, sonny, get a van.'

'Capital expenditure, that is,' said Sammy.

'It hurts, of course, but you can get treatment.'

'And a van needs a driver.'

'That'll make a steady job for a deserving ex-soldier,' said Boots, 'and we'll still save money.'

'Hold up,' said Sammy, 'I ain't running parish relief for your old mates in khaki.'

'My old mates saved you from being swallowed up by Kaiser Bill. Shake yourself, Sammy. A delivery van's a must.'

Sammy, who knew Boots never offered unprofitable ideas, said, 'All right, I'll see what Susie says.'

'Pardon?' said Boots.

'What did I say?' asked Sammy, opening a desk drawer and rummaging uselessly through it.

'I think you mentioned the manageress of the Brixton shop.'

'Oh, young Susie Whatsername, you mean,' said Sammy, keeping his head down.

'Not that old chestnut,' said Boots, and noted the obvious fact that Sammy wasn't his usual self. 'All right, out with it.'

'I happen to need an assistant,' said Sammy, closing the drawer. 'Look at me overloaded in-tray, and me overburdened business day. I'm totally disinclined to die from being overloaded and overburdened. So I'm takin' Susie on as me private secretary and personal assistant.'

'I see. Giving in at last, are you, Sammy?'

'I don't consider that an appropriate remark,' said Sammy. 'Well, a van and a driver. I'll give it me serious attention as soon as I've got time.'

'No need for that,' said Boots, 'just show the figures to your new private secretary and personal assistant. She'll make sense out of them. And tell her I know a bloke she can offer the driver's job to.'

'Would you be so good as to inform me who you think's in charge here?'

'I think it's going to be Susie,' said Boots. 'Smart piece of work, Sammy. Susie's a bright girl. She'll help you live a lot longer.'

'I like some of your jokes,' said Sammy, 'I don't like 'em all.'

'Buy a van, Sammy. I'm off now, I've got to see one of Rosie's teachers. Love to Susie.'

Boots walked through the afternoon fog to the school. Lights of crawling vehicles and the lamps of horse-drawn carts peered through the gloom. He thought about the family. Emily was more energetic than ever at twenty-seven, dashing off to her part-time job in the mornings, spending the afternoons doing things around the house, giving time to Chinese Lady and to four-year-old Tim in between, and participating in every evening activity. She adored Tim, of course, and indulged her delight in him by taking ages to put him to bed at night. She romped with him in his room. Chinese Lady wasn't too sure it was a good thing to get a child all lively at bedtime, but didn't interfere.

Emily enjoyed having Chinese Lady and Mr Finch living with them. Mr Finch had sold his previous house and bought a large one at the south end of Red Post Hill, close to North Dulwich station, some fifteen minutes' walk from Lizzy and Ned's house. At the same time, Boots and Emily sold their house, and Chinese Lady showed guarded pleasure when they all moved into the new house, a well-built Victorian residence. There were four bedrooms on the first floor, with a bathroom and a huge airing cupboard, to accommodate Boots, Emily, Rosie and Tim. Chinese Lady and Mr Finch lived downstairs, where there were five rooms, including a large kitchen. There was also a scullery, which Chinese Lady thought right, proper and wholly necessary. She and Mr Finch had their bedroom and their own cosy sitting-room, plus a study for Mr Finch. The remaining room, spacious, was used by Boots and Emily as a living-room, and on frequent occasions everyone gathered there. One end of the room was set aside as a dining area, and they all had tea there on Sundays. Most other meals they ate together in the handsome kitchen. Emily handed over control of the kitchen to Chinese Lady as soon as they moved in, and Chinese Lady happily took up the role she cherished. She was the natural guardian of family life and the dispenser of provender. She was happy to be a wife again, and if there was one other factor that also gave her pleasure, it was having two children around, Rosie and Tim.

Boots knew his mother was very happy that she had a whole family around her, including a husband. She and Mr Finch got on remarkably well, although they were completely different. She was a woman of elementary education and old-fashioned attitudes, and with a fixed belief in what was right and proper. Mr Finch had attended university, been an agent for German Intelligence up to 1918 and become a British citizen in 1920, having crossed to the British side before the war ended. Only Boots knew these things about him. Chinese Lady admired and respected him because she considered him a gentleman, and he admired and respected her because he thought her remarkable.

The house was a palace to her and Emily because of its huge bathroom, three toilets, large hall and magnificent garden. The arrangement might not have worked, but Emily willingly deferred to Chinese Lady in all things domestic, and Chinese Lady had too much commonsense to let her opinions, always frank, sound too much like interference. Emily was currently working on her in a wheedling way, for Emily still wanted her job to be a full-time one, and she needed Chinese Lady to look after Tim all day until he went to school. Boots knew Chinese Lady would be resistant to that, not because it would be too much for her, but because she had decided ideas about who should be the family breadwinner and who should be the home-builder. She still thought it wrong and unnecessary for Emily to be out at work at all, but did not say so to her.

Boots rode on the bus with his Rosie every morning, and Annabelle and Bobby boarded it on the way. All three children got off at the school stop, and Boots stayed on until Camberwell Green was reached.

Lizzy and Ned now had four children, Annabelle, Bobby, three-year-old Emma and one-year-old Edward. Lizzy lived in singular content. Ned's job with the wine merchants of Great Tower Street was now a very well-paid one. He and the children made Lizzy the hub of their existence, and ups and downs were taken in their stride. Lizzy made her family go regularly to church, and here Ned saw a little of her mother in her. Chinese Lady believed people experienced a sense of humility in church, and Lizzy was apt to say that a bit of religious humility was good for everyone. It stopped them thinking they didn't owe anything to their Creator.

Tommy and Vi were the delighted parents of six-months-old Alice, but couldn't afford to rent a house of their own. Vi was not too concerned about this and neither was Aunt Victoria. Tommy, despite his own equability, very much wanted something better for Vi than the flat they had in her parents' house. He had come across two engineering jobs, but neither offered as much as the wages of two pounds five shillings that

117

Sammy paid him for running the stall. He and Vi could have afforded to rent a house in Walworth, but they both preferred an area farther south.

Boots came out of his reveries as he arrived at the school. It was cloaked by the fog, the classroom lights a dim glow. He went in, made for the teachers' rest room and knocked on the door.

'Come in.'

He entered. Polly, standing, smiled at him, her bobbed dark brown hair shining, her eyes bright. Her yellow jumper and dark brown skirt were the last word in simplicity. The skirt, short, revealed slim legs clad in silk stockings. She only ever wore silk, refusing to grace her legs with anything else. Her teacher's pay was pocket money to her, for she enjoyed a generous allowance from her father, General Simms. She had met Boots five years ago and fallen for him, but she had had nothing from him except friendship, friendship of a provoking airy-fairy kind on his part. It was still difficult for her to settle just for that. Through his daughter Rosie she maintained contact with him. And his son Tim would be attending the school next year. She had met his wife Emily and thought her lively but plain. She could not think how on earth a plain woman had netted him.

'Hello,' said Boots. 'Any tea?'

'Stewed, like before?' said Polly. 'I'll give you stewed, you cheap comic. No, of course there's some, just made.' She took the cosy off the pot and poured two cups. She handed him one.

'Much obliged,' said Boots, and she looked him over in a wry way. His hat was on a chair, his overcoat hanging unbuttoned over his long frame, his sound right eye clear, his blind one looking lazy. She did not know any man who handled himself in easier fashion. Her father, one of the school governors, had met him

118

once. A lengthy conversation ensued, and her father said to her later, 'Damned hard luck, Polly, but shouldn't have let him slip you.' 'How the hell could I help it when I didn't get to meet him until it was too late?' retorted Polly. 'Bad organisation, Polly. Get the feller compromised. Your only chance, y'know, divorce.' 'You heinous old ratbag,' said Polly, 'but what a thrilling idea.'

She smiled at Boots again. 'Kiss?' she said.

Boots sipped his tea. She was always playing that kind of game with him.

'Christmas?' he said.

'Mistletoe stuff?' said Polly, wrinkling her nose. 'You're stingy even then. I hope your wife hates you.'

'She will if I go to bed with you.'

'I'll risk divorce if you will,' said Polly.

'Messy,' said Boots, 'and it'll be my divorce, not yours.'

'Yes, darling, I know, but you'd get me as a lovely compensation, and we could have some kids of our own. You like kids, I know you do. So do I. I'd like to have yours.'

'Sounds tempting,' said Boots. 'Why am I here?'

'Because I adore you. Why can't you adore me?'

'It's a mystery to me. You look the part and sound the part.'

'Couldn't you make love to me just once?' asked Polly.

'Easily. But I might get to like you. Can we stop playing games?'

'I don't play games, not with you.'

'Well, shall we be serious, then?'

'Oh, hell,' said Polly, 'seriously, then, and about Rosie. Mr Stokes has let me have the privilege of discussing her education with you.'

'Is it a privilege?'

119

'Of course,' said Polly. 'Don't you know how sweet and gifted your own daughter is?'

His own daughter? Boots had given Rosie his name, and she was entered in the school register as Rosie Adams, implying she was adopted. Boots and Emily had known it was impossible to pass her off as their natural daughter. The school authorities accepted she was adopted. Rosie herself never mentioned she was either fostered or adopted. To her, Boots and Emily were her natural parents, because they loved her.

'Polly, you know, of course, that—'

'I know she's yours,' said Polly, her back to the fire that kept the teachers' room warm on winter days. 'You've made her yours, and she adores you for it. Rosie's your very own.'

Boots looked at her. Polly made a face, as if she had been guilty of exchanging commonsense for sentiment.

'Polly, that's very sweet of you,' he said.

'Well, you see, darling, it really isn't a game,' she said. 'I wish I were yours too. But listen, Rosie is very gifted. She's too much of a natural scholar not to be given more than an elementary education. In fact, all children of talent should have the chance of higher schooling. Between now and Easter, 1927, when Rosie will be in her twelfth year, we have time to help her. As you know, I've been teaching her French out of school, and you've helped in that too. And Mr Stokes is willing to cram her in English Literature. Further, old thing, the school has been given the opportunity to offer one girl a chance to sit an examination in London for a scholarship to St Mary's College near Brighton. She would be sitting the exam with other girls, and she does need to have a sound basic knowledge of French. There are four scholarship places, and thirty-two girls will be competing for them in January 1927. I'm going to ask you to allow Mr Stokes and me to give Rosie the extra tuition and homework necessary to help her qualify for the exam. If she were among the four successful girls, it would mean being at St Mary's for five years.'

'Is St Mary's a boarding school?' asked Boots.

'Yes,' said Polly, 'but you'd only have to pay for little extras, everything else would be found. It's a very generous bursary.'

'I'll speak to Emily,' said Boots.

'Yes, I suppose so,' said Polly, who was never going to make Emily her best friend. She had a fanciful conviction that that green-eyed woman had swiped Boots when her back was turned. The fact that she had not known him then did not alter her conviction. 'But how do you feel about it yourself?'

Boots thought. It meant the family parting with Rosie for five years. But there would be the holidays, of course, and how could they deny her the chance of such a good education?

'Let's see what Rosie says, Polly. Can you call her from class?'

Polly fetched her. Rosie came in looking intrigued. Boots spoke to her about the scholarship exam, the tuition she would need, and the education she would receive at a school called St Mary's if she secured a place there. He did not say it was a boarding school, but he did say it was in Sussex.

'What d'you think, kitten, would you like to do a year's cramming and try for one of the scholarships?'

'Would you like me to, Daddy?' asked Rosie, his wish counting most.

'Yes, if you'd like it too.'

Rosie gave no thought to how far away the school was, or to the possibility of separation. She thought only of pleasing him.

'Then I'll try my hardest, really I will,' she said

earnestly. 'Of course, you're not to think it's no sooner said than done. I mean, with thirty-two girls at the exam and only four scholarships, I'd have to be pretty spiffing, you know.'

Boots smiled. No wonder some of the pupils here called her Lady Muck. He had been called Lord Muck himself by the street kids. Rosie's favourite adjectives were ripping and spiffing. She was a devourer of the school stories written by Frank Richards about Harry Wharton, Bob Cherry and Billy Bunter.

'All right,' he said, 'I won't think it's no sooner said than done.'

'Yes, it's best to be sensible,' said Rosie, 'and it's a good thing you can be.'

'Kind of you to say so,' said Boots, and Polly thought how attached these two were to each other. A bell rang. Classes were over.

'You can get your hat and coat now, Rosie,' said Polly, 'and go with your father.'

'Oh, we must wait for Annabelle and Bobby, Miss Simms,' said Rosie. 'Mustn't we, Daddy? I don't know what Annabelle would say if we didn't, except what a rotten swizz. I'd better go and find them.' She went.

'Isn't she adorable?' said Polly. 'Aren't you a lucky old daddy?'

'So-so,' said Boots.

The buses were running again, and Annabelle and Bobby were with Boots and Rosie when they boarded one. Annabelle hung back so that she could sit with her uncle. Rosie made no protest. She knew she did not have to fight for her father's attentions. She knew instinctively she was special to him.

That evening at the supper table in the kitchen, Chinese Lady said, 'Well, I don't know, I'm sure. It's a lot to ask of Rosie.'

'Oh, I want to try, Nana,' said Rosie.

'And you should, Rosie,' said Mr Finch.

'Them kind of exams don't bear thinking about for little girls,' said Chinese Lady.

'But, Nana, I'm a big girl now,' protested Rosie. 'I used to be little when I hadn't grown much, but I've put on years since then. Tim, sit up,' she said to her brother beside her. 'Mummy, just look at that boy, he's nearly got his nose in his plate. I don't know sometimes what we're going to do with him, do you, Grandpa?'

'Don't want nothing done with me,' said four-year-old Tim. 'Do I, Grandpa?'

'Something could be done about the gravy on your nose,' said Mr Finch, a man happy to have acquired a ready-made family.

'Yes, you've got a nice nose for a boy,' said Rosie graciously, 'you oughtn't to put it in your gravy.'

'I didn't,' said Tim, and got on with his dinner, which Chinese Lady still called supper. Emily, on his other side, wiped the spot of gravy off his nose. Tim looked at her. Emily gave him a smile and a wink. He offered her a little grin. 'There wasn't no gravy, was there?' he said.

'Any,' said Boots.

'See?' said Tim to Rosie. 'Daddy said there wasn't as well.'

'There isn't, not now,' said Rosie. 'Eat your dinner up, there's a good boy. Nana, I told Daddy and Miss Simms I could only try about the exam.'

'Well, I just hope it don't get to be a strain,' said Chinese Lady, presiding in as upright a fashion as ever.

'I think Rosie's up to it,' said Mr Finch.

'I don't know I'm too keen on that Miss Simms,' said Emily.

'Oh, but she's awf'lly nice,' said Rosie, 'and she likes

Daddy lots, she's always asking after his health. "How is your father, Rosie?" she says. "Is he well?" "Oh, he's vital with health," I say.'

'Bless us, that child,' said Chinese Lady, 'what's vital with health?'

'Vigorous?' suggested Mr Finch.

'Lor', the words she uses,' said Chinese Lady, and glanced at Boots.

Emily, who also had her eyes on him, said, 'I can't say he talks vigorous, just airy-fairy like he always does, and not tellin' you much.'

Chinese Lady said, 'I think I'd like to come and meet Miss Simms, Rosie.'

'Oh, she'd be thrilled, Nana,' said Rosie. 'I've told her lots about you, how you brought up Daddy and Uncle Sammy and Uncle Tommy and Auntie Lizzy, and made them a credit to you except Daddy, who turned out only fit for the music hall. I told her I expect you wondered sometimes what you were going to do with him.'

Mr Finch smiled. Rosie, only ten, was already capable of teasing her father deliciously.

'I wonder myself what I'm going to do with you, young lady,' said Boots.

'But, Daddy, I only said what I've heard Nana say lots of times,' protested Rosie, 'and Mummy and I don't mind about you only being fit for the music hall, and Miss Simms said it was a good thing some people were different from others or life would be awful boring. Honest, we don't mind a bit if you've been an aggravation at times. It's better than being awful boring, isn't it, Mummy?'

'Can't no one stop her talking?' asked Tim.

'I'm still not too keen on Miss Simms,' said Emily pointedly. She thought Rosie's favourite teacher had all kinds of false mannerisms.

'Good teacher, harmless female,' said Boots.

'Yes, I think I'd better come and meet her some time,' said Chinese Lady, suspicious of any lady teacher uncommonly interested in the health of Boots.

In their house in Walworth, Mr Brown said to Mrs Brown, 'Our Susie's feeling better, she's been down in the dumps lately and worrying me.'

'She was nearly down for good this morning, I can tell you,' said Mrs Brown. 'She fell out with Mister Sammy.'

'Yer jokin',' said Mr Brown.

'It wasn't no joke, love. Real cut up, she was, and told him she was leavin' her job. But he came after her, and she said they had a talk and that he's took her on as his personal assistant. Our Susie, would you believe. She won't have to go all the way to Brixton no more. I never seen her more happy.'

'Well, who'd 'ave thought it, Bessie, Mister Sammy promotin' our Susie like that. All the same, I get worried she ain't being courted. She's gone twenty-one, she don't want to be a workin' woman all her life.'

'Here, what d'you think I am, then?' said Mrs Brown, giving him a cheerful dig in his ribs. 'I'm a workin' woman, y'know.'

'Course you are, me old Dutch,' said Mr Brown. He put an arm around his amiable trouble-and-strife and squeezed her cuddlesome plumpness. 'What I meant was, ain't it time she was married?'

'She's only waitin' to be asked, Jim.'

'Eh? Who by?'

'Best I don't name any names, in case I'm wrong,' said Mrs Brown. 'Here, I had some woman call this afternoon, askin' after Mr Finch.'

'What, 'im that used to lodge 'ere years ago?'

'Well, there wasn't no other gent by that name, was there?'

'What, 'im that's now Mister Sammy's stepfather?'

'I s'pose that's who she meant, that woman. Peculiar, she was. I said he'd gone away years ago. Well, I didn't think I'd tell her about him and where he was livin'.' Mrs Brown spoke firmly. Walworth people were instinctively cautious when strangers came enquiring. Strangers might mean trouble, they might be debt collectors or arms of the law or dubious people. 'Very peculiar, she was, kept saying where was he and not takin' any notice of me saying he hadn't lived here for years. It was like she wasn't hearing what I kept saying. She tried to push her way in, would you believe. I wasn't havin' that, I pushed her out and shut the door on her.'

'Yer did right, Bessie,' said Jim. 'It don't do to be informin' to people like that. It's like openin' up the cupboard door and lettin' a skeleton out.'

'Oh, you don't reckon Mr Finch has got skeletons, do you?' said Mrs Brown. 'Susie said he's a nice distinguished gentleman. She met him at the weddin' four years ago.'

'You did right, old girl,' said Jim again.

That night Daisy Cook woke up. She slept in the room that had once been the bedroom of Miss Elsie Chivers, daughter of the murdered Mrs Chivers. She did not know that, nor did her family.

A woman was there, a dark figure of the night. She seemed to be drifting slowly around and she seemed to be sighing. Daisy uttered a frightened little squeal and rushed the sheets up over her head, burying herself. She heard a long-drawn sigh and the whisper of quick-moving clothes. When she uncovered herself minutes later, the dark figure was gone. She felt it had been a bad little dream, and when she went back to sleep the sheets were over her head again. Covering up kept bad dreams away.

Her mother, Mrs Cook, found the front door open when she came down in the morning. She simply thought someone in the family had been careless. One of her two growing sons, probably. She picked up the pewter can of milk from the doorstep, closed the door and thought no more about it. Open doors in Walworth worried no one, except that they let the fog in and the draughts.

CHAPTER ELEVEN

It was merely misty the following morning. The fog, relenting, had stolen guiltily away after two days of punishing the bronchial tubes of old and young people alike. At Sandringham, Queen Alexandra, the graceful and elegant widow of Edward VII, had just died. Loved by all the people, she had slipped quietly away in her eighty-second year. Many of London's working-men wore black armbands on this misty morning, such was the affection in which she had been held.

Susie, nevertheless, arrived at the Shoreditch factory with a spring in her step. She entered the office in a mood of fervent loyalty, ready to help in the work of putting it to rights. Faintly she heard the hum and clatter of sewing-machines in the workshop. Astonished, she regarded the office. There was no sign of that disgusting clutter of yesterday. Everything objectionable to the eye had gone. There was a woman down on her hands and knees, scrubbing the worn linoleum with a well-soaped brush. A pail of dirty-brown suds was beside her, a large flannel hanging over the lip of the pail.

'Good morning,' said Susie, who had a carrier bag with her. It contained an old dress and an apron, plus a scarf to protect her hair from dust.

The charring lady, wearing a scarf of her own over her head, looked up.

'Mornin', miss. Watch yer feet, ducky. Floor's slippery, like. Lor', lucky yer didn't come sooner. Dunno I ever seen any office more of a mess, and I seen a few, that I 'ave. George Robey could of sung a song about this one, I tell yer. All gorn now, though. Daft Dick's burnin' the lot in the yard. 'E ain't the brightest bloke this side of London Bridge, but 'e knows 'ow to build a bonny.' She meant bonfire. 'Likes a good bonny, does Daft Dick, and it ain't wise to let 'im get too near a ware'ouse if 'e's got matches in 'is 'andy-pandies.' The woman applied the flannel to the soapy floor. 'Yer want someone, dearie?'

'Yes,' said Susie, 'Mr Adams.'

The woman sat back on her heels, an apron of sacking enveloping her thin body, her worn face lined but good-humoured.

'My, yer a pretty young lady, aincher?' she said. She grimaced and adjusted her posture. 'That's me chilblains catchin' me. You got chilblains, ducky?'

'Not yet,' said Susie, looking around. The dust had gone as well as all the junk. The top of the desk was clear and clean, so was the top of the wooden filing cabinet.

'Crool, they are, chilblains. Mister Adams is in the shop – no, 'e ain't, 'e's 'ere.'

Sammy entered from the passage that led into the factory workshop. His overcoat was over his arm, his hat tipped forward, giving him the jaunty look of a man who had made a cheerfully satisfying start to his day. He placed his coat on the desk, lifted his hat to Susie and smiled at her. Watch him, she said to herself, he's got something up his sleeve.

'Morning, Susie. You've met our invaluable char, Mrs Turner? She's goin' to perform regularly for us at dusting and sweeping. But don't call her Mrs Turner, she's made known she only answers to Ma. Like Ma Earnshaw, the female greengrocery woman in East

Street market, you remember.' Sammy had nothing up his sleeve. His brisk and cheerful approach was simply that of a man accepting defeat bravely. If he had lost his battle by bringing Susie and her mesmerising blue eyes back to Camberwell, it was not in his nature to go about with a long face. True, he had thought last night he might still be· saved, that some acceptable bloke of Susie's acquaintance might pop the question to her and that she might say yes. Unfortunately, that thought was immediately superseded by an imaginative picture of Susie as Mr X's bride. It made him feel horrendously ill. 'Nice to see you, Susie.'

'Nice you haven't consulted your watch, Mister Sammy,' said Susie with cool flair.

'Eh? Oh, that. But slightly cheeky, Miss Brown. Ma, you finished here yet?'

'I almost nearly 'ave, Mister Adams,' said Ma Turner. 'I been held up a bit by me chilblains. They're something chronic this mornin'.'

'Wear woollen socks under your stockings,' said Sammy.

'Lor' luvaduck, Mister Adams, if I do that what chance 'ave I got of gettin' me shoes on? I asks yer, what chance?'

'Wear larger shoes, Ma,' said Sammy. 'I'll bring yer a pair from me Camberwell shop at trade price. Can't say fairer, and I don't want chronic chilblains crippling yer, it'd pain me Christian compassion, which Miss Susie Brown knows is a weakness of mine. Susie, you all right this morning?'

'Fine, Mister Sammy, specially as I don't have chilblains.'

'Pleased to hear it,' said Sammy, who thought she'd acquired style during her time as a manageress. I'm a drowning man. But I could still be saved. When I get to the stage of final surrender, she might turn me down. A frown injured his cheerful look.

'Something hurtin' you, Mister Sammy?' asked Susie almost demurely.

'Just a passin' thought,' said Sammy.

'Ain't she a pretty picture on a winter mornin', Mister Adams?' said Ma Turner, scrubbing again. 'Come trippin' in lookin' just like the Lord Mayor's fairy queen, she did.'

Susie laughed.

'Well, it's got to be said,' remarked Sammy, 'you do look as if you only need a coach and six white horses. Ma, look lively.'

'Now yer can't rush a good cleanin' job, or corners don't get done,' said Ma Turner. 'But there y'ar, all done.' On her knees, she wrung water from the enormous flannel into the bucket.

'Fine,' said Sammy, approving the results. 'Now be a good old girl and start the other job, the fact'ry floor. Get it swept and see that Charley Harry collects and burns the rubbish.'

'Yer mean Daft Dick,' said Ma Turner, climbing stiffly to her feet.

'That's him,' said Sammy, and she gathered up her flannel, brush and pail.

'Do a good job for yer, I will,' she said, 'seeing yer makin' it reg'lar work.'

'First cobweb I see I'll sack yer,' said Sammy.

'That ain't Christian, Mister Adams,' said Ma, 'that could be 'ard on a widder woman, that could.'

'Just don't cost me unwarranted money, Ma, that's all,' said Sammy, who always made it clear to newcomers that he expected a fair return for what he paid them.

'We'll get on, Mister Adams, you an' me,' said Ma, 'I likes yer.' She went into the workshop, limping a little on her chilblains. Susie heard a yell of greeting from one of the women machinists.

'Oi, watcher, Ma, how is yer, yer old scrubber?'

'She'll do,' said Sammy. 'Now, Susie—'

'Now, Mister Sammy.'

Sammy, suffering helplessness, said, 'Look, when I say now, Susie, it's just an uncomplainin' way of requestin' your undivided attention.'

'Yes, Mister Sammy, I understand,' said Susie, her smile forgiving, 'only could you excuse me requestin' you not to say it as if you're goin' to start learning me the ABC?'

'Oh, my achin' ears,' muttered Sammy.

'Pardon?' said Susie, and Sammy pulled himself together.

'As is no doubt visible to you, Miss Brown, this office has been cleared out and cleaned up. I telephoned Mr Morris yesterday afternoon, and he got a Charley Harry odd-jobber and charwoman Ma to go to work first thing this morning, which was to make up for your unfortunate sufferings of yesterday morning. I've had everything chucked out except the company books, which now repose in that cabinet. We are now in the highly advantageous position of being able to start from scratch, so I'd be much obliged to have you originate a system for keepin' advice notes, delivery notes, invoices and suchlike in a way that won't make it needful to turn the office inside-out to find them. There's the machinists' daily worksheets too. There's empty files in the cabinet for your use, writing paper, pens and ink in the drawer – oh, and on Fridays add up each machinist's worksheet and earnings, put their wages into envelopes and mark them accordin'. You'll be provided with the necessary cash by me. I am enquiring into—'

'Mister Adams, pardon me, I'm sure,' said Susie, 'but I am not agreeable to being banished again, specially not to Shoreditch. It's not what you said.'

'I don't find that word harmonious, Susie. Now why should I want to banish you?'

132

'Yes,' said Susie sweetly, 'why should you?'

'Perish the thought,' said Sammy. 'You'll be workin' in Camberwell, as promised. I just require you to travel to this office on Friday afternoons, check the worksheets, add up the earnings and make up the wages. I am enquiring into the needful necessity of findin' a strong-minded geezer to manage the place, which includes managing the machinists, which are women of vulgarity, impudence, blasphemy and shockin' language into the bargain. Mind, I don't mean they don't do first-class cuttin' and stitching.'

'Mister Sammy, regarding the filing systems and the other work you spoke of,' said Susie, 'kindly inform me why a manager can't do these things himself. I mean, he's goin' to be able to read and write, isn't he? He won't want me comin' in on Fridays to do the wages, which he could do himself if he could add up, which a decent manager ought to, besides lookin' after the machinists and their machines.'

'Ah,' said Sammy thoughtfully. 'Susie, your wordage is like you've been highly educated, and has had the desirable effect of givin' me a helpful idea concerning one of my close relatives. Good on yer, Susie love, you've come on a rare treat—' He coughed to clear his throat. Susie smiled. 'Yes, well, it's something to think about. Meanwhile, you'd better see what the workshop's all about.'

'Yes, I'd like to,' said Susie. He took her through. The place was very basic with its bare walls and its lack of all but the practical essentials. Susie saw Ma Turner at work with a broom, and long benches running from end to end. At the benches sat the seamstresses, women of all ages from twenty to fifty. Each had her sewing-machine and each was working away. They were all on piece-work. Shawls or scarves covered heads to keep hair out of the way, a few making do with a multitude of hairpins. They all looked thin and half-starved to Susie. There were at least forty of them, some rising above their depressing conditions to keep up a constant flow of chatter and gossip without ever once stopping their work. The windows were filthy enough to kill the better part of daylight, and the floor, littered with scraps of material, was of cold stone. A coal-burning stove in the middle of the workshop offered only a miserable amount of heat. But the machines hummed, whined and clattered, thin fingers pushing feverishly.

At the entrance of Sammy and Susie, several of the women actually stopped work to stare at Susie. Susie, a South London cockney girl in the process of bettering herself, looked to the seamstresses as if she was very much removed from the world of the working-class.

' 'Ello again, Mister Adams, Yer Lordship, 'oo's 'Er Ladyship?' asked one woman.

And two women sang, ' *'Ello, 'ello, who's yer lady friend, who's the little girlie by yer side? I've seen you, with a girl or two, oh, oh, oh, I am surprised at you. 'Ello, 'ello, what's yer little game, don't yer think—'*

'Shut up!' Sammy raised his voice. 'You're all sacked, the lot of you.'

All machines stopped and there was a shocked silence until the first woman spoke again.

'Gawd 'elp us, what for?'

'For impudence and downright disrespect,' said Sammy, given to establishing firm control of employees.

'Oh, yer can't do it, what about our 'ungry kids?'

'We've all got problems,' said Sammy.

'Oh, yer bleedin' 'angman,' gasped the woman.

Susie, shocked herself by Sammy's cruelty, saw a little grin flicker on his face.

'All right, Gertie, all right,' he said, 'kindly spare me a carry-on, it's your lucky day, you're all reinstated. But mind yer manners in future, and mind them in partic'lar when the Lord Mayor's daughter happens to be with me. Kindly accord her due respect.'

Every seamstress breathed with relief, every eye stared at Susie. Susie smiled.

'Oh, pleased to meet yer, me lady,' said a young woman, pale with anaemia.

' 'Owjerdo, madam,' said the woman called Gertie, thirty-five and the senior seamstress. 'It's a pleasure yer come among us.'

'Would yer give me regards to yer dad, 'Is Lordship?' offered a venturesome seamstress.

'Never mind all that,' said Sammy. 'Kindly listen. I'm requiring instructional information which will help me concernin' your welfare.' Mouths dropped open and gaped with incomprehension. 'Inform me first, Gertie, if you get breakdowns.'

'On these 'ere machines what come out of the Ark?' enquired Gertie, thin but resilient. 'Course we get breakdowns.'

'Have you got spare machines?' asked Sammy.

'Three,' said Gertie, 'and it's a sod—'

'Hold up,' said Sammy, son of Chinese Lady, a woman who thought it desecrating for bad language to sit on the tongue of a female, 'Miss Brown heard that.'

'Oh, beggin' yer pardon, Yer Ladyship, I'm sure,' said Gertie, 'but breakdowns is bleedin' inconvenient, to put it more acceptable, like.'

'Oh, I've known bleedin' inconveniences myself,' said Susie sweetly.

'Yer got a kind 'eart,' said Gertie, 'but it's crool, I tell yer, Mister Adams. With the breakdowns we get, we could do with a dozen spare machines. No machine, no work, yer know. No work, no pay.'

'Who repairs the machines that break down?' asked Sammy.

135

'Some geezer Mister Morris calls in, only Mister Morris ain't 'ere no more. Them three spare machines is being used now. I tell yer, Mister Adams, the 'ole bleedin' lot of machines needs doin' up proper, or yer'll lose money and so will we.'

'I don't like losin' money,' said Sammy frankly, 'it's unhealthy.'

'Starvation don't do our kids much good, neither,' said Gertie. 'Mister Adams, we're losin' bread money now.'

'I am takin' due note of that,' said Sammy, 'and will make it up to yer accordin'. This repairing gent, how long does he take to get here when he's required?'

'Now and again in a couple of hours,' said Gertie, 'but mostly 'e arrives termorrer.'

'I got you,' said Sammy. 'What about the cutting machines?' There were three cutting machines against a side wall.

'They don't give no trouble,' said Gertie.

'Right,' said Sammy. 'Now, kindly listen some more. I know what yer work's like. This fact'ry's been supplying my shops for five years, and yer stitching's earned you me heartfelt admiration. I do also know what yer average turnover is, highly satisfying. I'll make a deal with you. I'll see yer machines are kept in running order day in, day out, and you see you give me a turnover consistent with highly satisfying, and you'll all get a weekly bonus of half a crown. I can't say fairer—'

'Whadjer mean?' asked a woman suspiciously. 'What's a bonus?'

'It's extra,' said Sammy. 'It comes on top of your piece-work earnings and is related to being good girls and conscientiously efficient.'

'Extra?'

'What's 'e saying?'

'I dunno, it sounds Chinese to me.'

'Artful, they are, them Chinese.'

136

The seamstresses gabbled to each other.

Gertie said, 'Whadjer mean, bonus extra, Mister Adams? I ain't never 'eard of that round 'ere.'

'Well,' said Sammy patiently, 'if you earn ten bob for your week's piece-work, which represents a highly satisfact'ry endeavour, you'll get an extra half a crown, makin' twelve and sixpence in all.'

The shabby women of the sweatshop stared at him. Six full days a week they worked, from eight in the morning until six in the evening, and by dint of flying fingers and pedalling feet they managed to take home a wage of ten bob or so. An extra half a crown for no more work astonished them.

'Yer jokin', Mister Adams,' said Gertie.

'I never joke at business and suchlike,' said Sammy. He was not being philanthropic. He was always shrewd and calculating about what his employees and their efficiency meant to him. He knew how skilled these Shoreditch women were, and how important to the trade was first-class stitching. Just as important was the necessity of getting the garments into his shops at low production costs. There was also the question of reliability in respect of delivery, something Morris had fallen down on from time to time. Sammy knew he could get reliability from employees who had something extra to look forward to each week, and whose machines weren't always breaking down. Some sweatshops achieved reliability and low production costs merely by cracking the whip and keeping seamstresses in constant fear of losing their jobs. For all his obsessive need to make his fortune, Sammy had never operated in this way. He did not like keeping employees on the breadline. He did not shower gold on any of them, but he did pay them fair wages, and in return he expected and received a fair effort. He had his opinions about sweated labour. He kept them to himself, but he was

137

well aware these seamstresses were glad of any kind of job. He had grown up in Walworth, where conditions might have been a little better than they were in the East End, but where a job was still something to hang on to, however poor the pay. Handing out a little extra to Gertie and her thin-bodied colleagues would guarantee a mite more happiness and a more willing effort in respect of urgent orders. It might even make some of them smile a bit. They could joke, they could joke in caustic fashion, and they could fling vulgarities that would arouse screeching laughter, but they rarely smiled in the way of women who were enjoying their work. The work pressurised them, their fingers raced and their teeth grated with effort. In the summer they sweated and their hungry faces grew wet and shiny. Sammy often wondered what Chinese Lady would say if she knew how Adams Enterprises had been profiting indirectly from sweated labour and was now going to profit directly from same. Once she knew the factory was his, she was quite likely to take a tram across the river and see it for herself. If conditions for the women were as they were now, she would dismantle him piece by piece. He'd better do something about brightening it up and adding an amenity or two. All the women had now was a sink and a cold water tap, and a gas ring for boiling water for tea during their brief midday break. Their lav was a lean-to outside.

They were still staring at him. Susie had a little smile on her face.

'Mister Adams, yer really means it?' said Gertie. 'We're goin' to get an extra two an' six a week pervidin' we does yer proud with our rate?'

'You got my word,' he said, and Susie noted he said nothing about how it could ruin him. 'But listen, keep it to yourselves. If you don't, if you boot it about like a football and everyone gets to know, I'll likely be hacked to a fatal death by the geezers who run other fact'ries. I wouldn't like that, it'll hurt considerable. I don't mind yer feeling gratified, but I don't want any of you advertisin' it. I might be consequentially forced to cancel it. You all got that?'

'We got yer, Mister Adams,' said Gertie.

'Yer a gent,' said a young woman, 'and we'll do yer proud, yer won't have no fact'ry turnin' out better stuff than we will.'

'You get the orders, Mister Adams, you keep us goin' and we'll keep yer 'appy.'

'Bonuses start this week,' said Sammy, 'you'll get 'em with your Friday wages. Furthermore and so on, I'm puttin' in a manager in place of Mr Morris, presently defunct in a manner of speakin'. He'll treat yer right, he'll cop yer if yer don't treat him right, and he'll keep all yer machines in first-class order. You got a Charley Harry to do odd jobs for you, which is namely Daft Dick, I'm told, and you got Ma Turner who's goin' to keep yer clean and tidy. I don't like seeing an untidy workshop, it don't reflect well on me business, nor on me. Also, tea and biscuits will be provided morning and afternoon at my expense. I am beknown for suchlike Christian gestures, something highly appreciated by the Lord Mayor's daughter, this young lady here, who is Miss Susie Brown and my personal assistant.'

Susie did not know how she kept her face straight. She only knew what she had always known, that Sammy had his own way of talking to people. He now had these hard-working seamstresses in the palm of his hand, and he would get his pound of flesh without using a knife. It was ridiculous, of course, that he thought it a weakness to care for someone.

'Mister Adams,' said Gertie, 'you treatin' us to tea mornin' and afternoon, and with free biscuits too? You doin' that, Mister Adams?'

'Just see you don't diddle me when you hand the expense chits to the manager,' said Sammy. 'You diddle me and you'll all be on dry bread and cold water at your own expense.'

'We ain't goin' to diddle yer,' said Gertie, an efficient chargehand. 'When's the manager comin'?'

'Next Monday, probably.'

' 'E ain't a growler, is 'e?'

'He's recommendable as a gentlemanly geezer who'll keep your machines in order and treat you with love and kindness,' said Sammy.

' 'Ere, Glad'll like that,' said Gertie, 'she don't get much lovin', do yer, Glad?'

'Me old man's got a chronic back,' said Gladys.

'All right,' said Sammy, 'you can all get on with your work.'

They got on with it. Outside in the factory yard, smoke rose from a burning stack of piled rubbish. Ma Turner was still creating other piles with her broom.

'Mister Adams,' said Gertie, 'if the managin' gent ain't goin' to be 'ere till Monday, could I speak to yer about what orders we're d'reckly finishing and when yer gettin' Carter Paterson to call?'

'Mister Adams!' Ma bawled from the door leading to the office. 'Yer got a lady askin' to see someone.'

'Susie, would yer kindly see who she is?' said Sammy. 'If she wants a job, take her name and address.'

'Very good, Mister Adams,' said Susie. She found a woman in the office. She was dark, close to thirty, and with the hungry face and eyes common among many people in the East End. Her hat and coat were cheap, but she wore them with style, and her cracked shoes still shod her feet neatly. Under her arm she carried a large, cardboard-backed folio. 'Good morning,' said Susie, 'can I help you?'

'Good morning,' said the woman, 'is Mr Morris around?'

'Well, no,' said Susie, 'he's sold the business to Adams Enterprises Ltd.'

'Never heard of 'em. Who are they?'

'The Adams fam'ly, prominent in South London,' said Susie. 'The managin' director's Mister Sammy Adams.'

'Don't know him,' said the woman. 'Still, it's not my week. Wasn't last week, either. My life, I could drop dead and there'd still be a million people I'd never met. What's he like, this managing director?'

'Well, he's not started to eat people yet,' said Susie.

'Sounds promising. D'you think I could see him?'

'What about, a job?' asked Susie.

'Fashions.'

'Pardon?'

'All right, I know this isn't a fashion house, but you've got outlets for your own designs, I suppose.'

'I don't know Mister Adams has ever had his own designs,' said Susie.

'Well, I'm a designer.' The woman smiled a little bleakly. 'Well, I think I am, only most don't. Most of the London houses, I mean, and most of the manufacturers. Trouble is, we're ten a penny, and you've got to be a French poof to stand any real chance. If you're not, if you're just another female amateur, all you can do is hope and pray. I fall back on being a dressmaker, running up party frocks for small girls. About one a month, which hardly pays the rent. Is this Adams gent around?'

'He's busy at the moment,' said Susie. 'I'm his personal assistant.'

'Are you influential? I mean, would you like to see my sketches and ideas, and recommend me to him if they take your fancy? Is he adventurous, not afraid of taking chances? I think I'd have found Reuben Morris a bit conservative, but I thought I'd come and have a go at him, since I believe he has the potential with forty and more machinists here. Does your Mister Adams have panache?'

Susie had to guess what panache meant. She guessed that somehow it fitted Sammy. She said, 'Show me.' She was intrigued by being face to face with a fashion designer, even if she wasn't a French poof.

'I'm Lilian Hyams,' said the woman, and Susie placed her among Mr Greenberg's warmhearted fraternity. Times must be exceptionally hard if the Jewish rag trade men were closing ranks against their own. Or perhaps they discouraged enterprise in a Jewish woman.

'Don't the rag trade just copy French designs?' she asked, as Lilian Hyams placed her portfolio on the desk.

'Under licence, of course, or in a naughty way,' said Lilian, and opened the portfolio. Susie studied sketches in water colours as each page was turned, thinking the woman an artist as well as a designer. She studied some sketches at length, the water colours laid on over lightly pencilled outlines. Spring coats and summer coats alternated with summer dresses. Susie thought them very appealing, very stylish. Lilian gave a little commentary on each design. Susie noted neatly written details of materials. Silk, of course, and marocain, printed cottons, shantung and crêpe de Chine. Some of the colours were brilliant. A few Paris designers had been inspired by the magnificent colourfulness of the Tutankhamen discoveries. Susie saw that Lilian had used rich orange reds and golden yellows in some sketches.

Then a purple red dress leapt to her eye. Purple red? And terribly short? The hemline was two inches above the knees. And long strings of beads reached almost to the waist. Lilian waited for a comment.

'Well,' breathed Susie. To the right of the design,

hanging on the white of the drawing paper, were two matching purple garters, neatly sketched.

'Decorative accessories, to be seen if desired,' said Lilian.

'It's so short,' said Susie.

'Wait till the New Year fashion shows in Paris,' said Lilian. 'It's my guess they've decided to aim for the limit. This length.'

'Someone's told you that?' asked Susie.

'I should be so lucky. No, it's my own feelings. Should I gamble on my own feelings if I had the capital? I would. Would your boss?'

Fashions were already short, as short as most people thought they would go. Flappers among the Bright Young Things never wore anything longer than two inches below the knees. Susie's own hemlines were short. But two inches above the knees? That was blush-making.

'Crikey,' she said, the cockney surfacing, 'd'yer think Paris really will go the limit like that?'

'Something like that will be out by the spring,' said Lilian, 'I'd bet ten quid on it if I had ten quid. You're not sure yourself, are you? But at least you're more interested than anyone else I've shown it to. I've had horse laughs spilled over that design. But if your boss would risk it and put money into it, he could beat the Paris fashion houses themselves into the shops over here, he could be the first in the shops with this design and similar ones, and that would be at just the right time, after the Paris shows have all the flappers jumping about in excitement over the new lengths. That's the market to aim for, you know, the flappers' market. And they don't buy new fashions just one at a time. You didn't say, is your boss conservative, is he cautious?'

'No, he's not,' said Susie, and Lilian showed her sketches of similarly short designs. Beads and bangles

143

were prominent. Colours were radiant. 'You sure about the red purple? You're using it a lot,' said Susie.

'Outrageous, d'you think?' said Lilian. 'Flappers like the outrageous. They'll like the garters. They'll go with the Charleston. That's going to be all the rage in the New Year. What's your name?'

'Susie Brown.'

'Well, Susie Brown, you're the first personal assistant to a boss who's taken the time to look all through my portfolio. D'you think I could now see the boss himself? Is he fat, does he chew cigars, is he rude, middle-aged and bald, would a woman dress designer make him laugh his head off? Adams, you said? Could this be a Gentile firm now?'

'You don't mind, do you?' asked Susie, who had taken to the woman.

'I'll put up a fight,' said Lilian, and Sammy came in then, having discussed with the astonished Gertie how to brighten up the workshop and make things a bit more comfortable for the machinists.

'Mister Adams,' said Susie, 'I'm pleased to present to you someone who could be our own French fashion designer. Madame Lilian Dupont.'

'Come again?' said Sammy, and Lilian cast a smiling glance at Susie in appreciation of her quick turn of thought. Then she took a long look at Sammy. Her eyes opened wide. Tall, lean, and with a determined mouth and direct blue eyes, he was far from what she had imagined. He was even young. No more than twenty-four, surely. Young. Alive. Acute interest dawned and hope quickened. She was down on her uppers, she was broke and hungry. But Susie had given her the hope, and the sight of this young man fanned it. Perhaps with his air of alertness, he also had nerve and imagination. He had to have sufficient of those qualities if he consented to gamble on her instincts and intuition.

144

Susie explained. Sammy listened. He sat down at the desk and went through the portfolio, Lilian providing a commentary. Arriving at the first example of audacity, the purple red design, he showed a little smile and his eyes glinted. He looked up at Lilian.

'You're who?' he asked.

'Madame Lilian Dupont,' said Susie.

'I think you're havin' me on, Miss Brown,' said Sammy.

Lilian gave him her correct name and added, 'I think your personal assistant thought a French monicker might help.'

'Susie's a bright girl,' said Sammy, 'it wouldn't surprise me if she married one of those Russian Grand Dukes that's floatin' about in Paris, I hear.'

'Don't let's have any comical stuff, Mister Adams,' said Susie.

'Kindly continue,' said Sammy to Lilian, and Lilian talked about the January fashion shows in Paris, about the feelings she had concerning hemlines, colours and accessories, and about stealing a march on the French designers. She'd been to London fashion houses, she said, and to manufacturers, without arousing a glimmer of interest. That, she said, was because she wasn't a French poof. One fashion house had advised her to go to Paris and study the art of true fashion. Imagine English fashion houses having no faith in native designers except in respect of tweeds. Would Mister Adams care to comment on her portfolio? Did any of her designs interest him?

'Considerable,' said Sammy, slowly leafing through more pages.

'Considerable?'

'The previous gent in ownership of this business left behind a multitude of unusable articles, all of which my personal assistant referred to as demolishable junk,' said Sammy, 'and which included catalogues of designs dating back, in my opinion, to the time when fig leaves were popular. These selfsame catalogues are presently goin' up in smoke, with all the other articles ancient to behold, much to the pleasure of Miss Susie Brown. There's some designs, fairly reasonable, still in our workshop and coincidin' with orders my staff of seamstresses is workin' on. I was about to make known to Miss Brown the needful necessity of acquiring up-to-date designs from sources common to the trade, which task I am sure she would have performed with considerable flair and taste, being, as you can see, a young female woman of style and remarkability.' Sammy paused. Lilian was looking mesmerised, and Susie hardly knew how to contain herself. 'However, Madame Dupont, who needs designs from common sources when here in front of me admiring mince pies is an exclusive collection?'

'Mister Adams?' said Lilian, who had not met many like Sammy.

'I am speakin' of exclusive, I trust, if we take you on?' enquired Sammy.

'I should come to you and offer you designs not exclusive to you?' said Lilian.

'It's not what I'd like,' said Sammy.

'It's not what I'd do,' said Lilian. 'Mister Adams, am I reading you right? Are you actually offering to take me on as your designer?'

'I've seen designs, all sorts,' said Sammy. 'I don't recollect seeing any like these, which I would specifically class as superior. Adams Enterprises, however, have shops in Camberwell, Brixton, Peckham and Kennington.'

'I could adapt most designs to cheaper materials,' said Lilian, 'but with your own label you could aim to open up an outlet for dearer garments in West End shops and stores, couldn't you?'

'That thought is just crossin' my mind,' said Sammy, 'but I don't know about stealing a march on the French.'

'In respect of my shorter lengths?' said Lilian. 'There wouldn't be any point in trying to if you didn't believe in my ideas. A half-hearted commitment wouldn't work.'

'I don't go in for being half-hearted,' said Sammy, and made another study of the purple red creation. Susie knew he was taken with the portfolio and intrigued by Lilian's audacity. Looking up at the woman, he noted a wedding ring. 'You're married?' he said.

'I was,' said Lilian. 'My husband Jacob was killed in the war. On the Somme.'

'I'm sorry,' said Sammy, and thought about Boots, blinded on the Somme. The Somme had been horrendous. He looked at the design again, then at Susie, still in her hat and coat. The coat was three inches below her knees. Her shapely legs shone in rayon stockings. 'Susie—'

'Oh, no you don't,' said Susie.

'Don't what?'

'I'm not doing any leg show,' said Susie.

'Susie's religious,' said Sammy to Lilian, and Lilian smiled. 'I was merely thinking, Miss Brown, that if you removed your coat I could use my imagination concerning this partic'lar design.'

'That's all you could use,' said Lilian, 'until you had a sample made up. I could do that, if you're interested, and you should be interested in anticipating the French.'

'Well, Lily—'

'It's Lilian.'

'Yes, Hyams you said. Fine old fam'ly name, that, but I think for business reasons I'd prefer Dupont,

147

specially as it was offered up by Susie. Well, Lily, I tell you what, you make up a sample here. Today, if you don't happen to be otherwise engaged. Can you use a cutting machine?'

'Of course,' said Lilian, 'and a sewing-machine.'

'And have you got a pattern?'

'The patterns of all those designs are in the back of the portfolio.'

'I like a self-organised woman,' said Sammy. 'Select a material from our stocks. When you've done the cutting – wait, have you got a sewing-machine at home?'

'Yes,' said Lilian, impressed by the decisive nature of this personable young businessman.

'Then make the sample up there,' said Sammy. 'We don't want too many people knowing you've got certain ideas about the 1926 hemlines. This trade is thick with dubious geezers.'

'Mister Adams, you weren't born yesterday, and that's a fact,' said Lilian. 'Shall I make the sample up to Susie's size?'

'On behalf of my personal assistant,' said Sammy, 'I accept that convenient suggestion.'

'Mister Adams,' said Susie, 'I hope that don't mean I'm goin' to be turned into a clothes horse.'

'My ideas for your future don't include makin' a mannequin of you,' said Sammy, dropping his guard in another weak moment because Susie looked like a picture postcard in her red coat and navy blue cloche hat. He coughed. Susie felt a little spasm of delight. He just couldn't meet her eyes, he couldn't. 'Yes, well, if you could temp'rarily oblige so that we could see what the sample looks like on you, I'd be gratified.'

'Oh, lor',' said Susie, 'all those inches above the knee?'

'Kind of you, Miss Brown,' said Sammy, and gave Lilian another look. She seemed very happy about

148

things, but he noted her aquiline features and her hollow eyes, the all-too-common signs of a person down on her luck. She was fighting for survival, like too many others in the crowded jungle of the East End. And it was a harder fight for a woman. 'It occurs to me that before you select a material and cut it to pattern, Lily, we ought to consider some reviving refreshment. I'll take you both round the corner to Joe's eatin' place, and we'll try for some hot tea and a fried egg sandwich.'

'But it's nowhere near dinnertime yet,' said Susie.

'It's reviving time,' said Sammy. Lilian was perceptibly tempted by the thought of food. 'Afterwards, we'll make some detailed notes concerning how the firm is goin' to adjust to this new prospect, Susie, leaving Lily to go off home with her material.'

'Mister Adams,' said Lilian, 'I think I'm going to like working for you.'

'If I like what you turn out from that pattern,' said Sammy, 'I'll take you on definite and permanent. Our own label. Lily Dupont of Paris. How does that strike you?'

'It strikes me I'll love it,' said Lilian.

'Good. We'll meet you here tomorrow morning.' Sammy, coming to his feet, eyed her again. Jewish, of course. Well, he liked the fraternity. 'You don't mind I'm a Gentile?'

'I don't mind if you're Goliath the Philistine, you take me on permanently and pay me a fair salary, and you won't see me running off if Solly Bergmann makes me an offer. I like it that you liked my collection, I like it that you and Susie both took the time and trouble to consider it. Mister Adams, I also like you, both of you. I hope you'll both like me.'

Susie smiled. Sammy had made another Jewish friend, and had taken another step on his way up, she was sure.

149

CHAPTER TWELVE

The school playground of St Luke's was ringing with the noise of boys and girls. Rosie and Annabelle were seated on a bench eating their dinnertime sandwiches. It was too far for them to go home for a meal, as a number of other pupils did. Twelve-year-old Alfred Grimes approached, a grin on his face.

'Give us a bite, Rosie,' he said.

'I'll save you the crusts,' said Rosie.

'Don't want yer crusts,' said Grimes, 'give us a kiss instead.' He plonked himself down next to Rosie, slipped an arm around her waist and tried for a kiss. Rosie stuffed her half-eaten sandwich into his mouth. At the same time fingers took hold of his right ear. He gurgled a yell around the sandwich. He lifted his head and looked up into the face of Miss Simms.

'Depart,' said Polly, 'or I'll wallop you.'

He disgorged the sandwich into his hand.

'Me?' he said. That was the standard response of all boys affecting to suffer the injury of being misjudged. 'Me, Miss Simms?'

'You,' said Polly. 'Six of the best.'

'Blow me,' said Grimes, 'it don't bear finking of what can be done to yer when yer ain't done anyfink yerself.'

'Dear me, oh dear dear me,' said Polly, 'go and write out the word think fifty times, and then you and I will

150

go through its correct pronunciation fifty times immediately after classes. Go now, go, go, go.'

'Stone the bleedin' crows,' muttered Grimes, as he went on his way, 'yer try an' treat a girl to a decent kiss and this is what yer get. I ain't 'anding out none to that Rosie no more.'

Polly, who would have protected Rosie with her life, said to her, 'As soon as you and Annabelle have finished your sandwiches, will you both come into the hall for some rehearsal?' The school was to perform a Nativity play at Christmas, the play written by Polly herself. Annabelle was in the role of Mary, and Rosie was playing the innkeeper's wife.

'Yes, Miss Simms,' said Rosie. An upright-looking woman entered through the school gates.

'Oh, there's Granny Lady,' cried Annabelle.

'Miss Simms, it's our grandmother,' said Rosie, and both girls got up and ran to meet Chinese Lady, dressed in a brown coat and brown hat. She had stopped wearing black hats after her marriage to Mr Finch, thinking it only right and proper that respect for her late husband shouldn't be inflicted on her new husband.

'There you are, the pair of you,' she said, and gave each girl a pat.

'Nana, we're having our sandwiches,' said Rosie. 'Have you come to see us about something?'

Polly came up.

'I was just passin',' said Chinese Lady.

'Good morning,' said Polly. She had never met Boots's mother, but had heard much about her. She thought her pleasant-looking, but with a very firm mouth that seemed to suggest a no-nonsense approach to her family and to life. 'May I help you?'

'I was just passin',' said Chinese Lady again, shopping-bag with her. 'I thought I'd look in. I'm Mrs Finch, these are my granddaughters.'

151

'I'm Miss Simms,' said Polly, 'and happy to meet you, Mrs Finch.'

'It's nice to see what my granddaughters' school looks like. Goodness, what a racket them children are kickin' up.'

'We can escape that,' said Polly. 'I can take you round the hall and classrooms, if you'd like to see them. I'm having a little rehearsal of our Nativity play in ten minutes, but there's time to show you round.'

'Very kind,' said Chinese Lady. She gave Rosie and Annabelle another pat each, and went into the school with Polly. 'I hear you're goin' to give Rosie special lessons.'

'Yes.' Polly stopped at the door to the hall. 'She's such a talented girl.'

'Her father said it's all about a scholarship.'

'Yes, I did speak to Mr Adams about it,' said Polly.

'He's my only oldest son,' said Chinese Lady, examining a child's drawing pinned to a wall.

'Your only – ?'

'My oldest. Not that you'd think it sometimes.' Chinese Lady turned from the drawing and accompanied Polly into the assembly hall. The subdued light of the misty day seemed to linger outside the windows, as if reluctant to enter. The hall appeared to be stoically resigned to winter. 'Just like St John's,' murmured Chinese Lady.

'St John's?' enquired Polly.

'The Walworth school my children went to.'

'I see.' Polly, not realising she was under scrutiny, said cheerfully, 'Why wouldn't I sometimes think Mr Adams wasn't your oldest son?'

'He don't always look serious enough at life, and when he was younger, well, he had all the airy-fairy answers to everything you could think of.'

'Oh, he's still like that,' said Polly with the unguarded

frankness of a woman responsive to men of that kind. Clear almond eyes gave her a direct look.

'You've met him, of course,' said Chinese Lady.

'A few times,' said Polly, suddenly cautious.

Chinese Lady, looking around the hall, thought well, I can't say she's not polite and nice-speaking. She sounds almost like she's upper-class. But there's a minx trying to get out somewhere, and it's halfway showing in that short skirt of hers. I just don't know what sociability's coming to, girls and young women flaunting their legs outrageous. I'll never hold with lady teachers flaunting theirs, nor married women. There's Emily going off to work each morning in skirts and dresses nearly up to her knees. And that Sammy selling them in his shops to innocent young working girls. Well, they can't go any higher, it just wouldn't be decent, but I'd have something to say to Sammy if they did.

'Still, his wife takes things more serious, thank goodness,' she said.

'Mrs Adams? Yes, I've met her too, of course,' said Polly, who had been astounded at what she considered the plainness of Boots's wife, even if she did have enviable auburn hair. 'She's serious about everything?'

'Some things,' said Chinese Lady. 'Like her home and her marriage. Well, it's a nice large hall, and I'd best be going now, I'm partakin' with my daughter.'

'Wouldn't you like to see the classrooms?' asked Polly.

'Not now, Miss Simms, thank you, I've got to be at my daughter's by one. It's nice you're being a help to Rosie.'

When she had gone, Polly wondered why she had come at all.

People were pushing a bit in the East Street market in Walworth. It was often swelled by an influx of workers using their dinnertime break to look for bargains. Tommy, in charge of Sammy's glass and china stall, was by himself for the moment. His assistant, Mrs Walker, was giving her feet a rest in Toni's refreshment shop, while taking in a cup of tea and a sandwich. Sammy and Susie appeared at the stall.

'How's business?' asked Sammy.

'What can I show you, guv'nor?' asked Tommy. 'Tea service? Or some other fashionable weddin' present?'

Sammy quivered.

'Leave off,' he said.

Tommy simulated a peer of recognition.

'Oh, it's you,' he said. 'Ain't seen you down here for years. Couldn't think who you were for a moment. Hello, Susie, recognise you anytime, anywhere. Peachy, you are.'

'I like you too,' smiled Susie.

'Real treat to me optic nerves,' said Tommy. 'What's me young brother doing in this strange spot?'

'He's come to see you,' said Susie.

'I'm honoured,' said Tommy.

'How's your little girl?' asked Susie.

'Fat,' said Tommy. 'I'm told that means she's well-fed and healthy. I hope it don't mean it's permanent. A girl's a girl. A dumpling's a dumpling.'

'I like dumplings,' said Sammy.

'Yes, you tried to turn me into one when I was workin' on the stall for you,' said Susie.

Ma Earnshaw at her greengrocery stall called to Susie.

'Watcher, Susie me love, 'ardly recognised yer. My, aincher growed? 'Ow is yerself, eh?'

'All the better for seeing yer, Ma,' said Susie in old-fashioned cockney parlance.

'Real young lady, aincher? And that Sammy there, look at 'im, ain't 'e lordly?'

'Now, Ma, don't get fancified,' said Sammy, 'just keep the fog off yer cauliflowers.'

'There's ain't no fog got at my cauliflowers,' said Ma Earnsaw, 'pure lily-white, they are.'

Mrs Walker, arriving back from Toni's, said hello to everyone. Sammy asked her to hold the fort while he and Tommy and Susie partook of some needful refreshment themselves. They began a walk through the market, with Tommy asking if this was some form of reunion.

'Give over,' said Sammy, 'I don't go in for fam'ly cross-talk when I got serious business on me mind. Referring to present business, kindly meet my new private secretary and personal assistant, Miss Susie Brown.'

'Is that a fact?' asked Tommy. 'If so, I'm pleased for yer, Susie.'

'I'm pleased for myself,' said Susie.

'About time he rescued you from the wilds of Brixton,' said Tommy.

'Yes, it's been very trying,' said Susie.

'You take one step at a time,' said Sammy, 'not two. Or you fall over yerself.'

'Yes, Mister Sammy,' said Susie, and Tommy glanced at her as they forged a way through the crowds. He thought she looked stunning. She'd come a long way from her starved, ragamuffin look of five years ago.

'We'll have a talk at Toni's,' said Sammy, 'and a small amount of refreshments.'

'I'll just eat a cup of tea,' said Susie. 'I was, you recollect, considerably filled up with the reviving refreshments we had in Shoreditch.'

Tommy grinned. Susie had learned to match the verbiage Sammy indulged in at times.

'Now we've got a prolonged afternoon of business in front of us, Susie,' said Sammy, 'callin' at all our shops to talk to the manageresses about the future concernin' our own label, and I don't want you faintin' from lack of nourishment. We'll all have fried eggs and bacon, and you can say grace, if you like, to show we appreciate the blessings of being able to afford what lots of other people can't. That'll make you feel you can tuck in nice and religious.'

Susie smiled. Sammy had always fussed over what he considered was her tendency not to eat enough. He seemed to think she was still a hungry waif with bony knees and skinny ribs. Wait till he arrived at the moment when he would discover she had a lovely body. She was going to marry him, never mind if the thought of taking a wife turned him hoarse with fright at what it would do to his pocket. She just hoped she wouldn't have to do the proposing herself.

It was after one and there was only one spare table at Toni's. Sammy ordered at the counter, then they all sat down. Sammy at once addressed Tommy briskly.

'It's time you came off the stall, Tommy,' he said, 'it's time you had a manager's job. It don't look good, me with a brother still running a stall, and we got to re-arrange you and stop you talkin' about gettin' a job outside the firm. That don't look good, either. Now, how would you like to manage the garment fact'ry we've lately acquired? Managing includes makin' use of your engineering talents, seeing there's nearly fifty sewing-machines of various intricacy which require overhauling and keepin' in permanent running order, which they ain't been up to now.'

'That's not engineering,' said Tommy, but his eyes gleamed. Any kind of machine was interesting to him. He liked to know how any machine worked, how to dismantle it and put it together again. However, he added, 'And it don't hardly sound like a manager's job.'

'But it is, Tommy,' said Susie earnestly, 'you'll be in charge of everything.'

'Right,' said Sammy. 'You'll be in charge of all

156

machines, all the machinists and the office. You've got a tidy mind, you can read and write and add up, and you keep things in good order. Further, you won't have to work Saturday afternoons or Sunday mornings any more, which is going to please Vi considerable. It's my opinion that a tidy fact'ry's a more efficient one, as well as more of a credit to Adams Enterprises. Limited. Also further, you'll have desirable company in the shape of a French lady, our fashion designer.'

'Now, Mister Sammy,' chided Susie.

'All right, so she ain't precisely French, except we're calling her Madame Dupont,' said Sammy. 'I'll get a temp'rary to help Mrs Walker on the stall tomorrow so's you can come to Shoreditch with me and Susie and take a look at things. It's my pleasure to inform you that Miss Brown gave me the idea that pointed me at you, which is the sort of help I require from me personal assistant, and for which I duly credit her. Well, what d'you say, Tommy?'

'You talk a lot, but I like most of it,' said Tommy, 'and Vi's a consideration, as you mentioned.'

'I appreciate same,' said Sammy, 'even if the opinions of female women don't always make good business sense. Present company excepted, of course,' he added hastily.

'You said that just in time,' murmured Susie. Her foot touched his under the table. Sammy quivered and sat up straight. Susie smiled.

'Eggs-a bacon! Who's-a for eggs-a bacon?' Toni called from the counter.

Tommy and Sammy got up to fetch the plates, with knives and forks. Susie accepted hers, after all, because the aroma was irresistible, and because she had a lovely feeling Sammy was in a corner and she had put him there.

She kept looking at him while he enlarged on things

with Tommy. She liked his face very much, especially his firm mouth and his frank blue eyes, which always looked directly at people, even if they did shift about to avoid looking at her. She knew why he did that. He was afraid of loving her, he was afraid that loving her would interfere with his business career. How silly he was not to know that as his wife she would give him all the support he needed.

Tommy was saying, 'You won't mind if I ask about a manager's salary?'

'You're expected to ask,' said Sammy, 'that's good business sense.' He put his knife down and fished a slip of paper from his pocket. He handed it to Tommy. Tommy examined it. Sammy was offering him three pounds a week, plus an extra month's salary at Christmas. Tommy knew Vi would like to see him in a better job, and that Aunt Victoria would certainly like to see him off the stall.

'What prospects, Sammy?' he asked.

'Well, I'll tell yer, old cock,' said Sammy. 'Unlimited. We're going to market ladies' garments for our usual kind of trade and West End trade, all garments with our own label. I'm satisfied, and so is Susie, that in Madame Dupont we have acquired a fashion designer of remarkable forethinking.'

'Don't hand me left-over marmalade,' said Tommy. 'I may be dead ignorant about fashion, but I'm not mug enough to believe a notable fashion designer is goin' to work for any manufacturer who's never been heard of, specially not heard of in the West End. Come on, who is she?'

'I'll grant yer she ain't yet acquired notability,' said Sammy, 'but she will with us.'

'She's actually Mrs Lilian Hyams of Shoreditch,' said Susie.

'Battersea, actually,' said Sammy. 'She wrote her

partic'lars down for me.' Finishing his food, he called for a pot of tea for three. Toni called back.

'Pot? What-a you ask for? A pot, Mister Adams? Is-a a hotel I got here?'

'All right, three cups of tea,' said Sammy. 'Fresh.'

'What-a you doing, Mister Adams?' Toni waved his arms about in Italian fashion. 'First you ask for what-a I don't do, now you insult me. You hear that, Maria?'

Costermongers grinned, Toni's plump wife Maria smiled, shrugged, poured out three cups of tea from a large enamel teapot, and took them to Sammy's table. Sammy gave her bottom a pat, and Maria, giggling, returned to safety behind her counter. Susie gave Sammy a cool look.

'I don't think it becomes the managing director of Adams Enterprises to do things like that,' she said.

'I didn't do anything,' said Sammy. 'Tommy, I have to record it was Miss Brown who came up with a French monicker for our designer.'

'Duly noted,' said Tommy. 'All right, I'll come and take a look at things tomorrow.'

'Tommy, that's lovely, and you'll make a good manager, I know you will,' said Susie, 'and I'm sure Madame Dupont's goin' to be a boon to your fam'ly's future prosperity. Your nice mother'll be so pleased Mister Sammy's recognised your worthiness at last.'

'My what?' said Tommy.

'At last?' said Sammy, looking shocked. 'Kindly understand, Miss Brown, it's been shirts off me back to get where I have got. I have not been in no position to hand out advantageous prospects until now. It is not like handin' out cards at *Beat Yer Neighbour*.'

'No, Mister Sammy, I was only saying, like,' said Susie.

Sammy frowned at her. She smiled. He drank some tea. After they had parted from Tommy and were on their way to the Kennington shop, Sammy asked how she was liking her new position as his assistant.

'Bliss,' said Susie. The bliss came from being with him after two long years in the desert. 'I'm so glad you did what you did do for Tommy.'

'Well, like I said, it don't look good, a brother of mine only running a stall.'

'Can I say something personal?' asked Susie.

'How personal?' asked Sammy cautiously.

'Oh, only that yer lovely, really,' said Susie, 'yer got a real Christian soul inside yer, Mister Sammy.'

'Oh, gawd,' said Sammy.

Susie laughed out loud.

'If it works out all right,' said Tommy at home that evening, 'we can think about givin' your house back to you, Aunt Victoria.'

'Oh, you don't need to think about that yet,' said Aunt Victoria.

'Still, Mum, you want to call the place your own again sometime,' said Vi, who was lovingly happy for Tommy. He was such a good husband, so easy-going, and a pleasure to her whenever they made love. But she had known running the stall had long lost any appeal for him, if it had ever had any real appeal at all.

'You an' Tommy go ahead an' make what plans you want,' said Uncle Tom.

'Now they mustn't rush things,' said Aunt Victoria. 'Tommy having such a respectable job now, he can take a respectable amount of time to find a nice house. We don't want our neighbours thinking we're in unseemly haste to get rid of them. If they took their time, Alice would be grown more. Young parents don't want to move house when a child is only a mite.'

Vi caught Tommy's eye. He winked. They both knew her mother did not want them to move at all.

'We'll take our time, Aunt Victoria,' said Tommy, 'we cert'nly won't go next week. Nor won't we go till we've found just the right place and arranged a mortgage. Vi and me want to buy, like Boots and Ned, we don't want to rent.'

'Sensible,' said Uncle Tom.

'Well, all right,' said Aunt Victoria. 'Tommy, don't you think you should start calling us Mum and Dad?'

'All right, Mum,' said Tommy cheerfully, 'all right, Dad.'

Aunt Victoria looked flustered at that immediate response. Then she smiled. Aunt Victoria, obviously, had come to realise she hadn't lost a daughter, she had gained a son.

CHAPTER THIRTEEN

Susie, with Sammy regarding her as if she had just come out of a Christmas cracker, wasn't sure she was quite decent. Her knees, her legs. Lilian had chosen a dark red crepon, the most suitable material she could find among the factory stocks, and had made it up to near perfection. Waistless, it draped Susie's figure in stylish looseness, its pointed scalloped hem flirting above her knees. Her legs shone in black rayon stockings. Long strings of beads, bought by Lilian from a market, hung low.

'Oh, lor',' breathed Susie, who was certainly sure the effect of the design was not less than audacious, 'I don't know I could go to summer church in this.'

'We should gamble the flappers will?' said Lilian. 'We should. Susie, it looks a dream on you, you have perfect legs for such a style. Mister Adams, say something, even if only throw it away.'

Sammy inspected the short, sleeveless dress with new interest.

'You're lookin',' said Susie.

'Well, I am,' said Sammy, 'and that's a fact.'

'Oh, don't mind me,' said Susie.

'How does it feel on you, the dress?' asked Sammy.

'Short.'

'Kindly oblige me by performing a circle,' said Sammy.

162

Susie did a slow, self-conscious about-turn.

'Well?' she said.

'Crooked seam,' said Sammy, a perfectionist.

'Oh, no,' wailed Susie. She bent her right knee, lifted her leg and looked over her shoulder at the stocking seam. It was quite straight. She inspected her left stocking. The seam deviated a little. 'But that's got nothing to do with the dress.'

'Just thought I'd mention it,' said Sammy.

'Is that all you're going to say?' asked Lilian.

'I like it,' said Sammy. 'We'd better talk about a campaign, right?'

'Right,' said Lilian.

'Gambling's goin' to cost us.'

'But you know what you're gambling on.'

'Yes, the 1926 look,' said Sammy. 'Let's talk about it. Then I've got to get back to Camberwell, which hasn't seen much of me this week, and where I'm all behind, like the cow's tail. Sit down, Lily. You too, Susie.'

'Not in this dress,' said Susie.

'Susie, legs are going to be the thing in 1926,' smiled Lilian.

'Well, mine aren't goin' to be the thing in here while it's still 1925,' said Susie. 'I'll change. Mister Sammy, would you kindly go away for a little while?'

Sammy went outside. He regarded the drab street, grey in the misty morning. Tommy appeared. He had gone to his stall first, to make sure the temporary help promised by Sammy had arrived, and to talk to her and Mrs Walker about keeping the takings up.

'This is prospective?' he enquired, looking at the entrance to the office and factory and conscious more of a surrounding dinginess than of bright hopes.

'All right, some paint's needed, but you got to look farther than that,' said Sammy. 'I'll take you in as soon as Susie's finished dressin'.'

'Finished what?' Tommy grinned. 'What's she been suffering, a fate worse than death? Chinese Lady'll kill you, Sammy.'

'Kindly grow up,' said Sammy, and took his brother in. Susie was herself again. Tommy was introduced to Lilian, then to the workshop, where the Shoreditch seamstresses eyed him with delight.

'Yer new manager, ladies,' said Sammy, 'Mister Tommy Adams.'

'Well, I ain't never seen a more manly pair of trousers,' said one woman.

'I'm all yours,' said Tommy amiably, eyes already on the sewing-machines.

'No, she's 'ad 'ers,' said Gertie. 'That's Flora, and she 'as 'ers reg'lar every mornin'. It's Glad who don't get none, 'er old man's got a hurt back. Tell 'im, Glad.'

'You 'old 'is trousers, Glad, and I'll mind yer drawers,' said another woman.

'I'll mind me own drawers, if yer don't mind,' shouted Glad.

'Just can't satisfy some women, that yer can't.'

'It's occurrin' to me,' said Sammy in a deep growling voice, 'that yer beginnin' to think yer'll get paid just for being here. Well, yer won't. Any one of yer that doesn't reach her minimum quota will get her pay docked accordin', and will also receive the sack. Yer got that, I hope?'

'Gotcher, Mister Adams,' said Gertie.

In such fashion was Tommy introduced to the atmosphere of the workshop, and it did not take him long to discover that these skilled East End seamstresses, who worked for a pittance, never quite lost hope, any more than the hard-pressed people of Walworth did. There were little differences between the people of the East End and the people of South London, but they all

164

shared the same kind of cockney resilience.

He acquainted himself with the workshop machines. They were all fairly ancient, but every sewing-machine in the world was built to last a lifetime. Three machines here were out of action. He saw at once that as soon as he put them right, he could overhaul every woman's machine in rotation. That was a job to give him pleasure and satisfaction. He discussed with Sammy the office work required in all its aspects. Susie agreed to spend the rest of the week at the factory to help with current mail not yet attended to, and to start a filing system, a petty cash book and a sales ledger.

Sammy and Lilian agreed that various of her designs were to be made up and shown to buyers around the time when the French collections were on display in Paris. That was to impress buyers with the fact that Adams Enterprises were not offering copies of any Paris models, but the exclusive range inspired by their own designer, Lily Dupont. Lilian was high on adrenalin, totally captivated by Sammy's personality, his eccentric euphemisms, his belief in himself and his faith in her. They spent the whole morning in discussion. Susie opened outstanding mail and Tommy used the telephone where answers were needed, Sammy telling him what to say in certain cases. Sammy also saw to it that Tommy made his status known. Tommy obliged.

'This is Mr Adams, manager of Adams Enterprises in Shoreditch, speakin'.' So he opened each phone conversation. When he had finished with all necessary calls, he went back into the workshop to look at the three machines that were out of action, and to see if he could put one to rights for Lilian's use. Which he did. By the afternoon, Lilian was using it, her adrenalin higher. Sammy had given her an advance on her agreed salary; the workshop and its stock of materials were at her disposal, and she was in sheer pleasure at putting some of her own designs together. Not, however, any of the more audacious creations. The machinists would be bound to notice, and however much they were sworn to secrecy, one tongue would inevitably wag.

Gertie did what she rarely did. She left her machine to go to the office. Susie was out, buying books for the office, including a wages book. Sammy was at the desk, writing out an order for materials suggested by Lilian.

'Yer'll pardon me, guv,' said Gertie.

'What'll I pardon you for?' asked Sammy.

'That woman, the one you said's our designer. She's a seamstress?'

'Why you askin'?'

'It ain't right 'er makin' up samples if she ain't.'

Sammy cottoned on.

'She's a seamstress.'

'Worked in a registered fact'ry, I mean?'

'Of course.'

'Yer sure?'

'I'm sure,' said Sammy.

'It ain't fair if she ain't.'

'You've already said that. Don't say it again, Gertie. She's all right, you're all right. Push off now, you got work to do.'

'Well, if you say so, Mister Adams, good enough. I'll pass the word.'

Gertie went back to her machine. She had made her gesture, but Sammy knew the threat of a strike had not been present. None of them could afford to strike, and even if they did, it could easily be broken by simply taking on unemployed seamstresses. But they might have been awkward, they might have come up with sloppy stitching in a crafty way, a way that meant a finger could not be pointed at the guilty. If they were satisfied Mrs Hyams had been one of them in the past, they'd be happy. He had a word with Lilian later. She was able to inform him she had worked as a seamstress from the age of fourteen until she was married. She named three sweatshops. They might have been registered with the Inspector of Factories and they might not. There were any amount of tiny, back-street places in the East End unknown to the Inspectorate. It did not matter. Lilian had worked in sweatshops and that was good enough.

'Glad for you,' said Sammy.

'You're a welcome change as a boss, you are,' smiled Lilian. 'By the way, do you know any big buyers?'

'For West End stores and chain shops? No,' said Sammy frankly.

'We ought to know who they are by name,' said Lilian. 'It'll help if we don't look as if we've just come in from the outside.'

Sammy thought about his contacts. Mr Greenberg came top of his list.

'I'll make enquiries, Lily.'

'My life,' said Lilian, 'you're bouncy, aren't you? You don't mutter and scratch your head.'

'I've heard him mutter considerable,' murmured Susie, who was entering names from a list into the new wages book.

'I don't think I caught that, Miss Brown,' said Sammy.

'I didn't say anything, Mister Adams,' said Susie. 'Well, nothing of importance.'

Lilian smiled. They had an engaging freshness in their relationship, this extraordinary young boss and his attractive, articulate assistant. And there was something else between them. What was it now? Of

167

course. They were in love. Were they keeping it from each other? If so, why?

'Are you married, Mister Adams?'

Sammy looked for a moment as if the question hurt him. He was making notes on a scribbling pad of a hundred and one things he had to do. His pencil stopped moving.

'Pardon?' he said.

'No, he isn't married,' said Susie, neatly inscribing one more name.

'I happen not to have had time to go courtin',' said Sammy.

'It's expensive too,' said Susie.

'What is?' asked Lilian, fascinated.

'Courtin' and gettin' married,' said Susie. 'And it interferes with business.'

'Miss Brown, would you kindly not put uninformed words into my mouth?' said Sammy.

'Oh, dear, so sorry, Mister Adams, do pardon me, I'm sure,' said Susie, tongue in cheek.

'And speakin' of business,' said Sammy, 'could you come up with a few French words, if needful, Madame Dupont?'

'A few,' said Lilian, 'like *oui, merci* and montsewer.'

'Not too good,' said Sammy frankly. 'How about English with a French accent?'

'Do you mean Jewish English with a French accent?'

'You got it,' said Sammy. 'That's a winning combination in the higher ranks of the rag trade. Let's hear a sample.'

'Ze pen of my Aunt Fifi is in ze garden wiz ze fairies,' said Lilian.

'Promising,' said Sammy.

Lilian laughed, liking Sammy very much.

'You want I should go to French classes for you?' she asked.

'You do that, Mimi,' he said.

'Mimi I am now?' Lilian laughed again.

'Glad you mentioned it,' said Sammy. 'Mimi Dupont. I regard that highly. More French feeling to it than Lily Dupont.'

'I'm not sure I shouldn't put trousers on and call myself Raymond Dupont,' said Lilian. 'I've mentioned before, haven't I, that French designers are all men?'

'Not my mother's kind of men,' said Sammy, 'and accordingly of small account to me. It shouldn't be too injurious to our manly chests to mount a frontal assault on them and split their ranks wide open.'

'Ours?' said Lilian. 'Mine, Susie's and yours?'

'I was being figurative,' said Sammy. 'You keep your flag flying high, Lily. You've got Adams Enterprises behind you, which includes Miss Brown, whose audacious tongue ain't unbeknown to you.'

'Flattered, I'm sure,' murmured Susie.

'Don't mention it,' said Sammy. 'Lily, it has just occurred to me, we need a trade mark. Could you design one?'

'Eiffel Tower?' suggested Lilian. 'Little deep blue silhouette on a white silk label?'

'Proud of yer,' said Sammy, 'glad we met.'

'It's bliss to me,' said Lilian. 'Must get on now. Ta for the tea.'

Saturday morning. Ned arrived home from his half-day's work just before one. His children greeted him boisterously, Lizzy with a kiss. Lizzy, unlike her mother, was demonstrative. Ned announced that through the good offices of a colleague he had arranged to rent a seaside bungalow for two weeks in August next year. At Selsey in Sussex. The property was on the sea front, overlooking the sandy west beach. There was a long time to go before next year's school holidays arrived, but these seaside places were popular and needed to be booked well in advance.

'All in favour put their hands up,' said Ned.

Lizzy, Annabelle and Bobby put their hands up. Emma, three years old, thought about it. Edward, one year old, was interested only in winding his arms around his father's trousered tin leg.

Emma, having thought, said, 'Will there be donkey rides?'

'Oh, there's donkey rides at every seaside,' said Lizzy.

'A'right,' said Emma, and put her hand up.

'We'll call that unanimous,' said Ned.

'I call it spiffing,' said Annabelle. 'A seaside bunga- low all to ourselves.'

'There's another next door,' said Ned. 'Eliza, d'you think Boots and Emily and their lot would like to rent it for the same fortnight?'

'Mum and Dad as well?' said Lizzy, meaning Chi- nese Lady and Mr Finch. 'I bet they'd all love it, and we can all afford it. It's time everyone had a real proper holiday.'

'Well, I don't suppose anyone's too keen on an improper fortnight,' said Ned.

'Funny ha-ha,' said Lizzy.

Boots and Emily liked the idea very much. So did Chinese Lady. And Rosie thought it sounded awfully imperious.

'Imperious?' said Boots.

'Yes, isn't that a ripping word?' said Rosie.

'Is it the right one?' asked Boots.

'Of course it is, Daddy, it means urgent.'

'I thought it meant haughty.'

'Oh, bless me,' said Rosie, 'how can you call a holi- day haughty? You can call it urgent when you can

170

hardly wait for it, only imperious sounds better.'

'All right, I'll tell Uncle Ned to ask his friend if he'll put our names down for an awfully imperious bunga-low holiday.'

'Daddy, you're so comical,' said Rosie. 'Can I phone Annabelle and talk to her about it?'

'About my being comical?'

'No, about the holiday. Goodness, I don't know sometimes what we're going to do with you, do you, Mummy?'

'Live in hope, that's all we can do,' said Emily. Rosie darted out of their sitting-room to use the phone. 'Boots, I think we're bringing her up quite nice, don't you?'

'Well, she hasn't complained yet,' said Boots, 'and neither has her natural grandfather.'

Rosie's grandfather, Mr Tooley, visited once a month, on Sunday afternoons. His invalid wife had died two years ago, since when, with the agreement of Emily and Boots, he had kept in touch with Rosie by way of these monthly visits. Rosie liked him and behaved very nicely towards him, but Emily felt there was always a little apprehension below the surface, as if the girl suspected her grandfather might one day take her away. Emily assured her she need not worry. Mr Tooley was a man of integrity, a staunch friend to Boots, whom he liked and admired.

The woman in a dark brown cloche hat and a brown belted leather coat peered at the door in the afternoon darkness, took hold of the latchcord and pulled it. The door opened and she stepped into the passage, illumi-nated by a gas mantle in a pearly globe. She called in a gentle voice.

'Mrs Adams? Are you home?'

In the kitchen Freddy and Daisy were sitting at the table playing *Ludo*. Mr and Mrs Brown were down the market, Susie was out shopping for new shoes, and Sally was at the Brixton roller-skating rink with a girl friend.

'Who's that?' asked Freddy.

'It's someone in the passage,' said Daisy.

Freddy went to take a look. He saw the woman. She smiled kindly at him, her eyes softly clear behind her spectacles.

'Is that you, Sammy?' she asked.

'What, missus?' asked Freddy.

'Is your dear mother at home? She is such a good friend of mine.'

'Me mum's Mrs Brown, and I'm Freddy, yer know.'

'I wanted to tell your mother it will be all right for me to come in for Sunday tea tomorrow,' said the woman. Her smile faded and a little frown arrived. 'You aren't Sammy,' she said.

'No, I just said, I'm Freddy, and me mum's—'

'Everything is such a worry,' said the woman and murmured to herself. Then she said, 'Mr Finch will be coming to tea as well? Is he here?'

'Mr Finch?' said Freddy, bemused. 'Missus, 'e don't live 'ere no more, nor Mrs Adams. You said Mrs Adams first orf, didn't yer?'

'Dear Mrs Adams,' murmured the woman. 'Where is Mr Finch?'

'Dunno 'is address,' said Freddy, beginning to feel the caller wasn't all there, 'but yer could ask at the shop at Camberwell Green, the Bargain Bazaar. Me sister Susie knows the address, but she's out. Yer see, Mr Finch an' Mrs Adams, they're—'

'So kind, Mrs Adams, such a dear friend. Such a worry, to be without a husband. I must go. People look, you know, people look.'

Daisy ventured out from the kitchen. The woman smiled vaguely at her.

'She's Daisy,' said Freddy.

'Lizzy is such a sweet girl,' said the woman. 'Oh, dear,' she said, and murmured worriedly to herself, then turned and left. She wandered murmuring up the street.

'Cor, what a funny woman,' said Freddy.

'I dreamt a funny woman was in our 'ouse the uvver night,' said Daisy. 'Well, I fink I did.'

'Dreams is funny too,' said Freddy. 'Would yer like a cup of tea, Daisy, and a slice of me mum's fruit cake?'

'Oh, crumbs, not 'alf,' said Daisy.

CHAPTER FOURTEEN

'I still can't hardly believe it,' said Mrs Brown at Saturday suppertime. 'Our Susie bringing home three pounds a week as Mister Sammy's personal and private assistant, and goin' every day to Shoreditch with him to help with his new fact'ry and everything. I don't know when I've been more proud.' Mrs Brown smiled fondly. 'How much do bank managers get, Jim, and people like Navy captains?'

Mr Brown thought. 'Oh, four or five quid a week, I reckon,' he said.

'Fancy that, and our Susie gettin' as much as three. Ain't you grown up clever, Susie? Wait till I tell your brother William in the next letter I write to him.'

'I don't think I'll tell no one,' said eleven-year-old Freddy, whose brown hair always flopped over his forehead no matter what he or his mother did to it with a comb and brush. 'It's a bit embarrassin', y'know, Dad, 'aving a clever sister when all me best friends 'ave all got soppy sisters. Soppy sisters is more natural.'

'Oh, yer cheeky monkey,' said thirteen-year-old Sally, 'I bet all soppy sisters 'ave got even soppier brothers, I bet no girl's got a soppier brother than you. Can't we change 'im, Mum?'

'Oh, we wouldn't want to change Freddy,' said Mrs Brown, 'he's a nice boy, really.'

'Yuk,' said Sally, enjoying her hot faggots and pease

pudding with gravy from the pie shop at the end of East Street market. There was usually high tea on Saturday evenings, but Mrs Brown had treated her family on this occasion to celebrate Susie's promotion. A supper of faggots and pease pudding really was a treat, especially as there were two faggots each and a mountain of pease pudding.

'I been nearly all week gettin' the room next to Mister Sammy's office cleared and ready for Susie on Monday,' said Mr Brown. He applied himself with gusto to all the work he did for Adams Enterprises as their full-time odd-job man, despite his gammy leg, and he had added pride to gusto in preparing an office for Susie. 'Yer goin' to start work formal there on Monday, Susie?'

'I shall have that honour,' said Susie.

'Cor, yer do talk swell, Susie,' said Freddy, fond of his elder sister. 'Don't she talk swell, Sally?'

'I dunno where she gets it from,' said Sally, 'and I dunno I want 'er talkin' like that in the street to me with people listening. And I dunno it's fair 'er wearing silk stockings with me in rotten old socks or cotton stockings.'

'It's imitation silk, lovey, I've told you,' said Mrs Brown placidly. She was very much the indulgent mother, and always left it to her husband to apply the heavy hand, if the heavy hand was necessary. Unlike Chinese Lady, she could never have brought herself to box her children's ears, but Chinese Lady, of course, had had to be both father and mother to her four.

'Anyway, Susie's got ravishin' legs, which you ain't, Sally,' said Freddy.

'Oh, I don't have no legs at all, I s'pose,' said Sally, 'I s'pose I just walk about on me knees.'

' 'Old 'ard,' said Mr Brown, 'what was that word you used about your sister's legs, Freddy?'

'Ravishin',' said Freddy, looking pleased that he could pronounce it.

175

'I don't know I like it,' said Mr Brown.

'It's what the older boys say about 'em,' explained Freddy.

'Saucy devils,' said Susie.

'Well, Susie do have very nice legs,' said Mrs Brown. 'Modern fashions do suit yer, Susie love, but I don't know your grandparents wouldn't turn in their graves to see how short ladies' skirts is these days. My mother never showed any of her legs all her life.'

'P'raps she didn't 'ave any,' said Freddy.

'P'raps she was like me,' said Sally, sensitive about being short. ' 'Cording to Freddy, I don't 'ave any, neither.'

'Course you have, Sally,' said Mrs Brown, 'and pretty ones.'

'Yes, course you have,' said Susie, and ruffled her sister's curly hair. The kitchen was a warm and cosy place. She always felt they had inherited its welcoming family atmosphere from the Adamses. The range was glowing, the wooden bunker in the yard containing five hundredweight of newly delivered coal, all because she and her Dad were bringing home good and regular money. Pictures danced for her in the fire.

'Sally's gettin' very pretty, ain't she, Jim?' smiled Mrs Brown.

'She's me pretty little fairy,' said Mr Brown.

'I ain't noticed it,' said Freddy.

'Well, boys never notice how pretty their sisters is,' said Mrs Brown.

'Girls notice their brothers is little 'orrors,' said Sally.

'I don't mind being an 'orror,' said Freddy, 'but I ain't little.'

'You goin' out this evening, Susie?' asked Mrs Brown.

'I've got a library book to read,' said Susie.

'That young man from Brixton not goin' to call any more?' asked Mr Brown, wondering if his wife was right about Susie being in love.

'I hope not,' said Susie. 'I happen to have acquired distinctive uninterest in him.' A little laugh escaped her. Verbally, she was a faithful echo of Sammy sometimes, and she knew it.

'Still, it's a shame you don't have no one to take you out on Saturday evening,' said Mr Brown, and it occurred to Susie then that Sammy had never even offered. It was criminal. What was he doing now? Probably studying the accounts books his brother Boots kept for him.

'If you're all finished, I'll make a pot of tea,' said Mrs Brown. At which point the front door was opened by a pull on the old latchcord, also inherited from the Adams family. A voice called.

'Freddy? Can I come in?'

'Course yer can, Daisy,' called Freddy.

' 'Ere comes 'is sweet'eart,' said Sally.

Footsteps sounded over the floor of the passage and down the step into the kitchen. Ten-year-old Daisy Cook put her head in. From beneath her woollen hat shining black hair escaped, and her button-bright brown eyes beamed at the family. Her coat, run up by her mother out of a navy blue blanket, cuddled her plumpness, and her little nose was pink. Knitted black mittens showed pink finger tips.

' 'Ello,' she said, 'can Freddy come an' play?'

'If 'is legs ain't fell off,' said Sally. ' 'As yer legs fell off, Freddy?'

'Not lately,' said Freddy.

'I don't 'ave none meself,' said Sally in a bitter aside.

'What d'yer want to play, Daisy?' asked Freddy, getting up.

Daisy came right in and breathed a little excitedly.

'I got conkers, me dad give 'em me,' she said, and dug her hands into her coat pockets. She brought out four huge glossy horse chestnuts, two in each hand. 'An' I got two more besides. Yes, I got six, I fink.'

Freddy, impressed, gave her a pat.

'Crikey, they look like champions, Daisy,' he said. 'I'll get some string and a meat skewer.'

'You can 'ave four, if yer like,' said Daisy, 'an' I'll keep two.'

'No, three each, that's fair, and I'll conker with yer,' said Freddy.

They went out into the street and began their game of conkers under the light of a lamp-post. Daisy closed her eyes as she held the string of one conker and Freddy took a swipe at it with his.

'Oops,' she kept saying, each swipe striking a hit. Then came a miss.

'Your go, Daisy,' said Freddy, 'and I still ain't cracked yer.'

'Oh, lor',' said Daisy, and took her turn. Freddy's conker took a biff and cracked. The audience of street kids yelled.

'Yer done 'im, Daisy, yer done the champion conker of the Place.'

'Crikey,' said Daisy.

'Go on, Daisy, yer still got another go,' said Freddy, 'yer keep goin' till yer miss.'

'Oh, corks,' said Daisy, not sure she wanted to completely shatter the conker of the champion in front of the other kids. So she took a blind swipe. Her tough horse chestnut struck home, all the same. Freddy's conker split apart and fell from the string. The kids yelled in delight.

'Yer done 'im right up, Daisy, yer got a seconder!'

'Yer the champ now, Daisy!'

'I dunno she is. Freddy's 'it oners to make 'isself champ. Daisy's only 'it a seconder.'

'That don't matter. If yer beat the champ wiv a seconder, yer beat 'im.'

'But it don't make 'er champ, not till she beats 'im wiv a oner. Freddy being a oner champ don't give up being champ till 'e's beat by a oner. Yer got to be fair. Still, yer can do it, Daisy, yer got a real champion conker there.'

'Oh, I don't mind Freddy's still champ,' said Daisy.

'Give over, Daisy, don't talk like that, and yer still got a right to go first when 'e strings up a new conker.'

'You Jimmy! You Cissie!' A mother was calling from a front door. 'Come on in now!'

The kids began to melt away in case other mothers had the same idea. Cold or foggy, hot or rainy, the street kids still preferred to be out of doors most of the time.

'The kids was right, Daisy,' said Freddy, 'yer got a champion conker there.'

'Can we go an' sit on yer doorstep while yer put anuvver one on yer string?' asked Daisy.

'All right, come on,' said Freddy. 'I've got a gobstopper in me pocket, I'll share sucks with yer, if yer like.'

'Oh, I ain't tasted a gobstopper for ages,' said Daisy, 'I put all me 'a'pennies away for the country 'oliday fund.' The country holiday fund was something sponsored and organised by schools. Pupils who could afford it paid sixpence a week during term times, and were rewarded with a fortnight's summer holiday in a country village, boarding with villagers. It was a fortnight's bliss to Walworth kids.

'Come on,' said Freddy, and they went and sat on his doorstep. Daisy was Freddy's mate. They had once done *Knocking Down Ginger* together, all along King and Queen Street, and knocking on every door, Daisy in exhilaration and all flying feet as irate residents yelled after them. ' 'Ere y'ar.' Freddy fished the gobstopper out of his pocket. It was pink-tinted. He wiped flecks from it. 'You can 'ave first go, Daisy.'

179

Daisy popped the large sweet ball into her mouth and sucked in rapture. It rolled around her tongue and puffed out her cheeks. She gurgled something.

'What?' asked Freddy, working a meat skewer through a new horse chestnut.

' 'S'nice,' slurped Daisy. She took it out. It was all white. 'Oh, I been an' sucked all the pink off.'

'I don't mind,' said Freddy. He took it from her. It was shining wet. He put it into his mouth and sucked with boyish relish.

'Yer ever so kind, sharin' yer only gobstopper wiv me,' said Daisy.

'Well, you're me mate,' said Freddy, driving the skewer right through. He disgorged the sweet into the palm of his hand. 'Your suck, Daisy.'

'Fanks,' said Daisy blissfully, the gaslight of the lamp-post reaching out to faintly touch them. The gobstopper spilled sweetness down her throat.

'I s'pose we could get married later on,' said Freddy.

'If yer like,' said Daisy. 'Your turn, Freddy.'

Freddy rolled the gobstopper thoughtfully about inside his mouth, took it out and said, 'Can yer make apple dumplings and 'ot custard?'

'Course I can,' said Daisy. 'Well, not yet, not exactly yet, not exactly now.'

'It don't 'ave to be now,' said Freddy, 'I just 'ad faggots and pease pudding. Later on.'

'Yes, a'right,' said Daisy.

Freddy looked at the gobstopper, slightly decreased in size. 'Whose turn is it?'

'I fink it's mine,' said Daisy.

A shadow fell across the faint light. They looked up.

'Hello, Freddy,' said Sammy, spruce in overcoat and trilby hat. 'Who's yer lady friend?'

'Crikey, it's Mister Sammy,' said Freddy. He liked Sammy, although he had only met him a few times, when Susie had been working in the Camberwell shop.

'I was just passin',' said Sammy, 'and thought I'd take a look at the old place. How's the fam'ly?'

'In the pink,' said Freddy. 'This is me friend Daisy.'

' 'Ello, mister,' said Daisy.

'Yer best go in,' said Freddy, 'they're all 'ome.' He pulled the latchcord and opened the door. 'They're in the kitchen. Yer goin' to say 'ello to 'em, Mister Sammy?'

'Well, now I'm here,' said Sammy, and went through and knocked on the kitchen door.

'Who can that be?' asked Mrs Brown, about to pour tea.

'Daisy, I expect,' said Susie, and opened the door. Sammy offered a slight smile and cleared his throat.

'Good evening,' he said. Susie stared at him. He took his hat off. 'I just happened to be passin',' he said.

'I thought it was just happening to be an emergency,' said Susie, 'that the fact'ry had fallen down and you required me to help put it together again.'

'Now would I ask that of yer on a Saturday evening?' said Sammy.

'Yes, you would,' said Susie, hiding the delight she felt in seeing him.

'Mister Sammy, come in now,' said Mrs Brown. 'I don't know what Susie's doin', keepin' you standin' in the doorway. I just made tea, you must have a cup.'

Susie stepped aside, watching Sammy as he entered the kitchen. His tallness made the ceiling seem lower. She tried to catch his eye. He avoided the attempt. Oh, you Sammy Adams, you wait, she said to herself, I'll make you look me straight in the eye one day, I'll make you tell me you love me. You'd better love me when I've given you the best working years of my life, or I'll kick you to death.

'All very cosy here,' he said, 'just like the old days.

181

Pleased to see you, Mrs Brown. You all right, Jim? And how are you, Sally? Haven't seen you since you were in Peabody's. Little terror you were then. Now look at you. Pretty as a picture.'

Oh, the swine, thought Susie, all that cheerful chat for them, and not a word to me about my divine beauty.

'Do honour us by takin' a seat,' she said.

'Well, I was only passin',' said Sammy.

'You already said that.'

'Mister Sammy, you can sit next to me,' said Sally, who had developed an instantaneous crush. 'Yer ever so welcome to 'ave a cup of tea with us, and Mum's got some 'ome-made cake as well.'

'Well,' said Sammy.

'Yes?' said Susie, the light in her blue eyes a little dangerous.

'I happened to be on my way to the Tivoli in the Strand,' said Sammy, 'where there's this monster Hollywood film showing. *Ben Hur*. Featuring a popular Hollywood geezer name of Ramon Novvaro.'

'Ramon Navarro,' said Susie.

'Funny name, that, sounds Eyetie,' said Sammy. A cup of tea was pushed across the table to him. He was still standing. He accepted the cup and saucer. He sipped the tea. Susie watched him, eyes simmering. 'Well, in passin' I thought – this is first-class tea, Mrs Brown.'

'You thought in passin' that my mother's tea is first-class?' asked Susie.

'I was makin' a complimentary comment on the spot, Miss Brown,' said Sammy, who had come to a final conclusion for the twentieth time. 'What was I saying before that?'

'Lord knows,' said Susie, 'I don't.'

'Ah,' said Sammy. 'Ah, yes,' he said, and drank more

tea. He looked at the clock on the mantelpiece. Ten past seven. The last performance at the Tivoli began at eight. 'I thought as I was passin'' I might look in and request the pleasure of knowing that if you weren't otherwise engaged, Miss Brown, you might consider—'

'Thank you, how kind, I won't be a minute,' said Susie.

'Pardon?' said Sammy.

'I'll just get my hat and coat.' Susie disappeared. She was laughing to herself as she ran lightly up the stairs to her bedroom.

'What's she done that for?' asked Sally.

'To get ready to go to the pictures with Mister Sammy,' said Mrs Brown, quite sure she'd been right in the first place about who Susie was in love with.

'But Mister Sammy didn't accherly say so.'

'On the tip of my tongue,' said Sammy.

'Yer very welcome,' said Mr Brown.

'I heard it's a highly remarkable film,' said Sammy.

'I 'eard there's always queues,' said Mrs Brown.

'I happen to have acquired circle tickets,' said Sammy. 'It wouldn't look right, standin' in a queue with a young female woman as ladylike as Susie.'

'Crikey, can't yer talk 'igh-class?' said Sally, faint with admiration.

'Well, y'know, Sally,' said Sammy confidentially, 'when you get out into the world you meet all kinds, and it's needful to know how to talk to them. Me brother Boots, he can talk to anybody and not turn a hair. He learned, when he was being educated, that if you talk right, then people'll listen to you. If you talk slipshod, they mark you down as slipshod. I'm cockney all over, I got a feeling for Walworth and me hallowed years here with me fam'ly, but it's needful for me to offer the world a bit of style. And there's Susie, she's got style. She didn't have when she first started to work for me, which I hope don't offend you, Jim, but in five years she's collected as much style as if she'd been born a lady, which is a credit to you, Mrs Brown. You'll get style, Sally, when you're older. Being born poor don't mean you've got to stay poor, we've all got something we can offer, and it's up to us to see it don't go to waste. You're pretty, and you've got lovely curly hair and a sister who's an example to you. Your mum and dad'll help yer, like they've helped Susie. Don't get stuck in a ditch, just find out what you're best at and go to work on it.'

'But I'm growin' up all short,' said Sally.

'You've hardly started yet,' said Sammy.

'But I'm thirteen,' said Sally.

'All right, so you're thirteen. And you're something else. You're dainty. Not every girl is, and really dainty girls make good dancers.'

'Mum, that's it, I'll be a dancer!' cried Sally rapturously.

Susie returned in her blue cloche hat and a blue coat. She was freshly made up, new lipstick moistly glimmering.

'I am quite ready, Mister Adams,' she said.

'There, see what I mean, Sally?' said Sammy. 'That's style.'

'Have a nice time, Susie,' said Mrs Brown.

'So long, fam'ly,' said Sammy, 'I'll bring her back.'

Walking to the Walworth Road bus stop with him, Susie, who had decided just how she would conduct herself, slipped her arm through his. She felt him quiver a little. She smiled.

'Do you go out often?' she asked.

'Not often,' said Sammy. There was no fog, the street lamps glowed clearly, and the lights of trams, buses and the Walworth Road shops created a picture of brightness quite different from the greyness seen by day. 'Still, it's a nice evening tonight.'

'It's a surprise,' said Susie.

'What is?'

'The evening,' she said. 'Who'd have thought you'd take me out? I wouldn't. You haven't been drinkin', have you? I don't want to go to the Tivoli Cinema with a drunk.'

'I am mystified by such remarks, Miss Brown.'

'No, you're not, and don't call me Miss Brown. It's my belief you must have been drinkin' or a brick must have dropped on your head for you to actually invite me out.'

'I have not been drinkin',' said Sammy, as they crossed Walworth Road, 'and I do not recall any brick droppin' on my loaf of bread. It happened to occur to me that as you've been a good and helpful girl this week, it would become me to show me heartfelt appreciation.'

'Bless the man,' murmured Susie, 'I'll get a pat on the head next.'

'I didn't catch that,' said Sammy, as they arrived at the bus stop. The right bus came along almost at once, a number 68. It was packed with people going up West for the evening.

'Room for two only,' sang the conductor. 'One short, one long, one up, one down. You takes yer pick. Suit yer, mister and missus? You can cuddle up later.'

Sammy perforce had to separate from Susie. He went up to the top deck, Susie boarding the lower. 'I'll pay for Lady Hortense,' he said to the conductor.

'So yer should, me lord,' said the conductor, and winked at Susie.

'He's so kind,' said Susie, whose unexciting evening had turned into one of exhilarating cut-and-thrust.

They joined up again in the Strand, and made their way to the Tivoli. There were long queues slowly moving forward for the last performance. Sammy produced tickets obtained from Keith Prowse, agents, and Susie forgave him everything for the moment as they were led up to the circle by an usherette. The Tivoli was the handsomest cinema in the West End. To add to her excitement, Sammy bought her a box of chocolates from the tray of another usherette.

'I don't know I can hardly believe this,' she said, quite giddy.

Sammy, settling into the comfortable seat beside her, murmured, 'Well, it's like I said, Miss Brown, you've been a good, kind and helpful girl this week.'

The lights were up, the circle filling, and Susie kicked his right ankle with the side of her left shoe.

'Take that,' she said.

'Ouch,' said Sammy as an afterthought.

'Did it hurt?' she asked. They were whispering.

'Well, pain does happen to hurt a bit,' he said.

'Good. It was for callin' me Miss Brown. And I shan't offer you a chocolate.' She opened the box of Cadbury's King George chocolates while the lights were still up. She selected one and ate it. Delicious. She had never been happier.

'I'm partial to chocolates myself, y'know,' said Sammy.

'Oh, dear, hard luck, then,' said Susie. 'Oh, all right, just one.' She offered the box. Sammy took one with a caramel centre. 'Put it back,' she said, 'I like caramel centres myself.'

'It's upsettin' me,' said Sammy, 'you not givin' me a bit more kindness and gratitude.'

'I suppose,' whispered Susie, leaning close, 'I suppose you couldn't just say you're takin' me out and treatin' me and buying me a lovely box of chocolates because you happen to like me a bit? Oh, no, you couldn't say that, not the highly reputable Mister Sammy Adams. Give that chocolate back.'

186

Sammy popped it into his mouth, turned his head and looked at her. Susie held his glance. He saw her deep blue eyes bright with silent laughter, her lips slightly parted as if that laughter was about to spring forth. Sammy's confused emotions crystallised into one clear certain emotion as he fell hopelessly, helplessly and inescapably in love with her. Their eyes locked, faint colour flushed her face and a little pulse beat. The huge buzz of a thousand people waiting for the performance to start receded from their own little world of the moment.

Then Susie looked to her front, to the blank silver screen, her flush visible. The lights dimmed, the audience became still and sighed itself into expectant silence. Sammy sat back, arms folded. Susie sat breathless with the certainty that he loved her.

Ben Hur, with Ramon Navarro in the leading role and Francis X. Bushman playing Messala the Roman, was as powerful and moving a film as the critics had said. Dramatic, stirring and spectacular, the tale of a great wrong and a great revenge, it unfolded silently on the screen, but was accompanied by the telling virtuosity of the pianist. The chariot race, a pitiless contest, reached its terrible climax with Messala crushed and broken beneath iron wheels. At the crucifixion of Christ, the sky darkened to blackness, the blackness was sundered by the lightning of God, and Susie's tears ran as the dreadful scourging sores of leprosy vanished from the faces of Ben Hur's mother and sister because of their belief in the Son of God.

Susie's face was still wet, and women in the audience were dabbing their eyes, as everyone stood for the pianist's last piece of the evening, the National Anthem.

The bus back to Walworth was crowded with home-going cockneys. The continuing post-war depression was trying the people, and there were ominous

187

rumblings from trade unions, but somehow London's cockneys endured and survived, and they flowed into the West End on Saturday evenings to enjoy themselves, even with no more than a few bob in their pockets.

On the packed bus, Sammy said, 'Enjoy the film, Susie?'

'Oh, yes.' Susie was still in the land of Christ and Ben Hur, still emotional. 'I think I'd like to see it again.'

'Whenever you say,' said Sammy.

She wanted to tell him what a lovely evening he had given her, but the crowded lower deck was a discouragement to heartfelt talk. She was glad when they reached Browning Street and alighted from the bus. She said then, 'I've had a lovely evening, it was the best film I've ever seen, I don't know how to thank you – oh, I'm sorry I was so mean about the chocolates, except I was only teasing, really I was.'

'I know you were,' said Sammy, who was examining his feelings. 'Regular little tease you are, Susie. I don't know why I—' He broke off.

'Why what?'

'Pardon?'

He was doing it again, thought Susie, he was backing off. She ought to go to Boots and ask him to hit his brother over the head. Boots, she knew, was on her side.

'Never mind,' she said, 'you can have a chocolate when we get home.' She hadn't touched the chocolates all through the drama and emotion of the film. Nothing had diverted her attention from the screen. Sammy had sat quiet and absorbed beside her, and not once had he attempted to touch or grope. She had a feeling Sammy and Boots and Tommy were all like that, they'd all been brought up to respect girls, and they respected the mother who'd been responsible for that. But sometimes, of course, a girl wanted to be touched. Only by someone special, of course.

Reaching her front gate, she turned to Sammy.

'Same old house,' he said reminiscently.

'It's a happy house,' she said. 'You made it like that, you and your family. It sings sometimes, specially at Christmas. Houses are like that, aren't they? They never let go of the people who've made happy places of them. There's two families there at Christmastimes, yours and ours.'

'Susie?' Sammy's commercial soul was strangely touched.

'There is, you know. Oh, am I being silly? I expect it's the film. But you'll come in, won't you?'

'Is it a bit late?' Sammy had emotions of his own to contend with, because of his absolute certainty of what Susie meant to his life. At this particular moment she even meant more than his business. The realisation was quite shattering. So was the possibility that Susie's feelings for him might not be the same as his for her. Never having taken women seriously, except to make sure none got too close, Sammy was now on such unfamiliar ground that it was making him lose his way. His self-confidence as a businessman took him along sure-footedly, but his self-confidence as a man in love was almost nil.

Everybody said yes to Sammy, either at once or eventually. He was not equipped to cope with the devastating blow of having Susie say no to him. She could get vexed with him, haughty with him, and even answer him back. She'd ground him into the dust that foggy morning at the factory. He would have lost her if he hadn't gone after her and eaten humble pie. He'd never had to do that before, not with anyone, and especially not with a female woman.

I'll leave it, he said to himself, I'll work up to it. Yes,

that's what I'll do. I'll see if she comes over a bit loving now and again. Best to be a bit sure, best not to rush her.

Rush her? If Susie, who had known him over five years and was now twenty-one, could have read his thoughts, she would have hit him over the head herself, and without any help from Boots. As it was, she pulled on the old latchcord, opened the door and said, 'Of course you must come in, it's not as late as that, and Mum and Dad will still be up.'

'My pleasure,' said Sammy, feeling that a coward's decision had been a wise one.

Mr and Mrs Brown were waiting to hear how the evening had gone. Mr Brown had talked about what a surprise to have Mister Sammy call and take Susie out, and how educating he'd been in the way he spoke to Sally. It had done Sally no end of good. Mrs Brown had remarked what a clever girl Susie was, she'd played it very cool with Mister Sammy.

Susie recounted details of the film. Sammy interposed relevant comments. Susie said she'd make a nice pot of hot tea for all of them, and sandwiches for herself and Mister Adams, who had been very gracious taking her to the Tivoli and buying her a box of chocolates as well. Sammy said he'd only been given one chocolate and accordingly fancied a fried bacon sandwich. Mrs Brown said there were only streaky rashers. Sammy said streaky were best for sandwiches and that he'd fry them himself, which he did. The old gas stove was still being used, still in its place in the scullery. Susie, waiting for the kettle to boil, watched him. There were four rashers in the pan.

'You can cook as well?' she said.

'Being a bachelor, Miss Brown, I have—'

A kick arrived, from the toe of her shoe.

'Take that,' said Susie.

'What, again?' said Sammy, feeling it was definitely not loving.

'I mean it,' said Susie, 'I'll do it every time you call me Miss Brown. I don't mind at work, it's proper at work, but not at sociable times. Can you cook?'

'Being a bachelor,' said Sammy, turning the sizzling rashers, 'I have learned the needful necessity of cookin' for myself, and regard myself as comin' up to a highly competent performer. D'you like your bacon crisp, Susie?'

'In a sandwich, yes,' said Susie. A little smile showed. 'You're actin' like you're at home.'

'Oh, well, the feel of the old place, y'know,' said Sammy.

'Mum keeps it nice.'

'Well, you're a nice fam'ly,' said Sammy.

The kettle boiled and Susie made the tea, thinking how much she liked having him here. If he was smart and shrewd, he wasn't conceited. He had bounce and he had belief in himself, but he didn't go about full of conceit. He was still ever so droll. She supposed he would kiss her before the evening was over. He had better.

Everyone had a cup of tea. She and Sammy ate their bacon sandwiches. They all talked around the kitchen table. To Sammy it was a little like old times, even without Chinese Lady's searching eye and quick admonishments. The Browns were a happy family and knew how to make the kitchen a place of warm, homely hospitality. And that Susie. Remarkable. The style she had. She and Lizzy, two Walworth cockney girls who had known what real poverty was, had bloomed like flowers, Lizzy vivid as a rose in her colouring, Susie as fair as May.

It was almost midnight before he left. He said good night to Mr and Mrs Brown, and Mrs Brown said, 'It's been a pleasure havin' you, Mister Sammy.'

'Glad you and Susie picked yerselves a good film,' said Mr Brown.

'Oh, we're goin' to see it again,' said Susie, 'I happen to have received a kind promise from Mister Adams for next Saturday week.'

'Was it Saturday week we mentioned?' asked Sammy.

'You're so kind, thank you,' said Susie, and saw him to the front door.

'Been a nice evening,' he said.

'Lovely,' said Susie, lifting her face.

'Yes, well, see you Monday morning at the Camberwell offices,' said Sammy. 'Good night, Susie.' He put his hat on and left.

Susie, watching him go, breathed, 'Oh, I don't believe it. Not even a peck. Sammy Adams, you wait, you just wait.' She closed the door and leaned against it. She laughed.

There was still next Saturday week. And every day at the office.

Life was utterly wonderful.

CHAPTER FIFTEEN

There were five rooms directly above the clothing and linen shop by Camberwell Green. They had all been turned into offices. Sammy occupied one office, Boots another. The two largest offices housed the staff, four general clerks in one, three copy typists and a Jill-of-all-work in another. They were all girls. Sammy stuck to his opinion that girls were more adaptable and less demanding than young male clerks. And they cost less in wages.

There were further rooms on the second floor, all available for staff expansion. At the moment, Sammy had his flat up there.

At five minutes to nine on Monday morning, Boots put his head round the door of the little room that had just been turned into an office for Susie.

'Good morning, personal assistant,' he said. Susie, in a neat dark blue dress with a white collar, was regarding her little sanctum. It contained a desk, a chair, a filing cabinet, an Imperial typewriter, a wastepaper basket, two wire trays, empty at the moment, a telephone and two or three sundries. The window overlooked the main road and an inner door opened on to Sammy's office.

Susie, turning, gave Boots an affectionate smile.

'I'm so glad to see you, and over the moon to be back here,' she said. 'I just hope I can live up to my promotion.'

'You'll walk it,' said Boots. 'You're a treat. Glad to have you back with us.'

Impulsively, she said, 'Are you really? It's bliss to me.'

'Welcome home,' said Boots, and stepped in. He placed a wrapped sheaf of chrysanthemums on her desk. 'From the garden, and with Emily's good wishes as well as mine. You only need to pinch a vase from the typists' office.'

Susie, overcome, said, 'Oh, I could kiss you.' And she did, very warmly, with her arms around his neck. The inner door opened and Sammy addressed her.

'May I enquire, Miss Brown, as to the nature of the business you happen to be conductin'?'

Susie, startled, detached herself. And it mortified her to know she was turning a hot pink. The lurking smile in Boots's eyes reached his mouth. If no one else knew of Sammy's weakness for Susie, Boots had spotted it long ago.

For once Susie was unequal to the situation. Further, Sammy had a glint in his eye and was very straight-faced. All she could say was a limp, 'Boots brought me flowers.'

'We're not holding any horticultural show,' said Sammy, 'there's work to do. Kindly see me in my office.' He disappeared.

'Oh, lor', that's done it,' said Susie in dismay, 'my first day here and I'm goin' to get the push before I even start.'

'Well, don't forget to mention that as you're salaried, you're entitled to either a month's notice or a month's pay,' said Boots.

'Oh, don't,' begged Susie, 'it's not funny.'

'Yes, it is, it's very funny,' said Boots, 'but you'll win, Susie. Just look him in the eye.'

Susie went in. Sammy, seated at his large desk, had an enormous backlog of mail in front of him. All letters had been opened by Boots while Sammy had been busy at Shoreditch, and all mail requiring Sammy's attention

194

was what he was going through now, a pencil in his hand. Susie presented her defensive self.

'Mister Adams?'

'Brixton,' said Sammy abruptly, scanning a handwritten letter from a supplier. He liked to see every letter that arrived. It kept him up-to-date with everything that was happening.

'Brixton?' Susie sagged for a moment, then pulled herself proudly upright. 'The shop or the prison?'

'Prison?' muttered Sammy, keeping his head down.

'If it's back to the shop it's as good as the prison,' said Susie.

'Kindly be your age, Miss Brown,' said Sammy, refusing to meet her eye. He was suffering slight trauma. Susie and Boots kissing. Everyone knew ladies took a fancy to Boots. Was that why Susie had wanted to return to Camberwell? 'Did I say I was sendin' you back to our Brixton shop? I was merely about to inform you that the new manageress took over on Thursday and is doing very nicely.'

'I still don't like your growling look,' said Susie.

'My what?' Sammy leaned back and fixed his eyes on her white collar. 'What did you say?'

'You're wearing your growling look, that's what I said, Mr Adams.'

'I must point out, Miss Brown, that I am considerable shook up to catch my personal assistant disportin' herself in the arms of my office manager, whose name we both know but won't mention out loud in case Mrs Em'ly Adams gets to hear, which if she does will cause horrendous ructions. I don't want your fatally dead body littering up these offices. That's all, Miss Brown.'

'No, it's not, Mister Adams,' said Susie. 'I merely happened to give Boots a grateful kiss for welcomin' me with a gracious bouquet of flowers. I don't know anyone nicer than Boots, who's a pillar of shinin' light compared with someone else I know but won't name in case he gets more growling.'

'I will choose to ignore that,' said Sammy, compulsively raising his eyes to hers. Hers were a scornful dark blue. I knew it, he told himself, I knew I'd get turned upside-down and my business as well. And what does she mean by coming in on a cold November morning looking like a summer day in June? 'Just do me the favour, Miss Brown, of conductin' your kissin' out of office hours.'

'Shame on you, Mister Adams.' Susie had not only recovered, she was enjoying a sudden certainty that Sammy was jealous, actually jealous. 'I won't tell Boots what you said about him and me disportin', because we weren't, and because I don't want him givin' you a black eye. It wouldn't do the business any good, everyone seeing you goin' around with a black eye as if you'd been gettin' mixed up with hooligans.'

Sammy wondered what good it was doing him, being hopelessly in love with a girl who had a talent for giving him headaches.

'Go away,' he said, 'I'm havin' a fit, and I'd like to have it in private.'

'Yes, Mister Adams. Is there any work for me?'

'Work?' said Sammy vaguely. He felt floored. Susie regarded him tenderly. He caught the look. She smiled. His mouth twitched, just as Chinese Lady's did when she wanted to smile at something she should be frowning at. 'Work?' he said, rubbing his mouth.

'It's what I'm here for, isn't it?' said Susie.

'Yes. Right.' Sammy became brisk. He picked up a pile of letters he had already examined. 'Take these, read 'em, regard my pencilled notes, write out answers and get Lottie to type them. If I'm not here when they need signing for the afternoon post, you sign 'em as personal assistant to S. W. Adams, managing director. There'll be more comin' your way all day. Shoreditch has put us

196

behind here. You'll see I've suggested on some letters that you answer by telephone. They're the ones that concern prices, and such prices I've pencilled in. The first job I want you to take off my hands is answering correspondence. I'll help you with details until you're into the swing of things. All right?'

'Very good, Mister Sammy. There's files I can refer to?'

'These here offices happen to be full of well-kept files.'

'Very good, Mister Sammy. Who is Lottie?'

'Senior copy typist. The one with the Friday night Amami shampoo look.'

'Very good, Mister Sammy.'

Suffering cats, thought Sammy, I'm going to eat her in a minute.

'What's all this very good lark?' he asked.

'It's for formal business hours,' said Susie. 'Oh, can I take that vase on that sideboard there?'

'Pardon?'

'Thank you, Mister Sammy, that's very obligin' of you. It's for the flowers your kind brother graciously presented me with.'

Sammy muttered something highly uncomplimentary about his kind brother. Susie smiled, picked up the vase, and went back to her office singing to herself. Not until the door closed behind her did Sammy let a huge grin spread over his face. The monkey. He ought to sack her. He couldn't. It would be like cutting off his right arm.

Susie, at her desk, the chrysanthemums in the vase which she had placed on her window ledge, thought that working like this with Sammy was going to be joyful. Life was hard, especially for the really poor people, but even for them there were some happy days. But oh dear, for Sammy to have caught her kissing Boots wasn't the best start she could have made to this day. Never mind,

197

he had finished up trying not to laugh.

Her telephone extension rang.

'Hello?'

'Are you Miss Brown?' It was a girl's voice.

'Yes.'

'I'm Doreen. I do everything, like. D'you want Camp coffee or tea in the mornings, d'you take how many lumps of sugar and d'you want to pay tuppence a week for biscuits with your afternoon tea like everyone does?'

'Oh, thanks,' said Susie. 'I'll have Camp coffee in the mornings, one lump of sugar and, yes, I'll pay tuppence a week towards the biscuits.'

'A'right, Miss Brown. I do the telephone switchboard as well, and Mister Sammy said you'll be taking all calls for him when he's not here. I also do the correspondence filing and you can ring through if you want me to bring any file any time. I don't do errands, though, we don't have an office boy like we should.'

'I've got the picture, Doreen, thank you.'

'Yes, Miss Brown. Goodbye, Miss Brown.'

Susie heard giggles in the background before the line went dead. She smiled. She was past giggles herself. Happily she went to work on the letters.

At coffee-time, Boots introduced her to the rest of the staff, girls and young women. They all seemed very nice, even if their interest in her as personal assistant to Mister Sammy drew covert looks. Lottie, senior copy typist, was a blonde young woman, her bobbed hair too frizzy to lie in disciplined neatness around her head. She was the only one who was a little cool towards Susie. At eleven, she walked into Susie's office bearing letters and written answers. She put them down on Susie's desk.

'I can't read your writin',' she said, 'so I can't type what I can't read.'

'Just a moment,' said Susie, and called one of the other typists in. 'Norah, would you read that?' she asked, giving the girl one of her hand-written answers.

Norah quoted. 'Dear Sirs, In answer to your kind letter of the 9th of November, we confirm receipt of all goods except the knitwear for our Kennington and Peckham shops. Please telephone—'

'Yes, thank you, Norah,' said Susie, taking the answer back, and Norah went back to her work. 'It doesn't seem like my handwriting's all that bad, Lottie. You don't need glasses, do you?'

'Course I don't,' said Lottie.

'Well, I tell you what,' said Susie, 'I'll get Norah to do them, shall I?'

'But I type all Mister Sammy's letters,' protested Lottie sulkily, and Susie recognised a girl with her nose out of joint. She might also have seen her as a rival had she not been sure there were never going to be any. That telling moment at the Tivoli on Saturday, when she had held Sammy's eyes at last, had given her a breathless certainty that he was hers alone. Lottie Miles was just a silly girl. 'I'm his personal typist, I am, Miss Brown.'

'I know you are.' Susie gave the girl a winning smile. 'He told me to give these only to you. Could you manage them with a bit of a push?'

'Well, all right.'

'Thanks ever so much.' Susie smiled again, and that hurdle was cleared. It was odd but true, most girls didn't like women being in charge.

On the stroke of noon, Mrs Rachel Goodman entered Susie's office. Rachel, in a black astrakhan coat and a silver-grey fur hat, looked a warmly clad winter beauty. Susie knew her, having seen her several times in previous years. She would enter the shop, exchange light patter with Boots and then make her way up to Sammy's office. Boots had eventually come up with the information that she had been Sammy's only girl friend, but had inevitably married a man of her own race.

'Hello, Susie.' Rachel's greeting was a smiling one. 'Boots has just told me Sammy's appointed you as his personal assistant. My life, that's a promising curtain raiser to a career for a girl, isn't it? Best of luck.'

'Thanks,' said Susie, and Rachel crossed to the inner door in gliding grace, knocked and went into Sammy's office. The door closed on her. Seven minutes later, Sammy appeared.

'I'll be out for a while, Miss Brown. I am takin' a business acquaintance to lunch.'

'Yes, very good, Mister Adams,' said Susie coolly, and made a pencil note in a red-covered desk diary.

'What's that you're writing?'

'Oh, just a diary entry, Mister Adams. Twelve-five. Mister S. Adams, lunch with Mrs R. Goodman, a married woman.'

'What?'

'I won't tell Mr Goodman.'

'Oh, my suffering ears,' said Sammy, 'is that you saying that, Susie?'

'It's a diary for all your appointments, Mister Adams.'

'Well, you can rub that one out,' said Sammy.

'Very good, Mister Adams.'

'Jesus, you saucebox,' said Sammy, and went back into his office. From there he took Rachel across the road to Camberwell Green's high-class pub. At the marble-topped food counter, he surveyed the joints of cold meat available for sandwiches. Roast beef, pork, mutton and York ham were on offer. The white-capped chef, an array of carving-knives to hand, smiled at him.

'Mornin', Mister Adams.'

'How's yer luck, Ernie?' responded Sammy.

'So-so, yer know. Can I pleasure yer with a prime cut or two?'

'That yer can,' said Sammy. 'Ham. And kindly apply

200

unsparing mustard. Any kosher beef?'

'Don't upset me, Mister Adams. That joint is fresh kosher.' The chef pointed to a cold roast rib of beef. 'Or where would I be with some of me valued customers?'

'Only askin' on behalf of me business friend,' said Sammy. Rachel was seated at a table in the far corner. 'And she'd like mustard pickle of gen'rous proportions on a separate plate. Also, do us proud with your crustiest bread, Ernie.'

'Got you, Mister Adams.'

'Good on yer,' said Sammy. At the mahogany drinks bar, he ordered a dry cider for Rachel and a Guinness for himself. He carried the drinks to the table while Ernie prepared the sandwiches. He sat down beside Rachel on the leather-backed wall seat. Rachel slid herself gently close.

'Sammy darling—'

'Now, Mrs Goodman, try to remind yourself you're a wife and mother.'

'And could I remind you to come to Rebecca's next birthday party and do funny faces for her?'

'Cheers,' said Sammy, taking up his Guinness.

'Cheers, lovey,' said Rachel, and sipped her cider. 'And what's the idea of having Susie as your personal assistant instead of taking on a male manager?'

'I don't need a male manager, not in the offices. Boots is the Lord Factotum there.'

'Well, no funny business, Sammy.'

'Eh?'

'I'm all teeth when I'm jealous, lovey.'

'Here, hold on,' said Sammy, 'your life's your life, my life's my life. Am I jealous of Benjamin?'

'Yes, of course you are, aren't you?'

Sammy looked into deep, sultry brown eyes. It wouldn't do any good not to humour her. Rachel and her father meant much to him in his business world.

'Considerable,' he said, 'but I wasn't brought up to uncover me aching heart. Me old lady expects me and Boots and Tommy to stand up courageous to hurt and sorrow. Burnin' arrows pierced me to me vitals, Rachel, when yer married Benjamin, but did I reproach yer? I can say with remarkable integrity that I did not.'

'Ain't you the one and only?' murmured Rachel in delight. 'Sammy, I could eat yer. Now, tell me more about Adams Enterprises as fashion designers.'

'I have already informed you we are intendin' to manufacture our own designs,' said Sammy. 'It's now my pleasure, sport, to further inform you that all I need is a couple of grand.'

'That's all? Two thousand pounds?' Rachel shook her head. 'That's a fortune, sweetie. My daddy will have a heart attack.'

'Your daddy is a friend of mine. It's against my principles to be fatally injurious to my friends.'

'Ain't yer lovely, Sammy?' Rachel's velvet laughter softly bubbled. 'You want I should break it to my daddy gently?'

'A touch of lovin' preparation might help,' said Sammy. Then Ernie the chef arrived, bringing the tray himself. He set out the plates containing the sandwiches and the plate containing a generous portion of mustard pickle. He produced napkins and cutlery. Sammy gave him the customary sixpence for carving the meats.

'Pleasure, Mister Adams.'

'Mutual, Ernie.'

Ernie departed. Rachel and Sammy began to eat. They both had good appetites, and the large crusty sandwiches of new bread and fresh meats were works of art.

'Sammy, why aren't you asking me for the loan?'

'I am dead set on not askin' you, Mrs Goodman. It ain't right. It's takin' advantage of yer warm and noble heart, which kind of advantage has been known to happen

202

before. And yer warm and noble heart is something I hold in affectionate reverence, like I do your melting peepers and your highly good-lookin' female legs.'

Rachel, mouth full of new bread and kosher beef, pressed her napkin to her lips to stifle choking laughter. She chewed and swallowed.

'Oh, you crafty demon, Sammy, I could listen to you all day and you know it, even if you don't mean a word of it, you old ratbag.'

'Steady, Rachel, this here public house is now full of listening earholes.'

'I should blush after hearing you talk of your affectionate reverence for my highly good-looking female legs? Sammy, Sammy, tell me everything about your new venture and your faithful Rachel might buy a piece of it for two thousand.'

'You'd buy in on a gamble?' said Sammy, a gleam in his eye.

'I want to know what kind of a gamble it is, I want to know who this fashion designer is, what her credentials are. She's news to me. A woman fashion designer? Crazy. It's bitter to say so, but it's men who've got the gift for dressing us.'

'Never heard of men like that myself,' said Sammy, the mustard hot to his appreciative tongue, 'only heard of French poofs.'

Rachel's soft laugh arrived again. Every minute she spent with Sammy was delicious entertainment to her.

'All the same,' she said.

'Never mind all the same, Rachel, there's a first time for everything. Mimi Dupont's going to first-time the fashion world.'

'Mimi Dupont? She's French?'

'Well, I'll tell you, Rachel, but keep it all under your tit-for-tat. There's a shockin' amount of underhand goings-on in the rag trade, which me old lady would call

203

implorable, but I favour you with me deepest trust.'
Sammy could be very close-mouthed about his business,
but he trusted Boots, he trusted Susie and he trusted
Rachel. He gave her the details of his new venture,
including those concerning the fixed belief of Lilian
Hyams that her 1926 look was going to anticipate Paris
ideas.

'Bobbed hair, strings of beads and two inches above
the knee?' breathed Rachel. 'And frilly garters?'

'Sent you dreamy with bliss, has it?' said Sammy.
'Well, it'll suit a young Yiddish beauty like you, with
your remarkable handsome limbs.'

'I'm a wife and mother,' said Rachel. 'Benjamin probably wouldn't notice, but my daddy would, and he'd
have a fit.' But her eyes were a gleaming velvet. 'Sammy,
of course. The flappers would consider it the last word.
They'll trample each other to death to be first in the night
clubs with it. You'll form a subsidiary company? I'll buy
thirty-three per cent for two thousand pounds, lovey.'

Sammy considered it.

'It's fam'ly, Rachel,' he said.

'I know. I'll buy into your family, Sammy darling.'

'Why?'

'It's a dream of mine.'

'Twenty-five per cent,' said Sammy. He was incur-
ably family-minded. Boots, Tommy, Lizzy and Chinese
Lady all counted. Ten per cent each for Boots and
Tommy, ten per cent each for Lizzy and Chinese Lady,
and thirty-five per cent for himself, giving him a needful
advantage over Rachel, whose warm and noble heart
didn't get in the way of her shrewdness. Adams Fashions
Limited might well make the rest of the business look
puny.

'Thirty,' said Rachel.

'Agreed at twenty-five, yer sweet and lovely song of
me heart,' said Sammy.

'Oh, my God,' breathed Rachel, but shook her head and laughed. 'Why didn't I do it when I was fifteen?'

'Do what?' asked Sammy.

'Make you make love to me.'

'I didn't hear that,' said Sammy, 'and I am, in any case, dead against performing illegal activities with under-age female persons. Handshake, Rachel, on twenty-five per cent?' Rachel moved closer and they shook hands. 'Kindly lift your hip off my lap,' said Sammy, 'there's people lookin'.'

'People,' said Rachel, 'are spoilsports.' But she smiled. She was very pleased with things. She was in Sammy's business now. She was part of his life.

Mr Barry Somerville, son of the senior partner of Somerville & Partridge, Estate Agents, said, 'Thanks, Emily.'

Emily, having placed an up-to-date list of properties available for purchase or rent on his desk, said, 'I haven't had time to check it, I've only just finished typin' it. But it's just gone one and I must go, my mother-in-law always likes me home punctually to have lunch with her.'

'I know.' Mr Somerville, thirty and dapper, smiled up at her. He liked her efficiency, her willingness. He also liked her figure, her legs and her green eyes, even if she wasn't a raving beauty. 'Keep working on her. We really could do with having you full-time, and I'd like to teach you to help with valuations.'

'No chance, not till my little boy gets to school age,' said Emily.

Mr Somerville got up, saw her to the door of his office, touched her shoulder lightly and said, 'Well, keep working on her, all the same.'

Emily's quicksilver smile flashed in response to his encouragement, and she went. She was quite aware Mr Somerville fancied her. He was already talking about bringing mistletoe to the office at Christmas. She supposed it was flattering to be fancied at her age. She was twenty-seven and had been married nearly nine years. She'd given up her previous job in 1921 when she was expecting Tim. The man she worked with, Mr Simmonds, was very down in the mouth about her going. She had come to like him very much, and let him kiss her goodbye on the day she left. A light kiss had been intended, but it became warm and lingering, and a second kiss followed, and even a caress of her breast. Alarmed at her response, she hastily said goodbye and left. She was Boots's wife, and faithful to him, but the moment showed her that temptation could exist even for a faithful wife. She must make sure temptation did not arise with Mr Somerville, who was a dashing bachelor and liked her to use his Christian name when they were working together in his office. To call him Mr Somerville was so stuffy, he said, that it made him wince. He did not hide the fact that he liked her in the modern fashions, for legs as good as hers, he said, should be seen, not covered up. She told him he ought to keep such remarks to himself, specially as she was married. Nor would her husband be too keen.

But she liked him, he was breezy and outgoing, and he didn't actually pester her, he just had a frank eye for her and kept it that way. And he was set on getting her to work full-time. She had dropped various hints to Chinese Lady. Chinese Lady was not too responsive. For one thing, although she did not say so, she thought a wife and mother's place was at home. For another, Emily didn't need to be out working. Her job ought to go to some poor woman who really did need it.

When Emily got home on this particular day, she raised the subject again over their light lunch. Tim had had his meal earlier and was playing on the hall floor with his clockwork train set. It gave Chinese Lady the necessary privacy to speak her mind firmly at last.

'Em'ly Adams, I don't know what's gettin' into you. You've got a nice home, two nice children, and a hard-workin' husband. I wouldn't like to think you're dis-remembering your blessings, that you're thinking tappin' a typing machine all day would be more of a pleasure to you than your home and fam'ly.'

'But Boots is out all day, and Rosie's at school most of the day,' said Emily.

'Tim's here, so am I, so's the house. You can't expect to have everyone round you every hour of the day, but you can expect all of them to like comin' home to a place that a wife and mother's made warm and welcoming for them, which you can't do if you've only just come home yourself. Men have got their duty, and women have got theirs, and them duties is different, Em'ly, or a house wouldn't be a proper home any more. I don't like saying so, but it seems to me Boots ought to have a firm talk with you.'

'Mum, Boots hasn't ever minded me havin' a job.'

'You mean he's never said anything to upset you. Well, he wouldn't, love, would he? Boots likes peace and quiet, he likes it because peace and quiet is a godsend to him after all them guns and shells when he was in the trenches. Em'ly, you're a good girl, but be careful you don't take Boots too much for granted.'

'Well, I like that,' said Emily, getting cross with Chinese Lady for the first time ever, 'it's wives that get taken for granted.'

'It can happen the other way, Em'ly, and if Boots comes to feel you like your job better than your home and fam'ly, you might just lose his best affections.'

'What d'you mean?' demanded Emily.

'Boots is attractive to women, and I mean women, not flighty girls.' Chinese Lady thought of Miss Simms, the lady teacher who was always asking Rosie about her father, and who had suddenly become cautious during a certain conversation. Very striking to look at, she was, and high-class too, and wasn't she the daughter of an aristocratic lady who still did business with Sammy concerning an orphanage? Miss Simms must have known Boots as well as Sammy before she became a teacher. Chinese Lady thought there was a strong possibility that she was very partial to him. 'It's best to make sure you do the right things, Em'ly, and not the wrong ones.'

'Mum, I think you're being very unfair,' protested Emily. 'All right, suppose I do like my job? Boots likes his job, don't he? But he's not goin' to be told he's puttin' his home and fam'ly second, oh, no.'

'Em'ly love, I don't like to hear you not being sensible. A man's got to have a job, he's got to provide for his fam'ly, it's what a man's made for, and it gives him self-respect. I dare say Boots does like his job, but what he likes better is comin' home from it. Boots is a fam'ly man. I don't want to interfere, I'm only just saying be careful.'

'I don't see why—' Emily broke off as Tim came into the kitchen, his clockwork engine in his hand.

'Mummy, it won't go,' he said.

Emily turned in her chair and opened her arms to him. He scrambled willingly up on to her lap and she hugged him.

'You're not second to me, Tim love, you're first,' she said.

'Can you mend it?' asked Tim hopefully, offering the engine. Emily took it, looked it over and tried the key. It wouldn't move. 'I fink I overwound it,' said Tim sadly. 'Can you mend it?'

'I don't know it can be mended, darling,' said Emily.

'I best ask Daddy, then,' said Tim, and slipped from her lap. 'I'll just have to push it till he comes home.' And he went back to the hall.

'That's put me second to Boots,' said Emily wryly.

'Course it hasn't,' said Chinese Lady. 'Boys need their

208

mothers for some things, and their fathers for other things.'

'Well, I want you to know none of my fam'ly come second to my job,' said Emily.

'That's nice, Em'ly, I'm glad to hear you say that.'

Emily, of course, mentioned the matter to Boots, first asking him a direct question.

'Boots, do you or don't you like me havin' a job?'

'What brought that up again?' asked Boots.

'Just tell me.'

'I'm in favour of you doing what you like to do,' he said. 'I did say so before.'

'And supposin' I did it full-time?'

'If that's what you want,' said Boots.

'You don't sound too keen,' said Emily.

'Well, you don't need to do any job, and there's Tim and Chinese Lady, and the housework.'

'I could still do my share of the housework.'

'I know you could, lovey, but it wouldn't give you much time to yourself. Anyway, what brought it up?'

'Chinese Lady went and gave me a lecture,' said Emily. 'She told me I'm puttin' my home and fam'ly second to my job.'

'Well, you know Chinese Lady. She's got very fixed ideas about marriage, and about the ordained roles of husbands and wives.'

'It's 1925, not 1890,' said Emily firmly, 'and I don't like havin' to listen to a Victorian lecture. You better tell her that.'

'Pardon?' said Boots.

'Tell her,' said Emily. 'It's your place to stand up for your wife.'

'Don't be silly,' said Boots, 'just laugh it off.'

'You don't mind I'm upset?'

'I mind you taking Chinese Lady too seriously. She

might not be in favour of mothers going out to work, but she loves you, Em. That's all you need to remember, that she cares for you. Just settle for doing your job part-time until Timmy goes to school. It's a ready-made compromise.'

'Oh, you sound so upper-class sometimes you make me feel I'm not good enough for you,' said Emily crossly.

'That's even sillier,' said Boots. If anything was notable at the moment, it was Emily's improved speech. She was no longer a gabbling cockney, rushing her words, she had benefited from the way she had applied herself to her jobs, first in the town hall and now at the estate agents.

Her mood changed. She smiled ruefully.

'Oh, I'm sorry,' she said, 'it's just that I want you on my side.'

'Forming sides, taking sides, that's the start of family divisions,' said Boots. 'Not good, Em. Better to laugh some things off. Better to remember, as I said, that Chinese Lady loves you.'

Emily, touched by that, said, 'Well, I love her too, don't I? That's why it upset me.'

Boots gave her a cuddle. She pushed herself against him. When Rosie entered the sitting-room a moment later, she found them kissing.

'Golly,' she said, 'are you having happy ever after?'

'Yes,' said Emily.

'Spiffing,' said Rosie, pleased for the two people she loved the most.

CHAPTER SIXTEEN

The December day was murky. At eleven o'clock, Sammy entered Susie's office, his overcoat on, his hat in his hand.

'I am about to make a call, Miss Brown.'

'On the telephone, Mister Adams?' enquired Susie, busy with a heap of correspondence.

'I do not regard that as amusing,' said Sammy. 'I have in mind an important conversation with Mr Eli Greenberg at his junk yard off Newington Causeway.'

'Yes, Mister Adams,' said Susie, and consulted the desk diary. 'I don't have it recorded. I've got down that tomorrow Mr Entwistle of Manchester is comin' to see you at eleven-thirty, and on—'

'Turn it up,' said Sammy.

'But, Mister Adams, as your personal assistant it's highly needful for me to know your present and future whereabouts each day.'

'I do not consider it needful for you to give me sauce,' said Sammy, sternly hiding a grin. 'I think you'd better come with me and learn how to extract confidential information from Mr Greenberg without it costin' yer a packet.'

Susie's eyes lit up. Sammy had ways of making her very happy.

'Yes, Mister Adams.'

'Lottie's workin' on some letters?' he said.

'Yes, and I've most of these ready for her. I've got phone calls to make with some, I can do that when we come back.'

'Well, jump about, Miss Brown, I'm standin' here waitin' on yer competence.'

Susie could hardly believe her eyes when she and Sammy stepped through the door of the high wooden gates fronting Mr Greenberg's covered yard. She was confronted by great piles of every conceivable kind of household goods, some dating back to Queen Victoria's heyday.

'Jesus,' said Sammy, 'do my mince pies glimpse pianos as well under this lot, Eli?'

'Vun or two, Sammy, vun or two,' said Mr Greenberg, beard and hat both nodding in welcome to Susie. 'Vhat's your pleasure, my poy, a Bechenstein? You vant a Bechenstein, I got a Bechenstein. Sammy, vhat a cheering thing it is to have you visit me in company vith your lady friend. Vhy, never before has it happened, and do I remark her to be a sweet friend of mine too? Susie?'

'Miss Brown happens to be my personal assistant,' said Sammy. 'Give her your respects accordin'.'

'Ah, my respects, dear young lady,' said Mr Greenberg, lifting his hat to Susie, who smiled.

'Mister Sammy has been most kind,' she said.

'Ah, vhen vas Sammy not kind?' said Mr Greenberg. 'It has cost me money, my dear, but vhat is an emptied pocket compared vith the blessings of such kindness?'

'Your compliments, Eli,' said Sammy, 'are a pleasure to me ears, which have been suffering unbelievable lately.' Susie gazed in innocence at a stack of dismantled bedsteads. 'Well, now,' said Sammy for openers.

'Ah,' said Mr Greenberg in pleasurable anticipation.

'I wish to converse with you,' said Sammy.

'And vhy not, Sammy?'

'At no charge.'

'Of course, my poy. I vill forget time is money,' said Mr Greenberg, with Susie listening fascinated. A train rumbled by over the nearby railway bridge on its way to Blackfriars. A mountain of chairs trembled and quivered. Stacked saucepans vibrated. 'Come into my office, ve don't vant the next train to bury Susie under my stock of valuable brass fenders.'

His office was a small wooden hut that had been painted green twenty years ago. But its interior was surprisingly neat. He extracted a large red handkerchief and dusted the seat of a chair for Susie, who sat down.

Sammy said, 'My desire for converse concerns some friendly information I require, Eli.'

'Friendly?' Mr Greenberg looked cautious.

'Helpful,' said Sammy.

'Friendly information that's helpful I should supply free in times like these? Sammy, Sammy, vhat are you askin' of such a friend as I am? Already I am standin' here losing money.'

'I am only requiring names,' said Sammy, 'the names of buyers of ladies' wear for West End shops and stores.'

'The Vest End?' Mr Greenberg smiled in delight. 'Sammy, you are goin' to dig for gold?'

'Branching out, Eli, branching out with quality garments. Observe that I do not want to go into a class store and ask to see Mr Whatsit or Madam Howjerdo. I want to know names, I don't want to look like a pushing elbow. I want to sound familiar.'

'Familiar, Mister Adams?' enquired Susie.

'Familiar with the buyer, Miss Brown. Meaning I am able to ask to see Madam Hilda Ponsworthy or Mr Lionel Spriggs, giving the impression we are close to

213

bosom friends. First names accordin' are also required, Eli.'

'Ah, vhat is called vun foot in the door,' said Mr Greenberg.

'You got it, old friend,' said Sammy breezily.

Mr Greenberg raised his hands high.

'Sammy, Sammy, all this for friendship?'

'All what?' asked Sammy, and Susie thought oh, ain't he priceless?

'My life,' said Mr Greenberg, 'ain't vun foot in so many doors vorth a mite?'

'All right, how much?' asked Sammy. 'I know yer've rubbed shoulders with the trade for more years than I've been born with, I know yer can point yourself at an informative geezer.'

'Vell, now,' said Mr Greenberg, 'it might be I know a certain gent. But he von't expect friendship to interfere with business. It ain't done, Sammy. Did my father leave Russia vith the help of friendship or business? Business, my poy, vhich he expected. Vell, then, vhat d'you say?'

'Two quid,' said Sammy, 'one for your certain gent, and one for you, and I can't say fairer, not without it hurtin' me considerable.'

'Sammy, Sammy, are you trying to kill me vith kindness?'

'All right, you kill me,' said Sammy.

'Shall ve say tventy?'

'Twenty what?'

'Green vuns?'

'Oh, my bleeding heart,' said Sammy, 'did you hear that, Miss Brown? Now look what you've done, Eli, you've turned Miss Brown dead faint. All right, I forgive yer, old cock, I realise you spoke unthinking, only don't make it so that I can't afford to pay Miss Brown her wages. Use your smelling salts, Miss Brown.'

214

'Yes, Mister Sammy, thank you for your kind concern,' said Susie, 'but I am overcomin' my faintness.'

'There you are, Eli, now can you think up a friendly figure?' said Sammy.

'My poy, ain't tventy single smackers friendly?' countered Mr Greenberg. Sammy winced.

'Twenty smackers for names?' he said. 'That's fatal, and dying hurts, yer know. Moses would have left yer to the Egyptians, Eli. I tell you what, I'll double me original offer. Four quid.'

Mr Greenberg's red handkerchief reappeared. He blew his nose on it.

'I'm veeping for yer, Sammy, veeping. But I'll take three vhite vuns.'

'Fifteen nicker? Not from me you won't. All right, I'll give yer six quid, plus me trust and faith, which means six quid in yer mitt now.'

'Done,' said Mr Greenberg. 'I'm a poor man, Sammy, and times is hard, my poy, hard.'

'Don't I know it,' said Sammy, 'it's hardly worth being alive sometimes. Still, friendship keeps a bloke going.' He handed the money over.

'Vell, it's a comforting thing, friendship,' said Mr Greenberg, 'except vhen it pushes a poor man under a tram.'

'They're a sign of hard times too,' said Sammy.

'Trams?' said Mr Greenberg.

'Funerals,' said Sammy. 'I'll expect the list of names some time next week, Eli?'

'I'll ride up special, my poy.'

'Love yer, Eli. Well, come along, Miss Brown, and I'll find out if I can treat you to lunch. I might have enough for a stale loaf and some cheese.'

'Oh, just a crust will do for me, Mister Sammy,' said Susie.

He took her to the little SPO cafe under the bridge at

Waterloo Station, where they each had a plate containing sausages, mashed potatoes and fried onions, and the onions were truly luscious.

'Mister Adams, poor Mr Greenberg,' she said.

'Now, Susie, Mr Greenberg ain't poor.'

'I meant the way you teased him.'

Sammy popped sausage into his mouth and chewed with thoughtful relish.

'No, no teasing,' he said, 'just accepted custom, Susie love.'

Her blue eyes danced.

'Pardon, Mister Adams?'

'Pardon?' said Sammy.

'Yes?' she said.

'What?' he said.

'You spoke familiar, Mister Adams.'

'I accord you me respectful apologies, Miss Brown.' A kick arrived under the table. It struck his shin. 'Would you mind keepin' the pain out of my legs except for when we're socialising?'

'We're socialising now,' said Susie, and gave him a sweet smile. Their eyes met across the table. Sammy fell into hers, they were so vividly blue and large. He drew a breath. He looked at his fork. There was another piece of sausage on it. He muttered at it. Susie wanted to shriek with laughter. He was still doing those things. Looking, dropping his eyes, and muttering. It was hysterical, Sammy not knowing how to tell her he loved her. Sammy of all men. 'When we're socialising, Mister Adams, I'm goin' to kick you every time you call me Miss Brown or talk about respectful apologies.'

Sammy ate the piece of sausage, and followed with a forkful of fried onions. Then he said, 'I appreciate your sentiments.'

'I bet,' said Susie.

'But regardin' Mr Greenberg. My dialogue with him

is mutually harmonious. It is the agreed form of bargaining. It is a considerable pleasure to them to have a conversational carry-on when doing business. And you mustn't think, Susie, that the mention of friendship is all my eye and Betty Martin. It ain't. It is genuine. I've known Eli Greenberg all my life, also Isaac Moses, known as Ikey Mo, and his daughter Rachel. All lifelong friends, Susie, all genuine and reliable business contacts.' Sammy finished his tasty meal. The little cafe, clean and quite attractive, was a long-standing retreat for those who enjoyed a well-cooked, homely repast. It was full, but he and Susie had a small table to themselves. 'If I ever have to ask you to conduct a matter of business with Mr Greenberg on our behalf, you'll know how to talk to him and how to bargain.'

'Yes, Mister Adams, I'll tell him he's ruining us,' said Susie. 'By the way, I happen to have heard you used to go out with Mr Moses's daughter Rachel.'

'Just roller-skatin',' said Sammy.

'Yes, well, I don't think you should go out with her now she's a married woman,' said Susie, trying to catch his eye. 'It just don't look good, Mister Adams, not now you're a business gentleman of high repute.'

'My hearing's gone up the spout again, the ringing in me ears has come back,' said Sammy. 'I'd better ask you to repeat that piece of unsolicited wordage in case I got it wrong.'

'I was speakin' to your dear brother Boots—'

'My what?'

'Oh, he is a dear, Mister Adams, and he agreed with me that as your personal assistant one of my most important personal responsibilities was to protect your high repute. We'd best not take married women out to lunch any more, Mister Adams, we don't want people talkin'.'

'I ain't here,' breathed Sammy, turning his eyes up to

217

the ceiling, 'I'm somewhere else, havin' a fit. Have you finished them satisfying eats, Miss Brown?'

'Yes, Mister Adams, and I don't mind Miss Brown now we're talkin' about business.'

'Then perhaps you'll kindly accompany me into Waterloo Station. I desire to fall under a train.'

'Very good, Mister Adams.'

Outside he stood on the pavement with her. He looked at her through the murk of the day. Susie smiled.

'Susie Brown, you'll be the death of me,' he said. His mouth twitched, and as they walked to the bus stop he was laughing. Susie, laughing herself, thought the dismal day gorgeous.

That evening, Mr Finch had a private word with Boots, the one person in the family who knew his true background and his secrets.

'In a week's time, Boots, I shall be going to Belgium, and from there into Germany. With a German passport. I've told your mother I've a job to do for the Government in Belgium, of indefinite duration. I am, of course, being sent back into the field by Intelligence.'

'British Intelligence?' enquired Boots, his pipe going. They were in Mr Finch's study.

'A fair question,' said Mr Finch with a slight smile, 'but yes, you can believe it, old chap, British Intelligence.'

'As a former member of German Intelligence, you'll be going into the lions' den,' said Boots. 'Can I ask why?'

'Oh, to acquire information. Isn't that what it's all about for every agent?'

Boots looked slightly sceptical.

'What's important about information on Germany, a country down and out?' he asked.

'Down, Boots, but not quite out. And have you heard

of a political gentleman called Adolf Hitler?'

'I've heard of him,' said Boots. 'It's news to me that he's a gentleman.'

'A dangerous nationalist,' said Mr Finch, 'with a flair for oratory and rabble-rousing, and peculiar ideas about the superiority of Germanic people.'

'You've orders to take a close look at him, to join his political party, perhaps?' said Boots. 'That'll mean months in Germany for you, won't it?'

'I shall be sorry to miss Christmas with you,' said Mr Finch. There was more to it than an investigation of Adolf Hitler and his National Socialist Party. There was a certain General Hans von Seeckt, a Prussian of the old military caste, whose record during the war had been highly distinguished. He was now Commander-in-Chief of the limited German Army of 100,000 men allowed by the Allies. He was training that army of long-term officers and men to become an elite force of the finest soldiers in Europe, or so it was whispered. Its attitude, so it was said, was based on the principle of Aryan supremacy.

Mr Finch was to find out what General von Seeckt might be up to, to discover what, if anything, was being kept from the eyes and ears of Allied military observers.

'I thought you'd finished field work,' said Boots. He knew Mr Finch to be over fifty now.

'I had thought so too,' said Mr Finch, 'but when one's country calls, Boots, one does what one can.' He gave another slight smile. 'This is my country now, England is where all my affections lie. Believe that too. And it's a pleasure to know I shall leave your mother in the good hands of her family.'

Polly visited the house every Tuesday and Thursday evening to give Rosie tuition in French. Mr Finch let them use the quietness of his study. He was abroad now, in Belgium, everyone thought, except Boots. Christmas was close, and in the study one evening Rosie was persisting with the complexities of French grammar, an important part of the written exam she was to face in the future.

Boots put his head in.

'Camp coffee, Miss Simms?'

'Oh, very welcome, Mr Adams,' said Polly, finding it difficult always to be fairly formal with him in front of any member of his family.

'And tea for you, Rosie?' asked Boots.

'Oh, ever so grateful, ta,' said Rosie. 'It might save my life, you know. French grammar is killing.'

'You'll win,' said Boots, 'and I'll decorate you myself.'

'What with?' asked Rosie.

'Cocoa tin lid on a piece of string?' suggested Boots, and withdrew.

'Is your daddy fun, Rosie?' asked Polly.

'Oh, Nana always says he's always saying things no one ever understands except himself.'

'Well, that's fun, isn't it?' said Polly. 'Now, how about trying to paraphrase, "*Notre maison est assez grande pour nous*"?'

'Crumbs, Miss Simms, I don't even know what it means.'

'Yes, you do. "Our house is big enough for us." '

'Help,' said Rosie, but went to work.

Chinese Lady had made the inevitable pot of evening tea. Tim was enjoying a cup before being put to bed. He didn't like cocoa, he said it was yukky. Boots made a cup of Camp coffee for Polly, who had become addicted to its chicory flavour during her time in France and Flanders.

'Is that for Miss Simms?' asked Emily, seated next to Tim and caressing his tousled hair.

'She likes Camp,' said Boots.

220

'Well, it's nice she comes to the house to help Rosie,' said Emily, thinking of what Chinese Lady had said about Boots being attractive to women. 'But you don't have to run about for her.'

'Who's running about?' asked Boots mildly. 'Just performing a small service.'

'Still, it's my job really,' said Emily, 'I'm the skivvy.'

Chinese Lady looked pained.

'Oh, I've skivvied a bit myself in my time,' said Boots, and took the coffee and tea to the study.

'*Merci, mon père*,' said Rosie.

'Lovely,' said Polly, turning on her chair to receive the steaming cup. Her dress was hitched, knees showing, legs gleaming in her silk stockings. Boots thought about Sammy's new venture, Adams Fashions, soon to be launched as a limited company. Polly, slim of figure, neat of bosom and long of leg, was a natural for Lilian Hyams's 1926 look, though not during her school hours. She caught his brief glance at her legs. It induced excitement in her. She had thought, at her teachers' training college, that time and absence would cure her of her love for him. Instead, the moment she first saw him again she knew her feelings were incurable. She would have given a whole precious year of her life to have him make love to her. Just once, only once. Only once? How absurd.

'Daddy,' said Rosie, 'Miss Simms just told me I'd split a French infinitive.'

'Good for you,' said Boots, 'that's stupendous progress. Split a French infinitive? Amazing. Remarkable. Well done, kitten. And I suppose I ought to thank Miss Simms for helping you achieve it.'

'But it's not an achievement, Daddy, it's a howler,' said Rosie. 'Isn't it, Miss Simms?'

'Of a kind,' said Polly, 'and forgivable.'

Boots saw her out later. Parked in the road was a

high-bonneted Bullnose Morris, its hood up. It was Polly's car, a present from her father.

'You wouldn't like to whizz off with me into the dark yonder, would you?' suggested Polly, warmly wrapped in a winter coat of black leather.

'Ask me another,' said Boots.

'Aren't you ever going to make love to me?'

'Is it necessary? Won't someone else do? One of your many friends?'

'Oh, you sod, that's below the belt,' said Polly.

'Language, Miss Simms, language.'

'Pompous prig.'

'Fair comment,' said Boots amiably. 'But you're a lovely girl, Polly. Don't go to waste.'

'I'm not going to waste,' said Polly, 'I'm living a worthwhile life. Or haven't you noticed? Or do you mean I ought to be someone's wife? Well, I would be, you stinker, if that someone hadn't married some other woman when my back was turned. Why couldn't you have waited for me?'

'Never having met you, I'd no idea you existed. Come on, I'll crank your car for you.' Boots went to the car with her. She got in and switched on. He cranked. The engine spluttered. He tried again, vigorously. The engine fired. He put the starting handle back into the car. He leaned in under the hood. 'Good night, Polly, and don't think I don't appreciate what you're doing for Rosie.'

Polly kissed him full on the mouth.

'Love you,' she said, and drove off into the damp, misty night.

Boots went back into the house. He put his head into the study, thinking to ask Rosie how her cramming was going. Rosie, however, had already joined Emily and Chinese Lady in the kitchen.

The doorbell rang. He answered it, suspecting Polly had forgotten something.

It was a woman in a dark brown cloche hat and a brown leather coat. She wore spectacles. She had a soft enquiring expression on her face, and her face looked cold and pale.

'God Almighty,' he said.

The woman was Elsie Chivers. He had last seen her at Lizzy and Ned's wedding in March 1916, nine and a half years ago. Elsie Chivers, tried for the murder of her mother at the Old Bailey, and acquitted. And he had committed perjury on her behalf because at that time he was fascinated by her, a woman of soft myopic loveliness without her glasses, her voice a caress. Nearly ten years older now, she had changed little, except for a slight twitch and tremble to her mouth. He stared in helplessness at her. She smiled, a softly sweet smile.

'How tall you are,' she said. 'Such a fine young man, Boots. Oh, dear, it has been so worrying. Is my husband here?'

'Husband?'

'Mr Finch. Edwin.'

'Jesus Christ,' said Boots.

She was a woman tired and drained. Seated in an armchair in the sitting-room, her gloved hands hung limply over the sides, her body slightly drooping. Her head nodded. Her coat was off and he saw that her body was thin in its brown skirt and beige jumper. She was vague now, and incoherent, her answers to his questions making no sense.

'Where are you living?'

Her head came up.

'Hotel. Yes, hotel.' That was her first coherent reply. 'But with no one, you see, no one. I must find my husband.' The worried look appeared. She murmured to herself, and her head nodded again.

'Hold on,' said Boots, who now had worries of his

own, catastrophic worries. 'Hold on now.' He went into the kitchen and quietly advised Emily and Chinese Lady that Miss Elsie Chivers had turned up out of the blue. They gaped at him. Rosie looked puzzled.

'Who's Miss Chivers, Daddy?' she asked.

'An old neighbour of ours,' said Boots. 'She's not too well. I think—'

'You're jokin',' said Emily.

'He better not be,' said Chinese Lady.

'I'm not joking,' said Boots, 'I think she needs some strong coffee and a brandy. She's worn out.'

'Well, I'm amazed,' said Chinese Lady. 'Miss Chivers? I can't credit it. I'd best go and see her.'

'Could you make the coffee, Em?' asked Boots.

'I'll bring it in,' said Emily, charged with intense curiosity. Boots knew there was no way he could keep Miss Chivers to himself, but there had to be a way of preventing her from telling Chinese Lady she had come in search of Mr Finch, and that she had named him as her husband. Mr Finch, Boots remembered, had told him that Miss Chivers had married a Bavarian land-owner.

He went back to the sitting-room, Chinese Lady with him, and his mother took a long look at the woman in the armchair. Miss Chivers was leaning back, her eyes closed, her lids heavy.

'Miss Chivers?' said Chinese Lady, who had thoughts of her own. 'Miss Chivers?'

Miss Chivers opened her eyes. She blinked through her spectacles.

'Oh, my dear friend,' she said. Chinese Lady studied the pale face.

'Lord,' she said, 'what brings you here, Miss Chivers?' she asked.

'It is so nice to see you, so nice,' murmured Miss Chivers, who was not Miss Chivers, thought Boots.

224

'Where have you been all this time?' asked Chinese Lady, who always went straight to the heart of things.

'Boots is such a fine young man, isn't he?' said Miss Chivers, and lapsed into vague, wearied murmurings again. Emily came in with a cup of hot Camp coffee, strong and black. She gazed in intrigued wonder at the visitor.

'Miss Chivers, it really is you,' she said. 'Oh, you do look tired. Here's a cup of coffee.'

Miss Chivers took it. The cup and saucer trembled a little in her hand.

'How kind,' she sighed, 'how kind.'

'Steady now,' said Boots, and poured brandy into the coffee. He'd drunk coffee and brandy, or coffee and rum, in the trenches when there was a treat on, the spirits usually emanating from the company commander, Major Harris, a man of grey granite but, to Boots, an incomparable soldier.

Miss Chivers sipped the laced coffee. The slight tremble afflicting her mouth caused the liquid to spill a little down her chin. Chinese Lady looked distressed at that.

'Oh, poor woman,' she whispered to Emily.

'She's ill,' whispered Emily. 'Where's she come from?'

'I just don't know, and she don't seem in the right kind of way to say.'

Miss Chivers slowly drank the coffee, her chin wet and stained. Boots, taking the cup and saucer from her, wiped her chin clean with his handkerchief. She seemed not to notice.

'Can you tell me the name of your hotel?' he asked.

She lifted her head and looked up at him. He saw the eyes that had once held so much fascination for him, eyes so clear when seen through her spectacles and so soft, peering and myopic without them, holding even more fascination. She smiled.

'You're Boots,' she said. 'How is your dear mother?'

'Oh, lor',' breathed Chinese Lady, 'she's really in a bad way.'

'Boots, I think she'd better stay here for the night,' said Emily, 'we can let her have the spare room.'

Miss Chivers sank back. Her head dropped and a tired sigh came from her.

'Emily,' said Boots, when they were eventually in their own bedroom, 'would you go and bring me her handbag?'

'What?' asked Emily. She had looked in on Miss Chivers and found her fast asleep. After Rosie had gone up to bed, they had all talked about their unexpected visitor, although Boots had not talked quite as much as Emily and his mother. 'What d'you mean, her handbag?'

'I'd like to see what's in it.'

'You know what Chinese Lady would say to that, don't you? She'd say a man goin' through a lady's hand-bag is desecratin'.'

'I know, Em. But I have to tell you what I couldn't tell Chinese Lady, that Miss Chivers made a fairly lucid statement when I opened the door to her. To the effect that she was looking for Mr Finch, her husband.'

'Oh, my God.' Emily whitened with shock. 'No, it can't be. Boots, it can't be.' She went into painful thought. 'But I remember – oh, Lord, no – we all said at the time that she and Mr Finch had eloped. Boots, it'll give your mum heart failure, it'll give her a terrible time.'

'So would you go and get the handbag? I will, if you'd rather. There might be something in it, something a woman might carry about with her if the rest of her possessions were in an hotel.'

Emily stared at her husband.

'Yes,' she breathed, 'a marriage certificate. Yes. Wait.' She hurried out. She was back in quick time, with a brown handbag. She opened it and spilled the contents out on the bed. There were all kinds of things. A purse, a bottle of aspirin tablets, two crumpled hankies, make-up items, bus and tram tickets, loose coins, a spare pair of spectacles in a case, a fountain pen and other innocuous things. But no papers, no letters, no certificate. Boots turned the handbag inside-out without result.

'Hell,' he said, 'nothing. In the morning, Em, I'll take her with me when I leave for work. I can't leave her alone with Chinese Lady.'

'Yes, we can't risk that,' said Emily, green eyes enormous with worry. 'It might be something she made up about Mr Finch, but all the same we can't risk her repeating it to Mum. Oh, God, I hope she did make it up. Well, she's wandering in her mind, you can tell, so she might have. But suppose it's true?'

'Shattering, if it is,' said Boots. Tight-mouthed and grim, he thought. 'I'll have to try to get the name of the hotel out of her. There must be some clue in her possessions.'

'Yes, if she's married there has to be a certificate,' said Emily. 'Lord, if it is Mr Finch, he must have deserted her – Boots, he couldn't have, could he?'

'And committed bigamy with Chinese Lady?'

'Oh, God,' said Emily.

Boots returned everything to the handbag and Emily took it back to the spare room, placing it on the chair beside the bed. Miss Chivers was sleeping heavily. Emily and Boots had hours of broken sleep themselves, waking up and whispering worriedly to each other. Boots said it would be wise to give Miss Chivers breakfast in bed, not to let her come down and have Chinese Lady ask her questions. He'd get her out of the house as quickly as he could, on the grounds that he was going to take her back to her hotel. He'd name one.

They slept fairly soundly in the end.

Boots, woken by the alarm, came to with a start, and went at once to the spare bedroom in his pyjamas. He knocked. There was no answer. He put his head in. The room was empty. He went all over the house.

Miss Chivers was gone.

'Thank goodness,' breathed Emily.

'Only up to a point,' said Boots.

'Pretend she never came.'

'She's a wanderer, Em. She's only half in the real world. But she may wander back here again. How, I wonder, did she get to know our address?'

'Don't think about her, pretend she never came,' said Emily.

'Well, there's nothing we can do as things are,' said Boots, 'except wait until Edwin Finch returns.'

'Yes, we'll do that,' said Emily, 'we'll wait.'

Boots wondered how it would all work out. He wondered exactly what had happened between Mr Finch and Miss Chivers when they went off together in 1916. Both had had more on their minds than a thousand other people put together.

CHAPTER SEVENTEEN

Boots spent some time out of his office during the next few days to look for Miss Chivers. Sammy, with Susie looking after so much of his office work, was busily out and about, but still managed to find a moment to ask his eldest brother what he was up to. Family business, said Boots. What family business? Boots said he'd let Sammy know if he had to, but would keep it to himself if he didn't. Very informative, I don't think, said Sammy, and what about the real business, the business that paid a handsome salary? Boots said not to worry.

Chinese Lady, of course, was worrying at the mystery. Boots had noticed that the bus and tram tickets in Miss Chivers's handbag all related to journeys in South London. They pointed to the possibility that she was living in the area, but he could think of no hotel in places like Walworth, Kennington, Bermondsey or Camberwell. But he spent time looking for her there, searching the streets she had known so well for many years. A woman with a wandering mind might be drawn back to the environment of her past out of strange compulsion. He had reached the conclusion years ago that Elsie Chivers was guilty of the murder of her mother. It was not a conclusion of absolute certainty, but of suspicion and painful deduction.

He searched Walworth Road and the East Street market more than once in his attempts to find her. He walked around the little streets surrounding Caulfield Place and St John's Church. He went into the church, thinking she might be there.

He was in Caulfield Place one day. The kids were just coming home from school. They were sprightly. Christmas was coming. That always put a spring in young feet.

Freddy Brown saw the tall man in hat and overcoat, and recognised him, even though he had only seen Boots once. Susie often spoke of him and how nice he was.

' 'Ello, mister,' said Freddy.

'I think I know you,' said Boots.

'I'm Freddy, Susie's brother. We live in yer old 'ouse, yer know.'

'So you do. Is it all right, Freddy?'

'You bet, Mister Adams.'

'Freddy, have you recently seen a certain woman?' Boots described Miss Chivers, and also mentioned her cloche hat and leather coat.

'Crikey, yes, I seen 'er all right,' said Freddy. 'Ain't she a funny old girl?' Miss Chivers was in her early forties. 'She come and asked questions, yer know.' Freddy told Boots of the time when the woman had appeared in the passage and asked about Mrs Adams and a Mr Finch, and talked about coming to Sunday tea and didn't listen to nothing he said.

'I'd like to get in touch with her,' said Boots, 'I'd like to find out where she lives. If you see her again and your time's your own, is it possible you could get someone to ring me at the shop from the Walworth Road phone box while you keep your eyes on her? If it's out of shop hours, have the phone call made to my home. There's a couple of bob in it for you, and two extra pennies to keep in your pocket for the phone call.'

'Two bob?' Freddy's eyes lit up. 'Yer on, Mister

Adams. I'll keep me eyes on 'er, I'll keep 'er talkin', I'll invite 'er in, that's what, and me mum'll keep 'er talkin' as well. Me mum's a dab 'and at keepin' anyone talkin'. Course, I could just ask 'er where she lives, if yer like.'

'She might not tell you.'

'See what yer mean, Mister Adams, she's a bit funny all right.'

Boots took out his wallet, found a scrap of paper and used his propelling pencil to write down the relevant phone numbers. He gave it to Freddy, together with a florin and two pennies. He had a feeling that it was here, in Caulfield Place, that Miss Chivers was most likely to reappear. Was it the grisly and macabre nature of her conscience that had driven her to return to Walworth? He experienced a sense of deep pity.

'Right, Freddy, keep your peepers peeled, then, eh?'

'You bet, Mister Adams,' said Freddy. He could buy Daisy a Christmas present now, out of the two bob. A fair-sized rubber ball, which they could both kick about.

That evening, Boots advised Emily of his arrangement with Freddy Brown. Emily said that was a long shot, if you like. Better if Miss Chivers just disappeared again, and for good. Boots thought not every sleeping dog ought to be left to lie.

The following day was crisp and bright with winter sunshine, shop windows decorated for Christmas. At ten o'clock, a small dark blue motor van stood outside the Adams's shop at Camberwell Green. On each side it bore the painted inscription, 'JAMES BROWN & CO – FAMILY BAKERS – DAILY DELIVERIES'. Boots was inspecting it in company with an old wartime comrade, ex-Corporal Mitchell of the West Kents.

'I'm leavin' it with yer, guv,' said the driver.

'Fine,' said Boots, and gave him a tip.

231

'Bless yer, guv, merry Christmas to yer,' said the driver and went off.

'Well, there you are, Mitch,' said Boots, 'all yours, job and the van.'

'Ain't many sergeants like you,' said Mitch.

'We're all sods,' said Boots.

'Gettin' a permanent job ain't something I don't like to mention,' said Mitch, 'specially at Christmas time. Me old lady don't know if she's comin' or goin', she's that tickled. I've had bits o' jobs, I 'ad one that lasted six months once, so yer won't mind me mentioning this 'ere permanent job's a godsend.'

'Works both ways,' said Boots. 'You need us, we need you. All right, Mitch, hop up and try it.'

'I ain't 'andled four wheels since me Army days,' said Mitch, 'but this runabout won't give me no trouble.'

'Take it for a run round the block,' said Boots.

Mitch climbed up into the driving seat. Sammy came out.

'What's this?' he asked.

'A delivery van,' said Boots. 'Needs a sign-writer to work on it, that's all.'

'You crafty bleeder,' said Sammy.

'Now, now, sonny, it's a bargain buy at forty quid,' said Boots.

'I don't recollect signing no indent approving same.'

'Don't worry about that now, I've sent the cheque to Browns, and it's still a bargain. Remark the condition, my lad.'

'Sometimes,' said Sammy, 'I can hardly believe you're me own brother the way you slip in unapproved transactions when I've got me back turned.' But he walked around the van with a slightly proud look of ownership. He spoke to Mitch at the wheel. 'You from Browns?' he asked.

'No, from fifty-four Rodney Road,' said Mitch, 'and

was instructed to present meself 'ere by Sergeant Adams to take on the job of driving this box for 'is firm, which is Adams Enterprises.'

'I see,' said Sammy, 'you're an old Army mate of his, are you?'

' 'E's me sergeant,' said Mitch.

'Well, I'm Adams Enterprises,' said Sammy, 'and Sergeant Adams is me brother and manager.'

An open Morris car came rushing up. It jerked to a stop behind the van. From the driving seat, Polly Simms gestured frantically to Boots, who strode up to the car.

'Where's the fire?' he asked.

'Oh, God, it's Rosie,' gasped Polly, pale-faced. 'She fell down some steps at school. She's unconscious. I've just driven her to King's College Hospital. She's in casualty. You must come.'

Boots, stunned for a moment, shook himself and leapt into the car.

'Pick up Emily, at the estate agents,' he said.

Polly, teeth biting bottom lip, drove to the estate agents. Boots jumped out and ran in. A young woman in the front office looked up.

'Sir?' she said.

'My wife, Mrs Adams, where is she?'

'She's out with Mr Somerville, Mr Barry Somerville.'

'Where?'

The girl, seeing the look on Boots's face, said, 'She's gone to help with a valuation at fifty-four Denmark Hill—'

Boots was out and away. He gave Polly the address, and Polly, her mouth compressed, drove there at speed. It wasn't far. Boots leapt out again. Polly followed. The front door of the house was open.

'Emily!' Boots shouted from the hall. There was no answer. He looked into one room, then another. He entered the living-room, Polly behind him. Through the window he saw Emily. She was in the garden with Mr Somerville. He was kissing her, his arms around her. Polly sensed Boots turning rigid. She herself felt frozen with shock. She wished herself a thousand miles away.

Emily put her hands on Mr Somerville's chest and gently pushed him off.

'That's your Christmas come and gone,' she said.

'Emily!'

She turned her head, and she too froze in shock then. Boots was looking at her from the window he had opened.

'Oh, my God,' she gasped.

Boots, his face expressionless, said, 'Break that up, will you? Rosie's had an accident. She's in King's College Hospital. I'd like you to come. Miss Simms is here with her car.'

It was a short ride but a traumatic one. Emily did not know what to say. For the first time in her life her ready tongue lay helpless. It was impossible, the situation, because of the presence of a third party. Boots was curt in telling her about Rosie's fall. And Emily found herself saying, 'But she'll be all right, won't she, she'll be all right?'

Boots did not answer.

And Polly said nothing. She was angry now, and suffering. She was totally unable to understand why the wife of a man like Robert Adams could indulge in cheap kisses with another man. Polly had known a thousand cheap kisses herself, every one of them instantly forgettable. If the actions of Emily Adams made her angry, the humiliation Robert had endured in seeing his wife in the arms of another man made her suffer. She felt intensely for him.

She heard him speak then, quite quietly.

'Just say a prayer, Em.'

And Emily said huskily, 'Yes. Yes.'

At the hospital they spoke to a doctor in casualty.

234

'Severe concussion, of course, Mr Adams. But we'll see what the X-ray says. If there's a fracture, it'll show up.'

'A skull fracture?' said Boots.

'There may be no fracture at all. Call in later this afternoon.'

'Can we see her?'

'She's sleeping. We've given her a sedative. Best thing.'

'Is she sleeping, or is she unconscious?' asked Boots.

'Oh, she came to, but with a terrible headache, of course. She's a brave little girl. Yes, she's sleeping.'

'Can we see her?' asked Emily.

A nurse took them to the ward. Rosie lay asleep, with a huge black bruise disfiguring her forehead. Emily suffered distress, unhappiness and pain. She glanced across the bed at Boots. He looked tragic. He took life mostly in a whimsical way, as if he found its ups and downs amusing. An old comrade of his, a man called Nobby Clark, blind from the war, had once said to her when she asked him how he was getting on, 'Well, it ain't a garden of roses, Mrs Sergeant Adams, but it's good to be alive.' That was how it was with Boots, of course. It was simply good to be alive. It was painful to see him so set-faced, so sombre, his eyes on Rosie. She wondered if he loved Rosie more than he loved her. The thought that perhaps he did twisted the knife. Had she been taking him for granted? Whenever she did anything special for him, he'd say, 'Love you, Em.' Or, 'Love you, old girl.' She could not remember the last time she'd said she loved him. Now, on a day when Rosie had perhaps fractured her skull, he had caught her being kissed by Barry Somerville, an irresponsible bachelor. And so soon after this awful problem with Miss Chivers.

'Boots?' She spoke in a whisper.

235

'She's so young,' he said.

'Yes. I love her too, you know, and I am praying.' She reached out a hand across the bed, and emotions welled as he took it and squeezed it.

Leaving the hospital, he said, 'I'll call in again this afternoon, they'll have examined the X-ray by then.'

'Yes, I'll call in too.'

Polly, who had spoken to the casualty staff, was outside, in her car. Boots thanked her for everything and told her he and Emily would walk back to their work. Polly said nothing, she drove away, eyes burning.

Emily watched her go, then turned to Boots.

'Don't say anything,' said Boots.

'I must. It was only a stupid Christmas kiss. He brought mistletoe.'

'Yes, all right. Leave it, Em.'

'I can't. It didn't mean anything. He gets silly ideas. It would only mean something if I got silly ideas myself. Did she see too, that woman?'

'Leave it, Emily,' said Boots, as they turned left into Denmark Hill, in the direction of the shop.

'We've got to talk,' said Emily.

'I don't see why, if it didn't mean anything.'

'I just want to know you believe that.'

'I believe you.'

'I want you to believe something else, something important,' said Emily. She stopped, took his arm, and made him stop too. 'I want you to know I love all of you. Rosie, Tim, Chinese Lady, Dad, and you. It wouldn't matter if I had the best job a woman could ever have, and all the money in the world, my fam'ly would still mean more to me than all of it. Only no one believes me. I just like being busy, doing things. Oh, men are so stupid.'

'You've set yourself up, have you, Em, as an expert on our imperfections?'

236

'I'm unhappy, I'm suffering for Rosie, I'm mad at myself and that stupid, stupid man. And don't be upper-class with me. Hit me.'

'Do me a favour,' said Boots. His mind on Rosie, he was not disposed to discuss who was stupid and who was not. 'Give Somerville a message from me. Tell him you're my wife. Tell him that if he's that much in need to get one for himself.' A little gleam of the hidden steel surfaced. 'Tell him that if he continues to fancy you, I'll knock his bloody head off. You got that, Em?'

It shocked Emily. It almost frightened her. Boots meant it. She had never heard him speak like that before, nor had she ever seen his eyes look so steely.

'I don't like this,' she said, oblivious of people passing by.

'Tell him, Em.'

'I'll tell him.'

'You'd better,' said Boots.

'Then I'm going home to talk to Chinese Lady.'

'Why?'

'Because she's the fam'ly, because I've got to, and because I don't like you like this.'

'You're my wife,' said Boots, and went walking on to the shop. Emily had a terrible feeling that in some way she was going to lose him. She crossed the road, she walked fast to the estate agents. Mr Barry Somerville was back. She marched straight into his office, and word for word she delivered her husband's message to him.

Mr Somerville sat up.

'Emily—'

'And what's more, I'll kill you too. If you've done anything to my marriage, I'll kill you!' She marched out and she went home to talk to Chinese Lady.

Chinese Lady listened in silence, then regarded Emily a little sadly.

237

'I'll get my hat,' she said.

'Your hat?'

'I'm going to the hospital to sit with Rosie. Rosie's a child, and she's hurt bad. You and Boots, you're grown-ups. What's happened was bound to happen, with you comin' home each day with tales of Mr Somerville saying how good you are at this, how promisin' you are at that, and what he's got in mind for you, and Boots lettin' it go on and not seeing what it was goin' to lead to. Well, he's been pulled up with a jerk, I'll be bound. Of course you didn't like him speakin' to you like that, but what did you expect? Did you expect a bunch of roses, Em'ly Adams?'

'Oh, that's not fair,' protested Emily.

'You said that to me once before,' said Chinese Lady. 'I told you then, and I'll tell you again, you and Boots got duties to each other, and responsibilities, and it's not responsible for him to be so airy-fairy about things and for you to encourage men to kiss you. Now don't tell me there was no encouragement, it might not have been deliberate, like, but it was there, it's no good always blaming the men and calling them stupid. There's stupid women, Em'ly, as well as stupid men, so don't go about thinkin' it's all on one side.'

'Oh, anyone would think I went to bed with Mr Somerville!'

'Well, that's usually the next step. I'll get my hat and coat and go and sit with Rosie. You stay and look after Tim.'

'Mum, you're being awfully hard on me.'

'Wait till I see Boots, I'll be a lot harder on him. It's his fault mostly. If either of you think I'm goin' to sit back and see a fam'ly marriage break up, you've both got another think comin'. There's goin' to be no broken marriage in my fam'ly, nor broken Commandments.'

'I'll come down later meself,' said Emily. 'Oh, it's a

238

rotten rotten day, Rosie looks so bad. Mum, I don't want a broken marriage, honest to God I don't. I never seen Boots look at me the way he did.' She put her face in her hands.

There was the lightest pat on her shoulder.

'There, he'll get over it, and there's wives who've done far worse things than you, Em'ly love.'

Emily, strong-minded though she was, burst into tears. Chinese Lady comforted her.

'I'm afraid you can't, Mrs Finch,' said the ward sister.

'Don't be afraid, because I'm goin' to,' said Chinese Lady. 'She's my granddaughter, she's a hurt child.'

'She's still sleeping, and the visiting rules—'

'I won't interfere, I'll just sit with her. She ought to have someone there when she wakes up. I'll stay until her father gets here.'

'Matron will have my head.'

'I don't want to get you into trouble,' said Chinese Lady.

'Go in, Mrs Finch.'

'That's kind of you. Well, it looks a nice cheerful ward. And there she is. You just get on with things, sister.'

The ward sister smiled resignedly. Chinese Lady, seating herself at Rosie's bedside, gazed in concern at the huge black bruise. Rosie lay with her eyes closed, her breathing interspersed with what sounded like the sighs of troubled dreams. Chinese Lady removed her gloves and took hold of the still hand that lay over the blanket. She held it gently throughout her vigil, discouraging talk from any of the other patients. She did not want to be obtrusive, only to be there if Rosie woke up.

In the middle of the afternoon, the girl's hand lightly stirred and her lashes lifted. Chinese Lady thought her eyes looked blurred.

'There's a good girl,' she murmured.

239

There was a faint, painful sigh from Rosie. Her heavy lashes blinked.

'Nana?'

'Yes, it's me, Rosie.'

'Nana—' Another sigh. 'Oh, I've got an awful head.'

'Bless us, that's a nuisance.'

'Yes. Awful.' The lashes dropped and the sedated girl went to sleep again.

Chinese Lady looked up as someone looked in. Sammy. The ward sister was shaking her head at him.

'Just a quick peep, be a sport,' said Sammy, and crossed to the bedside, hat in his hand. 'Mum? I heard, of course. How is she?'

'She just woke up, then went off again. We just have to wait and hope, Sammy. Nice you've come, nice you remembered Rosie.'

Sammy looked down at her girl. He frowned.

'Boots is regular cut up,' he said. 'He'll be here soon, he's been frettin' all afternoon. Have they looked at the X-ray yet? Boots'll burn his top if they don't have the result when he gets here.'

'I didn't think.' Chinese Lady relinquished Rosie's hand and got up. 'You sit with her, Sammy, while—'

'I've only got a few minutes.'

'I didn't finish speakin'.'

'Sorry, old girl.'

'You sit with her and hold her hand. I'll go and see a doctor or someone. If that X-ray's been done, I want to know what it says. It's no good you goin', you'll try to sell them sheets and blankets. That won't do Rosie no good.'

Sammy sat down and Chinese Lady went in search of up-to-date facts. She looked for the ward sister. She might know by now. The ward sister was missing for the moment. Chinese Lady went to casualty.

Sammy took hold of Rosie's hand, thought how

warm it was, and how ugly and painful the bruise looked.

'Buck up, Rosie love, you'll win,' he said, 'your mum and dad are counting on that. So am I.'

The next one to arrive was Polly. She had had a terrible afternoon. The ward sister, around again, was very firm this time. Sammy got up and joined Polly in the corridor.

'Sammy, you're here?' she said. 'God, does that mean she's bad? Does it?'

'Steady,' said Sammy. 'I don't really have time to be here, but I made time. I don't know if she's bad or good. I'm just hoping. You don't look all that good yourself.'

'Thanks very much,' said Polly, 'but I've had a bloody awful day, and I feel responsible.'

'Now, Polly, don't say things like that. You can't stop kids from falling over. Not even God can. Kids are always falling over.'

Polly, trim but haggard in a cloche hat and buttoned coat, smiled wanly, then bit her lip as Boots appeared.

'I had to come,' she said.

'I'll take a look at her, then find the doctor,' said Boots. The ward sister reappeared.

'We really can't have this,' she said, 'so many of you.'

At which point, Chinese Lady returned, her back straight, her step sprightly.

'So there you are,' she said to Boots. 'And good afternoon, Miss Simms.'

'I'm so terribly sorry about Rosie,' said Polly.

'It's bad concussioning, that's what it is,' said Chinese Lady. 'I just seen the doctor.' The ward sister exclaimed and departed with a swift rustle, wanting to find out for herself. 'Rosie don't have a fracture, Boots. She'll be kept in a few days, but she'll be all right. What a blessing.' Chinese Lady raised an eyebrow as Polly turned away, biting on a lip that was actually trembling. One never thought of weakness in a woman who had seen the hell of France and Flanders as an ambulance driver. 'There's a—'

'It's official?' said Boots. 'There's no fracture?'

'I don't like this interrupting,' said Chinese Lady. 'Still, I can understand. No, there's no fracture. There's a place where we can all have a cup of tea – Boots, what're you doing?'

Boots was giving her a warm kiss on her cheek.

'Good on yer, Granny,' he said.

'There's no need—'

'I got you, Boots,' said Sammy, and kissed her other cheek.

'That's it, make exhibitions of yourselves and me too, never mind it's a hospital.'

'Love yer,' said Boots, and slipped into the ward to take a look at Rosie.

'I don't know what you must think, Miss Simms,' said Chinese Lady.

Polly faced up to the emotional problems she experienced so often in her relationship with this family. Their background was plain, simple and unvarnished cockney, their love of life extraordinary. In going regularly to the house to cram Rosie, she had come to know their enthusiasms, their laughter and their loyalties. For her, Boots stood out, of course, an ex-Tommy, a man of infectious whimsy who could pass muster in any house in the land. His mother was a reactionary Victorian, an incredible character, with searching eyes and knowing eyes. Polly was sure that Mrs Finch, formerly Mrs Adams, was aware of how she felt about Boots. She stood up to that awareness now.

'I think, Mrs Finch, that people who make exhibitions of themselves on occasions like this are the best kind of people. I'm so relieved about Rosie, so glad for all of you. I feel I shall never let Rosie out of my sight again.'

Chinese Lady gave her a kind but level look. The vitality of Rosie's teacher looked as if it had taken a drubbing. Chinese Lady did not know Polly had witnessed Emily's indiscretion. Emily had left out any mention of Polly. Chinese Lady only saw a woman whose feelings had badly suffered solely on account of Rosie. For all that she felt Polly Simms needed watching, Chinese Lady could not help liking her.

'I think you need a cup of tea too, Miss Simms,' she said. 'Come along, we'll go to the tea room. My hooligan sons can join us there.'

'I don't know I've got time,' said Sammy.

'I'm not havin' any argufying, I want to speak to you. I'm hearing tales about you designing ladies' clothes. I don't like the sound of that, it don't sound decent or proper. When Boots comes out, bring him with you. Come along, Miss Simms.'

Sammy grinned and waited for Boots. Polly went with Chinese Lady, and by the time they reached the tea room Polly had a curiously tingling feeling that this resilient and protective Victorian mother had accepted her as a family friend.

Chinese Lady, of course, believed in keeping close to anything that might be a threat to family unity.

'We'll walk part of the way home,' said Chinese Lady later. 'We can talk better than on a bus. Em'ly should be with Rosie now. You didn't wait for her, I noticed. She'll have had Tim with her.'

'We'll go together this evening, at visiting time,' said Boots.

'Still,' said Chinese Lady, walking through the darkness of the cold, crisp December evening in her proud, busy way, 'I think you might have waited, just to please Em'ly.'

'I'm seeing you home.'

'I'm not an old woman yet, I can see myself home.'

'It's not the kind of thing I promised your husband.'

Chinese Lady reflected, little knowing Boots was wondering if she had a husband.

'Well, it's nice Edwin was thoughtful concernin' me,' she said. Boots silently winced. The situation was playing havoc with his peace of mind. He had got to find Miss Chivers. 'Still, you mustn't think it's the cold air that matters, it's the fog. And it's not foggy, and I've got something to say to you.'

'Yes, Emily spoke to you. She said she was going to.'

'Yes. Well, it wasn't a great sin she did. I don't want you to go about thinkin' it was. Men have always got an eye for women. Most men have got respect for married women, but some haven't. Some think married women get taken for granted by their husbands and will enjoy being flirted with. The trouble with married women goin' out to work is that they come up against men like that Mr Somerville of the estate agents, and it makes them lose their heads. Not that Em'ly's a woman who'll lose her head easy, but you know she don't think much of her own looks, specially not when she puts herself up against our Lizzy and our Vi, or that young lady who's come back to work for Sammy in Camberwell. I disremember her name—'

'I don't think so, old girl, I think you know she's Susie Brown.'

'Oh, yes, that's her. I went to the shop yesterday and happened to see her.' Chinese Lady was casual, so Boots, of course, knew how her mind was working. 'I noticed she speaks much better and has got very elegant, like.'

'I'm with you,' said Boots, 'I'm following. Have you told Sammy you've decided?'

'I don't know what you mean. It's a grief to me you still say things no one understands except yourself. I hope you get to understand about Em'ly, she was very upset when she got home. I wouldn't like to think I brought up my only oldest son to be uncaring. Now, I don't want any nonsense from you about all this. It was silly of Em'ly to go to an empty house with that man and let him kiss her there. In an office or a fact'ry at Christmastime, well, people do bring mistletoe, but lettin' it happen at an empty house, it was wrong of Em'ly and she knows it. Em'ly's a good girl, really, and a lovin' mother, even if she has got strange ideas about she ought to have a job when she shouldn't and needn't. I been surprised all along you wasn't more firm with her, a man's got a duty to be firm with his wife sometimes, same as a woman's got a duty to put her husband in his place when he's lordin' it. I don't hold with men actin' like lords of creation, and never will. Well, I was saying before you interrupted me about Em'ly not thinkin' much of her own looks – Boots, now what're you doing?'

'Taking your arm, old lady. It's dark along here.'

'No, it isn't.' The window lights of houses emitted a cosy glow. 'I'm not ninety yet, so stop your fussing.' But she let him take her arm. 'Where was I? Yes, our Em'ly. Not thinkin' herself much to look at, and havin' a husband who's so airy-fairy she thinks he don't mind what she gets up to, she's bound to let herself be flattered by a man like Mr Somerville. I don't hardly know any husband more airy-fairy than you, Boots. Em'ly can't know where she is with a husband who don't do his duty by being firm, it's like children get when no one tells them what's right and what's wrong, they don't know where they are. Em'ly's been talkin' all the days God's give her about havin' a full-time job, and I been sorely grieved to see you sittin' there and not puttin' your foot down like a proper husband should. What you saw goin' on between Em'ly and that Mr Somerville is your own blame. Boots, you listening?'

'I'm listening.'

'Well, I can tell you Em'ly went back to her office and give Mr Somerville an earful, like you asked her to, but when I heard what shockin' language you used to her, your own wife, as well as givin' her a very nasty look, I near fell down with shame. What your dad would of said, or Edwin either, don't bear thinkin' about. Speakin' like that and lookin' at Em'ly so nasty, it's near to hooliganism and it upset her something chronic. You sure you're listening?'

'Carry on, old love.'

'If I thought you had one of them sly smiles of yours on your face, I'd give you a real talking to. Now, I don't want you ridin' no high horses, my lad, I don't want no unpleasant atmospheres. I know it's not been the best day you and Em'ly ever had, but God's still been good to you by makin' sure Rosie wasn't fractured. When we get home I'll start doing the supper, and by the time we're sittin' down to it I want to see you and Em'ly lovin' each other.'

'Over the supper table?'

'What? Is that one of your low music hall jokes at a time like this and you my own son?'

'Yes, all your own work, old lady. And Dad's too, of course. Come on, there's a bus on its way and here's the stop. You've walked far enough, and I promise Emily and I won't disgrace the supper table.'

Her mouth twitched. Standing with him at the bus stop, she said, 'I don't know how I ever come to have a son who's always saying one thing and meaning another. Anyway, Boots, I'm not havin' no fam'ly upsets, I'm not havin' any of my fam'ly being fractious with each other. It's not good for none of us, specially not for the children.'

'You're a wise old girl, old lady.'

'You and your old lady. After supper, you and Em'ly can go and see Rosie together. Together. Have you got that, my lad?'

'Yes, got it, Mum. I'll be firm.'

The bus pulled up. Chinese Lady boarded it with a satisfied look.

Emily arrived home with Tim not long after her husband and mother-in-law.

'Boots is upstairs,' said Chinese Lady. 'Did Rosie wake up?'

'Yes, she kept wakin' and goin' off again,' said Emily. 'It's such a relief it's only concussion.'

'She'll be more awake later, they won't give her another sedative yet awhile. There, I'll see to Tim. You go upstairs and take your hat and coat off.'

'Yes, upstairs where Boots is. The penny's already dropped, Mum.'

Boots had washed and freshened up. Emily entered the bedroom resolved to stand up for herself. Boots regarded her soberly. Her mouth tightened.

'Did Rosie wake up?' he asked.

'On and off, like I just told Mum.'

'We'll go and see her together after supper.'

'Will we?' said Emily, stiff-faced.

'Yes. Orders from Chinese Lady. Come here.'

'That's another order?' said Emily, taking her hat and coat off.

'Yes. Come here.'

She approached him, tense in defence of herself. He put his arms around her.

'What's this for?' she asked.

'Christmas,' said Boots and kissed her firmly on the mouth. Emily collapsed against him. 'All over, lovey,' he said.

'Oh, I been havin' a rotten day.'

'All over,' he said again, 'and we have to love each other over the supper table.'

'Oh, don't joke.'

'No joke,' said Boots, 'it's another order. From

Chinese Lady. We talk rhubarb, Em. She talks sense. She made me realise our little troubles hardly rate a mention compared with what might hit her if Miss Chivers does turn out to be the first Mrs Finch.'

'I've got a terrible feeling that if Mr Finch is a really dark horse, Miss Chivers might not be the first herself,' said Emily.

'Jesus Christ,' said Boots.

CHAPTER EIGHTEEN

Rosie's one concern, while recovering, was that she might not be home for Christmas. The school had broken up, and Annabelle and Aunt Lizzy were visiting.

'Of course you'll be home, darling,' said Lizzy, 'the nurses told us so.'

Rosie, still with a tender head that went thump if she moved it too quickly, said, 'Oh, but they have to say gracious things, Auntie, it's in case they don't want you to know you're next door to death.'

'You're not next door to death,' said Lizzy, looking like a Christmas card in her deep blue cloche hat and warm red winter coat.

'No, but I'm next door to not being home for Christmas, Auntie, and that's death,' said Rosie.

'Oh, I'll come and spend Christmas Day in here with you,' said Annabelle, 'and we could—'

'Don't say it,' said Lizzy, 'you're not goin' to die together in here, you pair of pickles. We'll all be with Granny Lady and bursting with health unless some I could mention eat too much and get sick.'

'Auntie, I haven't bought presents yet,' said Rosie. 'Oh, what a blessed nuisance having a head like this. I just hope it didn't knock my brains about and get them all mixed up. Auntie, I've got saved-up money, really, and I made a list. Could you—' She winced as a little dart of sensitive pain struck. 'I expect you're awfully busy, but—'

'I'll get them for you,' said Lizzy.

'Oh, and could I whisper to Annabelle?'

'I won't listen,' said Lizzy.

Rosie whispered to Annabelle.

'Goodness,' said Annabelle, 'she'll like that. I know where to buy one.'

Lizzy affected innocence.

Going down to the shops at Camberwell Green after leaving the hospital, Lizzy stopped with Annabelle outside the theatre. Camberwell Green still boasted a theatre, and still promoted mainly music hall turns. Now the annual pantomime was being advertised. This year it was *Dick Whittington*. Annabelle eyed the posters excitedly.

'Oh, there's a conjuror too, Mummy.' Conjurors fascinated her. Rabbits out of a hat were simply spiffing.

Lizzy noted the fact that, along with other turns in the pantomime, Rainbould the Master of Magic and his assistant Vivette would be performing.

'Annabelle, let's,' she said. 'A fam'ly pantomime party. We'll go and see Uncle Boots and Uncle Sammy, and we'll get tickets for Uncle Tommy and Auntie Vi, and Granny Lady too. We'll all go, the whole fam'ly.'

Sammy, arriving in his office from Shoreditch, was a man perpetually busy. He looked lean, fit and clear-eyed, for perpetual motion that related to business, his business, did for him what climbing a mountain did for other men. Boots came in as soon as he sat down.

'Ah,' said Sammy.

'Ah?' said Boots. 'I believe that's an interjection mainly used by bank managers.'

'That's educated talk, Boots. You're good at that.'

'You're not short of your own kind of chat,' said Boots.

'I do me best, y'know. Now, it's me pleasure to inform you that Christmas Eve – oh, how's Rosie?'

'Out in two days,' said Boots.

'I'm joyful,' said Sammy. 'Well, on Christmas Eve, Madame will be here to show us samples of her first collection.'

'Madame?'

'Madame Mimi Dupont, called Lily Hyams previous. Camberwell, I thought, not Shoreditch. Yer can't believe the eyes that creep up around Shoreditch. We shall have the honour of receiving our benefital shareholder, Mrs Goodman—'

'Rachel, your old love, you mean, and beneficial, not benefital.'

'Same difference,' said Sammy, 'but kindly don't pain me with references to what ain't relevant. Also, do me the favour of remembering I'm your own brother, and refrain accordin' from acquaintin' Chinese Lady with details of the Christmas Eve display, or she'll come round and set fire to everything.'

'If you don't refrain from trying to teach me how to suck lemons,' said Boots, 'I'll break your leg.'

'Granted,' said Sammy. 'We shall discuss the samples and prospects, you, me, Mrs Rachel Goodman and Fifi—'

'Fifi?'

'Mimi. My personal assistant, Miss Brown, will also be present on account of if she's left out I might not get to see Christmas Day.'

'Pardon?' said Boots.

'Did I say something?'

'Nothing that I don't understand. Christmas Eve, right, I'll be here.'

'You certainly will,' said Sammy.

'New Year's Eve, you'll be there,' said Boots, and placed two tickets for the pantomime on Sammy's desk.

251

'What's all this?' asked Sammy.

'Tickets for this year's pantomime. New Year's Eve performance. Two bob each. Four bob for the pair. Pay Lizzy. She bought them for the whole family, this afternoon.'

'Well, I like a panto, I won't say I don't,' said Sammy, 'but I don't know I'll have time.'

'You'll have time. The evening is by royal command.'

'Whose command?'

'Chinese Lady's,' said Boots, 'as spoken by her herself when Lizzy phoned her from my office earlier.'

'All right,' said Sammy, 'but I don't need two tickets.'

'Yes, you do. One's for Susie.'

'I do not recall—'

'Nothing to do with your memory,' said Boots. 'It's orders.'

'Orders?'

'Chinese Lady's. Tell Sammy he's not to come by himself, it won't look sociable, she said. Tell him to ask that nice young lady who works privately for him.'

'She's pushing me,' said Sammy.

'Susie is?'

'No, yer clown, Chinese Lady. She'll have me churched the day after if she can.'

'I don't think so,' said Boots, 'I think she favours a spring wedding.'

'Kindly note I am not in the mood for comic chat of a highly personal fashion,' said Sammy.

'It's no joke, Sammy. Chinese Lady passes on those kind of orders directly from God.'

'What kind of orders?'

'Spring weddings.'

'I'm hysterical,' said Sammy.

Susie knocked and came in, looking the impeccable secretary in a stylish white blouse and dark blue skirt. She consulted her wristwatch. An air of reproof arrived. Boots studied the ceiling.

'You're late back, Mister Sammy,' she said. 'It's four-fifteen, and you told me half-past three.'

'My movements happen to be elasticated, Miss Brown.'

'Yes, Mister Sammy, very well. Christmas week is very elasticated, of course. I've ordered the port for Christmas Eve. There are forty letters waitin' for your signature.'

'You sign 'em,' said Sammy, regarding her cautiously and looking for a sign of a little loving. 'And ah, yes, let me see. Now what was it?'

'It'll come to you, with the assistance of the nice young lady who works privately for you,' said Boots, and went back to his office.

'May I enquire who this young lady is?' asked Susie. In the office, she conducted herself to plan, exercising a businesslike air that sometimes induced that muttering mumble in Sammy, much to her delight. 'I do not recollect being told about her.' She could take him off with no effort at all.

'Listen,' said Sammy, 'that high-falutin' gent, who happens to be my only eldest brother, has a nasty weakness for failing to be serious at times, which is every day.'

'I won't hear a word against him, Mister Adams,' said Susie, 'he's adored by all of us.'

'Oh, he is, is he?' growled Sammy. 'Well, if I catch him being adored in office hours there'll be ructions that'll blow the roof off.'

'Really, Mister Adams, such a fuss about our hero-worship, I'm surprised at you,' said Susie.

It wasn't possible, thought Sammy. She'd been a woebegone, hungry-eyed, skinny young cockney waif five years ago. Look at her now. And listen to her. The Queen of Sheba couldn't have been more regal. Gawd help me, if I ask her and she does say yes, she'll have me on toast for the rest of my life. I won't be able to say no to anything she asks for, she'll end up with all I've got, including every shirt off my back.

'Where was I?' he asked.

'You were going to tell me who the young lady is who works privately for you,' said Susie.

'Didn't I make it clear Boots meant you?'

'Oh, the dear man,' said Susie, 'to call me nice, would you believe.'

'I'll remind you, Miss Brown, that on a considerable number of occasions I've called you nice myself. Also good, kind and helpful.'

'Yes, Mister Adams, thank you. I want you to know—' Susie paused.

'All right, let's hear it, I know it's goin' to make my ears ring,' said Sammy.

'I want you to know I'm very very happy working here,' said Susie. Sammy coughed, rubbed his mouth and looked at his desk. He had a thousand things to do, and as always she took his mind off all of them. Susie's eyes grew warm and loving. He was a terrible coward, but such a darling. 'I'll go and sign the letters. Oh, that list on your desk is of people you have to phone.'

'Yes, right,' said Sammy. 'By the way, I happen to have acquired tickets for the Camberwell theatre pantomime on New Year's Eve. Would you care to accompany me?'

Her eyes danced.

'New Year's Eve? The pantomime? Oh, Mister Sammy, I'd love to.' Susie lost her businesslike mask.

'It's with the fam'ly,' said Sammy, 'we're all goin'.'

'Oh.' Susie adored his family. His brothers were gorgeous, and she didn't know anyone more loveable than his mother, nor anyone lovelier or more infectious than his sister Lizzy. 'The Tivoli again with you tomorrow,

254

and the pantomime New Year's Eve? Mister Sammy, why are you so lovely to me?' That was a request to him to declare himself.

Sammy coughed again and said, 'Well, I was thinking that in appreciation of your considerable worth—'

'Oh!' Susie, in spirited vexation with him, stalked out. Sammy's phone rang, and he was immediately wrapped up in a profitable business conversation.

She forgave him again during the second visit to the Tivoli, which was even more exciting than the first. He actually called for her in a taxi, bought her an even sweller box of chocolates, saw her settled comfortably in her seat, and even went so far as to tell her he was highly gratified to know she was the most stylish young female woman in the audience.

'Mister Sammy, you can have a chocolate for that, a caramel centre. Oh, lor', though, the money you're spending on me when you've got all those ruinous business expenses.'

'You saucebox,' said Sammy, 'I'll take two caramel centres for that.'

She laughed. She liked him so much when he was droll. She looked at him as he helped himself from the proffered box of chocolates. She liked his clean look very much, and the manly lines of his face. She liked the way he challenged life, the way he bargained, and the way he left competitors trailing in his wake. The people who worked for him really did have to work, but no one ever complained, because if you did a good job for Sammy Adams, you had a job for life. The Shoreditch machinists were stitching for their lives, for their promised bonuses, and Sammy kept them going not only because of the bonuses, but because of the way he talked to them. He gave them cockney talk, and he laced all his threats with a mixture of sugar and vinegar that made them shriek with laughter. Susie liked going to the factory with him, to see how improved in look it was, and to see Tommy, for whom she had much affection.

The lights went down, and Susie absorbed herself again in the tense and emotional drama of *Ben Hur*. At the end, when the whole audience was charged with emotion, she found she was gripping Sammy's hand tightly. She could not remember when she had taken hold of it. She felt his fingers press hers as the screen went blank.

They stood for the National Anthem. When it was over, Sammy handed her something. His handkerchief.

'Blow your nose, Miss Brown,' he said.

It was a taxi again for the journey home. As it carried them over Waterloo Bridge, Susie kicked his ankle.

'You did that last week,' said Sammy.

'Yes. I never makes promises I don't keep. You're terrible, takin' me out, being lovely to me, and then calling me Miss Brown.'

'Well, Susie—'

'Yes?'

'You're nice to be out with.'

'Yes?'

'I won't come in when we get you home—'

'You will,' said Susie.

'I've got some multiple financial figuring to work on.'

'No, you haven't, you've just made that up. Besides, Mum's doing us a late supper of eggs and bacon.'

'Eggs and bacon? That's different,' said Sammy.

Susie smiled. Everything was fun when she was out with Sammy.

At midnight, with the weather chill and damp, they were at the open door and Sammy was about to say good night.

'I was thinking,' he said.

'Yes?' said Susie.

'Yes, I've been thinking.' He had. He had made his

decision. He would ask her Christmas Eve. Christmas Eve was always a time of goodwill, when most people had loving feelings towards each other, and some port inside them as well. And he could fall back on more port if she said no. 'I'll have to speak to you some time, Susie.' He lightly patted her arm. 'Good night, Susie.'

He'd done it again, thought Susie. He'd left her unkissed. But he was going to speak to her some time? When was some time?

CHAPTER NINETEEN

On the day before Christmas Eve, Boots's office phone rang. He picked it up.

'I think Oliver Twist wants to speak to you, Mr Adams,' said Doreen.

'Who?'

'Well, it's some boy.'

'Put him through,' said Boots.

' 'Ello?' said a young voice.

'Is that Freddy Brown?'

'Yerse, Mister Adams. Cor, ain't phones funny? Mister Adams, she's been again. Me mum's out Christmas shoppin', yer know, so I couldn't get 'er to talk to the lady. She kept saying she was goin' to come to Christmas dinner, an' I kept saying won't yer come in, so's I could get me sister Sally to phone yer. Only she just stood on the doorstep talkin' away till she said she'd got to see to 'er muvver and then go an' see Mr Finch—'

'And she's gone, Freddy?'

'I got 'er address, though, Mister Adams. I just said to 'er, "Where'd yer live, missus?" An' she come right out an' said, "Twenty-one Westmoreland Road." So I fought I'd phone you right away. Cor, Mister Adams, fancy talkin' to yer like this, I never used no phone before.'

'Freddy, have you told your family about this lady?'

'I ain't told no one. Well, I felt she was trouble to yer,

like, and I wasn't goin' to say anyfink unless she turned up again—'

'Good on yer, Freddy, you've earned that two bob. Leave it with me now, and thanks a lot. Merry Christmas.'

'Yer a sport, Mister Adams,' said Freddy and hung up.

Boots rang Emily at home. It was three in the afternoon. Freddy, of course, had broken up for the Christmas holiday.

'Boots?' said Emily.

'Listen, love. Our lady of trouble may be on the way to you right now.'

'Her?' said Emily.

'That's the one. Don't let her get inside the door. I'm afraid that means you'll have to put your hat and coat on and intercept her at the end of the road.'

'Yes, love,' said Emily. 'I'll take Tim for a walk. I know what to do if she turns up. I'll handle her, I'll put her on a bus. Trust me.'

'I'm going down now to Westmoreland Road. Young Freddy Brown has found out where she's staying. There's a chance she may have gone there first, and another chance she may have forgotten about visiting us again.'

'Yes, go there, Boots, see what you can find. Lord, I hope you don't find the worst.'

'We've got to know, Em.'

'Yes, we've got to, but I don't want to.'

'We'll see.'

It was not far to Westmoreland Road. A tram got him there in minutes. The street lamps were alight, the afternoon damp, and little eddies of shifting fog swam in the dusk. He knocked on the door of number twenty-one. He knocked twice without getting an answer. The latchcord, such a familiar thing in Walworth and

Camberwell, invited a tug. He tugged and the door opened. The passage was gloomy. He closed the door and made his way up the stairs. The house smelled of polish, a sure sign that the tenants were people of pride, however poor. Having made up his mind that Miss Chivers was a lodger here, he made straight for the upstairs back room. The landing was dark. He struck a match, turned the handle of the door and went in. The match went out. He struck another and lit the gas mantle. The room sprang into light. There was no fire burning and the room was cold. He saw the bed. It was neatly made, and the room was perfectly tidy. He had felt he might find untidiness and some neglect. One could relate that to a woman not quite right in her mind. He doubted then if this was her room. This might not even be where she lived. The address she had given Freddy might easily have been something she pulled out of her vague mind. Certainly, it was not an hotel. That too could have been a vague something.

An item standing on the mantelpiece caught his eye. It was the back of a photograph frame, a small frame. He picked it up and turned it, and a snapshot of Mr Finch came into sharp, clear being. He put it down and closed the door. He looked around. He opened a cupboard. A suitcase stood on the floor. He brought it out and placed it on the bed. He sprang the locks. He lifted the lid. Possessions. Little delicate ornaments, carefully wrapped in tissue. Little jewellery boxes. A ribboned bundle of letters. A flat inlaid box containing a mani-cure set. A leather wallet. He opened it. He saw German banknotes. He extracted two folded documents of fine, thin paper. One was Miss Chivers's birth certifi-cate, the other a marriage certificate, issued in Munich in the Republic of Bavaria, and dated 21 September 1917. There was her name, Elsie Maud Chivers. And the name of the bridegroom, Walther Hirst Lansberg.

Except that this had been crossed out by a single, wavering line of ink, and above it, in equally wavering fashion, had been inserted, '*Edwin Finch*'.

That, thought Boots, in great pity, was the wishful thinking of a woman who had married a German called Lansberg, but would have preferred Mr Finch, a lapsed German and a man who had given her all the supportive strength of his being after the murder of her mother.

Boots's relief was intense. The foundation of his trust and belief in his stepfather had proved solid. And his mother had no worries. He tidied up, and he left, catching a bus that would carry him straight to Emily. Miss Chivers had not turned up. Nor did she at all.

Christmas Eve morning.

Emily was at work, Mr Barry Somerville subdued and quietly businesslike, Emily cool, efficient and thinking of a happy family Christmas.

Chinese Lady was mixing the Christmas pudding, using rich old ale to bind everything. Lizzy was in the kitchen with her, making stuffing for a gigantic turkey. A turkey. Some people sometimes ran to a chicken for Christmas, but only the rich were known to have turkey. Sammy had been presented with this twenty-six-pound bird by a customer who supplied lingerie to his ladies' shops. Sammy had presented it in turn to Chinese Lady, for the family's Christmas dinner. Chinese Lady had asked him how much he was charging her for it. Sammy said that was the kind of question that gave him a pain. Chinese Lady said it never used to. Sammy said he was profoundly pleased to hand it over free and for nothing. Chinese Lady said she'd always known he was really a good boy at heart, and that she hoped some nice girl would recognise it.

'I'm on to you, Ma,' said Sammy.

'I don't know what you're talking about,' said Chinese Lady.

All the family would be there for Christmas dinner, including Aunt Victoria and Uncle Tom. Only Chinese Lady's husband would be absent. She hid her little sadness about that. No one knew just how much she liked having a husband again. To make up for his absence, she had just received an affectionate letter from him.

Rosie was home and taking it quietly. She was under strict orders from Boots. Annabelle was with her and they were writing their Christmas cards in Chinese Lady's little sitting-room. Tim was in the other sitting-room, playing with his cousins Emma and Bobby. Three-year-old Emma was giving the two boys a terrible time. Tim and Bobby both felt girls ought to be sent to live on a desert island.

Lizzy's youngest child, Edward, was toddling about in the kitchen, making use of his grandmother's skirts and his mother's legs to steady himself whenever the floor didn't behave as his childish mind thought it should.

Vi was out shopping with her mother, and her mother was proudly wheeling the pram in which infant Alice lay warmly covered up to her button of a nose. Uncle Tom was at his work, laying gas pipes in Peckham.

Tommy was at the factory in Shoreditch, keeping one eye on the machines and the other on the machinists. He had confiscated a bottle of gin.

Polly was at home, going restlessly from one room to the other. Her father, General Sir Henry Simms, who had once had the audacity to argue with Field Marshal Douglas Haig during the war, asked her why she wasn't out and about. Polly usually spent Christmas Eve rushing around London with long-established friends, friends who thought her enthusiasm for teaching fiendish kids a scream.

'Is that a serious question?' asked Polly.

'Best I can do,' said her father, tall and iron-grey.

'Well, look, old bean, you'll make more of a success reading your *Times*.'

'It's bad, is it, Polly?'

'You don't require an answer to that, do you?'

'Gad, no. Treat it as an expression of sympathy. But would you like to go to India for a year?'

'To get over my blues?' said Polly. 'Yes, I'd like it very much. It's a ripper of an idea. I'd love to go and eat my heart out with the flies, the punkah-wallahs and the Indian elephants. There's only the school and the kids to leave behind.'

'It's not on?' said General Simms.

'It's not on,' said Polly.

Lady Simms put her head in.

'Diana's on the phone, Polly. She'd like you to lunch with her at Romano's.'

'I'm not in,' said Polly.

'Where shall I say you are?' asked Lady Simms, step-mother.

'Purgatory.'

'Very well,' said Lady Simms pacifically. 'You can come and help me decorate the orphanage Christmas tree this afternoon.' And she went to advise Polly's friend that Polly had a headache.

Sammy spent the morning in his office with Boots, Rachel, Lilian Hyams and Susie. His office was radiant with colour, for Lilian had brought the best part of her collection. She met Rachel and Boots for the first time. She thought Rachel sultry and striking. She thought Boots fascinating. 'One mother to have two like Sammy and Tommy, and another like Boots, I should believe that?' she said to Rachel. And Rachel replied, 'Yes, I have asked myself, is it fair?' She recognised the fashion

263

designer as a re-charged live wire, a woman who, discouraged by fixed attitudes, had had the good fortune to encounter Sammy, a man who could infect people of promise with his own energy, vitality and enthusiasm. Sammy could identify winners and losers. He had seen the woman, Lilian Hyams, as a winner. He had seen the promise in the girl Susie Brown even when she had been all huge eyes, sharp cheekbones and skinny frame. He had hung on to Tommy, a young man of honesty and skill, until he could place him with advantage in a job in which he could excel. Tommy could manage machines, and Rachel had no doubt he could manage the machinists. Boots, of course, had been a winner from the beginning. Sammy was the creative builder, Boots the one who held everything together. Sammy, a dynamo, electrified people. Boots could get all he wanted with a sly smile and a whimsical comment.

Rachel felt nothing could stop Adams Enterprises becoming big business. Their ladies' shops were already well-known, their scrap yards run by astute men whom Sammy seemed to have plucked magically out of the air. Men who ran scrap yards for a parent company could fiddle with ease, but Sammy rarely made a misjudgement, and in any case the man in overall charge of the yards was Fred Scribbins, Sammy's most loyal servant.

As for Lilian Hyams's collection, Rachel considered it original, imaginative and colourful. She asked, however, why Sammy had not arranged for the hire of a mannequin. Sammy replied that mannequins talked, and that in any case Miss Brown's kind services were available. Susie said she did not recall being asked. Sammy told her to have another port. (He had ideas of getting Susie mellow.) Susie said too much port went to her head. Sammy said he was pleased to hear it. Susie made a face. But Sammy had made her part of the team, and although she did not really like taking on the role of mannequin, for she was no exhibitionist, she consented to model a number of the designs. Rachel made comments that were shrewd and generally enthusiastic. Sammy's comments increased Lilian's belief in him as a man who could meet a challenge. Boots put in a word or two from time to time. Rachel had only one real criticism, of a spring coat, which she dismissed out of hand as being too fussy. Lilian listened to all comments. She was there to listen. Listening was more beneficial than arguing. She was not showing her collection to acknowledged experts of fashion, but Mrs Rachel Goodman was a woman who dressed beautifully, Sammy had a natural eye for what would sell, and his eldest brother, she felt, would know what looked good on a woman. Sammy had put his faith in her, and she was willing to put her hopes in the judgement of the three of them.

In respect of the star dress of the collection, the short purple dress with the fringed hem, Susie modelled it a little self-consciously. Going into her own office with Lilian to put it on, she said, 'Oh, lor'. Well, if I die, you'll send me a wreath, won't you, Boots?'

'Two,' said Boots. 'One out of affection, one out of admiration for your bravery.'

'I like the first reason best,' said Susie.

'I am not in approval of funeral talk,' said Sammy, who really meant he was not in approval of a flirtatious exchange between Susie and his brother.

The dress evoked a low, warm whistle from Rachel. Long strings of beads adorned neck and bodice, and reached to the waist. The purple silk shimmered, and a narrow matching bandeau with a single black feather encircled Susie's fair hair. Frilly garters peeped through the fringed hem of the dress. She was pinkly self-conscious about the garters, not her style at all, but

Sammy thought her irresistible in Lilian's 1926 look. Boots thought her delicious but sensitive. Rachel took a very long look, then said, 'My life, should we worry that in the country women will still wear tweeds? In London, the flappers will scratch each other to be the first to wear this. It's audacious, Sammy, and that is the rallying flag of the flappers, audacity. You're certain, Lilian, that it's going to pre-empt the French designers?'

'It's a feeling I have,' said Lilian.

The atmosphere was one of exciting challenge. Sammy poured more port. It was midday. Boots, declaring himself impressed, went to his office to make a phone call.

The butler, finding Polly in the conservatory, informed her she was required on the phone. There had been six previous calls for her from friends, and she had been unresponsive to all.

'I'm not at home,' she said.

'Very good, Miss Polly. Hi will advise the gentleman accordin'.'

'What gentleman?'

'A Mr Robert Adams—'

'I'll take it. In the library.' Polly was swift in getting to the library extension. 'Hello, is it true?'

'Is what true?' asked Boots.

'That you've actually phoned me. God, I hope it's not to do with orphanage business. I'll kill you if it is.'

'Merry Christmas,' said Boots.

'As if you care.'

'I care enough to ask if you'd like to share a turkey sandwich and a bottle of French wine with me at the pub. It'll be crowded out, but they're holding a table for me at one o'clock in the sandwich bar. It's not the Savoy, and it wouldn't surprise me if you were already fixed up, but—'

'Are you inviting me out? Am I actually listening to an invitation? I never have before. I think you'd better start at the beginning again, old love.'

'If you can't manage it—'

'Don't spoil it with negative speech, darling. I'm tottering with rapture.'

'Is that what a turkey sandwich on Christmas Eve does to you?'

'It's what an invitation from you does to me.'

'One o'clock, then, in the sandwich bar?' said Boots.

'Yes, if I can get up. I've fallen to the floor. But don't go, I've plenty of time to get there by one. Talk to me. You can't be busy. Nobody does much business on Christmas Eve. God, I've been so bored. No school, no kids, no dreams.'

'What sort of dreams have you been looking for?'

'Don't ask dreary questions, sweetie, that makes you too much like other men. Be what you always have been, provoking, frustrating, stinking and adorable.'

'D'you think, over our sandwich, we can have a sensible conversation?' suggested Boots.

'Hell, I hope not,' said Polly, revitalised. 'I like our kind of conversation. I can have sensible conversations with MPs, archbishops and other boring people, I don't want them with you. I'd like a lifetime of our kind of dialogue, with not one sensible word spoken by either of us.'

'You'd like me as a village idiot, would you?'

'Join the club, darling, I'm one myself.' Polly paused. 'Is it intruding too much to ask about you and Emily?'

'Emily's fine.'

'Hate her,' said Polly, 'hate her for what she did to you.'

'When you get to know Emily, you'll find you can't hate her.'

'You clown,' said Polly, 'I'll never like any woman who sleeps with you.'

'See you at one,' said Boots, and rang off.

At ten to one, Susie was in her office, trying to come to terms with the effects of three glasses of port and the necessity of preparing letters for Lottie to type. Lilian had returned to Shoreditch with her collection, ex-Corporal Mitchell driving her in the firm's van. Rachel, much though she would have liked to lunch with Sammy, knew she must go home and take her little girl Rebecca off her father's hands.

'*Shalom*, Sammy. Good luck.'

'Likewise, and spoken from me heart, Rachel.'

'Bless you,' murmured Rachel, and kissed him and left.

Sammy entered Susie's office. It was colourful with little Christmas decorations. So were the offices of the typists and clerks.

'Ah, Miss Brown,' said Sammy, 'I thought on this auspicious occasion of Christmas Eve, it behoves me to ask me invaluable personal assistant to lunch at the expense of my private pocket. In the upstairs room of the pub, where there is an aspidistra and a potted palm.'

'Upstairs room? The private room? Mister Adams, really, should you? Lord above, Mister Adams, what will people say?'

'I am indifferent to un-Christian gossip,' said Sammy who, having made his momentous decision, was accordingly firm.

'But my mum's not, nor my dad,' said Susie. 'I just simply couldn't, not a private room, Mister Adams. Private rooms are for fast women.'

'Eh?' said Sammy.

'Well, all right,' said Susie, the port making her feel

warm and rosy with well-being and entirely capable of holding her own with Sammy. 'But I'd best cover my face and head with a scarf when we go in and come out.'

'None of your sauce, Miss Brown,' said Sammy. 'I am not noted for escortin' young ladies into dubious places. Kindly put your hat and coat on.'

'Yes, Mister Adams.' Susie smiled. Sammy saw blue eyes swimming with dreams, or so they seemed to him. He wondered if his future meant he would be waking up to them each morning.

He took her across the road to the pub. Susie bobbed and danced on high heels, humming 'Miss Peggy O'Neill' to herself. They entered the pub by a side door and climbed the stairs to the upstairs room, reserved for small private gatherings. Usually, it was never used on days like Christmas Eve, when the pub was far too busy coping with bar trade. Ernie, the sandwich bar chef, had put in a word on Sammy's behalf, however. In the window, draped by green velvet curtains, stood a huge aspidistra on a bamboo table. In a smaller side window stood a potted palm. In the middle of the room a mahogany table was laid for two.

'Be seated, Miss Brown,' said Sammy.

'Excuse me, I'm sure,' said the rosy Miss Brown, 'but are we socialising, Mister Adams?'

'It's my pleasure,' said Sammy, as she sat down.

'I hardly like to kick you at Christmastime,' said Susie.

'None of that, Susie. I am in a considerable serious frame of mind.'

'Oh, lor',' said Susie, 'it's goin' to be lecturin' and growlin'.'

Ernie came in bearing a tray containing two plates of a hot turkey lunch. He set the plates before the customers.

'Yer'll excuse me hurry, Mister Adams, I got a bar that's bustin' at the sides, like. I'll send Johnny up with any drinks yer want.'

'Susie?' enquired Sammy.

Susie, trying to focus on her turkey lunch, said murmurously, 'I'll 'ave a port, if you'd be so kind.'

'You sure?' said Sammy.

'A port,' said Susie.

Sammy ordered a beer for himself. A little man brought the drinks up, and left them to their lunch. Susie had no trouble with the port, but seemed vague about the exact purpose of her knife and fork.

'Merry Christmas, Susie,' said Sammy, and cleared his throat and drank some beer.

'Oh, same to you, Boots, I'm sure,' murmured Susie, and managed to fork a piece of turkey into her mouth.

'Pardon?' said Sammy.

'You're sweet,' said Susie, and blinked to focus on him. 'Oh, lor', you're Sammy.'

'It is my good fortune to be my dear old lady's favourite son on account of my kind nature. I ain't Boots. You got that, Miss Brown?'

'Who said Miss Brown?' Susie drank more port.

'Now, Susie, kindly pay attention. We'll be busy this afternoon, I'm takin' you round our shops, to the stall and to Fred's scrap yard, and then to the fact'ry. We are droppin' in on one and all, as is my custom at Christmas, bestowing good wishes and bonuses, which is done in appreciation of their work, but not forgettin' to tell some there's room for improvement. It will take time, and I am accordin' sharing this table with you for thirty minutes in order to acquaint you beforehand with certain feelings of mine, not excludin' my honourable intentions. I am hopin' – Susie?' He stared at her across the table. She was sitting back. Her chin had dropped, her head and hat bent. She was gently asleep, lulled into dreams by the morning's port. 'I don't believe it,' breathed Sammy. 'It wouldn't happen to a dog, but it's happened to me, Sammy Adams. Is it right? No, it ain't, and it's not even decent. Chinese Lady, she's done it on me. How'm I goin' to get her back to the offices?' He put his knife and fork down, got up and went round to Susie. He lifted her chin. Beneath her cuddling cloche hat her fair hair peeped and her sleepy eyes opened. She smiled dreamily.

'Oh, I do feel lovely,' she murmured and drifted off into warm seas again.

'Done it on me,' said Sammy.

The port.

He laughed.

In the sandwich bar, Polly sat with Boots at a small corner table. The place was loud and hearty with Christmas spirit, and there was a crush of people at the marble-topped sandwich counter. Polly's friends might have thought it screamingly bourgéois, but to Polly it was life among the people, just as her time in France and Flanders during the war had been life and death close to the raw, earthy Tommies of the trenches. If it had made a brittle woman of her, it had also taught her what ordinary men and women were made of, except that she had long given up thinking them ordinary. Nor was it remotely ordinary to be eating turkey sandwiches with Boots in a Camberwell pub. It was rescuing her from restless boredom. So many things were boring that did not have anything to do with Boots or Rosie or the school. Her knee touched his under the table.

'Am I crowding you?' he asked, refilling her wine glass.

'Please do,' said Polly, refusing to take her knee away. 'Exactly why am I here? Oh, I'm not complaining, old bean, far from it. But why am I here?'

271

'So that I can thank you for all the private tuition you're giving Rosie, and for taking such good care of her by getting her to the hospital so quickly.'

'Have you forgotten I was an ambulance driver for four years?' Polly's smile was brittle. 'I love Rosie. If I had a small share of her, I'd have a large share of you. You can have all of me.'

'That's far too much,' said Boots.

'You've forgiven Emily, haven't you?'

'We haven't quarrelled, no.'

'You mean you've settled for peace and quiet,' said Polly, maroon coat unbuttoned, round black fur hat softly crowning her head. 'You're an old softie, Robert. You're all the same. My father's the same. It's a form of cowardice. You should all have gone to war on the politicians after the last man had got back from the hellholes. Everything to do with blood and guts you all left behind, buried in the trenches. I'd have marched with you on Parliament, so would a thousand other women like me.'

'Are there a thousand like you? As many as that? Terrifying.'

Polly laughed, then put a hand on his arm. A man not far from them got up and left the bar. 'Listen, darling, could we have a lifelong friendship? It need not be platonic, I'm very easy about that, but I'd like it to be lasting.'

'Is this a serious conversation?' asked Boots.

'Well, it's not a boring one, at least. No, really, dear old sport, if you ever need silly old me, just call and I'll come. God, is that hackneyed?'

'Not to me,' said Boots. 'What are you doing over Christmas?'

'Participating in the rites of being utterly charming to a select gathering of ancient relatives on Christmas day. On Boxing Day, my father and step-Mama are off to Nice for a month.'

272

'In that case,' said Boots, 'my mother would like to know if you'd care to join us for Boxing Day tea.'

Polly stared and said, 'Would you mind repeating that?'

'She feels the family should show its appreciation of the way you're giving up your time to cram Rosie. It's not been enough to give you coffee on those evenings. Boxing Day tea will be like Sunday tea. It's a religion with my mother. Everyone sits up straight and no jam is allowed until you've eaten at least one slice of bread and butter. And you must pass the cakes or jam tarts before you take one yourself. Do you like winkles?'

'Oh, my God,' said Polly, big-eyed and fascinated.

'Pins are provided with the winkles. Do you like toasted crumpets with butter? It used to be margarine. It's butter now.'

'What are you doing to me?' asked Polly.

'Boring you and putting you off?'

'Darling, I'm entranced.'

'About pins and winkles?'

Polly laughed.

'Love the thought,' she said.

'It's a cockney feast,' said Boots.

'I'll come,' said Polly.

'You can say no.'

'I'm not going to say no.'

'You're for it, then. You'll have to wear a party frock—'

'A what?'

'Party frock. We always have a Boxing Day party as well as a Christmas Day one. The kids insist. After tea you'll have to play party games, like Tail the Donkey, Hunt the Slipper, Forfeits—'

'Forfeits?'

'The men like Forfeits. The girls usually find they have to do things that make them show their legs. My

273

mother allows this, as legs are traditional at party games.'

'Crazy,' said Polly.

'You're not keen?'

'I can't wait. I'll put my legs up against Emily's any day. Or is it all a joke?'

'It's no joke, it's dead serious. And there are no exceptions. Rosie and Annabelle won't allow them. Nor will I. And we usually finish with a knees-up.'

'Say that again.'

' "Knees Up, Mother Brown," ' said Boots with a straight face.

'Hysterical,' said Polly.

'And watch out for Postman's Knock,' said Boots.

'I haven't played Postman's Knock since I was ten.'

'Being rusty is no excuse. Rosie and Annabelle won't accept that. Nor will I. In between, a hot supper will be served. Don't call it dinner or my mother will think you're trying to turn things upside-down. Have you got a party frock with a red sash?'

'I had one when I was eight.'

'Well, make do with one of your Bond Street creations. Rosie and Annabelle might pass it.'

'I think I'm going to love Boxing Day,' said Polly.

Mrs Brown, opening her front door in answer to a knock, found Mister Sammy standing there, one arm around Susie, whose head was resting on his shoulder.

'Sorry and all that, too much port, Mrs Brown,' he said. 'My fault, but I'd be grieved if you thought I'd been careless about Susie. It's just that we do pass the port round at Christmas.'

Mrs Brown, seeing a taxi outside the house, its driver waiting, said, 'Oh, but it's kind you brought her home in comfort, Mister Sammy, and only two o'clock as well, when she should still be at work.' Mrs Brown was too philosophical a woman to make a fuss about Christmas drinks, even if it was a little bit of a shock to know Susie had had one too many. 'Susie, you been havin' too much port and no lemonade with it? Susie?'

'Been lovely,' murmured Susie.

'I'll see to her, Mister Sammy.'

'I'd be gratified,' said Sammy, 'I've got a hundred calls to make. I'd also be obliged if you'd tell her my mother's invited her to tea on Boxin' Day, which if she can come will be a pleasure to one and all. I've put her Christmas bonus in her coat pocket, I don't think she knows it's there.'

'Been lovely,' murmured Susie, as her mother took hold of her.

'Merry Christmas, Mrs Brown,' said Sammy. 'Must push off, I'm considerable belated with my calls. Susie?'

'Mmm?' said Susie, befuddled with an excess of well-being.

'Merry Christmas, Susie.'

'Been lovely,' said Susie dreamily.

'It's no blame to you, Mister Sammy,' said Mrs Brown, 'when a girl's come of age, like, it's her own blame.'

'Did it on me,' murmured Sammy wryly.

'Pardon?'

'So long,' said Sammy, and went.

'Oh, Mum.' Susie, having come to by half-past three, was aghast at herself. 'Lord above, what'll he think of me? I left all that work not done. I don't know how I'm goin' to look Mister Sammy in the face. Did he really say his mum's invited me for Boxin' Day tea?'

'He said his fam'ly would be that pleasured to have you, love. What got into you, all that port and all?'

'Everything was so exciting,' said Susie. 'I bet he won't even look at me on Boxin' Day. He took me to lunch, and then I didn't remember anything. Oh, he's goin' to be all growling, I'm sure he is. Me, his private secretary, goin' one over the eight. I'll have to cut my throat or take poison. It's awful, he'll never—' Susie, looking down at the kitchen range, broke off.

'Never what, lovey?' said Mrs Brown, mixing the pudding.

He'll never ask me to marry him now, thought Susie, I know he won't, he'll never marry anyone who gets tipsy in his offices on Christmas Eve.

'Oh, it doesn't matter,' she said.

'That's yours,' said Mrs Brown, pointing to an envelope on the mantelpiece. 'Mister Sammy put it in your coat pocket, and I took it out for you.'

Susie opened it. She drew out two crisp white fivers and a note written in a hurry by Sammy.

My compliments, and your bonus, Miss Brown. That's business. S. W. Adams.

Merry Christmas, Susie, see you Boxing Day for tea at my mother's, if you're free. Four o'clock. That's socialising. Love, Sammy.

Love, Sammy? And a whole ten pounds bonus? Ten pounds?

'Mum, look, a bonus of ten pounds.'

'Lawks alive,' gasped Mrs Brown, who had never seen two five-pound notes all at once.

'I'm goin' back to work,' said Susie, 'I've got to, it's only fair. I can work till six and do some late shoppin'.'

'Susie, I don't think Mister Sammy wants you to—'

'No, it's only right,' said Susie, and she went back to Camberwell, where the other girls were in high spirits and Boots was at work in his office. No one asked where she'd been. She sat down and attended to a stack of letters, writing out replies that Lottie could begin typing first thing after Christmas.

Love, Sammy.

276

Her head was a little like a floating puffball from the after-effects of the port, but was back to normal after Doreen had given her a strong cup of tea. Boots sent all the girls home early, electing not to argue when Susie told him she was staying until six. She was secretly hoping Sammy would be back. He wasn't. She left with Boots at five-past six, all the letters ready for Lottie.

'Did you receive an invitation for tea on Boxing Day?' asked Boots.

'Oh, yes. I'll love to come.'

'Love to have you. Merry Christmas, Susie.'

'Oh, you too, and all your fam'ly.'

Sammy left Shoreditch a little after six, in company with Tommy and Lilian. The machinists had left at six in rapturous disbelief, each with a bonus of five bob. Money of this kind left the firm's till as an outgoing investment.

Tommy took Lilian and Sammy home with him, where Aunt Victoria gave everyone a supper of poached fresh haddock with two poached eggs for each, and a great pile of crusty bread and butter. Lilian was touched. Tommy just didn't like to hear she was living on her own in one room in Battersea, and Vi and Aunt Victoria had happily arranged to entertain her for supper. She stayed on a while. Extrovert, she took the atmosphere of a Christian family on Christmas Eve in her stride, and liked the gentle nature of Tommy's wife.

It was Vi who saw Sammy out at ten to nine.

'Well, I tell yer, Vi, yer a treasure,' said Sammy in old-time fashion, 'and you got another little treasure in Alice. And yer mum's turned out a real homely female woman. You and Tommy all right?'

'Tommy's a dear,' said Vi, as placid as Emily was spirited.

277

'I'm considered fairly kind and lovin' meself,' said Sammy.

'You're considered smart,' said Vi.

'Kind of yer to say so, Vi.'

'Gertcher,' said Vi. 'Oh, but me and Tommy'll have enough saved by the spring to put down a big deposit for a house mortgage. We've been saving for ages, and now he's got his new job – Sammy, thanks ever so for that, and Mum couldn't be more proud now she's got a son-in-law who's a manager.'

'Well, Vi old girl, I didn't do Tommy any favours. It's fifty-fifty and mutual as well. Tommy knows what doing a good job's all about, and I know when I'm gettin' a good return. Also and further, I like his wife considerable, which is you, Vi. I like havin' yer in the fam'ly.'

'Oh, I better give you tuppence,' said Vi.

'What for?'

'Well, you still charge for getting a kiss, don't you?'

Sammy grinned. In his boyhood he had never kissed or allowed himself to be kissed without charging a penny.

'Merry Christmas, Vi, see you at dinner tomorrow,' he said, and kissed her. Then he went back to his office. It did not worry him that the place had a hollow ring, that he was the only one there, that it was Christmas Eve, some shops still open, carol singers abroad with their lanterns and pubs alive with revelry. Business fascinated him. He sat down at his desk to commence work on a multitude of matters. A letter stared up at him from his blotter, a letter from Susie.

Dear Mister Sammy, I don't know how to thank you for such a generous bonus, I really don't, but I'm terribly grateful. Also, Boots told me I'm invited to Boxing Day tea with your mother and family, which overwhelmed me with pleasure. I came back to the office at four, I felt I had to, I wanted to show I'd forgiven you for getting me drunk. I'm sure your intentions weren't dubious, which they are with certain men who've fallen from grace, I'm sure you're a trustworthy business gentleman as well as a reputable one, so I'm not going to say anything about how you poured all that port wine into me. I've done all the letters and they're ready for Lottie as soon as she gets in after Christmas. I wish you a very happy Christmas and I really do forgive you, Yours sincerely, Susie Brown.'

Sammy grinned. That Susie. The saucebox. She was trying to turn him upside-down.

I'll get you, Susie, I'll make you Mrs Sammy Adams, even if it costs me the lifeblood of my business.

CHAPTER TWENTY

Chinese Lady had her own reasons for inviting Miss Simms and Susie to the Boxing Day party. She did not divulge them, but at a quarter to four she addressed her family. They were all in the large sitting-room, where the old piano stood in the corner.

'Now, when our lady guests arrive, we won't have any larks, if you don't mind,' she said. 'Miss Simms is a respectable teacher and high-class, and that nice Susie Brown is comin' on to be as ladylike as our Vi, which I'm pleased Tommy noticed in good time. So we won't have any larks, I don't want Miss Simms or Susie to think I've got hooligans in my fam'ly.'

'Larks? What larks?' asked Ned.

'In my position, I can't afford larks,' said Sammy. 'It might get about.'

'Vi and me haven't met Miss Simms,' said Tommy. 'Would she do Bible readings?'

'Bible readings?' said Annabelle. 'At a party? Ugh.'

'We could ask for the Old Testament,' said Boots, 'there's blood and thunder in that.'

'I'll give you Old Testament, my lad,' said Chinese Lady.

'Nana, we could have some small larks, couldn't we?' said Rosie, her forehead showing the receding bruise. 'Only small ones. Daddy was splendiferous yesterday, doing Pass the Orange with Auntie Vi.'

'We don't want your Auntie Vi lookin' like she's been dragged through a hedge backwards again,' said Chinese Lady.

'Hooligan, that's what your daddy is, Tim,' said Lizzy.

Four-year-old Tim looked at his father and gave him a shy grin. Boots responded with a wink.

'Granny Lady,' said Annabelle, 'I quite like our hooligans.'

'Yes, they've all got saving graces, haven't they?' said Rosie. 'We have to count our blessings, Nana. About their saving graces, I mean.'

'I haven't noticed any,' said Emily.

'Nor me,' said Lizzy, giving toddling Edward a cuddle.

Vi said, 'Isn't it awful, Bobby, your daddy and all your uncles goin' to perdition one day?'

Five-year-old Bobby thought. Tim asked, 'Have they got train sets there?'

'Course they have,' said Bobby. 'My daddy said so. We're going there together.'

'Who said you was?' asked Tim.

'My mummy,' said Bobby.

Emily's laughter pealed. They had all enjoyed an hilarious Christmas Day party, and Emily was quite ready to enjoy more fun at this Boxing Day get-together. Her quicksilver energy always unleashed itself at family parties. During the progress of this one she was to make friends with Polly Simms. Chinese Lady had advised her to. Emily, of course, was going to make up her own mind about that.

Boots, answering a ring on the front doorbell, admitted Susie into the hall. Outside, the afternoon was dark, damp and foul. Susie compensated with her glowing colour.

'You're in the pink, I see,' said Boots, taking her hat and coat.

281

'Pink?' said Susie, thinking the hall and the house grand.

'Your nose,' said Boots.

'Oh, it's not, is it?'

'Fashionable at this time of the year,' said Boots, 'but cover it up, or all the girls will want one like it.'

Susie laughed and Boots gave her a Boxing Day kiss. Susie, in impulsive affection, hugged him for it just as Sammy appeared.

'Again?' said Sammy.

'Oh, don't be mean,' said Susie, 'it's Christmas.'

'It seems to be goin' on all the time, Miss Brown,' said Sammy. 'I'll see to her, Boots, I have formally informed the company I am takin' her to inspect the kitchen of this palatial residence. This way, Miss Brown.'

'Pardon?' said Susie.

'You're surprised?' said Boots. 'Don't be. We always insist on new visitors inspecting the kitchen.'

'But I haven't paid me respects to your mother,' said Susie.

'Later,' said Sammy. 'Kindly accompany me, Miss Brown.'

Boots, his smile close to the surface, went back into the sitting-room. Susie, wearing an ultramarine dress quite new, lifted cool blue eyes to Sammy.

'Very well, Mister Adams, but I hope you don't have any ideas about growling at me.' She went with him. The handsomeness of the kitchen made her sigh. 'Oh, I never saw any kitchen so posh,' she said.

'Never mind that,' said Sammy. 'What I am concerned about, Miss Brown, is my shockin' discovery that you're a little Turk.'

'Well, I don't know what my parents are goin' to say to that,' said Susie. 'I wasn't found in some Turkish baths, you know.'

'Kindly don't give me no innocent looks,' said Sammy.

'Really, Mister Adams, you're conductin' yourself very growling, and I don't know what your mother must be thinking, me not paying respects to her.'

'I have informed my mother I am obliged to deal severely with you,' said Sammy sternly, who thought that in ultramarine blue and with her hair newly shingled, Susie could knock 'em for six down the Old Kent Road.

'Oh, you're goin' to hit me now, are you?' she said.

'You saucebox,' said Sammy, 'what d'you mean by writing down in black and white that I poured a gallon of port wine into you?'

'Really, Mister Adams, I thought that was over and done with after I'd forgiven you for makin' me unconscious with drink.' Susie put her nose in the air, giving not the slightest hint of how much she was enjoying herself. 'It's not hardly my fault if it's still on your conscience.'

'See that?' said Sammy, pointing upwards. Susie lifted her eyes and found mistletoe depending from the ceiling. Sammy swooped. 'Oh—' He cut her off. Susie went dizzy. He was kissing her. It lasted for ever, or almost for ever. Bliss and colour suffused her, and when the end of the world had been reached her face was as flushed as the sky at final sunset. 'Oh,' she gasped faintly, 'did you hit me, then, was that what it was?'

'My eye and Betty Martin,' said Sammy, 'you're still at it, you're still banging my ears about.'

Susie, exhilaration overcoming faintness, drew herself up and said, 'Sammy Adams, you kissed me.'

'Yes, and I'm likely to do it again, any minute, Susie Brown.'

'Very well, Mister Adams, I'm only your helpless employee and a defenceless girl, and if I don't let you I suppose you'll sack me and really hit me. I hope you'll be able to live with your unChristian conduct, makin' me drunk on Christmas Eve and hittin' me on Boxing Day.'

'Oh, my achin' head,' said Sammy, and roared with laughter.

Annabelle put her head round the door.

'Uncle Sammy, Granny Lady says if you don't kindly come and present Miss Brown to the family, she'll come and see what you're up to. Hello, Miss Brown.'

'Hello, Annabelle,' smiled Susie.

'We're comin',' said Sammy.

'Uncle Sammy?'

'What's up?' asked Sammy, ushering Susie to the door.

'Uncle Sammy,' said Annabelle gravely, 'you've got lipstick. And you're ever so pink, Miss Brown.'

Susie knew all the family. They greeted her like an old friend, and she felt quite swamped by the warmth and affection. It made her eyes misty. Sammy's mother was very kind and welcoming, and said how pleasured she was that Sammy had such a ladylike assistant. Tommy kissed her very affectionately. So did Ned. Emily was sparkling, Lizzy vivacious, Vi charming. And Susie thought what a lovely young girl Rosie was, despite her forehead still showing a faint bruise.

Chinese Lady intended to serve tea at four-fifteen, but by four-thirty Polly had still not arrived. At twenty to five she asked what had happened to her.

'She's forgotten, I expect,' said Emily.

'Oh, she wouldn't be casual like that,' said Lizzy, who liked the schoolteacher because she was so good with the schoolkids.

'Well, we can't wait and do nothing,' said Sammy crisply. 'Phone her, Boots. If she's forgotten, I recommend a large helping of tactfulness. We don't want to lose the orphanage business, it's a steady income for the Camberwell shop.'

'You and your business,' said Lizzy, 'you ought to be hung out to dry with the orphanage blankets.'

'She might of had a collapse comin' here,' said Chinese Lady.

'I'll phone,' said Boots. He and Sammy both had the number of Lady Simms's house. The butler answered, informing Boots that Miss Polly had left in her car at just after four. Boots disliked the sound of that. Her family's mansion-like house in Dulwich was no more than a six- or seven-minute drive away. She was half an hour late. Boots asked the butler if he knew whether Polly had intended to drive straight to North Dulwich.

'I was hinformed by Miss Polly at where she would be at this evening, sir, and was not given no himpression she was hobliged to call in somewhere else on her way. May I henquire if we are to be in concern?'

'I'll let you know,' said Boots, and hung up.

'I don't like it,' said Chinese Lady when Boots recounted the conversation.

'Boots, didn't you speak to her parents?' asked Ned.

'They left for the South of France today,' said Boots.

'Which they won't get to until tomorrow morning,' said Ned. 'It's in our lap.'

'I'll get my hat and coat,' said Boots.

'I'll come with you,' said Sammy.

'Yes, you best go and see,' said Chinese Lady.

'I'll go with them,' said Tommy.

'We don't want everyone leavin', Tommy,' said Chinese Lady, but saw Boots give him a nod. Yes, Tommy knew most about cars, of course, being an engineer.

Boots took a torch, and the three brothers, over-coated against the damp cold, made their way along the road in the direction of Dulwich. Street lamps cast misty light. Behind drawn curtains, house lights dimly glowed. There was no one about. People were tucked into their homes, seated around their coal fires, the toys and games given as Christmas presents the focal point of family enjoyment.

At the end of the road they turned into Half Moon Lane, eyes peering and searching the darkness. Boots stopped.

'Half a minute,' he said. They had just passed a half-demolished house at the end of the road. The remains of the residence stood in a third of an acre of overgrown grounds. He turned back, Tommy and Sammy with him. He switched on the torch and flashed its beam over the road. The beam swept the immediate stretch of road, then the pavement. He held the torch steady. The wet pavement was marked by the muddy streaks of skidding tyres. The beam traced the course of the streaks to the open front of a neglected garden. A forest of weeds lay crushed in two parallel lines.

'God,' breathed Tommy.

Boots moved forward, and the beam of light played over tangled undergrowth and came to rest on the back of a car, its bonnet close to the rubble of demolition. Boots knew what had happened. It was so typical of Polly. Only at school was her behaviour constrained. Outside of it, she was as mad as ever. The misty darkness of the wintry afternoon and the greasiness of the roads would have held no terror for a woman who had driven her great square box of an ambulance over the torn, muddy roads of France and Flanders. She had taken this corner in reckless defiance of conditions and she had run out of road. No one had seen her, no one had heard her. These were not the crowded, close-packed streets of Walworth.

The thoughts travelled fast through his mind as he ploughed his way around the crashed car, the wet undergrowth soaking shoes and trousers. He pulled open the driving door. Sammy was behind him, Tommy on the other side of the car. He played the torch. There she was, huddled over the steering wheel, arms limp, round fur hat squashed down over her head. Fragments of glass glittered in the fur. The windscreen was smashed. The passenger door, slightly buckled, was wrenched open by Tommy.

'Won't be moved, Boots. Hit the rubble. I think the front axle's gone. Hell, she looks bad.'

'Run back home and phone, Tommy. Call an ambulance.'

An ambulance for Polly.

Tommy dug himself out of the undergrowth and ran. Leaning in, Boots carefully brought Polly back against the seat, Sammy holding the torch. Polly's face was white and waxy, eyes closed.

'Don't like it,' said Sammy tersely.

Boots said, 'Polly?'

She opened her eyes. Cloudily, they saw him.

'Been a hell of a day, old sport . . . and so cold . . . so cold . . .'

Her eyes closed. Boots felt a strange, intense affection for this brittle, extrovert woman who had lived with the sound of the guns for four long courageous years, and conceived a lasting love for the bitter, caustic men of the trenches. Her Tommies, she always called them.

'*Watcher, Polly, old girl, come to pick up Bert, 'ave yer? Well, there's 'is left leg and there's 'is tin lid. Dunno where the rest of 'im is.*'

Boots had heard that kind of comment from soldiers to women ambulance drivers.

There was no blood, but he could smell some. Blood he could always smell.

'Sammy, get round to the other side. Give me some light from there. She's bleeding and we've got to find where.'

'Got you, Boots,' said Sammy, and tramped his way round to the open passenger door, from where he gave

287

Boots light from the torch. Polly was inert, her head heavy, shoulders sagging.

'Hold her, Sammy – gently now.'

Sammy, reaching in, pressed Polly's left shoulder back, keeping her upright in the driving seat. He shone the torch over her. Boots's nostrils tracked the blood. He opened up her fur coat. She was wearing a plain russet-coloured dress of simple style, not a creation to stun. Boots saw wetness. He drew dress and slip up. Blood pulsed. There was a savage gash above her left knee, the stocking ripped. The gear lever, he thought.

'God,' said Sammy, 'her life's running away, that's a foot long, that gash.'

'Hold her, Sammy.'

Sammy held her, gently but firmly, and left the rest to Boots. It was Boots's moment. He was a man who had been wounded three times, and then blinded. Sammy saw the soldier in his brother go to work. He took Polly's shoes off. He unclipped her stockings and removed them, working fast. He discarded the soaked one. He tore a large button from her fur coat, his wrench savage. With the button and the right stocking he made a tourniquet around her left thigh, above the gash. He used a propelling pencil from his inside jacket pocket to tighten the stocking. It bit into Polly's strong, smooth thigh.

'Hell, that's tight, Boots,' said Sammy.

Boots held the tourniquet and watched. The slowly pumping blood from a ruptured artery gradually diminished. He made another turn. The pumping stopped, to become a small seeping. He tightened a little more and fixed the tourniquet.

'Hold on, Polly,' he said. Sammy gave him a look. Boots's expression was a strangely bitter one. Boots was thinking of Major Harris, his commanding officer, who had bled to death in Trones Wood on the Somme because that German grenade had blasted fiery light before he could apply tourniquets to legs riddled above the knees. He covered Polly's legs, drew her fur coat to and buttoned it up. Polly did not move or speak or moan.

'Worth saving, if we can, Sammy,' he said.

'I know,' said Sammy. 'Up to Tommy now.'

Boots sucked on his pipe and watched Polly. Sammy lit a cigarette.

Tommy had been quick, literally barging his way into the house the moment Emily answered his summons. The ambulance arrived not long after Tommy got back to the car. It rushed Polly to hospital. Boots went with her. Sammy and Tommy both thought he should. They returned to the house, where Sammy phoned Lady Simms's butler. Everyone was upset by the news, but Emily understood about Boots going with Polly to the hospital.

'Yes, someone's got to decide if her parents need to come back,' said Chinese Lady. The evening was any old how. 'I'll put the kettle on. I hope some of you will sit down to a bit of tea.'

Rosie and Annabelle shed a little tear for their teacher.

'Well?' said Boots.

The doctor on duty in casualty looked him over.

'What's your blood group?' he asked.

'It was A positive when I was in the Army,' said Boots.

'Good. Come this way. You don't mind, do you? She needs a generous transfusion. She'll have a chance then. Who applied that tourniquet?'

'I did,' said Boots, going with the doctor.

'Well, if she lives, she can thank you.'

The evening was well advanced, and the damp mist had turned into wet fog as a million chimneys emitted the smoke of coal fires into the cloudy sky. But there was some faint colour back in Polly's cheeks. Her neatly bobbed hair looked dark against the white pillow, and her eyes were open.

'Good as new,' said the doctor, and left Boots to have a couple of minutes with her. She looked vaguely up at him, she focused, and a little smile touched her mouth.

'Did it in,' she said. Boots nodded. She smiled again, faintly. 'What've I got?' she asked.

'A hundred stitches and two ruined stockings. And they think you've caught Rosie's complaint. Concussion. Your fur hat saved you from worse.'

'My head's lousy,' said Polly. She frowned and thought. 'Stupid wheels left the road,' she said. 'Who dug me out?'

'Sammy, Tommy and self,' said Boots.

'Good old sport,' she sighed.

'There's a silver lining,' said Boots, 'you've missed the torture of Forfeits and Postman's Knock.'

'I was counting on not missing that.'

'Time's up, Mr Adams,' said a nurse. 'That's all.'

'Except for this,' said Boots, and gave Polly what she had missed in Postman's Knock, an affectionate, comradely kiss on her lips.

'There's a good old scout,' she murmured, and her eyes closed.

Sammy took Susie home after a somewhat disjointed evening, although it had been a relief to all when Boots returned with the news that Miss Simms was recovering, not dying. Emily had asked why he had been so long at the hospital. Boots said it wasn't every day that Polly made a mess of herself and her car, so he'd stayed to hold her hand. In a manner of speaking. Emily gave him a searching look. Boots gave her a smile. But she knew that smile of his. It didn't always mean what it seemed to. For the first time the firmness of their

290

marital ground felt a little unsteady beneath her feet. She supposed if she could be tempted, so could he, and that Polly Simms, with her glittering, artificial smile and her silk stockings, was a temptress all right.

Oh, blow and bother, am I going to have to watch my husband and that Polly Simms?

Susie and Sammy caught a bus. It trundled slowly through creeping, rising fog. Susie said she was so sorry about Miss Simms. Sammy said no, be glad for her, she could have been a goner and would have been if Boots hadn't done a fast first-aid job on her.

'Some people think Boots is airy-fairy, but don't you believe it. He only seems as if he is. Well, all right, he does take most things a bit easy, but not when the kettle's boiling over. Dubious geezers is well advised to stand clear then.'

'I think he's lovely,' said Susie.

'Well, I know you're on a kissing relationship with him, of course.'

'I'll kick you, Sammy Adams, and on this public bus too.'

'Which behoves me to say, Susie Brown, it's a grievous pain to know my own kind self has to put up with you being on a kickin' relationship with me. It ain't partic'larly Christian, y'know.'

'Really, Mister Adams, I don't know anyone who sometimes deserves kickin' more than you. And I bite as well. Sometimes.'

'Fares, if yer please, and if it ain't disturbin' yer too much,' said the conductor, making a sudden appearance. Sammy fished out coppers and the conductor clipped tickets. 'Is the young lady yer Christmas present, guv?'

'Not yet,' said Sammy, 'and she's still givin' me problems.'

'I got some of them. Me feet's perishing, to start with. And me missus put burnt Yorkshire pudden on me plate with the Christmas beef. I dunno, life don't 'ardly seem worth gettin' up for sometimes. Still, I've 'eard it's an improvement on being dead.' The conductor moved along. 'Fares, if yer please, ladies an' gents.'

'Cheerful old Charlie, that one,' observed Sammy. He was sitting with Susie at the back of the top deck, a dozen other passengers way down from them. He felt a little sober on account of Polly and her crashed car, but it did not affect the pleasure of being with Susie. 'It occurs to me,' he said, as wet fog and the dim glow of street lamps slid by, 'that new plans for you next year is needful and likewise necessary.'

'What plans?' asked Susie.

'Pardon?' said Sammy.

'What plans?'

'New Year's Eve,' murmured Sammy, talking to himself.

'New Year's Eve?'

'Highly appropriate now Christmas Eve's been and gone,' said Sammy. Yes, he thought, the pantomime and the revelry. But no port, not for Susie. By New Year's Eve, he'd be in firm command of himself, and have the right words ready. *I am concerned to know, Miss Brown, if you would do me the honour of becoming my wife.* No, considerable honour? No, great honour? No, loving honour. Right. Loving honour. There ought to be a touch of that. 'Yes, New Year's Eve,' he said in decisive cowardice.

'Pardon me, I'm sure, for not knowing what you mean,' said Susie. If the evening had not been hilarious, because of poor Miss Simms, there had been all the pleasure of being with the family she liked so much. And Sammy had given her the kiss of a lifetime.

The trundling bus began to pull up.

'Our stop, Susie,' said Sammy. He was off the bus first. He gave her his hand. She liked that. He was well brought up. He took her cautiously across the foggy road to Browning Street. She put her arm through his.

'You haven't said what plans you've got for me, or what New Year's Eve means,' she said.

'I'm just hoping, Susie Brown, that on New Year's Eve you'll lay off the port.'

'And I'm just hoping you won't pour none down my throat,' said Susie.

Sammy laughed. He guided her through the fog to her door. He kissed her, lightly this time.

'You're a lovely girl, Susie. Good night,' he said, and left her glowing.

CHAPTER TWENTY-ONE

Emily, back at work the following day, took completed letters to Mr Barry Somerville at twenty past twelve.

'Thank you, Emily. Enjoy your Christmas?'

'Yes, thank you.' Emily, in a dark green costume and neat white blouse, had an acquired elegance that took Mr Somerville's eye as usual. Her trim figure, her personality and her marvellous green eyes discounted the plainness of her thin cheeks and pointed chin.

'I saw your husband on Christmas Eve, in the sandwich bar of the pub,' he said in friendly fashion. 'He seemed to be enjoying himself too.' He felt, of course, that if Emily's husband had a piece of stuff on the side, it was an infernal cheek for the man to take umbrage with him.

'With drink?' said Emily, eyes cool.

'With a rather attractive lady,' said Mr Somerville junior.

'Yes, I know,' said Emily, coolness changing to contempt. 'A friend of ours. He was invitin' her to tea with us on Boxing Day. Good morning, Mr Somerville.'

She left his office. She put her hat and coat on. The other girl said, 'Where you going?'

'Home,' said Emily.

'But it's not one o'clock yet.'

'Tell Mr Barry Somerville hard luck,' said Emily.

She crossed the road. The day was misty again, but

not wetly misty. High above, the sun was trying to break through. She walked to the Bargain Bazaar and through the shop, saying good morning to the manageress on the way. She went up the stairs and into Boots's office. He was at his desk, his hand in his hair, fiddling with his scalp, a fountain pen in his hand. He turned his head.

'Emily?' He came to his feet. Emily realised her husband had very nice ways with him. He always came to his feet for a member of her sex.

'Boots.' She went close to him and kissed him.

'What's that for?'

'Oh, just to show you. Boots, you offered for me to work for the firm. Is it still on? Oh, just mornings, of course, just something more than all-day housework.'

'You'd really like that?'

'Ever so much. It's safest.'

Boots smiled.

'Does safest appeal to you?'

'Yes, it does, when it's safest for me and you.'

'Well, I suppose we ought to take care of what we've got,' said Boots.

'And we've got a good marriage really, don't you think so?'

'Good enough for us to keep working at it,' said Boots. His phone rang. He picked it up and answered it. Emily quickly recognised there was someone obstreperous on the line. Boots didn't get vexed or impatient, even though he obviously kept being interrupted by the angry voice. He calmed the caller down in the end.

'What was that all about?' asked Emily.

'Oh, a supplier trying to suggest we'd promised to pay on delivery instead of asking for the usual twenty-eight days' credit,' said Boots, and Emily wondered if all her husband's calmness and airy-fairy front didn't hide a much deeper man than she'd thought.

'I been a bit worried about you lately,' she said.

'Worried?'

'Yes. Boots, you're not in love with Polly Simms, are you?'

'Not yet,' said Boots.

'Oh, what d'yer mean, not yet?' she flashed.

'I'm not in love with Polly Simms yet.'

'That's not tellin' me what you mean!'

'Yes, it is. It's telling you I'm still in love with you.'

Emily shook her head at him and smiled wryly.

'Oh, yer cuss,' she said, 'you're always doing that to me.'

'Doing what to you?'

'Takin' the ground from under me feet,' said Emily, and kissed him.

A tap on the door preceded the entry of Doreen, carrying a file.

'Oh, sorry, beg yer pardon – oh, sorry, Mrs Adams.' She fled.

'She's not used to seeing us rubbing noses,' said Boots.

'I don't care,' said Emily.

'About the job,' said Boots.

'Yes, I'm serious, honest,' said Emily. 'Is there one for me? I mean a proper one, not one that isn't.'

'We don't place lady applicants in improper positions, Em. Sammy wouldn't allow it, and Chinese Lady would pull the place down.'

'You'll be the death of me and Chinese Lady with your comic stuff,' said Emily. 'Boots, I do shorthand-typin' now, you know.'

'I do know,' said Boots. 'You're going to be a godsend. We're expanding fast. Sammy wants to transfer the shop below to other premises and convert the space into more offices. The Council's refused permission. They won't allow change of usage. Sammy's still going to transfer the shop business to other premises. Just around the corner of the Green, in Camberwell New Road. Then he'll cut the shop space down to a third and just sell children's clothes. That'll take care of no change of usage. It's a large shop and deep. Two-thirds of it will convert to two offices. For more staff.'

'But how long will that take?' asked Emily.

'Oh, you can start now,' said Boots. 'In here, with me. I'll order a desk for you, and a typewriter, I'll give you dictation and also a little bookkeeping work. I'm run off my feet, and you'll be our first shorthand-typist. I'll talk to Sammy about what we'll pay you. Sammy might want to grab you for your shorthand-typing, but with Susie in charge of all his correspondence, it won't do for you to take dictation from her.'

'I don't mind working with a woman,' said Emily.

'You'll be working for her. You're the wife of a director. You can't work for an employee, Em. For Sammy and me, yes. Got that, lovey?'

'I got you, Boots,' said Emily. That was something Boots and Tommy and Sammy often said to each other. It went back to their days as Walworth cockneys.

'Well, stick with us, Em, and you'll be a director yourself one day.'

'Me a director?'

'You've got brains, love, and Sammy likes as many family brains in the firm as possible. In addition, a fancy dress and an elegant pair of legs on the board will make it better-looking.'

'Lucky for you you mentioned my brains,' said Emily, 'or I might've thought you was lookin' forward to the Can-Can at directors' meetings. But I can really start next Monday week, say?'

'You're on,' said Boots.

'Bless yer. Yer still good for a girl, ain't yer, Boots?

I'm off home now. I'll tell Chinese Lady I'm comin' to work for the firm. In the mornings.'

'I think in my lunch hour I'd better pop in to see Polly.'

'Yes, well, all right,' said Emily, 'but don't get into bed with her or I'll kill you.'

'You can't,' said a nurse.

'Can't what?' asked Boots.

'You can't visit a patient, not at this time of the day.'

'I keep having these problems,' said Boots.

'We keep having ours,' said the nurse.

Boots rubbed his chin. The nurse eyed him warily. He smiled.

'Mine give me a headache,' he said.

'So do mine,' she said.

'Well, I'll only be a minute,' said Boots.

'You won't,' said the nurse.

'I'll just slip in when your back's turned.'

'I'm not turning my back.'

'Don't blame you,' said Boots, 'you've got a perfect front.'

'My word, that's too much,' said the nurse. 'Sister is with Matron. I shall go and report you to both of them.' And she turned her back and walked crisply down the corridor. Boots slipped into the ward. Several female patients, sitting up in digestive repose after their lunch, eyed him with interest. Another nurse eyed him with suspicion.

'Dr Adams,' said Boots, 'to see Miss Simms. Ah, there she is.' His hat in his hand, his overcoat over his arm, he approached Polly. Polly, who had seen him and heard him, wanted to shout with laughter. Shock and concussion were going to keep her hospitalised for a few days. Her head still felt a little tender, her leg a little sore. Otherwise, she was fine, apart from being bored out of

298

her wits. The arrival of Boots charged her with adrenalin. She lay with her head and shoulders resting on heaped pillows.

'Oh, good morning, Dr Adams,' she said.

'How are we today?' asked Boots.

'You'd better take a look,' said Polly. 'Nurse, would you put the screens up, please?'

The nurse came over.

'Well, I don't know—'

'What d'you mean, you don't know?' asked Polly. 'I'm not going to be examined in public, I hope.'

'But I don't know Dr Adams, and no one's said—'

'Well, I know him,' said Polly, 'he's my personal physician.'

'But Sister James hasn't said—'

'Look, don't muck about, darling. What kind of a hospital is this?'

The nurse looked at Boots. He responded with a nod of gravity.

'I'm sorry, Dr Adams,' she said, and wheeled the screens into position around the bed. Boots looked down at Polly, her bobbed hair slightly ruffled by the pillows. Her smile was full of silent laughter.

'Monkey,' he murmured.

'Monkey yourself, you started it. I heard you. Oh, joy. Besides, you look like a doctor in your grey suit. My, how very distinguished. You can examine me now. Not all over. Just my bosom. It's slightly bruised but otherwise perfect. Do examine it thoroughly, won't you?'

'We're better, are we?' said Boots.

'Certainly not. I'm ill. My leg's a swine. Oh, hell, I think I'm going to have a scar. I'm badly in need of your bedside manner. It's bliss to see you, darling, really. Are you going to examine me?'

'Not today, Miss Simms, I'm pressed for time, but glad you're all in one piece.'

299

'Your doing, darling. They told me about the tourniquet, and the blood transfusion. You gave some of yours. I'm joyful. You're going round and round in my veins. Jolly giddying that is, old sport. Were my legs a mess, or did you like them?'

'Did it all with my eyes shut, Polly. I've had your car towed away for repair. Your butler's got all the details. But ride a bicycle from now on or I'll worry about you.'

'I like the idea of you worrying about me.'

Whispers outside the screen suddenly culminated in the rise of a sharp voice. The screens were opened up and the formidable presence of Matron Ramsey was revealed.

'Must dash, Miss Simms,' said Boots, 'I've got my surgery and an outbreak of mumps.'

Polly, the silent laughter bright in her eyes, watched him sidle adroitly past the Matron and two nurses. One nurse was trying to hide a smile. Boots was out of the ward before the Matron could catch her outraged breath.

'Miss Simms,' she said.

'Sorry, old thing,' said Polly.

'I won't have this kind of behaviour.'

'Sorry, dear lady,' said Polly.

'Who was he?'

'No idea,' said Polly, 'never seen him before.'

'But you said he was your personal physician,' protested the second nurse.

'I wasn't seeing straight. Isn't concussion rotten on the eyes?'

The outraged Matron said, 'Good heavens, did he examine you?'

'No,' said Polly. 'Worse luck,' she murmured.

'Pardon?'

'What a bounder, though,' said Polly. Matron quivered. 'My father, General Sir Henry Simms, may be visiting tonight. He's on his way back from the South of France. Fred telegraphed him.'

'Fred?'

'Our butler.'

'Ah,' said Matron, 'I see. Yes, very well.'

Polly smiled. It was quite useful sometimes, her father being a baronet. She hoped her leg wouldn't be badly scarred. She always felt both her legs belonged to Robert. In a certain way. One day that certain way would arrive. One day. Or one night.

Susie had a busy day. Sammy was conspicuous by his absence. He was with Lilian at the Shoreditch factory, absorbed in the promise and potential of his biggest venture, and pouring all available capital into Adams Fashions. He did not appear in his Camberwell office until nearly five-thirty. Susie went in to see him.

'Good evening, Mister Adams.'

'Good evening, Miss Brown,' said Sammy at his desk. He glanced up. 'Is that a new office dress?' It was dark blue with white cuffs and white collar.

'I have only worn it on and off for several months, Mister Adams, includin' when I was banished in Brixton.'

'Well, it suits you on, I won't give an opinion when it's off.'

'I am gratified you noticed it, Mister Adams,' she said. 'After several months,' she added.

'Quite so,' said Sammy, leafing through papers in his Gladstone bag.

My, thought Susie, we are getting a posh man of business, aren't we, Sammy Adams darling.

'It suits you,' she said.

'What does?' asked Sammy.

'Quite so,' said Susie.

Sammy, extracting papers and keeping his face

straight, said, 'I am takin' no notice of that, Miss Brown. I happen to have concluded it don't advantage me to exchange verbal wordage with a female woman.'

'Well, no, of course not, Mister Adams, us female women are ever so much smarter, aren't we?'

'I didn't hear that, Miss Brown.' Sammy perused the papers.

'You ought to see a doctor about your ears, Mister Adams.'

'I know that. They're full up with ringing bells. But I haven't got time. Madame Dupont sent her regards, by the way.'

'Yes, thank you, Mister Adams.' Susie felt that in leaving Brixton she had exchanged dull old routine for moments of heavenly delight. 'I'd like to tell you before I go that all outstandin' letters have been done and signed and put in the post. And my new typewriter's come and—'

'What new typewriter?'

'Oh, Mister Adams senior ordered it for me.'

'Mister Adams who?'

'Your eldest brother, Mister Adams. Boots.'

'I'm watching you, Miss Brown, and I'm listening to you, and I've got ringing bells again.'

'Oh, dear, couldn't you try cotton wool soaked in warm olive oil?' asked Susie, looking earnest with concern.

'No, I couldn't. I'll just cut me head off and throw it away. Regardin' the typewriter, I don't recollect signin' the indent.'

'Oh, I'm so sorry, Mister Adams, I think Boots just went and ordered it. I've bought myself a Pitman's Typin' Manual, and I'm staying on each evening to teach myself touch-typin'. Touch-typin's best, Mister Adams, and I can learn it quicker this way than at evening classes. It's ever so consid'rate of you to let me practise here in my office.'

302

'Susie Adams—'

'Pardon?' said Susie.

'Now what've I said?' Sammy was past all help. The pangs of love were crucifying him.

'You called me Susie Adams.'

'It's all that ringing,' said Sammy. 'It makes me unconscious.'

'Oh, Susie Adams come out unconscious, Mister Sammy?' she enquired, blue eyes wide and innocent. She could have told him how much she liked the sound of Susie Adams.

'Never mind,' said Sammy. He muttered a bit. Susie smiled. He looked at his pocket watch. 'It's too late, I suppose, for someone to make me a cup of tea and find me a biscuit?'

'Yes, everyone's just goin',' said Susie.

'All right, never mind,' said Sammy, and got down to his papers again. Susie gazed lovingly at him.

'I'll do it,' she said.

'You're a lovely girl, Susie.'

It caught at her breath, that endearment, it was spoken so easily, so nicely, and with a little upward glance and a little smile before he bent his head again. Susie knew then that she loved him very much, because it almost hurt. She made him a pot of tea, took it in on a tray, with several biscuits, and placed it on his desk. He was so absorbed by then that he only murmured his thanks. She didn't mind. He was always going to be a man of business, but what you had to remember about him was that for all his ambition he didn't tread people into the ground, and however high he rose he was never going to leave his family behind.

Susie very much wanted to be part of that family.

In her own office she began to teach herself the first basic rudiments of touch-typing.

*   *   *

'Tommy?' said Vi, when he arrived home from work the following day.

'Watcher, Vi,' said Tommy, kissing her.

'I just missed,' said Vi. 'Well, nearly three weeks, actually.'

'Missed?'

'Oh, you know, silly. Tommy, I think we might be goin' to have another baby.'

'Help,' said Tommy.

'Aren't you pleased?'

'I ought to be, it's a consequence of me virile manhood.'

'You can say that again,' said Vi.

'You're welcome, Mrs Adams. Give us another kiss.' Vi, always responsive, kissed him warmly. 'But it's a bit soon for you, Alice only being seven months.'

'Just tell me, are you pleased?'

'I'm gladsome for both of us. Yer a lovely wonder, Vi, you're me own private Empire Day and me own Vilma Banky.' Vilma Banky was a film star who had played opposite Rudolph Valentino.

'All that?' Vi laughed.

'I'll do the cookin',' said Tommy.

'I shan't tell Mum and Dad till I know for certain.'

'That makes sense,' said Tommy. 'Still, I think I'll go and tell Alice.'

'She's in her cot – wait a minute, what d'you mean, you'll tell her? She won't understand a word you're saying, not at seven months, you silly.'

'Course she will,' said Tommy, 'she's an Adams. Chinese Lady don't allow any Adams to be born that don't understand another Adams.'

'I think all the Adams are a bit barmy,' said Vi.

'Who said that?' asked Tommy from the door.

'Me,' said Vi. 'Barmy nice, though, not barmy peculiar.'

'I'll tell Alice that as well. Good on yer, Vi love.'

'Good on you too, Tommy love.'

CHAPTER TWENTY-TWO

On New Year's Eve, the whole family attended the pantomime at the Camberwell Palace Theatre, except for little Alice and young Edward, both of whom were with Aunt Victoria and Uncle Tom. Aunt Victoria had actually invited everyone round after the performance was over, and to have a drink and see the New Year in.

The pantomime, *Dick Whittington*, was like all of its kind, full of nonsensical dialogue, terrible jokes, tinselled costumes, foul villainy, traditional songs and contrived absurdities, all of which delighted the audience, especially the children. Everything was magic to the children. Minor music hall stars played the main parts, but the cat, of course, was everybody's favourite. There was a magician too. He came on while the rest of the cast and the scene shifters prepared for the entry of Dick into London. He was dressed in black, with a top hat and black stick. He did conjuring tricks and made magic, producing things out of nowhere, even out of the ears of little girls and boys whom he induced to come up on the stage. He had a lady assistant, Vivette, who wore a kind of basque that shaped her voluptuous form, and flesh-coloured tights that sheathed her legs and handsome thighs. Chinese Lady, Tim on one side of her and Bobby on the other, took silent umbrage at such a revealing costume, and thought the people who whistled at it very common and vulgar. Vivette was very sweet to the boys and girls who let the magician pull cards or eggs or pennies out of their ears. Her smile for them was flashing, and she gave each of them a sweet as she led them off.

Boots thought the magician past his best. He fumbled some of his sleight-of-hand stuff, and his disappearing tricks were very old hat. His lady assistant's permanent smile looked very fixed at times. She wore a tinsel star in her wavy mass of auburn hair. Boots found himself watching her, wondering why he thought there was something familiar about her. The auburn hair, as darkly fiery as Emily's, ought to strike a chord, but didn't. He concentrated more on her round face and round eyes.

The familiar something resolved itself just as the act came to an end. He glanced at Rosie beside him. She was clapping, her face alight with the pleasure of a girl entertained. Rainbould the Master Magician bowed, then turned and flourished a hand at Vivette, who responded to applause and more whistles by blowing kisses. Rosie clapped her too, then whispered to Boots.

'Eyes off, Daddy, Nana's going to have something to say about her not wearing a blouse and skirt.'

Boots gave his foster daughter a smile. Rosie winked at him, and Boots knew she had not recognised her natural mother. The auburn hair was a wig, of course, and beneath it was the round face of Milly Pearce, the woman who had deserted Rosie, her illegitimate daughter. Boots was sure he was making no mistake. Rosie had been a mere child of five then, and her picture of her mother would have quickly faded. He wondered if Chinese Lady had recognised the woman. Or if Emily had. Or Tommy and Sammy, for that matter.

As the magician and his assistant began to withdraw to the wings, the theatre manager came quickly on to the stage.

'Ladies and gentlemen, a moment, please. If Mr Samuel Adams is in the house, would he be so good as to come to my office immediately. Thank you, thank you, the show will now go on.'

'Excuse me a tick,' said Sammy to Susie, and Susie nodded, wondering what could be up.

In the theatre office, the manager advised Sammy that the Shoreditch police had telephoned to say his factory was on fire.

'Eh?' said Sammy.

'They thought you should know. One of your workers reported it to the police.'

'Christ,' said Sammy, and ran, just as he was, in his suit, with no hat and no overcoat. Outside the theatre, he was lucky. It was New Year's Eve and there were London taxis about. One took him all the way to Shoreditch, and at speed under the promise of a generous tip.

Gertie, thought Sammy. She lived nearest the factory, and he had told her only this afternoon that he was going to the pantomime. He fretted and he worried. He had to rest his hopes in the quickness of the fire brigade. All the machines and the collection, all that material, material that was awaiting the first orders he and Lilian hoped to obtain for her collection. And many completed garments in cheaper material for his own shops, but not to be released to them until the Paris show began.

He saw the glow in the sky before he reached the factory. As the taxi turned the corner of the street, he saw the flames and the hoses of the firemen spouting arching streams of water. A policeman stopped the taxi before it reached the edge of a watching crowd. Sammy got out, quickly paid the driver and pushed himself through the crowd.

Gertie, the senior machinist, saw him. She hurried up to him.

'Oh, gawd 'elp us, Mister Adams, it's goin' to burn to the ground. That Daft Dick, the bleeder, he ain't never been safe with matches in 'is mitt. Morris did it on yer when 'e sent Daft Dick along to keep the yard clean. 'E's kept it clean all right, and 'e's made 'is bonfire 'eaps all right with cardboard boxes and every bit o' stuff Ma's swept orf the fact'ry floor. Mister Adams, is it goin' to sink yer?'

Sammy, watching the blazing factory and the playing hoses, felt as sick as a dog. Adams Fashions was all going up in fire and smoke.

'Bloody hell,' he said.

'Me too,' said Gertie, hair a tangle, arms crossed over her chest, hands clasping and digging at her thin arms. 'I'm cryin' me bleedin' eyes out. Yer didn't deserve this, Mister Adams.'

Sammy watched the high, leaping flames that shot sparks and smoke, flames that were consuming and destroying building, machines, benches, stockroom, everything. The hoses played, but he knew the firemen were fighting a losing battle. The factory was a roaring furnace. Glass exploded.

The faces of the crowd were lifted to the blaze, eyes glittering in red reflection of the blaze. There was something horribly fascinating about a fire such as this. It drew people and it held them mesmerised and rooted. It even excited some, such was the awesome spectacle of elemental destruction. The sparks soared in mockery of the firemen's efforts, and the heat scorched the night. A remaining section of the roof crashed inwards and a million fiery sparks leapt upwards.

'Jesus Christ,' said Sammy.

'I never seen nothink more crool,' said Gertie. 'No fact'ry, no jobs, no wages, an' yer losin' a packet, Mister Adams. There ain't no insurance can make up for this. Yer've only got the stuff.'

308

'There's no stuff I'm goin' to get out of this lot,' said Sammy.

'Oh, we got the materials out, an' the garments,' said Gertie, 'but the machines, there wasn't no time, and most was too near the fire.'

'What?' said Sammy. 'Say that again,' he said, and put an arm around the thin shoulders of the gaunt woman who had given him loyal service from the day he took the factory over. 'Say that again.'

'Me old man, 'e seen it first,' said Gertie, amid the shouts of the fire brigade chief and the roar of the blaze. ' 'E was comin' back from the jug an' bottle with our New Year's beer, 'e'd 'ad a couple of days' work at the docks an' said 'e'd treat. 'E saw Daft Dick runnin' away, the bugger come out by way of the office an' front door. Me old man smelled smoke. 'E went in, Daft Dick 'aving left the door open. 'E saw the fire right at the end of the fact'ry, a bleedin' great pile of rubbish flamin' away against the wall, an' 'e smelled petrol. 'E come runnin' across to me an' we got neighbours out an' some of the machinists, an' I told one of 'em to run an' tell the coppers to get the fire brigade. Then we all run into the fact'ry. It was goin' up down the end, Mister Adams, gawd, it was, an' me old man said buckets of water wasn't goin' to do no good. But the stockroom next to the office wasn't in no danger, not then, so I said let's get the stuff out while we can. So we did, we sweated blood, but we got it all out, all the finished garments an' the rolls of material, ev'rythink, we didn't leave nothink. It's all in our 'ouses, an' if anyone's nicked any of it, me an' me old man'll get it back for yer. Yer been a good boss to us, Mister Adams. Oh, I told Mrs Bernstein what run for the coppers to tell 'em to see if they could get a message through to yer at the Camberwell Palace, where you said yer was goin' for yer fam'ly New Year. Gawd, look at it, Mister Adams, don't it make yer 'eart

309

bleed? We'd've got the machines out if we could, well, some of 'em, but they're bleedin' weighty an' the place was gettin' too 'ot by then, an' the smoke, I never seen smoke like it, we was coughin' an' spittin', an' me old man said right, ev'ryone out, and then the fire brigade come an' they 'ad us out sharpish. Is it goin' to sink yer business, Mister Adams?'

'No, it isn't, Gertie. Nor you.' Sammy had thought only the finished samples of the 1926 dress design were safe. Lilian had them at home. She had run them up herself at home. In secret. To know that the whole collection had been saved, that all other garments and all materials had been saved too, brought Sammy's resilient nature to the surface. There was nothing to be done about the factory and all the machines, except to pass the headache to the insurance company. But there was something to be done about Gertie and the machinists. 'Gertie, where's yer old man?'

' 'E's over there, tryin' to cheer Gladys up. I'll 'ave to watch 'im with Gladys.'

'What happened to the jug of beer?'

'Eh? The beer? Gawd, we didn't stop to drink no beer,' said Gertie. Other machinists, shawls over their shoulders, were edging up, shocked, shaken, and despairing of their jobs.

'All right,' said Sammy, 'let's go and have some beer now, and I'll talk to you. Let me meet yer old man.'

'Bert!' Gertie shouted. Her husband, in a flat cap, trousers, jersey and tied scarf, came across. He had muscular shoulders. The rest of him was lean and wiry. Physically, he was typical of a docker. His life was hard. Dockers were counted as casual labour. Sometimes there was work for many, sometimes for some, and sometimes for only a few. 'Bert,' said Gertie, ' 'ere's Mister Sammy Adams.'

' 'Ow is yer, guv?' said Bert. 'Yer bleedin' copped it tonight.'

'Nice to meet yer,' said Sammy, and shook the docker's hand vigorously. 'Nice to know yer. Yer got some beer, I believe. I'd be pleasured to participate.'

'It ain't much,' said Bert. 'Well, it ain't as much as it was, seeing what got slopped on me run across 'ome. Still, there's maybe enough for you, me an' Gertie.'

'That'll do me,' said Sammy. 'Could yer get someone to go to the jug and bottle for a large bottle of brandy? Here's a quid. Never mind the change. We'll dole the brandy out to whatever machinists are here, if they could come across to your house.'

' 'Ere, you all right, guv?' said Bert. 'You got yer fact'ry burnin' to the ground an' yer doling out quids for brandy?'

'I'm all right,' said Sammy.

One of the machinists went for the brandy. About to leave the scene with Sammy and her husband, Gertie suddenly said with bitter venom, 'There 'e is, there's Daft Dick. Look at the bugger.'

Sammy saw him. The man had edged his way to the front of the crowd. He wore an old shabby mackintosh, belted, but no hat. His shock of wiry hair stood up. His face was shiny, his expression exultant, his eyes on the flames.

'Leave him,' said Sammy.

'Aincher goin' to do the bleeder?' asked Gertie.

'Not now,' said Sammy, and went across the street with her and her husband to their small, flat-fronted house.

'It ain't no palace, Mister Adams,' said Gertie, 'and we only got the kitchen stove alight.'

'I was brought up in a kitchen,' said Sammy. 'Best place in a house. Lead the way.'

It was small, the kitchen, but the glowing stove and

the homely nature of the room were more than good enough for Sammy. On the table, covered with green baize, stood a brown jug, three-quarters full of ale. Bert rushed his gawping children up to bed. Gertie put cheap thick glasses on the table. Sammy sat down. The machinists, a dozen of them, arrived to crowd into the kitchen doorway. Gertie poured the beer, and she and Bert sat down at the table with Sammy. The machinist who had gone for the brandy returned with it, pushing her way through. She placed the bottle on the table.

'Yer only got six bob change, Mister Adams,' she said, proffering it.

'Well, that's seventy-two pennies,' said Sammy. 'Share it out among all yer kids. Can yer uncork the brandy, Bert?'

Bert got a cheap corkscrew from a dresser drawer and pulled the cork.

'There y'ar, Mister Adams is treatin' yer to a nip each,' he said to the machinists. 'Do yer good, it ain't been yer best New Year's Eve. But leave a nip each for me an' Gertie an' Mister Adams, or I'll crown yer with the bottle.'

The bottle was passed round. The pale-faced machinists gulped from it. They coughed, they turned red.

' 'Ere's yer good 'ealth, Mister Adams,' said Gertie, lifting her glass of beer, 'yer need it.'

Sammy took a long swallow of the beer.

'Now,' he said. 'First, you got a job for as long as yer want with me, Gertie, and so have the rest of yer. I am in—'

'But you ain't got no fact'ry,' said Gertie, 'you ain't got no place for us to 'ave jobs in, nor machines. You ain't goin' to get no money from no insurance company for months.'

'An' they'll fight yer for every penny you ask for,' said

312

Bert. 'They got more takin' ways than payin' ones, guv, I tell yer.'

'We'll see,' said Sammy. 'I am concerned now to advise yer all I am in considerable appreciation of what yer did in clearing out the stock room, and it won't do me any good not to say so. You all got the stuff in yer homes?'

'We 'ad to do our bit for yer, Mister Adams,' said Gladys, a woman of thirty-five and still with some of the prettiness she had owned as a young woman.

'We couldn't just stand about,' said another machinist.

'That Gert, she run us off our feet,' said another.

'An' Bert, 'e got all our old men sweatin' at it,' said Gladys, 'an' my old man with that back of 'is an' all. But we 'ad to save somethink for yer, Mister Adams.'

'Yer been fair to us, Mister Adams,' said Gertie, 'yer been the best bleedin' boss I ever knowed, an' yer give us a good manager in yer brother.'

'Lovely feller, 'e is,' said another machinist. 'Keeps yer at it, mind, but a lovely bloke. Pass the bottle back, Maggie.'

'Pass it 'ere,' said Bert. A few mouths took further swigs before the bottle reached his hand. 'Mister Adams?'

Sammy finished his beer, dried the inside of the glass with his handkerchief and Bert poured him a generous noggin. He poured Gertie one, then himself. He passed the bottle back to the machinists.

'You've got part of the stockroom stuff here, Gertie?' asked Sammy.

'Me livin'-room's full of it,' said Gertie, the brandy tinting her cheeks. 'Want to take a look at it?'

'I am acceptin' your word,' said Sammy.

'We rushed about with it,' said Gertie, 'but treated it gentle, like. There ain't nothink ruined, Mister Adams.'

'I believe yer,' said Sammy. 'Well, then, you all want to keep workin' and I want it selfsame. If I put machines into yer houses, could yer work at home?'

'I'll work in me coal-'ole,' said Gladys. 'I don't 'ave to, but I would.'

'We've got one problem,' said Sammy, 'a place for new cutting machines. A shed would do, but it's got to be central.'

'I'll get yer the 'ire of a shed, guv,' said Bert.

'You're on, Bert,' said Sammy. 'Now, I'll give yer the loan of our van an' driver. I want someone who's got the room available to keep all the materials. I'll pay rent for it. The driver will collect for cuttin' work and deliver to her or her or her accordin'. Savvy?'

'Got yer, Mister Adams,' said Gertie.

'It's not goin' to mean the kind of turnover I'd like,' said Sammy. 'It can't be expected when you're not all under one roof, but I have considerable faith in yer willingness and a high regard for your co-operation, which has been a credit to yer so far. With the assistance of a certain business acquaintance of mine, who is notable for his remarkability, I'll get the new machines delivered to yer houses as quick as I can, but yer'll understand I can't pay yer any wages till yer start workin' again. At home. However, to compensate for loss of business revenue in misfortunate circumstances like these here, there is an insurance clause—'

'What's a clause?' asked a woman.

'A bit of wise thinking when takin' out business insurance, which in this case will allow me to pay yer fifty per cent of yer wages while yer waitin' for yer machines to arrive.'

'We get paid while we ain't workin'?' said Gertie. 'Yer jokin', Mister Adams.'

'It occurs to me,' said Sammy, 'that I have had occasion more than once to advise all of yer I do not joke

314

about business. I need yer skill, you need yer wages. It is mutually serious. All right, now, you girls get off to yer homes and see the New Year in with yer fam'lies.'

'God bless yer, Mister Adams,' said Gladys, 'yer a gent, you are. 'E copped yer, 'e did, that Daft Dick, but yer still on yer uppers and smilin'.'

'I ain't smiling,' said Sammy, 'but also I ain't on me downers. Yer'll all get an extra bonus at the end of yer first week's work at home in appreciation of what yer did to save me stocks. And I'll leave it to yer to acquaint all the other machinists with me proposition about workin' at home. A happy New Year to yer.'

'An' to you, Mister Adams.' The relieved machinists melted away.

'The bleedin' perishers,' said Bert, 'they swiped the bottle.' He rushed after them and brought it back. 'Guv'nor?'

'I'll go another,' said Sammy, and Bert poured a little more for all three of them. He looked at Sammy.

'I know yer been good to me Gertie,' he said. 'She ain't said how good, and yer maybe let slip then what yer didn't mean to just now, about bonuses. Yer been doin' that, guv, paying 'em bonuses?'

'Givin' due regard to yer natural question, Bert, I'm obliged to answer that I ain't saying.'

'You Bert, you ain't saying, neither,' said Gertie, 'you forget you 'eard it, or I'll wrap yer Sunday braces round yer neck an' strangle yer.'

'She would too,' said the docker, 'so I'll tell yer, Mister Adams, I've clean forget you said anything. All the same, yer a gent. What yer goin' to do about Daft Dick?'

'I'm not goin' to do anything,' said Sammy, 'but you could maybe favour me. He's not daft, he's a firebug, he likes the feel of matches in his hand. I wouldn't be disagreeably surprised to hear you knew someone who'd hammer his fingers.'

'Got yer, guv,' said Bert. 'I'll lay 'e ain't goin' to be able to strike another match for the rest of 'is life.'

'Just his fingers,' said Sammy. 'I am averse to hearing his loaf of bread has been bashed in. My mother wouldn't like it.'

'That's lettin' 'im orf light,' said Gertie.

'Not when the coppers get after him,' said Sammy. 'How much, Bert?'

'Five bob,' said Bert.

Sammy gave him four pounds.

'You and Gertie keep the change,' he said.

'Look,' said Bert, 'what we done we did on account of Gertie saying we 'ad to, which was on account of you treatin' 'er an' the girls right.'

'I owe yer both,' said Sammy. 'You know it, I know it. Cheer up, Gertie, we'll get another fact'ry built.'

'I'm cheered up already,' said Gertie. 'Any more brandy, is there?'

They finished the bottle between them. Sammy sat talking and thinking. Then he said, 'Right. Been a pleasure, considering. Now I've got to go and let Mrs Hyams know what's happened and what's happening.'

Gertie and Bert saw him out. He shook hands with them, wished them a happy New Year, and went striding away south in search of a taxi. He had to let the family know, as well as Lilian. And there was Tommy, without a proper job for the time being.

It was late when he reached Aunt Victoria's. The family had had their New Year drink, but not in the most convivial of moods. Boots had gone to see the theatre manager and been told the reason for Sammy not returning to his seat.

Lizzie and Ned had taken their children home, but Boots and Emily were still there with Rosie and Tim. Susie had felt that under the circumstances she was

316

outstaying her welcome, but it had been compulsive to stay in the hope Sammy would put in an appearance before time completely ran out on her. Tommy was sombre, Vi upset. Uncle Tom and Aunt Victoria were doing their best to be consoling. Chinese Lady was straight of face.

Sammy described the fire and the complete destruction of the factory. He recounted how all the stock had been saved and what he proposed to do to get production going again. Further, he and Lilian Hyams would proceed with the launching of Adams Fashions by introducing them, as planned, to West End shop and store buyers. That would take place in a few days. No one was to worry.

'What started the fire?' asked Chinese Lady.

'A box of matches in the hands of a dubious geezer,' said Sammy.

'I knew it,' said Chinese Lady. 'That's what comes of havin' a fact'ry in the East End.' Chinese Lady considered the East End was like foreign parts, and that Jack the Ripper's birth certificate was probably highly dubious.

'Sammy, you talkin' about the fact'ry handyman, Daft Dick?' asked Tommy.

'A misfortunate acceptance on my part of the previous owner's choice,' said Sammy. It was Reuben Morris who had sent Daft Dick along. 'Which grievous error I freely admit. Yer learn hard lessons in hard times.'

'But I thought he was harmless,' said Susie, suffering for Sammy.

'No, I'd say he was biding his time,' said Sammy.

Boots, looking thoughtful, said, 'Get yourself a car, Sammy.'

'How did that creep in?' asked Emily.

'Daddy's ticking, Mummy,' said Rosie. Tim, tired out, was asleep in an armchair.

317

'We don't want Sammy breakin' his neck in no car,' said Chinese Lady, 'specially after he might have just missed being burned alive.'

'The van's indispensable in its present use,' said Boots. 'Get a car, Sammy. You make a hundred journeys every month. Tommy will show you how it works, and he can use it, or you can use it, for carrying the cut materials to your machinists.'

'A car does sound nice,' said Aunt Victoria, already thinking of mentioning to her neighbours that her son-in-law's brother owned a car.

'Comin' up in the world, that is,' said Uncle Tom.

'You can talk about it at the office tomorrow,' said Chinese Lady. 'It's time now we all went home.'

'I'll take Susie,' said Sammy.

'I'll be all right,' said Susie, not her usual bright self because of the fire and the blow it must have been to Sammy. Also, he had been going to tell her tonight of the new plans he had for her. Everything had fallen flat, a bit like it had on Boxing Day evening. She hoped the Adams family hadn't entered a bad luck period. 'There's no need for anyone to come with me.'

'Now, Susie,' said Chinese Lady in a proprietary way. She had, of course, already made up her mind that Susie would make another ladylike daughter-in-law. 'Boots is seeing me and Em'ly and the children home, Sammy is just about fit to see hisself home, and Tommy will see you home.'

'Yes, I'll take her,' said Tommy, 'you look whacked, Sammy.'

'Yes, you go with her, Tommy,' said Vi.

'All right, see you in the morning, Susie,' said Sammy, feeling frankly drained, 'and you can come with me to Mr Greenberg, he being a very helpful gent who can lay his hands on anything, including best-quality second-hand industrial sewing-machines.

318

Which means, if you know Eli Greenberg like we know him, it ain't goin' to be necessary to buy new ones.'

'But my office work,' said Susie.

'I'll come in and help tomorrow,' said Emily.

'Yer will, Em?' said Sammy.

'The fam'ly comes first in a crisis,' said Emily.

CHAPTER TWENTY-THREE

New Year's Day, 1926, opened to rain. It had been raining buckets all over the Continent, and the rivers of Europe were flooding towns and villages. Chinese Lady, over breakfast, said that was what come of living in Frenchified countries instead of a God-selected country like England. And like Scotland and Wales too, she said, in her loyalty to the United Kingdom. But not Ireland. Ireland was a pack of trouble. She wouldn't be surprised, she said, to hear that all that Continental rain was falling on Ireland too, and that all them troublesome Irish were swimming for their lives. Boots said if they were, they'd all be swimming this way and probably end up on Blackpool beach. Tim looked awed at this. Rosie stifled giggles. Chinese Lady said someone whose name she wouldn't mention would be better getting off to his work before he brought the house down with his music hall jokes.

Emily left to go to the estate agents. She entered the premises in crisp fashion and said to her colleague, 'When Mr Barry Somerville comes in, Mary, would you tell him I won't be in myself, not this morning, we've got a fam'ly crisis. I'll hope to be in tomorrow.'

She had given in her notice, anyway. Umbrella up, she crossed the road and walked to the offices of Adams Enterprises, going up the side stairs adjacent the shop. She entered her husband's office.

'All right?' said Boots.

'What's it they say? See you got your priorities right? Yes, I've got mine right, Boots. You dictate and I'll do the shorthand-typin'.'

Boots had offered to look after Sammy's correspondence, with Emily's help, leaving Sammy and Susie free to devote themselves to the problems caused by the fire. The post was all opened, he had given out work to the copy typists, and had a pile ready for dictation. Emily was to use Susie's office and Susie's new typewriter. Emily, always brisk, wasted no time. Within two minutes she was seated, notebook open, pencil sharpened, legs crossed. Boots observed her legs and the sheen of her stockings. That, he thought, was probably one of the first reasons why Somerville had come to fancy her.

'You're showing off,' he said.

'I'm daft to ask,' said Emily, 'but what d'you mean, showing off?'

'Kindly adjust your skirt,' said Boots.

'Oh, yer chump,' said Emily, 'get on with it.'

Boots got on with it. After six letters, he said, 'How we doing?'

'I think I'm goin' to like it.' Emily smiled. 'I'm glad I think I'm goin' to like it.'

'It's to be your own choice, Em. No coercion. Right?'

'I got you,' said Emily.

'Good on yer, old girl.'

'Not so much of the old girl, old boy. Get on with it.'

Susie's first job that morning was to telephone the insurance company while Sammy was busy using the other line. She spoke to a clerk in the claims department, the policy in front of her. His first response was to say, 'Who?'

'Adams Enterprises,' repeated Susie, and went on to give details. To which he said, 'A fire? Well, I don't know. A fire, you say?' Susie, in no mood to play second fiddle to a voice vague with doubt and laziness, said, 'Kindly don't waste my time. Mr Adams will expect a claims form by first post tomorrow, and the date when the fire assessor will inspect. Sorry to have woke you up, what a crying shame, but you can go back to sleep now.'

When Sammy had finished his own phone calls, he summoned her. Susie, hat and coat on, went into his office. Boots arrived through the other door at the same time.

'Morning, Susie. Listen, Sammy.'

'I'm in a hurry,' said Sammy, shovelling himself into his overcoat, 'but I'll spare you a minute of me valuable time.'

'I can only spare you thirty seconds myself,' said Boots, 'that's all Emily's allowing me. I haven't finished dictation yet. This fire. That firebug. Adams Fashions. Exclusive collection. Think about the possibility that someone put the box of matches into Daft Dick's hand. It's a cut-throat trade, sonny, and someone might be thinking there's not room for you in it. One more thing. Mitch is going to find you a high-class, first-rate and commendably desirable second-hand car. Take care of Susie. It's wet outside.' Boots returned to his office, leaving Sammy gaping. Recovering, he let a little grin appear.

'Who was that, Susie?'

'That was Mister Adams senior,' said Susie.

'You sure? I thought it was God havin' a sharp half-minute with me.'

'Yes, Mister Adams senior can be very impressive,' said Susie.

'I'm not being provoked by that, Miss Brown.' Sammy buttoned his coat up and put his hat on. 'Come on, let's catch a bus.' They left the office and descended the stairs, emerging into the street. 'There you are, one

322

comin'.' He walked smartly to the stop, Susie bobbing along beside him with quick clicks of her heels. 'Make a note, Miss Brown, that we're to enquire into the possibility of devious actions by competitors unknown. And make another note that if it's true we ain't goin' to take it lying down. Which means God might send his troops in.'

'God?' said Susie, their arrival at the bus stop coinciding with the arrival of the bus. 'God, Mister Sammy?'

'Boots,' said Sammy.

They boarded, seating themselves in the lower deck. Susie was stifling laughter. Sammy enquired what was funny.

'Oh, you are,' she said. 'I know it's serious, the fire and everything, but I'm so glad you can wake up laughing about it.'

'Who's laughing?' said Sammy. 'I'm not.'

But he was meeting the first day of 1926 in a challenging mood and was not without cheer. He had his worries, but he also had the uplifting knowledge that he had far more friends in the East End than he had thought. He also had Susie beside him. He could, of course, have dealt with Mr Greenberg on his own, but Susie's presence was a pleasure. Susie had never let him down. She's had funny moments, but so did all women. It was a paralysing weakness, being in love with her. He had never included that kind of thing in his calculations. Other men got hit by a hammer, but it had never occurred to him he'd get knocked flat himself. It took his mind off business. It made him think of coming home at night to Susie, Susie in a pretty apron and serving up steak-and-kidney pudding. Or Susie in a black silk nightdress – no, don't think of that.

A warm hip was touching his, a warm voice floating into his ear.

'Penny for your thoughts, Mister Sammy?'

'Pardon? Ah, yes, about Mr Greenberg.' He spoke to her about Eli and industrial sewing-machines.

They came off the bus and out of the rain into Mr Greenberg's covered yard. They caught the well-known rag and bone man before he took off with his horse and cart.

'Morning, Eli,' said Sammy.

'Good morning, Mr Greenberg,' said Susie.

'Ah, good morning, Sammy, good morning, Susie,' said Mr Greenberg from beneath his round black hat. 'A vet vun, ain't it? And a sad vun.' He pulled out his large red handkerchief and blew his nose sorrowfully. His beard curled in sympathy. 'Sammy, such a grievous fire I have heard about. Vhat can I say? Vas it insured, my poy?'

'Fully covered,' said Sammy.

'Vhat a relief to all of us, and vhat a pleasure to see Susie, ain't it? A picture, Sammy, a picture, ain't she? Such a sveet vife she vhould make, even for our Prince of Vales.'

'Leave off,' said Sammy, 'I ain't proposin' to introduce her to no Prince of Wales.'

'Very vise, Sammy. Vill you both step into my office?'

They entered the old green shed that served as his office. He dusted a chair and begged Susie to be seated.

'Thank you, Mr Greenberg,' she said.

'Now, my dears, vhat can I do for you? I am a poor man, but vhat is money between friends? Money ve can do without, ain't it? Did not Moses say the poor shall inherit the earth?'

'I thought that was Jesus,' said Sammy.

'Jesus or Moses, Sammy, vhat is the difference to you and me?'

'Don't worry, Eli old cock, we're not after a loan. We're here to put some valuable business in your way. Mind, I could negotiate direct with certain suppliers myself, but it would take time, and I don't have any to spare, I've got Adams Fashions takin' up all of it. Susie, acquaint our friend with details.'

'Oh, a pleasure,' said Susie. 'Dear Mr Greenberg, we've come to ask how long it will take you to acquire on our behalf fifty highly recommendable first-class second-hand industrial sewing-machines which won't fall to pieces at first go.'

Sammy grinned. Mr Greenberg peered.

'I should be hearing this from Susie?' he said in pleasure.

'Also, Mr Greenberg,' said Susie, blue eyes making him sigh, 'we'd be awf'lly obliged if you won't ask a price that will ruin us, as we're near to that already on account of the fire.'

'My life,' said Mr Greenberg, mittened hands waving about, 'vhat have you been makin' of a girl so young and pretty, Sammy?'

'We are also in the market for three cutting machines,' said Susie. 'In prime condition, of course. For everything, Mr Greenberg, we're open to an askin' price of two hundred pounds.'

Mr Greenberg clutched at his heart and turned pale.

'Susie, Susie,' he said hoarsely, 'I am hearing this from friends? Two hundred single green vuns for fifty sewing-machines and three cuttin' machines?'

'Yes, it's a valuable order,' said Susie.

'I ain't saying it ain't, Susie.' Mr Greenberg took his hat off and fanned his beard. 'But valuable ain't too valuable vhen it gives a poor man a heart attack.'

'Can you get 'em, and at express speed immediate and forthwith, that's the point, Eli,' said Sammy.

'I am acquainted vith promising sources, to be sure,' said Mr Greenberg, replacing his hat, 'but at a fair price, Sammy, a fair price. Shall ve say three hundred pounds, vhich vould include cost of time?'

'That's upping it considerable,' said Sammy, 'and I don't think me personal assistant is too impressed.'

'We could go to two hundred and twenty, Mister Sammy,' said Susie.

Mr Greenberg shook his head reproachfully. They began to bargain. Out in the street a taxi pulled up. Rachel alighted, paid the cabbie and entered the yard. She knocked on the shed door. Sammy opened it. Rachel, in a shining cream-coloured raincoat and matching rain-hat, looked up at him, the velvet lustre of her brown eyes reflecting the wetness of the day.

'Sammy, my God, your factory,' she said in pain.

Sammy turned. 'Take over, Susie. Excuse me, Eli.' He came out of the shed, closing the door behind him. Susie saw him through the little window, and she also saw Rachel, the woman who had once been his only girl friend.

'Sammy, I phoned your office as soon as I'd looked at our morning papers,' said Rachel. 'Boots told me I might find you here. I had to see you. I'm devastated. Has everything gone?'

'The fact'ry's gone,' said Sammy, 'and the machines. But not the stock.' He detailed events and what the machinists and their husbands had done for him. Rachel took a deep breath. 'We're not done for,' said Sammy, 'the investments are still good, Rachel.'

'I should stand here with tears in my eyes about money?' she said. 'They're for you, you idiot. Or they were. Now I don't have a breaking heart. You've still got everything that's important at the moment. I thought you'd been left with nothing except the insurance. Do you know what it means that you've still got what's most important?'

'Yes, I know,' said Sammy, 'it means I've got a staff of machinists that need taking care of. And I'd like to say, Rachel, that you're a love for comin' here to be consoling.'

Rachel smiled a little moistly.

'That's my Sammy,' she said. 'You're soft, aren't you, under all that flannel you dish out. You're a man, Sammy, you've been brought up as a man, and you belong to the best family that ever came out of Walworth. You're my kind, Sammy, and I'm your kind, and I'm going to be with you every step of your way up, without doing any harm to anyone. You get me, Sammy?'

'I get you, Rachel.'

'It's special, what we've got. Ain't it?' Rachel was what she was born, a Jewish cockney with a warm heart, and Sammy was what he was, a man of Walworth, and Walworth was the resilient heart of the cockney world this side of the river. 'Ain't it special, love?'

'Right,' said Sammy. 'Which means it ain't something you'd tell Benjamin or I'd tell me future wife.'

Rachel shook a gloved finger at him.

'Listen, you clown, don't talk to me about any future wife. When it happens, I'll come to the wedding, but I'll be wearing black. You hear that, Sammy?'

'I hear you, Rachel.'

'Good. It's so you'll understand. Never mind the fire, you can build a new factory and you can still pre-empt the French designers. Oh, and my daddy sends his sorrow and regards, and asks me to tell you a friend of his has vacant premises in Islington.'

'I'm beholden to Isaac,' said Sammy, 'but it's got to be Shoreditch. I've got fam'lies in Shoreditch, me machinists' fam'lies, and I owe 'em, Rachel.'

'Only round the corner, Sammy. Well, as good as. Cheap rent.'

'It's a thought.' Sammy's eyes gleamed. 'Got insurance cover for that too, as well as fifty-per-cent wages for the girls when they're not working on account of unfortunate happenings.'

327

'Who's a clever, thoughtful boy, then?' smiled Rachel.

'I'll speak to me chief machinist. She and the others might not mind walking the extra footage to the next parish till the new fact'ry's up. Tell Isaac I'll look in on him this afternoon.'

'He'll be able to tell you he knows of a lease on a shop in Oxford Street that will be on offer in two months' time.'

'Oxford Street?' The challenge of that brought the gleam back to Sammy's eyes.

'Near Selfridges,' said Rachel. 'I was going to phone you about it today. Adams Fashions in Oxford Street, Sammy, think of that. If it's not Regent Street or Mayfair, it's still the West End.'

'Tell Isaac I'll definitely look in on him this afternoon.'

'My word,' said Rachel, 'I like the way you're bouncing back, Sammy, and I like it that you know where you're going and how to get there.'

'I like it that you and your father have got consideration for a Gentile.'

'My daddy loves you, Sammy, and wouldn't care if you were a Buddhist monk with two heads. Do you mind if I rush now?'

'I'm touched to the cockles of me heart that you came, Rachel. Help yourself to my best regards.'

'Sammy, Sammy, I get best regards from my grocer.'

'I get groceries from mine.'

'My, aren't we witty? *Shalom*, lovey.'

'Bless yer, Mrs Rachel Goodman.'

She left, and Sammy went back into the shed, where Susie and Mr Greenberg had settled, of course, on two hundred and fifty pounds cash and no questions asked, particularly about Mr Greenberg's sources of second-hand supply.

'Ah, Sammy,' he said, 've are now comin' to delivery charges.'

'Yer pulling a fast one, Eli,' said Sammy.

Mr Greenberg spread his hands in gentle protest.

'Sammy my dear, for new machines, no delivery charges. For second-hand, nothing is for free, ain't it? Also, dear me, delivery not to vun single address, but many. Vell, I vill arrange it for fifteen green vuns.'

'Delivery's when?' asked Sammy.

'Three days vill do?' said Mr Greenberg.

'Three days?' Sammy regarded his. long-standing friend fondly. 'That's a winner, Abraham old love. I ain't goin' to reproach yer for skinnin' us a mite, but I will tell yer delivery might be to just one address, an Islington fact'ry. I'll let yer know. Shall we say a fiver for same?'

'Two vould be sveeter and fairer, Sammy.'

'Oh, I think six pounds would be very fair, Mr Greenberg, don't you?' said Susie.

'Eight?' said Mr Greenberg.

'Very well, dear Mr Greenberg, seven,' said Susie.

'Done,' said Mr Greenberg, 've all know times are hard.'

'We're all suffering together,' said Sammy. 'Still, I'm proud of your influential talents, Eli.'

'Ah, my dear Sammy, vhat is the vorth of a deal when it ain't been conducted vith love and friendship?'

'There's the profit, that's always a consolation,' said Sammy. 'A happy Christian New Year to you, old sport.' Sammy shook hands. 'Shall we go, Susie?'

'Goodbye, Mr Greenberg,' said Susie, 'and thank you.'

'A pleasure, Susie.'

They left, making their way to a tram stop.

Susie said, 'An Islington fact'ry?'

'An empty one,' said Sammy, 'known to Mr Isaac

Moses, father of Mrs Rachel Goodman. We'll have to see if our machinists don't mind goin' the extra distance until we've built the new one. It's a hard life they live, Susie, and I ain't inclined to do any pushing. Well, let's get there.'

She walked through the rain in her brown cloche hat and her German-made leather coat, her umbrella a black, dripping shield that kept her glasses dry. She stopped at the entrance to Caulfield Place. It was wetly grey, its gutters running with water. She was talking vaguely to herself. Passers-by, hearing her, felt sorry for her. Some people got like that, they talked aloud to themselves.

She frowned and shook her head.

'Not now,' she said, 'not now, it's not the right time.' And she went on in a wandering way.

CHAPTER TWENTY-FOUR

In the wetness of the day they surveyed the sodden mounds of grey ashes. Twisted and contorted clusters of blackened iron and steel sprouted from the glistening grey heaps. The brick walls were devastated, fallen girders at obscene angles. Passing people, shabby with poverty, stopped to look and to mutter. A destroyed factory meant more unemployment.

Susie felt harrowed. Sammy felt philosophical. The temporary use of another factory helped, and so did the mental picture he was painting of a new building full of light, with decent amenities and radiators. Some schools had radiators and a hot-water plant. If schools could, his new factory could. He'd have to find out the running costs. But this lot had to go first. The damaged walls had to be pulled down and the site cleared. He had bought the freehold from Mr Morris on behalf of Adams Enterprises, the company's first venture into property ownership.

'It's awful,' said Susie, 'and so dispiritin'.'

'It's not good, but it could be worse,' said Sammy. 'It's a blow, I grant you, but there's consolations. Like Eli Greenberg and Isaac Moses both comin' to our rescue. And there's you too, Susie, which is a considerable consolation.'

'This is so sudden,' murmured Susie.

'Pardon?'

'Thank you, Mister Adams.'

'I'm on to you, Susie Brown.'

'On to me? I don't know what you mean.'

'Little Turk you are, Susie. It's leadin' you to a shockin' fate. Not today. Today's a bit mournful. But it could easily happen tomorrow, or the day after.'

'What shockin' fate?' asked Susie.

'You'll find out. I just hope it won't make you run a mile in record time. Come on, let's go across and see Gertie.'

Susie, now reading him like a book, went across the street with light dancing in her eyes, and hoping that her shocking fate wouldn't be too long delayed. Imagine he could be so dynamic in business matters and so hopeless about saying just a few special words.

Gertie was in. So was her husband Bert. He hadn't been called at the docks this morning, so he had come home. Gertie brought the visitors into the small kitchen. It was warm enough from the stove fire, but Sammy thought it had a kind of bare look, like Mother Hubbard's cupboard. That came, he knew, from poverty and a hand-to-mouth existence. The resilience of cockneys like Gertie and Bert would have surprised him had he not grown up among such people. He introduced Susie to Bert, who was down on his knees beside the grate. In the grate stood a triangular iron foot. On the upper foot was a boy's boot. There was a large square of boot leather on the floor, from which Bert had cut two soles. He'd got the leather from the docks. It had fallen off a ship. One sole was on the boot, a nail protruding. He got up to shake hands with Susie. His worn, rugged and lean face creased into an admiring smile.

'Blimey, it's a pleasure to meet yer, Miss Brown, yer the one I 'eard was the Lord Mayor's daughter.'

Susie smiled. 'I ain't no Lord Mayor's daughter,' she said.

'Don't you believe it, Bert,' said Sammy, 'she's given my ears more than a few tannings. No work today?'

'Dock labour's casual, bleedin' casual,' said Bert.

'Well, when there's no work for you,' said Sammy, 'would you do a job for me? That site's got to be cleared. I could use contractors to clear it in a few days. But there's no hurry until the insurance is settled and I know what I'm gettin'. You'll need a cart or a lorry, and some mates to help you. You can take your time. Give you forty quid to do the job, plus cost of hiring the cartage. You pay your mates out of the forty quid. What d'you say?'

'I'll say yer on, Mister Adams, that's what I'll say.'

'Also,' said Sammy, 'when the new fact'ry's built, I'll give you a job. That's if you won't mind handin' in your docker's card. You can be responsible for fact'ry maintenance, which will include keepin' it warm in the winter, decent all the year round, and makin' sure unpleasant geezers don't set fire to it.'

Bert's mouth fell open.

'Yer been an' poleaxed 'im, Mister Adams,' said Gertie, 'and 'e ain't goin' to get his breath back for a while. So I'll speak for 'im. Yer got yerself a man what'll do a good job for yer. 'E don't keep me in fur coats, like me old mum 'oped 'e would, but 'e can do a job good as any man. There y'ar, Bert, yer can straighten up now, Mister Adams don't want you lookin' as if yer goin' to fall over. Yer a gent, Mister Adams, an' I don't mean a fancy gent, an' when yer come up with them new machines yer promised, me an' the girls'll do yer proud workin' at 'ome.'

'Glad you mentioned that,' said Sammy, and put the alternative to her, the factory in Islington. It was a bit of a walk, but without the problems bound to be experienced by each machinist working at home. She could think it over, she could talk to the others, but he'd like a decision by tomorrow.

'We'll go there,' said Gertie.

'You sure? Look, tell you what, Gertie, I'll pay any tram fares that's necessary.'

'We won't say no to that,' said Gertie. 'It ain't the walkin', it's what it does to yer shoes. You take the fact'ry, Mister Adams, then yer'll get the turnover yer want.'

'Makes sense to me,' said Bert.

'Glad yer come to,' said Gertie.

'I'm all ears,' said Bert.

'Yer 'andsome brother come 'ere earlier, Mister Adams,' said Gertie. 'Lorst all 'is paperwork in the fire, yer see, all the order details specially. So he went orf to yer Camberwell office to telephone people an' yer shops, so 'e can get all them details, which we gotter 'ave. It won't be no use guessin'. Mister Adams, when will yer be puttin' the new machines into Islington for us?'

'Three days, I hope,' said Sammy, 'and I'll get you all back at work the day after, with brother Tommy's help.'

'Bleedin' lovely,' said Gertie. 'Oh, beggin' yer pardon, Miss Brown.'

'Don't mention it,' smiled Susie.

'Bert done a call on 'is way back from the docks, Mister Adams,' said Gertie. 'Like yer wanted, come tomorrer or the day after, Daft Dick ain't goin' to be able to strike no more matches. That right, Bert?'

'Right,' said Bert.

Susie gave Sammy a straight look.

'What does that mean?' she asked.

'No idea,' said Sammy. 'Didn't you make a note of something, Miss Brown?'

'Oh, about enquiring into things suspicious?' said Susie.

'That's it,' said Sammy. 'Listen, Bert, forget the aforementioned arrangement. It's occurred to us you

334

might instead like to enquire into what set Daft Dick off. Well, yer never know, someone might have put the matches into his hand, with the promise of a quid or two.'

Bert was on to that immediately.

'I gotcher, Mister Adams. The rag trade ain't never been like a dance of sugar fairies, not in the East End it ain't. It's more'n likely you been too good at it. Too good for other people, yer see. So I gotcher, Mister Adams. Leave it to me.'

'Good on yer,' said Sammy. 'We'll get all stock out of your houses, Gertie, on the day the machines are delivered to Islington. I'll phone Carter Paterson. They can pick up the lot at one go. And you better take this, Bert.' He took two fivers from his wallet and handed them to Bert. 'That's an advance for the clearing job. Start when you like, after the fire assessor's been tomorrow.' The insurance company had phoned after Susie's call. 'Leave it to you. Those brick walls have got to come down, of course.'

'No trouble,' said Bert.

'Good. I'll be coming around. So long for now. So long, Gertie.'

'Good luck, Mister Adams,' said Gertie. 'Oh, would yer like to know Mr Morris 'as started up again, in a fact'ry near 'Oxton Road?'

'Is that a fact?' asked Sammy.

'Did you squeeze 'im, guv?' asked Bert.

'He was in financial straits,' said Sammy. 'I favoured him with a deal. I do deals, I ain't partial to squeezin'.'

'I was just askin',' said Bert.

'I know yer was, Bert,' said Sammy. His little grin appeared. 'Good question, though. So long.'

Walking to the tramways, Susie said, 'Excuse me, Mister Adams, but I must ask what was meant about Daft Dick not being able to strike any more matches. I don't think I liked the sound of it. It didn't sound charitable or Christian.'

'I'm thinking at the moment about other things, Susie, such as calling on our Madame Dupont concerning arrangements to introduce our range to buyers in the West End. The Paris shows start soon.'

'Yes, but what about poor Daft Dick?'

'I've just been very considerate in respect of the bleeder—'

'Really, Mister Adams, I don't expect that kind of language from our managing director,' said Susie. The rain had stopped and two shawled women peered at them from an open doorway.

'My, yer a couple of fancies,' said one woman.

'Granted, missus,' said Sammy, walking on with Susie.

'Dolled-up rent collector and 'is bit of Sunday lamb, they look like,' said the second woman.

The street was a wet brown and grey, the flat-fronted dwellings grimy with London soot, the smoke from chimneys rising listlessly. A woman with a pillowcase full of wet laundry from the local bagwash fumbled for the latchcord of her front door. Sammy halted to oblige her. He gave the cord a tug and the door opened.

'Ta, yer a gent, mister, and a posh one too,' she said. She had the pale complexion of the East End, but her dark brown eyes were brilliant and her full mouth very kissable.

'Yer welcome,' said Sammy, lifting his hat to her.

'Same to you.' She winked at him. 'Knock any time yer like and ask for Amy. I'm Amy. Only don't knock Sunday afternoons, me old man's around then.'

'All right, no Sunday afternoons,' said Sammy. 'See yer Friday morning if it suits yer.'

'I can't 'ardly wait,' said Amy, and went in. Sammy resumed walking with Susie.

'You didn't say what time Friday morning, Mister Adams. Shall I put down eleven o'clock in your appointments diary?'

'It won't be Sunday afternoon, that's for certain. I'll get me livelihood injured. Right, now we'll take a tram to the City, find a JP eatin' house and partake of their individual steak-and-kidney puddings before goin' to Battersea to see Mimi.'

'Yes, Mister Adams, quite so.'

Sammy grinned. That Susie. Few people were going to get any change out of her. She was a ladylike knock-out. No wonder Chinese Lady was regarding her as highly favourable.

In the restaurant in the City, where there were white cloths on the tables and the individual steak-and-kidney puddings were luscious with meat and gravy, Susie harked back to Daft Dick and her suspicions.

'I wouldn't like to think you'd do him bodily harm,' she said.

Sammy chewed and thought. He was not going to ask the police to charge the miscreant. If the fire brigade declared it was an arson job, the police could take it from there. But nobody had been doing any sifting work today. The insurance company would get interested if arson was mentioned. That would delay settlement. They'd investigate the affairs of Adams Enterprises. And they'd find those affairs far too healthy for him to need his factory being burned to the ground.

'I don't go in for doing bodily harm personally, Susie. My mother wouldn't stand for it. All I've done is arrange for Bert to take a look at Daft Dick. Now how'd you feel about Adams Fashions opening a shop in Oxford Street?'

'Oxford Street?' Susie's blue eyes sparkled. 'Oh, how excitin'.' The restaurant was almost full, City clerks predominating, the clatter of knives and forks a metallic accompaniment to the chatter of conversation. 'You're not kiddin', are you?'

'The lease is comin' up on offer in two months, or so I was reliably informed earlier by Mrs Rachel Goodman during my business conversation with her.'

'Oh, thank goodness,' said Susie. 'I was so embarrassed, thinking Mr Greenberg was thinking you were consortin' with a married woman in his yard.'

Sammy eyed her across the table. Susie offered him a look of innocence.

'Kindly note, Miss Brown, I don't like gettin' a ringing in my ears when I'm enjoying steak-and-kidney pudding. Further note, you saucebox, that I don't consort with any female woman of a married kind.'

'I should hope you wouldn't, Mister Adams,' said Susie. 'Oh, but a shop in Oxford Street, that's really excitin'.'

'Thought you'd like it,' said Sammy.

'Oh, yes. I—' Susie's fork halted halfway to her mouth, and she gave Sammy a suspicious look. 'Excuse me, I'm sure,' she said, 'but you're not goin' to ask me to be the manageress, are you? Because I won't. I've only been your personal assistant for five minutes. I hope the new plans you've got for me don't mean I'm being banished again, even if it is to Oxford Street.'

'I don't know where you get all these banishing ideas from,' said Sammy. 'Did I say Oxford Street was for you, now did I?'

'You'd better not,' said Susie, 'or I'll throw what's left of my pudding over your waistcoat.'

'Eat it up, Susie, it won't do my waistcoat any good,' said Sammy. He coughed to clear his throat. That made Susie give him a different look. 'I'm not in favour of deprivin' myself of your personal assistance. Far from it.' He eyed the cruet. Susie eyed him. 'By the way, I don't want you to think I'm askin' a nosy question, but are you a marrying young woman?'

'Pardon?' said Susie, slightly quivering.

'Are you in favour of gettin' married?'

'Not to anybody I'm not,' she said, 'but I am to someone special.'

'Well, yes, I can see that's a fair point.' Sammy cleared his throat again, the small residue of his meal lying neglected on its plate. 'It reminds me that my old lady is in favour of everyone gettin' married. Anyone who doesn't is a kind of untidy piece of furniture to her. Of course, we owe a lot to our parents for gettin' married, or we wouldn't be here.'

'Mister Adams, that's an awful shame.'

'What is?' asked Sammy.

'Your mother thinkin' you're like an untidy piece of furniture.'

'You saucebox,' said Sammy, and gave her a direct look then. It raised slight colour in her. 'I'd be obliged, Susie Brown, if your parents would invite me to tea next Sunday week.'

'Mister Sammy, you can come to tea any Sunday you like, you know that. You only have to say. Why d'you want to come next Sunday week?'

'Well, the Paris shows will be well over by then, and Adams Fashions will have got off the ground. Also and further, I'll be wantin' to speak to your parents.'

'Oh,' said Susie, quivering again.

'Oh what?' asked Sammy, optimistic rather than confident.

'I don't know. Just oh.'

'I thought of arrivin' at four, if that's convenient.'

'Four. Next Sunday week. Yes.' Susie actually felt a little dizzy. It lasted for the rest of the day. It was present while they were with Lilian Hyams in Battersea, and while Sammy was receiving details from Mr Isaac

339

Moses concerning the Islington factory and the lease on the shop in Oxford Street.

When she finally arrived home in the evening, her mother thought she looked as if something rather exciting had happened to her. Sally asked if she'd lost a penny and found the Sheik of Araby, popularised by the song. Freddy said the Sheik of Araby wasn't much of a find, he only had a tent to live in and his horse shared it with him. When Susie went up to her room, Mrs Brown, naturally intrigued, went up after her. Susie was looking into her dressing-table mirror.

'Susie, has something nice happened after that awful fire?'

'I don't know,' said Susie.

'Don't know?'

'Well, I know Mister Sammy's makin' light of the fire, Mum. He's bounced back so cheerfully you'd think it hadn't happened.'

'Well, I expect that's what you're pleased about, lovey,' said Mrs Brown.

'Oh, he did say he'd like to come to tea Sunday week, so I invited him.'

'Sunday tea? Mister Sammy?'

'He said he wants to speak to you and Dad.'

'Susie, oh, my goodness, what about?'

'Ask me another,' said Susie.

This is your last chance, Sammy Adams, she thought, before I take Dad's chopper to you.

CHAPTER TWENTY-FIVE

The Paris fashion houses opened their salons to the world. The trade unions of Britain, seething at the injustice of low wages, long hours and continuing unemployment, thought the interest in fashions disgusting. The flappers did not.

On Thursday, Susie bought all the morning papers on her way to the office and rushed into Sammy's sanctum with them.

'Sammy, look!' She forgot business formality in her excitement.

'Good morning, Miss Brown. You have arrived distinctly refreshin', I see.' Susie wore a bright yellow jumper and a dark blue skirt. Spring daffodil, thought Sammy. 'I'm already lookin', by the way.'

The morning newspapers were on his desk. He had bought them too.

'But can you believe it?' Susie was radiant.

'It's in front of me eyes,' said Sammy. 'Our Mimi Dupont's anticipated the Frenchies.'

'Well, say something human,' begged Susie.

'Eureka,' said Sammy.

There they were on the fashion pages of every newspaper, photographs and sketches of the 1926 look proposed and created by the designers of Paris, with descriptions of the colours, the styles, the materials and the innovations. The colours sounded dazzling, the day dresses and dance dresses were all waistless, with rounded or pointed scalloped hems, or inserted flared pieces, like draped handkerchieves. And there were the abbreviated hemlines, the daring short-short look. Knees were in. Bobbed or shingled mannequins, poised on catwalks, were in haughty display of long legs and peeping knees.

Susie could hardly contain her excitement. Sammy was smiling. Lilian Hyams arrived, and she too was carrying the morning papers.

'Lilian, you did it, you were right,' laughed Susie, bubbling and sparkling.

Sammy, on his feet, said, 'I'm pleasured to congratulate you, Mimi.' And he kissed his designer. Lilian, no longer with hunger in her eyes, received the kiss enthusiastically.

'My life, such a smacker, Mister Adams.'

'Yer welcome,' said Sammy.

'You believed in me, you and Susie. And where's that handsome buck Tommy?'

'Islington fact'ry,' said Sammy, 'gettin' it fixed up. The machines arrive tomorrow.'

'Tomorrow's our day?' said Lilian.

'Tomorrow,' said Sammy, 'we go in and knock the West End buyers for six.'

That was Sammy's optimistic belief. But the day was a disaster, a fiasco. No one had ever said no to Sammy. At least, not for long. Lilian had harboured little doubts, little qualms, but had placed her trust and hopes in Sammy's infectious dynamism, supreme self-confidence and arresting personality. The collection was hung carefully in the van, and the van was driven by ex-Corporal Mitchell around the shops and stores of the West End. Lilian sat in the back, guarding the samples. Susie and Sammy sat next to Mitch, Sammy in his best grey overcoat and suit. Susie, hair newly dressed, looked lovely, but was all nerves. She was bravely prepared to model the collection, but was by no means an exhibitionist, nor could she contrive the haughtiness of professional mannequins.

She was not called upon to model a single one of Lilian's creations. Adams Fashions had never been heard of, nor had Mr Sammy Adams or Madame Mimi Dupont. Sammy had the list of buyers' names procured for him by Mr Greenberg, but for all the good it did him it might as well have been a list of East Street stall-holders. Adams Fashions were plainly regarded as interloping amateurs whose rightful place was Petticoat Lane. Susie, introduced as the firm's mannequin, was stared at by buyers' assistants as if she belonged to a dubious second-hand clothes stall. However, even if Sammy had hired a professional mannequin it would have made no difference. Not one buyer bothered to appear. Most, in any case, were busy studying the implications of the new Paris fashions, and some, of course, were in Paris.

'Do go away.'

'Who are you?'

'We've no interest in you.'

'Don't be absurd.'

'Please leave.'

'Where is your fashion house?'

'You're wasting your time. And ours.'

'Do go away.'

By late afternoon, total failure was obvious. Sammy's teeth were gritted, Lilian was brooding, and Susie felt sick with acute disappointment.

'All the same,' said Sammy, 'I ain't done for yet. I can't afford to be done for, but I'll admit me pride is suffering.'

Lilian went home with a headache. Neither her

portfolio nor any of her designs had been given a glance. Mitch drove Sammy and Susie back to Camberwell. They arrived in the offices a little before five. Boots came in to enquire about results. Sammy, in a brief exposition, revealed that results were nil, nothing and bloody hollow. Boots looked at Susie. Susie looked a nicely dressed and charming young lady. But she did not, he thought, look like a mannequin of flamboyant gestures or haughty carriage.

'Wrong presentation, probably,' he said. 'New tactics required. I'll make a couple of phone calls.'

He made them from his own office.

Polly was home, her leg healing rapidly, the stitches out, and the school still on Christmas holiday. The phone rang in the drawing-room. She answered it.

'How are you, Polly?' asked Boots.

'Is that my hero?'

'D'you want one? I'll find you one. How's your leg?'

'Leg singular? I happen to have two, old bean, and they're both visionary. I'm visionary everywhere, except for an unfortunate contusion on my left thigh. Not my best moment, that, letting my snorting beast run away with me. I think I was in too much of a hurry to get to Postman's Knock. Aren't you sweet to ring me?'

'My motive's suspect,' said Boots, 'I'm after something.'

'At last,' said Polly. 'Where d'you want to have it? Brighton?'

'I'm after what you can do for me as a well-dressed flapper, Polly. I think you're a customer at some of the best shops and stores in the West End.'

'Oh, you're interested in my ravishing undies? That's naughty, Robert old sport, but so exciting.'

'Leave off,' said Boots, and explained in detail Sammy's venture into fashions and how it had culminated in today's fiasco. Polly, who knew nothing about

344

Adams Fashions, was vastly intrigued.

'So Sammy fell flat on his face,' she said. 'Hysterical, darling. Has it put years on him?'

'It will do if he can't solve the problem.'

'No problem, old love. Harriet. She's the answer.'

'Who's Harriet?'

'Well, you've asked me, haven't you, if I can wangle things. Harriet de Vere, chief buyer for Coates, the West End store. That's not her real name. It's Bird. Her husband was Lieutenant Clarence Bird, killed in the war, poor devil. We knew her family. My father helped her to get a job with Coates immediately after the war. He's a shareholder. Leave it to me, sweetie, I'll see that Sammy gets the right kind of introduction to Harriet.'

'Bless you,' said Boots. 'And there's something else.' He explained what the something else was. A mannequin job, not only for her but for Sammy's friend Rachel Goodman as well. Polly yelped with delight.

'Crazy,' she laughed, 'crazy. Utter fun. No, wait a moment, are you sure this woman Lilian Hyams can design wearable stuff? I'm not pouring my perfect body into rubbish, not even for you, Robert.'

'Come in tomorrow morning and see for yourself.'

'Love to. Do you like her designs yourself?'

'I like the fact that I know they'd suit you, and that you'd suit them.'

'Is that good or bad, I wonder? But look, can't you use professionals?'

'I think they'd turn their noses up at working for an unknown designer.'

'They would. I won't. Darling, what a lark. I'll slay Harriet. I hope.'

'Adams Fashions will think the world of you, Polly.'

'Blow Adams Fashions, I'm doing it for you, sweetie, you know that. Now tell me what I get out of it.'

'I'll ask Sammy.'

'Miserable beast. Some husbands like to be faithful, I know, but you're ridiculous. Oh, come on, hero mine, at least present me with the order of your number one concubine.'

'Order presented,' said Boots. 'Turn up tomorrow in seven small veils or transparent Turkish pantaloons.'

'And then?'

'Tales of Arabian nights on Saturday morning in Camberwell, what else?'

'No wonder your daughter Rosie says your mother has never known what to do with you,' said Polly.

Boots rang Rachel next.

'Hello, you dear man,' said Rachel, 'to what do I owe the pleasure? The triumph of Adams Fashions? But I thought Sammy was going to give me the news himself.'

'He's speechless at the moment.' Boots described Sammy's day of disaster. Rachel expressed bitter disappointment. Boots said there was still a ray of hope and told her about Polly, who was going to arrange for Sammy to see the chief buyer at Coates. 'I think it's got to be one step at a time, Rachel. If he can do a deal with Coates, that's as good a beginning as we can expect.'

'Coates?' said Rachel. 'I should say it was.'

'You can help.'

'How?' asked Rachel.

'Well, you're good to look at,' said Boots. 'Striking, in fact.'

'Steady,' said Rachel.

'You're a natural for catching the eye, standing, sitting or walking. So do a mannequin job for us at Coates. Not by yourself. With Polly. She's also striking.'

'You're joking,' said Rachel.

'You only need to be yourself. Polly will put on an act. You don't need to. Have you ever been to a fashion show?'

'One or two, by special invitation.'

'Good. Susie's a lovely young lady, but mannequin stuff isn't her style. She's charming, but not extrovert. Polly is totally extrovert. You're self-assured. You get that from simply being beautiful.'

'You old dog,' said Rachel. 'You want me in Lilian's designs? I should be so outrageous? My daddy will sorrow for me. My life, my legs.'

'Yes, nice and long. Exactly what's called for. Many thanks, Rachel.'

'I'm helpless,' said Rachel. 'Your mama has much to answer for. One such son is enough. Two are one too many. Three are impossible. So how can I not do it? Monday?'

'Can you be here by half-nine?'

'For you and your family, and for me too, yes.'

'That's what I call a friend,' said Boots.

'That's what I call a sacrifice,' said Rachel.

On Saturday morning, Polly purred, gurgled and exclaimed over Lilian's collection. She tried on a number of designs that fitted her. She adored the audacious 1926 look. The injury to her thigh, covered by lint and a plaster, did not obtrude, it was too high up. Susie thought her theatrical but utterly right. Sammy thought her exciting, and Lilian saw the difference her posturings and mannerisms made to each garment. She did not simply wear them. She exhibited them.

Won over to a Monday performance, she advised Sammy she had been in touch with Harriet de Vere, and Sammy was to be there, with Lilian, at half-past ten.

'And you'll be here at half-nine on Monday morning?' said Boots. 'That's when Rachel's arriving.'

'The other half of the act?' said Polly.

'You'll like Rachel,' said Boots.

'She must be as crazy as I am,' said Polly.

347

'You're both gilt-edged,' said Sammy, 'you're both good friends.'

'Friendship has a lot to answer for,' said Polly.

The night darkness had not yet lifted at seven o'clock on Monday morning. Caulfield Place lay in silence, its pavements damp, the lamp outside the printing factory casting a misty glow. Light glimmered behind the curtains of some bedroom windows, where men were sleepily rising to prepare for an early start to their day's work.

The latchcord of a house door stretched to a pull and the door opened. In the dark passage a match was struck and the flame applied to a candle upright in its holder on the hallstand. The holder was lifted, and the candlelight illuminated the passage and the stairs. Shod feet began to quietly ascend the stairs.

Daisy, a light sleeper, awoke to the sound of a creaking board. There were never any creaks at seven in the morning. The creaking began only when her father went down to the kitchen to make tea and bring it to everyone, which was never before half-past seven. Daisy's subconscious reacted to a change in the pattern. She sat up in the darkness, the bedroom chill with January cold. A landing floorboard creaked. She heard a murmuring voice, the tones the soft ones of a woman. Was that Mummy? What was she doing up?

Daisy scrambled out of her bed and pattered over the lino in her bare feet to the door. She opened it. She saw her then, a woman with a lighted candle in her left hand, a long knife in her right hand. She was at the door of the front bedroom, where Daisy's parents slept. She was muttering.

Daisy screamed.

'Mummy, Mummy! Daddy, Daddy!'

It was her brothers, one fifteen and the other seven-

348

teen, who appeared first, charging out of the middle bedroom in their nightshirts. The woman did not struggle. She merely looked perplexed as the knife was wrested from her hand.

The police came a little later in answer to a summons. And at the police station a doctor was called to examine a woman who did not know her own name, but whom Boots and his family would have recognised as Elsie Chivers.

Harriet de Vere, chief buyer for Coates, was changing expression. She had been guardedly tolerant at first in her willingness to do a favour for Polly, an old friend and occasional customer. She was beginning to stare now, and so was her assistant.

Polly, of course, was a natural. She could have asked for a more spacious stage than the chief buyer's office, but she nevertheless performed with a dramatic range of gestures and movements. Her long cigarette holder was like a slender wand of black and silver in her right hand, her left hand rippling along her strings of beads. Around her bobbed hair was a purple bandeau with a black feather. The waistless day dress of bright purple that draped her body had a fringed hem that flirted just above her knees. Her legs were clad in black silk stockings. Her chin was lifted, her expression fixed and haughty. She moved with theatrical deliberation, aloof and red-lipped. Rachel, lush and sultry, glided to meet her in a dance dress of blazing tangerine, its scalloped hem lightly moving around her knees. Her strings of beads swung in her left hand, her right hand caressed the air. Her bandeau was silver, her feather matching her dress. She eschewed fashionable aloofness in favour of her rich smile and white teeth.

Harriet de Vere, impeccable in a dark grey tailored costume and white blouse, had returned from Paris on

349

Friday evening. She looked now as if she could not believe her eyes. Her assistant was rooted. Lilian stood well back, other creations over her arm. Sammy stood beside the assistant, hat and overcoat off, watching with new-found optimism as his amateur mannequins for the day met in studied deliberation. Close to the window, they were as far from their audience as they could get. Polly planted a chaste and haughty kiss on Rachel's cheek, and they murmured to each other.

'Dear God, what am I doing?' asked Rachel.

'No idea,' said Polly, 'but you're doing it rippingly, old thing.'

'Is anyone laughing?'

'No one.'

'Looking?'

'Everyone. Delicious, don't you think?' Polly turned and glided towards Sammy. Rachel weaved a half-circle, her smile vivid. Each moved differently. Legs were brilliant. It was simply not possible to ignore the effect each woman created. If Polly was perfection as a flapper, Rachel was representative of beauty in dazzling colour. To Polly it was exhilarating fun, a gorgeous lark. To Rachel it was time for a prayer. Polly was a mannequin to the manner born. Rachel was a sultry, provoking exponent whose smile hid her feelings of sacrifice.

The chief buyer's assistant took a deep breath. Harriet de Vere caught Polly's eye. Polly smiled.

'You're surprising me,' said Harriet, a woman of thirty. She looked at Sammy. 'I'll give you ten minutes, Mr Adams.'

But Sammy, Lilian, Rachel and Polly were still in Harriet's office long after ten minutes had elapsed.

Polly and Rachel had lunch at the Ritz. They had established a rapport.

350

'How long have you known the Adams family?' asked Polly.

'Since I was fourteen,' said Rachel. 'I'm a Jewish cockney.'

'I'm upper-class,' said Polly. 'Cheers, old thing.' They touched wine glasses and drank to each other. 'What a performance. Why did you do it?'

'I'm a shareholder,' said Rachel. 'Why did you?'

'I was asked,' said Polly, 'and had no idea how to say no.'

'Ah, Boots, of course,' said Rachel. 'I have my own problems with Sammy.'

'Have you and I got something in common?' asked Polly. 'Do we both want something we can't have?'

'I should answer a question like that?' smiled Rachel.

'What a life,' said Polly, and they laughed together.

Susie had spent the day at the office, unable to bear the possibility of being present at another fiasco. For his part, Boots wondered if it wasn't time Sammy made up his mind about Susie. The bonehead was obviously besotted with her.

Susie felt more comfortable working at her desk. She had not felt at all comfortable about the possibility of exhibiting herself as a mannequin for Sammy. She prayed he would not come back today wearing his previous tight-mouthed look of failure.

He was not back at all by the end of her working day. She went into Boots's office to say good night to him. She felt very low at having to wait until tomorrow for news. When she mentioned to Boots she was going to have a rotten night worrying, Boots said, 'Well, while you're tossing and turning, Susie, think about what the inebriated general said when he was waiting to hear whether his troops were flat on their backs or still standing up.'

351

'What did he say?'

' "In my condition, no news is good news." '

'Oh, that old chestnut,' said Susie.

'It's all we've got, love, so hang on to it.'

The phone in the general office rang after Susie had gone. As everyone else had also departed, Boots went in to answer it, feeling it had to be Sammy.

'Adams Enterprises,' he said.

'Ugh to Adams Enterprises, Robert old darling.'

'Hello, Polly.'

'I hoped I might catch you. Pleased with Polly, are you?'

'Should I be? I'm hoping so.'

'Sammy hasn't phoned? No, I suppose not. He talked just before lunch of going to Islington with Madame Pompadour, the designer. There's a contract coming up from Coates of Knightsbridge.'

'Tell me.'

'I'm at the Ritz. I've just had a pot of tea and some rounds of toast. I'm wearing one of your designer's day dresses. It's a knockout. Everyone's been looking. The colour, you know, a purple gold. Sounds hideous? Well, it isn't. And over lunch here, Rachel was slaying upper-class flappers in fiery tangerine. Hers and mine were both presents from Sammy. Dearie, that brother of yours, what he can do with the English language has to be heard to be believed. Listen, sweetie.'

Boots listened. The buyer at Coates had fought a losing battle with her own reactions, with Lilian's portfolio and samples, and with Sammy's eccentric English. After fifteen minutes, she was no longer a free woman. She was trapped. But of course, said Polly, the fact was the captive Mrs Harriet de Vere knew the collection was irresistible. Polly and Rachel were requested to try on other designs. Lilian brought more from the van, parked outside the store. Sammy pointed out that if the collection as a whole didn't stand up to the new Paris fashions, he would eat his way through Tower Bridge, whether it was up or down. Polly thought that by this time Harriet, whose business name showed where her prejudices lay, had become a little stupefied. But she was still smart, and began to talk about an exclusive contract. Sammy demurred on the grounds that it would limit the horizons of Adams Fashions. Mrs de Vere, jolly handsome, you know, said Polly, confessed she was a war widow and suggested Sammy should call back when the store closed and accompany her to her Kensington flat, where they could còntinue discussions without interruption. Meanwhile, she would lunch with him and Lilian. She was set by then on an exclusive contract for Coates. She mentioned they had branches in the swankiest shopping areas of Exeter, Bristol, Oxford, Bournemouth, Eastbourne, Brighton, Guild-ford, Bath and God knows where else. It was an attempt to stun Sammy. Sammy, of course, could see the advantages. He couldn't possibly meet other contracts on his present basis of production. But he refused to be stunned. He simply said he'd spend the afternoon doing costing so that he could have figures to present to her at her flat in the evening. He not only had all the answers, he looked so distinguished he was hardly believable.

'Where did he get that look? He was only a flash barrow-boy a few years ago.'

'He decided to become a reputable business gent,' said Boots. 'Is there more to tell? If so, carry on.'

'Willingly, old love. My foot's in your camp.'

'Mrs de Vere suddenly said she didn't want to upset anyone, and then proceeded to upset Lilian by saying she had to be sure there was no possibility the designs had been copied from the French. Sammy asked if she meant pinched. Mrs de Vere said with respect that such things happened. Lilian said they hadn't happened in this case. Further, the Paris shows were only just over. Further, she had never been outside England. Sammy said behold, and took a letter from an envelope clipped inside the back of the portfolio. It was a letter from a solicitor stating in clear terms that the designs, twenty-four in number, had been inspected by him on 17 December 1925, that he had stamped and initialled each one in confirmation and had photograph copies in his office.

Sammy then showed Mrs de Vere that each sketch in the portfolio bore the solicitor's stamp and initial on the reverse. He said there were so many suspect characters operating in the rag trade that when he had taken on Madame Dupont it was needful to protect her honour and reputation. Polly said Rachel looked as if she was splitting her sides at this. Mrs de Vere looked satisfied in a jolly pleased way, she having taken to Sammy by then. It was odds on she might want to nibble his ears when she got him to her flat. Rachel said later, over lunch, that Sammy would fight anything like that.

'Now are you pleased with me, Robert old sport?'

'Enraptured,' said Boots.

'Well, then?'

'Love you, Polly.'

'Say that again.'

'Love you, just as much as I love Lizzy.'

'You swine, Lizzy's your sister.'

'You're not complaining, are you, Polly? I'm not.'

'Listen, stinker, I'll be a sister to you when I'm ninety, never before. Oh, well, see you Thursday evening when I restart cramming Rosie. Had fun today. Sammy's a knockout. Toodle-ooh, old top.'

'Many thanks, Polly.'

As Boots put the phone down, Mitch put his head in.

'I'm back, guv. I got to bring the stuff up from the van. I just come from Islington. Yer kid brother said I wasn't to take it 'ome. I dunno, it's all go.'

'All right, bring it up, Mitch. And look, on your way home, would you drop a note in at Susie's house for me?'

'Lay it in me mitt, sarge.' To Mitch, ex-West Kents, Boots would always be his sergeant first, his employer second.

Susie opened the delivered note.

'Susie. Have a sound night. Sammy won. But leave the port alone. Boots.'

The following day, florists deposited a huge bouquet into the arms of the butler at the residence of General Simms. The bouquet was for Polly. With it was a brief note from Boots.

'Thanks, love.'

A similar one, with a similar note, reached the arms of Rachel.

The same day, Boots, turning the pages of the *South London Press*, the local newspaper, came across a news item that reported the detention by the police of a nameless woman following a disturbance at a house in Caulfield Place, Walworth.

And later, Boots received a phone call from Freddy about the incident.

'They copped 'er, Mister Adams. Daisy told me last night. It was 'er all right. Daisy said she 'ad a knife, a long one. She went in Daisy's 'ouse an' Daisy 'eard 'er comin' up the stairs. Cor, ain't she a queer one? They'll put 'er in the mad 'ouse, I reckon. You there, Mister Adams?'

'I'm here, Freddy. Thanks for ringing.'

'I fought you might like to know.'

'Yes, thanks. I'll pay you for the phone next time I see you.'

355

'Oh, yer don't 'ave to worry about that, Mister Adams.'

'So long, Freddy.'

'Any time, Mister Adams.'

The call gave Boots food for deep thought. She'd gone right over the top. She'd taken a knife into the house in which she had lived with her mother, and in which her mother's throat had been cut. She had become a woman haunted by the event. His conclusion about her became a conviction. What did 'nameless' mean in that newspaper report? That her troubled, haunted conscience had taken refuge in forgetfulness? Amnesia? Was that the word? What good would that do her? Her possessions, her birth and marriage certificates were in an upstairs back room of a house in Westmoreland Road. The landlady there would not let that room stand empty for long, and the police, of course, would do their best to find out all they could about the woman they were holding. They would ask around in Caulfield Place, and some of them would recall the unsolved murder and the woman who had been tried and found not guilty. They would take another look at her. And her birth and marriage certificates would inevitably come to light.

What would he do?

He could help her no more. She would end up in an asylum, for the law could not try her again.

Remembering her as she had been, during the years of his youth, the long-suffering daughter of an intractable and impossible mother, Boots sighed for her.

CHAPTER TWENTY-SIX

The contract to supply Coates of Knightsbridge and all their branches had been agreed and was being drawn up at speed under the supervision of Harriet de Vere. Coates were to launch Adams Fashions and its label. The factory at Islington was working full out, Lilian was on the way to being made as a designer, and Sammy was on the way to making his fortune. Susie was ecstatic.

'I need a new secretary,' said Sammy.

'I'm unsatisfactory?' she enquired, knowing she wasn't.

'You're valuable as my personal assistant,' said Sammy. 'We can make a secretary of a shorthand-typist. A good shorthand-typist. All these offices are bunged up with work. Boots needs more staff, I need more staff. The secretary'll be for you, Miss Brown.'

'Oh, Sammy, stop calling me Miss Brown when we're together.'

'Very good, Miss Brown, quite so,' said Sammy.

'Now you're mockin' me. Oh, did you say a secretary for me?'

'Your forthcomin' status requires you to have a secretary.'

'My what?'

'You're not goin' to be just anybody,' said Sammy. She was going to be Mrs Sammy Adams, whatever it

357

cost him. His phone rang. Doreen said Mrs de Vere was on the line, and put her through.

'Sammy?' said Mrs de Vere.

'Good morning, Harriet,' said Sammy, and Susie's eyes began to spark. That woman. She was always phoning Sammy. And there he was, calling her Harriet when he hadn't known her for five minutes. Susie listened to him answering unnecessary questions about production and delivery, which had been agreed on already.

When he put the phone down, Susie said, 'I'll talk to that woman in future, she's takin' up too much of your time.'

'Good idea, Susie. You do that. I got a horrendous feeling she's after my incorrupted body.'

'You don't fancy that?'

'She'll eat me,' said Sammy.

Susie laughed then. It pealed from her. Sammy grinned.

'Being eaten could be ever so painful,' she said.

'We'll handle her, Susie, between us. In the right way, mind. She's the icing on our cake now.'

'Duly noted, Mister Sammy. You mentioned my forthcomin' status. What's it mean?'

'I'll advise you at an early date.'

Early? Susie thought. Sunday tea? When he was going to speak to her parents?

Doreen knocked and put her head in.

'Someone wants to see you, Mister Sammy,' she said.

'Who?' asked Sammy.

'He just said he's Bert.'

'Send him in.'

Bert, Gertie's husband, came in, cap in his hand, suit shabby but shirt clean.

'Thought I'd best come an' see yer, guv,' he said. 'Morning, Miss Brown.'

'Good morning, Bert,' said Susie.

'Right, that's what you were, Mister Adams, right,' said Bert. 'The bleeder took a 'andful o' notes as well as a box of matches. I 'ad to tread on 'is plates o' meat a mite. 'E 'owled something shockin', but 'e come up with the goods. Wasn't Morris, guv. Two large geezers and a big fat one, the fat one in the background, like.'

'Fat Man?' said Sammy. 'Him again?'

'It ain't Morris's fact'ry what Morris 'as set 'isself up in, it's Fatty's,' said Bert. 'Morris is just runnin' it for 'im. I just found that out. I got eyes an' ears round corners, guv. I come to see yer on account of Daft Dick tellin' me, with tears in 'is eyes on account of his feet 'urting bad, that yer Islington fact'ry's goin' to get done. Goin' to be smashed up and set fire to. Tomorrer night.'

Sammy sighed. The Fat Man, Ben Ford, had tried to close him down when he first opened up here in Camberwell. Boots had used old comrades to prick the balloon. Fatty hadn't forgotten that, and now he was extending his business into the East End, he was after getting his own back. Dangerous, that was. For Fatty.

'Bert, yer a friend. Here, you've come all this way, so use this to buy yourself a pint and a sandwich across the road.'

'Don't want that, guv, I never come for it and I ain't takin' it.'

'Good enough,' said Sammy, and put the pound note back into his wallet.

'Gertie an' the girls is goin' great guns in Islington,' said Bert. 'Gertie says they're singing. See yer again some time. So long, Miss Brown.'

Sammy spoke to Boots, and Boots spoke to Mitch. Mitch began to contact old comrades.

'Just this one game, Daddy,' said Rosie that evening. She and Boots had settled themselves down in the

sitting-room for a game of draughts. 'Then I'll do homework, I promise.'

She would keep the promise. But she would enjoy the
game first. She enjoyed any activity with her foster-
father. Emily and Chinese Lady were in the kitchen
with Tim at the moment. Rosie had Boots all to herself.
They began the game, Boots making quick moves,
Rosie dwelling on hers. She had some of his men cornered after a while, and he did some dwelling then, one
hand in his hair, the other on the table.

'Well,' he said.

'Got you there, Daddy,' she said. He smiled. She put
her own hand over his and gave his fingers a love
squeeze. She sometimes couldn't help demonstrative
little gestures like that.

The doorbell rang.

'I'll go,' she said.

On the doorstep stood two people, a man and a
woman. The man wore a black Bohemian hat and a
flashy caped overcoat. The woman wore a fur coat and
a green velvet hat. Her lips were red, her face heavily
made-up. The time was seven-fifteen. They had to be
on stage for their first entrance at eight forty-five.

'Good evening, young lady,' said the man, and the
woman stared intently at the girl, noting her prettiness.

'Good evening,' said Rosie, disliking the way she was
being looked at.

'Is Mr Adams home?' asked the woman, smiling with
artificial brilliance.

'Yes, he's my father,' said Rosie.

'Is he?' said the woman, round face a trifle plump.
'Ask him if he'll talk to us.'

Rosie went to the sitting-room door.

'Daddy, a lady and gentleman want to talk to you.'

Boots went to the door. He recognised the woman at
once. Milly Pearce, Rosie's mother. Her real name was

360

Tooley. He told Rosie to go and talk to Tim in the kitchen. Rosie, who had not seen her mother for well over five years and did not recognise her, went to the kitchen. Boots brought Milly Pearce and her male companion into the sitting-room.

'D'you know me?' asked Milly.

'I know you,' said Boots, 'and your friend. You're both performing in pantomime at the moment.'

'You've got my daughter,' said Milly. 'I saw my father last Sunday and he told me about Rosie and where she was. He had to, me being her mother. I was expectant of him caring for her.'

'Yes, I saw the note you left on your kitchen mantelpiece,' said Boots.

'Well, I was in great stress at the time, I couldn't take care of her myself, not then, which Mr Rainbould knows.'

'You're Mr Rainbould,' said Boots to the master magician.

'I have that honour, sir,' said Rainbould, 'I am he. I am happy to meet you, knowing you've taken good care of Milly's daughter. We can't, alas, stay long, we are due at the Camberwell Palace in a little while. You are probably well acquainted with my name and reputation. Milly is my well-known assistant, her stage name being Vivette. Ah, yes, and now that she's no longer pressed by ills and misfortune, she naturally wishes to have Rosie back.'

'We called tonight just to let you know,' said Milly, remembering how she had fancied Boots and how he had kept turning her down. 'We thought it was only fair to do that, to let you know. We'll come and collect her later, at the end of the pantomime run, near the end of the month. Rosie was always a dear pretty girl, I was tragic not havin' the means to provide for her, but I'm better off now, havin' paid all my debts, and

Mr Rainbould is natur'lly prepared to see she has a lovely future on the stage.'

Emily came in then, having talked to Rosie about the callers. Her quick eyes at once took in the overdressed look of the woman and the flamboyant airs of the man. She searched the woman's face, and her wide firm mouth compressed.

'You're Milly Pearce,' she said stiffly.

'And you're Em'ly Adams, I'd know your face anywhere.' Milly was vinegary in her snide reference to Emily's plainer features. 'You and your husband's got my little girl Rosie. I was telling him I'm in a position to take care of her myself now. I thought my parents would look after her, I was surprised to hear you two had her. I didn't give no permission for you to. Still, she looks all right, so I'm not goin' to complain. Of course, me and Mr Rainbould haven't come to take her right now—'

'You're not takin' her at all,' said Emily.

'Alas, dear madam,' said Mr Rainbould, holding his hat over his heart, 'her mother has prior claim to her under the law of the land.'

Boots, steely, regarded the prize pair in hard, sharp suspicion. He thought about their act, the man visibly past his best. Drink was probably something to do with that, if his florid complexion was anything to go by. And the woman had little to offer apart from her theatrical tights and her artificial smile. They were probably down on their luck, with engagements few and far between. The woman's round face was coarse beneath its powder, her mouth sullen. Boots reflected on what might be the real reason for their call and their threat.

'How much?' he asked.

'I beg your pardon?' said Milly, her aged fur coat bristling.

'How much?' repeated Boots.

'Don't offer them money,' said Emily, green eyes flashing. 'She doesn't even have a father for Rosie, nor a husband for herself. The courts won't take Rosie away from us and give her to a woman who works on the stage and doesn't have a husband.'

'Mr Rainbould is my husband,' said Milly.

'I do indeed have that honour,' said Mr Rainbould, running his tongue over his bottom lip as if in need of liquid refreshment. 'And I am willing, of course, to be a father to Rosie and to see to her future. It will be a privilege.'

'Very well,' said Boots, 'by the end of January, then. Bring clothes for her, and shoes. You'll naturally wish your privilege to extend to providing her with a wardrobe.'

'I must say, sir, that sounds a trifle small-minded,' said Mr Rainbould, 'and not in keeping with the handsomeness of this abode.'

'This abode belongs to my mother and step-father,' said Boots. 'If you'll call again at the end of this week, we'll have Rosie ready for you.'

'Here, look,' said Milly crossly, 'there's no call to be in a rush to settle things. We've come here friendly, just to talk about it, which you can't say's not fair. We don't mind comin' again to talk more about it and settle it so there's no hard feelings.'

'We must go now, Milly my love,' said Mr Rainbould, certain he was not going to be offered a whisky, a constant consolation for a master magician who had never been fully appreciated.

'I've got a mother's feeling for Rosie,' said Milly. 'I've suffered tortured times thinking about my little girl.'

That was too much for Emily.

'Oh, you cheeky bitch,' she said, 'you left Rosie alone in the house, you went off not caring a thing about her. This is the first time you've shown your face. Well, it's not goin' to do you any good, you're not goin' to have Rosie, nor put her on any stage all painted up.'

'Really, my dear Mrs Adams,' said Mr Rainbould in a pained way, 'that is a little uncharitable. Milly and I will naturally sympathise with your desire to keep Rosie.'

'Course we will,' said Milly, 'but I hope I won't be spoken to in a common way again.' She addressed herself to Boots. 'We'll come again Sunday morning and have another talk, if that's convenient.'

'Yes, work out how much by Sunday,' said Boots.

'My dear sir,' protested Mr Rainbould.

'I'll see you out,' said Boots.

After the master magician and his powdered assistant had gone, Emily said fiercely, 'They're not havin' Rosie, she's ours. I feel like I gave birth to her myself. What got into you, talking about givin' them money?'

'It's what they came for, Em.'

'They didn't say so.'

'No. They went through the overture. On Sunday the curtain will rise and the performance will begin. They're down on their luck, old girl, and the last thing they want is to be lumbered with Rosie.'

'I'm not so sure, and you can be too clever by half sometimes,' said Emily. 'They could be thinking of using her on the stage now. She's such a pretty girl, they could be thinking of dressin' her up in tinsel and spangles and using her in disappearing acts. Help, they were the pair we saw at the panto on New Year's Eve, only her hair was different.'

'A theatrical wig,' said Boots.

'Look, don't count your chickens.'

'I hope they do want money. Legally, we've no hold on Rosie. But we would have if we adopted her by her mother's consent. Tarty Milly would have to sign her over, of course. How much, I wonder, is her signature on the dotted line going to cost us? She'll get nothing unless she does sign.'

'Just don't take it for granted she don't have her own ideas about Rosie, but if you're right, she might ask for what we can't afford.'

'We'll have to afford it,' said Boots.

'Well, I'm not partin' with her, not even if we have to go through the courts,' said Emily.

'Bless you,' said Boots. 'Not a word to her, of course.'

'As if I would. I'll go and make some coffee and tell Rosie she can come and finish her game of draughts with you. And when Tim starts school later this year, I'll come and work full-time for you. Well, up to half-past three in the afternoon, when I'll go and collect him and Rosie then. Chinese Lady says she don't mind me workin' for the fam'ly firm. I want to, anyway.'

'Sure?' said Boots.

'Yes.' Emily smiled. 'I likes yer for me boss.'

The ex-Servicemen of the West Kents and East Surreys, with a few Old Contemptibles, crossed the river by way of Blackfriars Bridge in the early evening, and reached Sammy's Islington factory just after the day's work was finished and the machinists had gone home to Shoreditch. Tommy had also gone. Boots had told him not to hang around. But Bert was there. The factory urn was full of freshly made hot tea. Mitch was in charge of the old comrades, who had done a job for Sergeant Adams once before. They drank tea and they waited. They did so in the darkness. They had to wait until after midnight. They heard the saboteurs then. They opened the main doors of the factory, poured out and met the enemy head-on. They used leather truncheons. They drew blood and they cracked a bone or two. No one came out of nearby houses. No one who woke up emerged to interfere. They all stayed put and minded their own business. It was over and the old comrades well away with Bert by the time the first copper's whistle sounded.

On Sunday morning, Boots opened the door at eleven o'clock to Milly Pearce and Mr Rainbould. Or perhaps it was Mr and Mrs Rainbould. If they were married, the significance of that to Boots was in the fact that it gave Milly a stronger claim to custody of Rosie. They assured him they were willing to be reasonable, although they protested the moment he asked them how much they wanted in settlement of the matter. Chinese Lady was at church with Tim and Rosie, and neither Boots nor Emily wanted to endure a prolonged discussion. They wanted it settled before church was over. So how much?

Mr Rainbould made pained gestures and Milly kept saying, 'Well, really.'

'Make up your minds,' said Boots.

Mr Rainbould managed to say that to deprive a mother of the pleasure of being reunited with her only child should mean offering her recompense. It was not what she had wanted, but if Mr and Mrs Adams were so set on keeping the dear little girl, Milly would not show a hard heart.

'Isn't that so, my love?'

'Well, yes,' said Milly.

'I repeat, we are prepared to be reasonable,' said Mr Rainbould.

'How reasonable?' asked Emily.

'Ah,' said Mr Rainbould.

'The thought of takin' money, well, I don't know,' said Milly. 'Like Mr Rainbould said, it wasn't what we had in mind.'

'It's a difficult decision to make,' said Mr Rainbould, and passed a silken handkerchief over his forehead.

'It's hardly decent,' said Milly, 'my own little girl and all.'

'Well, how decent is fifty pounds?' asked Boots.

'Oh, yer disgustin' man,' said Milly indignantly.

'Really, sir, that is farcical,' said Mr Rainbould. 'A moment.' He drew Milly aside and they whispered. She fished in her handbag, took out her hankie and dabbed her eyes. 'Don't upset yourself, my dear,' said Mr Rainbould, and looked up, his florid face shiny. 'My wife, Mr Adams, is heartbroken. What could recompense that? It hurts us both to concede a financial settlement, or to even think about it.'

Their performance, thought Boots, was first-class.

'Yes, of course,' he said, 'but give it a go.'

'If, sir, for the sake of not disturbing Rosie's life, there must be a settlement,' said Mr Rainbould, 'we suggest a thousand pounds.'

'You horrid creatures,' said Emily.

'Madam, it is not your heart that is broken.'

'Five hundred,' said Boots, 'and that's our utmost limit.'

'Ah,' said Mr Rainbould again, and Milly's floury face showed the glimpse of a quick, greedy smile.

But she said, 'Well, I don't know, I just don't know.'

'Make no mistake,' said Boots, 'it's take it or leave it.'

Emily eyed the pair in disgust. Boots was right, it was money they'd had in mind from the start. It's as plain now as the nose on my face, and that's as plain as anything could be.

'Allow us, sir, a natural distress,' said Mr Rainbould.

'I've never been more distressed,' said Milly, and dabbed at her nose. 'But – well, all right.'

'On condition you sign the necessary papers approving our adoption of Rosie,' said Boots. 'Otherwise, not a penny, and you can take yourselves off and apply to the courts.'

'Where we shall fight you,' said Emily.

'The courts?' Mr Rainbould permitted himself a shudder. 'Come, madam, do we wish to line the pockets of lawyers?'

'If you agree to the adoption,' said Boots, 'you have my word the money will be paid to you in full as soon as the papers are signed.'

'We don't want a lot of rigmarole,' said Milly.

'Just the minimum,' said Boots, 'and it won't hurt.'

'Oh, all right,' said Milly.

'Where we goin' to get five hundred pounds from?' asked Emily when she and Boots were alone. 'We only have about two hundred savings.'

'We'll borrow the rest from the firm,' said Boots. 'Sammy will agree to a director's loan. He's riding so high at the moment that he'll hardly feel the pain.'

'He had a flush and a bit of a cough yesterday morning at the office.'

'The flush of success and the strain on his vocal cords,' said Boots.

'Did you get Mitch up to something on Thursday?' asked Emily.

'Nothing out of the ordinary,' said Boots.

CHAPTER TWENTY-SEVEN

Just before Susie and her family sat down to Sunday dinner, a boy from Camberwell arrived with a letter. Susie, taking it from him at the door, saw that it was addressed to her. She recognised the writing on the envelope. Sammy's. She ripped it open and took out a brief note from Sammy.

'*Dear Susie. Laid out with a sore throat. Lost my voice. Can't come to tea. Regards and apologies to your mum and dad. Don't want to risk passing it on to everyone. Sorry, Susie. Love, Sammy.*'

'Are you goin' back to Mister Adams?' she asked the boy.

'Not likely I ain't, I'm goin' 'ome to me dinner,' he said.

'Did you see Mister Adams when he gave you this letter?'

'Only 'is bonce. Out of the top winder, it was. He dropped the letter down, wiv a tanner. He waved 'is 'and about. So I called up, "I gotcher, Mister Adams." I knows 'im, yer see.'

'All right,' said Susie, and the boy went off at the double. Susie addressed the printing factory. 'I'm not havin' this, Sammy Adams, oh, no. It's just one more way of being a coward. I'm comin' after you, Sammy Adams, and bringing my dad's chopper with me.'

*　　　*　　　*

369

It was half-past three when Susie, in her best Sunday coat and hat, entered through the door at the side of the shop, went up the stairs, passed the main door to the offices, and climbed the next flight to the second floor. There she knocked loudly on the door of Sammy's flat.

Sammy staggered out of bed, wrapped himself in his winter dressing-gown of dark blue wool with white piping, tottered into the lobby and opened the door.

'Oh, dear,' said Susie, 'oh, you poor thing. Oh, dear, I am sorry.'

Sammy, his hair tousled and untidy for once, his chin lacking the usual attentions of his morning razor, his face flushed, blinked at her in the way of a man who didn't quite know what had hit him.

'Go away,' he croaked.

'Certainly not,' said Susie. 'Oh, dear, dear, dear. Look at you. What have you done to yourself, left your vest off somewhere, I suppose. Not at Harriet's, I hope. Go on, back to your bed, and I'll take your temperature.' She stepped in and closed the door. Sammy backed off.

'Go away,' he croaked again, 'you'll catch me germs.'

'I'm not daft, I gargled with a throat disinfectant before I came out. Come along.' She took his arm. 'Where's your bedroom?'

'I ain't sure,' said Sammy, hoarse and husky, but he managed to find it. Susie hustled him in.

'Come along, back into your bed,' she said. She pulled the blankets and sheet down, and Sammy got in, still in his dressing-gown. She covered him up and tucked him in. 'Oh, dear, we are poorly, aren't we?' she said.

'I ain't a pretty sight,' croaked Sammy.

'Nor was I when I had mumps and you pushed your way in,' said Susie. She opened her large handbag and took out the family thermometer.

'Here, hold up,' said Sammy, sounding hoarser.

'Open your mouth.'

'I'm all right.'

'Of course you're not. Open your mouth.'

'Look, I—'

Susie popped the thermometer in. Sammy muttered around it.

'Don't start growling, you'll snap it,' she said. 'Or swallow it. Hand.' Sammy sucked ferociously at the thermometer. 'Hand,' repeated Susie. He gave her his hand and she felt for his pulse. She had no idea how to correctly check a pulse rate. She was simply putting Sammy through it. 'Oh, dear, if only Harriet could see you now, we really are poorly, aren't we? Now don't fidget. One, two, one, two – oh, lor'. Never mind, it's not as bad as mumps.' Sammy growled, and the thermometer rolled about. Susie smiled lovingly. 'I'm goin' to mix you two Beecham's powders and then make you a hot lemon drink. I've brought two lemons. Are you a bit feverish?' She placed a hand on his forehead. The coolness of her fingers was balm to Sammy's flushed brow. 'Well, you're not on fire,' she said. She took the thermometer out and peered at it. She could at least read a thermometer.

'Just don't worry,' said Sammy, 'I don't mind dying quietly.'

'I'll come to your funeral, if I've got time,' said Susie. He had said that to her once. 'But I think you'll be all right. Your temperature's short of the hundred.'

'Don't like you catchin' it,' he croaked, and glowered as she patted his pillows. She smiled. His little grin arrived. 'You Susie,' he said.

'You Sammy,' she said, and looked around the room. It was nicely furnished, if you liked mahogany. 'Well, I'll go and mix the Beecham's. I'll find the kitchen.'

She found it. It was surprisingly neat and tidy for a

371

bachelor. She warmed some water in a kettle, found a glass in a cupboard, and shook in the contents of two powders. She carried the glass to him.

' 'Orrible,' said Sammy, regarding the mixture with distaste. His voice was almost gone.

'Sit up,' said Susie, 'or you'll pour it all over your face.' Sammy sat up and took the glass. He drank the mixture at one go, to get it over with. 'There,' said Susie, taking the empty glass from him, 'aren't you a good boy?'

Sammy almost fell dangerously ill at being called a good boy.

'Susie Brown, I think you're comin' it a bit.' The words scraped his throat.

'Don't talk,' said Susie, 'I can't make out what you're saying, anyway. You sound like sandpaper fightin' a nutmeg grater. Just use this.' She picked up what she had seen on his little bedside table. A writing block and pencil. Typical. She could imagine him waking up in the middle of the night and jotting down a business idea or a reminder. 'While you're still sittin' up, just write.' She gave him the block and the pencil.

'Write what?' Sammy made himself heard.

'What you were goin' to say to me after you'd spoken to my mum and dad.'

'Eh?'

'Write it, then I'll go and make you the hot lemon drink.'

'Eh?'

'Just write it down, Sammy Adams.'

'Well, it hurts talkin', I can tell you,' he said, and bent his head over the pad. He wrote. Susie took the top sheet, ripping it off. She read his words.

'Would you kindly marry me before I pass on?'

'You'll be lucky,' she said.

'Pardon?' said Sammy in shock.

372

'It's not good enough,' said Susie, and gave the sheet of paper back to him. Sammy gaped.

'Susie, you turning me down?'

'I'm turning that down,' said Susie, 'it's just not good enough.'

The penny dropped. He had a headache and a fiery throat, but the penny managed to drop. He wrote more and handed her the sheet. She read the new words.

Dear Susie, business comes second to you. I loved you when I first saw you, it's given me a terrible time. Now it's making me ill. Do a life-saving job and marry me. You're an angel. Love, Sammy.

'That's better,' said Susie. She folded the sheet of paper and put it into her handbag. 'I'll make the hot lemon drink now. You can lie down again, you needn't sit up again until I come back. Oh, dear, how the mighty's fallen.'

Sammy watched her disappear again. That Susie. What was she up to? She hadn't said yes and she hadn't said no. He lay back. The Beecham's powders began to work. His headache slowly eased and the fire in his throat cooled a bit. Suppose she said no? Suppose she just said she was flattered to be asked, but didn't want to marry him? I'll jump off Tower Bridge. No, that wouldn't do the business any good, nor me either. Was there someone else? Did she have a crush on Boots?

She came back after ten minutes, her coat off, her blue cloche hat cuddling her bright hair, her royal blue dress new, her legs clad in dark blue silk. Silk. It's deliberate, that's what it is. Deliberate. She knows I can't talk, she knows I'm not myself, and she's brought herself here in a new dress and silk stockings.

'You Susie—'

'Stop croaking,' she said, the glass of hot lemonade in her hand.

'I'm croaking all right, I'll be gone in an hour.'

'I'll go and fetch the vicar,' said Susie, 'but first you'd better drink this. Sit up, come along.' Sammy perceptibly growled. 'Stop swearing. Sit up.' He heaved himself up and took the glass. 'You should drink lots, and stay in bed for a few days. Don't go out in the cold or you'll be worse before you're better. I'll see to things in the office and keep in touch with Tommy at Islington. I'll pop up here from time to time and nurse you a bit.'

Sammy, sipping the hot drink, almost choked on it.

'You'll what?'

'And I'll see you get some food. Bovril, porridge and rice puddings will be best. And lots of oranges. I'll make you a nice little tea in about an hour, and read to you as soon as you've finished the lemonade. Reading to the sick is soothing, I read that somewhere. Is the lemonade sweet enough? I found your sugar in the tea caddy. Your tea's in the sugar caddy.'

'That's it, drive me barmy,' said Sammy. The lemonade, tingling and biting, did wonders to his throat. He finished it. She took the glass from him and placed it on the bedside table.

'There, you can lie back again now,' she said.

'What's the point? I'm done for.' But he lay back and watched her. She took a book from her handbag, a book with a colourful picture on its cover. She sat down in a chair and crossed her legs. The silk stockings ran with gleaming light. Mother O'Reilly, thought Sammy, she's running rings round me.

She opened the book and leafed through it.

'Oh, here's a really nice story, with a nice endin' too,' she said. 'You'll like it, it's very soothing.' She began to read. 'Once upon a time in the land of daffodils and tulips, and of egg-cups made with marzipan, there was a Princess called Petal—'

'Bloody hell,' said Sammy.

The open book was lowered a fraction. Blue eyes looked reproachfully at him.

'Is that nice, Sammy Adams?'

'There's a lot more of it to come while I'm still alive. When I'm gone—'

'Don't be silly now,' said Susie, 'you can't go yet, not till after Easter.'

'Easter?'

'Easter Saturday.'

'That's a good day to go,' muttered Sammy.

'Not for you it isn't,' said Susie, 'there's the wedding.'

'Wedding?'

'Ours,' she said. Sammy stared at her. He knew then that she was laughing at him. Her expression was quite grave, but she was laughing all right, it was there in those eyes of hers. He knew something else too. The skinny waif he'd given a job to over five years ago had grown into a woman who was always going to be one up on him. It didn't bear thinking about. But look at her. She was worth every penny of a fortune, as long as there was some left for overheads.

'Susie, you witch.' He was croaking again. 'You've been havin' me on.'

'No, only hittin' you with me dad's chopper,' she said. She reached and squeezed his hand. She laughed. 'Oh, Sammy, you are lovely,' she said.

'Not by a long shot,' said Sammy, 'but I think I'm goin' to recover.'

Mrs Stubbs of Westmoreland Road, an honest woman, went to the police station to report that her lodger, a Mrs Adams, had gone missing and had left behind a suitcase containing valuables. Mrs Stubbs said she'd taken it on herself to open the case because she was worried, especially as her lodger had been a dreamy kind of woman. The police investigated, and turned the

375

suitcase inside-out. What they found was of much interest to them. And Mrs Stubbs's description of her missing lodger pointed them to the woman they had released from custody into a hospital. They made no charges. She belonged where she was, in hospital.

The next edition of the *South London Press* carried a report that the nameless woman who had been arrested for disturbing the peace was actually Mrs Elsie Lansberg, formerly Miss Elsie Chivers, who had been acquitted in 1914 of the murder of her mother. She had suffered a nervous breakdown and was now in hospital.

Boots, for all his determination to leave things alone, went to the Walworth police station. Emily accompanied him. They had a very interesting conversation with a detective-sergeant, who informed them in the end that the matter was quite out of police hands now, and that Mrs Lansberg was currently an inmate at the Maudesley Hospital, Denmark Hill. Boots and Emily went there, and a doctor permitted them to see the former Elsie Chivers.

She was sitting beside her room window, hands in her lap and gazing at the wintry scene outside. She wore a soft brown dress that was a little loose on her thin figure. She turned her head as Boots and Emily entered. Through her spectacles her eyes were clear and untroubled, but unknowing.

Boots spoke.

'Hello, Elsie,' he said, and he smiled at her. Her brow puckered. She gazed up at him. 'Emily's here too,' he said. 'Old friends, you know.'

Her brow smoothed out, a little sigh escaped, and she gave him another look. Her eyes expressed recognition and delight. She came to her feet, took her glasses off in the way of a woman sensitive rather than vain, and placed them aside.

'Oh, dear, I'm not at my best, am I?' Her hands

fluffed at her hair and smoothed her dress. Again she looked at Boots, and he saw what had once been so familiar to him, and so enchanting, the myopic misty softness of her eyes. And if she was ten years older, she still had a loveliness. A smile of affection touched her mouth. 'Yes, it's Boots, dear dear Boots.'

And Emily stared in astonishment as she embraced Boots and kissed him full on his lips, like a woman whose inner anguish had dissolved in a flood of emotional and resurgent happiness. But Boots, of course, had always been her favourite, as well as the young soldier whose evidence at the Old Bailey had shown the court she could not have murdered her mother.

But everything had played on her mind, poor woman.

'It's all over, Elsie,' said Boots gently, 'it's all over. No more worries. You've people here to care for you now.'

'Why, look, and there's Emily,' she said, 'and such a picture.' She took Emily's hand and squeezed it, then kissed her softly on the cheek. 'You are Emily, aren't you?'

'Well, I always have been,' said Emily, 'and I'm so pleased to see you.'

'I've had so many strange dreams, Emily.'

'All over now,' said Boots again, and asked lightly and casually, 'What happened to your husband, Herr Lansberg?'

'Dead, you know. Oh, dear.' She sighed again. The dreams took hold of her. 'I must get on, I really must, there's so much to do at home, and my mother is never well. Oh, dear.' She took up her spectacles, put them on and sat down again to gaze at the wintry view once more. Boots, remembering his youthful love for her, felt pain. He touched her shoulder in the lightest gesture of good-bye, and then he and Emily left.

On their way home, Emily said, 'She'll always be in some strange world of her own.'

377

'I hope it's a kind world as well,' said Boots.

'Boots, you don't think perhaps she was guilty, after all, do you?'

'Perish the thought, Em,' said Boots, who was always going to keep certain conclusions and convictions to himself.

Chinese Lady and her grandson Tim got off the bus and walked towards the school, she holding him firmly by the hand. The March afternoon was crisp, bright and invigorating, and she had thought it would be nice to get out with Tim, meet the children from school and share the bus ride home with them. Emily was working on today, with her approval. That was much better, Emily working for Boots in the family firm and enjoying it. It was always better for any wife to work in her husband's offices, if she had to work at all. The firm was so busy, and Boots was being overwhelmed, all on account of Sammy's success with ladies' fashions. That Sammy, the things he got up to in ladies' wear. Chinese Lady paused in her reflections, thinking she hadn't got that quite right. Something told her Boots would show one of his sly smiles if she said it like that. Still, it was nice him telling the family Emily was a perfect godsend in the office. Well, she'd been that to the family for years. Mind, she and Boots had been given something to think about over that bit of silliness with Mr Somerville. It had pulled them up short. Emily might not be the best-looking woman in London, but she was very lively, and men liked that in a woman. She had a good figure too, and men liked that as well. Boots wasn't so airy-fairy about his marriage now. Good thing too. Wives gave a lot in marriage. Not many men gave as much.

Imagine Sammy coming to his senses at last. Making money was all very well, but it wasn't everything.

Well, he'd seen that, and he'd done himself proud in picking Susie. He'd never find anyone more suited to him, nor anyone who could handle him better. That young man needed handling or he'd start chasing the moon. An Easter wedding and all. He'd bought Susie a lovely engagement ring from one of Mr Moses's new jewellery shops, and Mr Moses himself was coming to the wedding, with his daughter Rachel. And Mr Greenberg, of course.

Vi and Tommy would probably always be the happiest couple in the family, because Tommy was the most considerate of the boys and Vi was so placid it didn't take hardly anything to make her contented. Tommy would get on well as the factory manager, especially when the new one was built. Sammy had had trouble getting the insurance company to settle. They'd said they weren't too happy about the cause of the fire. Sammy went round to their head office and told them not to lay that one on him or he'd sue them. Susie went with him, and said afterwards that Sammy paralysed them with a speech that lasted fifteen minutes. They were going to settle now. Chinese Lady thought she'd have to go and see the new factory when it was up, just to make sure it was a credit to the family and the workers. She'd heard tales about East End workshops and how machinists were paid starvation wages. No son of hers was going to be allowed to pay wages like that to his machinists.

It wasn't hardly believable, the name of his fashions company and the name of his designer actually being in the papers, on the fashion pages. Adams, that was the name at the top of one page. That was his dad's name. Chinese Lady felt sad that Daniel hadn't lived to see what his sons had made of his name.

Lizzy and Ned were doing fine. Lizzy was living all her ambitions as a wife and mother in her house with its own bathroom and garden. She'd been invited to go with Ned to a celebration of his firm, and Ned had had to buy her an evening gown, a real silk evening gown, for the occasion. Lizzy looked like one of them Buckingham Palace debutantes in shimmering gold silk, and you could see Ned was proud of her. Lizzy was scared that in her nervousness she'd drop her aitches, and Ned said that if she did he'd better drop his too, just to let people see they were two of a kind. But Lizzy rose to the occasion, apparently, and Ned said she was as good as Eliza Doolittle at the ball. Lizzy asked who Eliza Doolittle was, and Ned said she was a flower girl who turned into a duchess in a play by Bernard Shaw. Lizzy said she didn't want to be a duchess, just Mrs Ned Somers. She and Ned and the children were going on holiday in the summer with Boots, Emily, Rosie and Tim. Chinese Lady was going too, with her husband Edwin.

It was nice. Edwin was coming home at Easter, and in time for the wedding. He'd written to say so. The letter had come in a Government envelope, like others. She felt happy about that. She'd missed him. He'd be surprised to know Elsie Chivers had turned up. Poor woman, she was in hospital now with a nervous breakdown.

Sammy actually had a motorcar now. A new one. Chinese Lady wasn't sure she held with motorcars. Horses had always been all right as far as she was concerned, and a lot safer too. Nor did they break down or need filling up with petrol. Some man needed a good talking to for inventing motors. They weren't what a woman would have filled the roads with.

After Sammy's wedding to Susie at Easter, all her children would be married. She'd have no more worries on that score. They'd all be settled. Her boys had been fortunate. Vi, Emily and Susie, what mother's sons could have better wives? But all of them had had to be given a bit of a push. That was the way with young men, most of them couldn't always recognise the gold that was staring them in the face. Lizzy as a girl hadn't needed any push at all. Lizzy had known right from the time she first saw Ned. Still, everyone was right as rain now. Chinese Lady felt that Daniel would be happy and proud of all of them.

She stopped at the school gates, still keeping a tight hold of Tim's hand. The schoolchildren were just coming out of their classes. From the gates she watched them. Children. They were all precious, those who belonged to poor parents just as much as those who belonged to the better-off. They were walking or running or scampering, these children. There was Bobby, a bundle of energy, and there was Annabelle, such a bubbly girl and getting so like Lizzy in her looks. She was with Rosie, of course. They were always together.

And there was Miss Polly Simms, a lady's daughter who'd become a teacher and who had an eye for Boots. But Chinese Lady couldn't help liking her, especially as she'd been an ambulance driver during the war. Four years she'd spent picking up wounded soldiers. You could like any woman for that, but liking her for herself was something else. Life was strange, really, you could never tell which way it was going to lead men and women. Miss Simms came of an aristocratic family, and Boots was like his dad, a man of Walworth, a cockney, even if he did speak what Emily called upper-class posh sometimes. Being what he was, though, didn't make any difference to Miss Simms. Chinese Lady knew that. Miss Simms was often at the house, giving lessons to Rosie, and if you caught her off guard, when she was looking at Boots, you could see how she felt about him. Emily must have seen it too, because she was like a tigress sometimes when Miss Simms was in the house. But Boots had never been a man to lose his head. Except he had once, when he'd gone off to join up behind her back. But he wouldn't lose his head over Miss Simms, except over my dead body, thought Chinese Lady.

'Nana!' Rosie came running. She was the adopted daughter now of Emily and Boots. What a palaver it had been. All kinds of people poked their noses in when a child was being legally adopted. Rosie had put up with the fuss awfully well. Everyone could see she didn't even know her natural mother. Unnatural, more like. It was all over now, and Rosie knew what adoption meant. It meant no one could take her away from Emily and Boots, it meant they loved her and wanted her. She'd get to that advanced school all right, Miss Simms said she would walk the exam. The world was going to open right up for Rosie, and Rosie deserved it because she gave so much happiness to Emily and Boots.

'Hello, Rosie, love. And there's Annabelle. My, don't you both look pretty? Get hold of Bobby, Rosie, before he gets into a fight. You're all comin' on the bus with me and Tim. Oh, good afternoon, Miss Simms.'

Polly, arriving, at the gate, smiled and said, 'Good afternoon, Mrs Finch.'

'It's nice seeing you, specially as I wanted to ask if you'd like to come to tea on Sunday.'

'I'd love to,' said Polly, but her smile was wry as she regarded the children, Rosie, Annabelle, Bobby and Tim. They all belonged to this upright, old-fashioned and remarkable woman who still wore high-necked Edwardian blouses. Everyone who meant most to Polly belonged to Mrs Finch, particularly Boots, Rosie and Lizzy. Polly had a happy relationship with Lizzy, the mother of Annabelle and Bobby. But what was her life to be if she spent it merely in their shadows, more especially the long shadow of Boots? She must break the invisible chains. She knew famous men and notable women, she knew lords and ladies, yet she could not divorce herself from this family, Mrs Finch's family. After all those traumatic years in France and Flanders, amid the sound of the guns, she could have more than she was getting now, surely.

'Oh, could I come too, Granny Lady?' asked Annabelle.

'Everyone must come on Sunday,' said Chinese Lady, and smiled at Polly. 'Don't have another motorcar accident on the way, Miss Simms, my fam'ly don't like to lose their friends.'

'Specially not special friends,' said Annabelle.

'Am I special?' asked Polly, her smile brittle.

'Of course,' said Rosie. 'Isn't she, Nana?'

'Of course,' said Chinese Lady. That was the best way, to make a special friend of Miss Simms and see she didn't bring upsets to the family. 'When you grow up, Rosie, and you, Annabelle, you'll get to learn about the war and your soldier daddies, and what they owed to ladies like Miss Simms and their ambulances. Ladies like Miss Simms are very special. Come along now. Bobby, put your cap straight. I don't hardly know any time when it hasn't looked crooked. Don't fidget, Tim, we're goin' now. Goodbye, Miss Simms. Don't forget on Sunday. Four o'clock.'

'Goodbye, Mrs Finch, I'll be there.' Polly's smile was very brittle as she watched them go on their way, the children's grandmother holding the hands of the two small boys.

A special friend? Very special? Sunday tea with the family? Was that enough?

'Miss Simms?' A twelve-year-old girl, wanting to ask a question, came to look up at the popular lady teacher. 'Could I – oh, Miss Simms, you look like you've got something in your eye.'

'Oh, just a mote, Hilda.'

THE END